THICKER THAN WATER

THICKER THAN WATER

A Cape May Trilogy: Book One

By Laura Quinn

"From every wound there is a scar, and every scar tells a story. A story that says I survived."

—FR. CRAIG SCOTT

PROLOGUE

Cape May, New Jersey, 1906

It was the kind of summer day people look forward to all year. Late June, the afternoon sun was still high on the horizon, and the beach was scattered with cottagers enjoying themselves. An older gentleman in a bowler hat flew a kite. A family walked the waterline, their young children splashing in ankle-deep waves, each squeal louder than the last every time another one rolled in, while their mother casually twirled her lace parasol. Another group had just finished a picnic and gone to one of the nearby bathhouses to change into woolen swimsuits for a quick dip of their own.

The dunes were several yards back from the water. Their tall grass and craggy shrubs shielded the landscape from the sea before them and the promenade behind. Huddled between the mounds were a little boy and girl. One would have to look closely to find them, precisely the point. Their clothing was tattered and threadbare, the soles of their shoeless feet, black. He wore a newsboy cap two sizes too big; she- limp, plaited pigtails.

The girl clutched her stomach, greedily eyeing up the picnic basket.

"I'm hungry, Danny," she whimpered, her sunken blue eyes pleading with him for something- anything- to dull the ache in her belly.

The boy frowned, his smudged face looking much older than his seven years let on. His own stomach felt like it had rocks in it. It was well past suppertime, but the only thing they'd eaten was some wild beach plums they picked yesterday.

Danny slowly shook his head. "Stealin's wrong. You know that, Shannon."

"I don't care." She crossed her arms against herself, her lower lip in a full pout as she sighed. "They'll prolly just throw it out anyway. What's the difference?"

"I'll think of somethin'." An assurance not only to her but to himself.

Shannon cast her gaze on the ocean. "Pa's been gone a long time, Danny. What if he don't come home this time?"

"He will. Always does."

"But," she gulped. "What if…"

Danny took her hands in his own, soothing her palms with his thumb the way their mother used to before tucking them into bed. His sister stared down at her feet. After a few moments, he saw her shoulders relax and knew what he had to do.

He reached into the pocket of his knickers and pulled out a gold watch. He'd put off parting with it for as long as possible, but he could count Shannon's ribs through her calico dress, and his own arms were twigs. Tarnished though it was, the pocket watch would fetch him a pretty penny- more than enough to tide them over until Pa returned to port, God-willing with a hull full of flounder. He swallowed hard and glanced at the dunes, thinking himself lucky the Blue Pig casino was just two blocks from the ocean. Their bellies would be stuffed in no time.

His sister snatched the watch. "No, Danny! You can't- I won't let you."

"Give that back!" He made a grab for it, but Shannon was too quick, tucking her arms behind herself as far as she could. "Aw, *c'mon.*"

"No." She shook her head so violently he thought it'd snap right off her neck. "It's from Ma."

"Exactly. She wouldn't want you to starve, Shannon. Neither do I. Now, gimme it."

This time he simply held out his palm, but she backed away.

"Bad enough Pa sold the locket she gave me." Her voice trembled. "This is all we have left. Please Danny," she begged as her eyes welled up, "I miss her. I miss her so much."

He missed her too. Terribly. He'd give anything to hear the sound of her voice just one more time.

"Okay," he relented, and she threw her tiny arms around him. Danny pulled her in, her tears flowing freely now. He brushed a greasy blonde braid over her shoulder and leaned in closer. "We have each other," he assured her. "I'll always take care of you, Shannon. Always."

She broke the hug, using a sleeve to wipe her nose. "Promise?"

Danny grinned. He traced an index finger over the leftover scrap of rope now serving as his suspenders. "Cross my heart."

"And hope to die?"

He shot her a quizzical look, and she poked him in the ribs.

"And hope to die," Danny pledged.

That was the first time his sister smiled- really smiled- since their Ma had passed.

"I hope you don't though," Shannon was quick to add.

"Well," he chuckled, "that makes two of us."

CHAPTER 1

Ten Years Later

No sooner had Remembrance Day passed and Cape May was abuzz preparing for the Fourth of July. It was all anyone could talk about for weeks, the *Star and Wave* promising "a gala day on the waterfront." To this end, the resort did not disappoint.

Jutting a thousand feet over the mighty Atlantic, the Iron Pier was alive with the spirit of American patriotism. Spectators crammed both sides of her lower levels. They cheered under an ink-black, cloudless sky- a perfect canvas for the coming fireworks display save for the sliver of moon glistening off the water.

Up on the third tier, the new electric lights switched on, illuminating the massive ballroom as the orchestra continued warming up. The place was splattered in red, white, and blue. Banners and bunting draped the banquet tables as well as the grandstand. More flags peeked out from the red rose centerpieces on the guest tables, all while a gargantuan portrait of Woodrow Wilson looked on approvingly.

None of this mattered to Danny Culligan.

All he could think about was his sweetheart, Jennie. *Jennie Martin.* He felt himself grinning like an idiot and forced his mouth to imitate the stern thin line of the men around him. She should be arriving soon. Any minute now, he imagined.

Class differences forced the couple to see each other in secret for years. But tonight? Tonight, he'd finally be able to hold her in public. It was also his best shot at impressing her millionaire father.

Danny was a hard worker. He wasn't rich by any means but knew he could prove himself worthy if given the opportunity. He'd show the older man just how much his daughter was cherished. Hopefully, by next July, Jennie would have a new last name.

Knowing their future was on the line, the punch bowl was all too inviting. But Danny didn't want to have liquor on his breathe in the event Mr. Martin turned out to be a teetotaler. Instead, he checked his pocket watch and frowned- only five minutes had passed since he last looked. He shoved it back in his jacket and turned his attention to inspect his fingernails.

Neatly trimmed. Not a trace of fish. Good.

Danny scanned the room. Nothing.

Where is she?

He chewed the inside of his cheek, then glanced down at his feet. Could've buffed his shoes a bit more.

"Stop fidgeting," his sister scolded as he went to reach for the watch again.

"I'm not," he mumbled.

"You are." She turned to face him head-on, wearing her usual confident smirk as she helped him square his shoulders. "You didn't expect the Martins to be here yet, did you? Her aunt likes to make an entrance."

Danny shrugged. Shannon was usually right. That he was older needn't matter. Irish twins born ten months apart, she was his closest confidant.

"How was the parade," he asked to distract himself.

His sister rolled her eyes. "Overdone." She gestured to their surroundings. "Just as this is. One of the floats even had a pyramid of shells from that munitions plant on Higbee Beach."

"No kidding?"

"No," Shannon quipped, lips tight. "So wasteful for just one day. But, hey, if the cottagers want a parade, they'll have a parade. And in two months' time they'll be gone for the season. Moved on with their lives just as they always do."

He felt the slight keenly. "Stop it, Shannon."

"Stop what?"

"Putting her down."

"I wasn't."

"You were and you know it."

This was neither the time nor the place for them to have this discussion. Again. Shannon would always remain part of his life. True, she'd be in a different role, but Danny would never abandon her. How could he? She was the one who patched him up after Pa was in one of his dark moods. The one who knew how to cover the bruises and, where she couldn't, how to lie about their origin. Shannon knew him better than he knew himself. Except where Jennie was concerned.

"Can we talk about this more at home?" he asked in a quiet voice.

Up went the barrier he knew so well. With an icy glare, she drifted a few steps away from him, smoothing her skirts before leaning casually against one of the columns.

Several minutes passed, and there was still no sign of Jennie. Danny grasped the watch again. Clenching and unclenching it, he stole a glance at Shannon to see if she was watching him and was surprisingly hurt to find she wasn't.

Arms crossed against herself, his sister scowled at the portrait of President Wilson as if she wanted to slap him. Shannon always felt everything so intensely, as if the whole world were against her. Danny hated quarreling with her. Deep down, he knew, even if he danced with Jennie all night, completely wowed her father, he couldn't be truly happy knowing Shannon was upset with him.

Hands in his pockets, he strode over and followed her gaze. "His nose is a bit off, don'tcha think?"

"Leave it to you to make jokes at a time like this."

"Like what?"

Shannon clicked her tongue and shook her head in disgust. "German U-boats patrolling the coast. Yacht club full of Navy ships. And *we're* the ones who have to live with it."

She inched closer, drawing her chin up, a caged look in her blue-gray eyes. "I worry about you," she whispered.

"Shannon—"

"No, I do. Every time you leave port. And when the war comes…."

"Not gonna happen. Wilson's a pacifist."

Her eyes flashed. "Perhaps you've been too busy mooning about to pay attention, brother. He's also running for re-election. It's been over a year since the *Lusitania*. This ball? These people? They want justice. But it's not their kind who gets drafted."

So that was it, then. She was afraid he'd go off to fight and never come back.

Danny regarded her thoughtfully. Her blonde mane was piled high atop her head, with just a few loose tendrils accentuating her high cheekbones and swan neck. She certainly wasn't a little girl anymore. Not on the outside, anyway.

"Remember our promise?" he asked. "It's still true."

Shannon looked down at her hands in respite. It was then he realized the family resemblance. How had he not seen it before? They never spoke of her, but Danny couldn't help himself.

"You look just like her."

"Who?"

"Ma."

Her cheeks flushed. "You really think so?"

"From what I remember, yeah. Spittin' image." He cupped her shoulder and nodded. "She'd be so proud of you. I sure am."

Shannon gave him a playful bump with her elbow. "Layin' it on thick, aren't we?"

"I mean it."

"Well, then," she grinned, "I'll take the compliment."

"Good." Danny smiled, too. "Y'know Shannon," he added, "If you let yourself, you just might have a nice time tonight. Think you can do that for me?"

"I'll try. Best I can offer."

"That's my girl."

He knew it was asking a lot. That he was pushing his sister well out of her comfort zone. But if Danny were to put his best foot forward with Mr. Martin, he needed his conscience clear.

At the podium, the conductor tapped his baton. Lights dimmed. Voices hushed.

Danny peeked at his watch before surveying the crowd. Everything was blurry, as if the ballroom had suddenly been lowered into the sea. Girls checked their dance cards, faces giddy, their laughter was garbled. The orchestra began the first stanza of Strauss's *The Blue Danube*. That, too, sounded off- like his ears were clogged.

Couples brushed by to the dance floor, and Danny's chest tightened. He and Jennie were supposed to be out there with them. He grabbed the watch again, but his palm was clammy, and he couldn't get a tight grip. *What's happening to me?* Meanwhile, his heart thundered against his ribcage. Faster and faster and faster. Too afraid to care whether it was gentlemanly or not, he gulped, uselessly tugging at his collar for any chance at precious oxygen.

Just then, the double doors of the main entrance flung open. The Martin party had finally arrived.

Every eye in the room turned to Jennie's aunt, Gertrude Callaway. Dripping in diamonds, the matriarch was escorted in on the arm of her son, Hugh. Tiffany tiara, cascading ear bobs, three rows of studs on her dog collar, cuffs over the gloves on each wrist, a belt to minimize her middle-aged waist- even the chandeliers couldn't compete. All Danny could see was Jennie.

His smile was momentary, his relief- fleeting. She was on the arm of another man.

CHAPTER 2

"Ready, Miss Martin?"

Jennie swallowed the bile rising up in her throat and plastered on her most demure smile. To her escort, she replied, "Joseph, thank you for filling in for Father. The family is most appreciative."

"Happy to be of service," her companion smiled- the triumphant assurance of a king.

I'm sure you are. Now, let's get this over with.

Joseph York the Third was the last person Jennie thought she'd be attending the ball with. Her cousin's friend from Harvard, Mr. York deserted his usual Newport set and took a suite at the Stockton Hotel for the season. Her aunt, of course, was delighted. With no family of his own in town, it was only natural for him to join their party. Old money, like her mother's side. Not that Jennie needed a reminder- Gertrude herself sufficed daily. Tall, dark, and indeed handsome, he was sure to make some deb 'an excellent match.'

Just not her. She'd long since lost her heart. Didn't expect to get it back anytime soon either.

Joseph no sooner led them into the ballroom when her cousin approached.

Cocktail in one hand, Hugh slung his free arm over the other man's shoulder. "There's some alumni here I think you should meet. Wanna talk about the team's chances next season."

"Oh?" asked the barracuda.

Hugh's brown eyes twinkled. "You don't mind, do you Jen?"

"Of course not."

"I'm taking them out on the *Crusader* day after tomorrow," Hugh told Joseph as they walked away. "The striper are running if you care to join us." Her cousin looked back over his shoulder and gave Jennie a wink.

"Thank you," she mouthed, and he cocked his head in acknowledgment.

Jennie bit her lip, her hazel eyes frantically searching for Danny. Maybe -just maybe- she prayed, he hadn't arrived yet.

No such luck. There, along a column in the far corner of the room, two sets of piercing blue eyes stared back at her- one in horror; the other, pure rage. She took a purposeful step in their direction when a silken hand grasped her shoulder.

"Your dance card, dear," Gertrude leered.

No. Not now, she didn't have time for this. Jennie's hand shook as she perused the pamphlet.

"How is it already full?" she asked, searching her aunt's face for an answer, a trace of emotion even, yet Gertrude's mouth remained in the same thin line as always.

"You know you can't be left with these decisions. You're not out yet, dear."

"I don't even know half these names."

"All good families, I assure you. Though I'm sure you recognize Mr. York's."

"How could I miss it?" Jennie scoffed. "He claimed five dances. Couldn't you have at least added Hugh to the list?"

Gertrude's eyes darted around them. "Remember yourself, young lady," she growled. "You have a duty to this family just like the rest of us. This little mishap in the papers will blow over much more smoothly if we shoulder the burden together, do you understand?"

Jennie understood, alright. Understood that she didn't have any control over her own life. Hoping he'd see she was detained, she threw a quick glance in Danny's direction. Hands in his pockets, he looked down at the floor.

She swallowed hard; she'd never hurt him purposely. Surely he knew that. Tonight was supposed to be about *them,* about finally being together in the open instead of sneaking around. Her declaration to her father, to Gertrude, to the world, that -out yet or not- she was spoken for.

Jennie had to fix this right here and now, thoughts of tearing up the dance card fueling her resolve. Once Danny heard her explanation, every-thing would be back on track. Of course, he'd forgive her. Right?

"Look at me when I'm speaking to you," her aunt commanded. "Answer the question."

"Yes," she mumbled.

"E-*nun*-ciate."

"Yes, Aunt Gertrude. I understand."

"Good." Gertrude gave a curt nod of approval. "Stick to the script and you'll do just fine. Now, dear, if you'll excuse me, I must make my rounds."

Jennie's cheeks blazed. Though not specific to Father, the headlines were damaging enough considering his thick accent. It started when the *New York World* reported the German-American Alliance supported the Kaiser's war effort, which was absolutely preposterous. Still, the press spilled blood in the water and created a feeding frenzy among the other papers. How could they print such lies? Fearmongering, that's what it was, pure and simple. She was proud of her heritage- proud of her father and the company he'd built. He was only a child when he left Bavaria. Alone, for that matter. If the papers could lie, Jennie supposed she could, too. Her mantra about Father being home under the weather slipped out with frightening ease.

She looked over at the column again, but both Culligans were gone.

Five minutes in, the ball was already a complete and utter disaster. Still, Jennie had a role to play, and the pressure was on. Until she could speak with Father about her feelings for Danny, she had to perform.

◇⟫═◗ ◖═⟪◇

The night dragged on and on. One boring conversation after the other, most of them about Father- her suitors fishing to estimate the size of her dowry. She smiled and nodded; laughed at all their terrible jokes. Any innocent bystander would think she was having a fabulous time. This was good because, somewhere amongst the crowd, Gertrude was watching her like a hawk.

All the while, Jennie kept her eyes peeled for Danny. To keep herself sane, she allowed her mind to wander, daydreaming she wasn't really dancing with Mr. Jones ("of-the-Baltimore-Joneses"), but him. Danny. *Her* Danny.

Most nights, they simply lay together by the lake. Her head on his chest, he'd pet her hair as they traced the constellations, never ceasing to find brave Perseus and Andromeda. Danny told her stories about the pirates that used to land on the surrounding shoreline, and, knowing he'd pull her closer, Jennie pretended to be afraid.

They both wished the giant elephant attraction Jumbo was still around. Jennie had seen its sister in Atlantic City, but he'd never been that far up the coast. "We'll go there sometime," she promised.

"Miss Martin?"

The spell was broken, and she found herself staring back at a very perplexed Mr. Jones.

"Yes?"

"I asked if you cared for some punch."

Jennie glanced at the buffet to hide her embarrassment. She saw Shannon enter the ladies' bathroom out of the corner of her eye. Finally- this was just the kind of chance she'd been waiting for.

"No, thank you." Smoothing her arms along her corseted bodice, she added, "I'm actually feeling a bit fatigued. Would you excuse me while I freshen up?"

Jones bowed, and Jennie seized her moment, hastily borrowing a pencil from one of the staff on her way to the lavatory. Once inside, she retrieved a calling card from her purse and scribbled as fast as she could.

Darling-I can explain.

The Spot. Same time.

All my love. ~J

There. Now, all she had to do was wait for Shannon to come out. The longest minute in the world passed. She couldn't have missed her, could she? Then what would she do?

Her feet swelled in her heels, so she plopped down on one of the velvet settees. Might as well take advantage of it while she could. Tempting as it was to hide out in the bathroom all evening, her aunt would eventually come looking for her.

Two girls about her age entered, and Jennie tilted her head in acknowledgment. It was better for her to appear aloof- she couldn't risk getting caught up in conversation right now- though, apparently, there was no chance of that.

"Kraut," one of them sneered on her way to the mirror.

Jennie balled her hands in her lap. *They're just jealous.* Of what, though? Empty-headed boys, who only cared about her money?

"I heard her father won't even show his face," said the taller of the two in a loud whisper.

Her companion nodded. "Well, *I* heard they're going back to Philadelphia." She pinched her nose. "The *stench* of it this time of year."

"I know. Why, it's almost as bad as...Liberty Cabbage."

Both girls snickered.

"Come now, ladies," said a third voice, "don't you have anything better to talk about?"

Jennie looked up, speechless. *Shannon?* She certainly didn't expect to be defended by someone who was shooting daggers at her only hours before.

The tall girl raised an eyebrow through the mirror. "Excuse me?"

Shannon eyed the girl up and down. "Those shoes with that dress? Inexcusable." Her opponent's nostrils flared, and Shannon cackled. "Truth hurts, doesn't it?"

"Well, I never!" the girl spat, grabbing her friend by the elbow. "Come on, Harriet."

Jennie intended on waiting until their footsteps faded to offer her thanks when the other woman spoke first.

"Don't get any ideas." Shannon's voice had a harder edge to it now.

"Pardon?"

"I did it for him, not you. He left, by the way. Not that'cha care."

"But I do!" Jennie was on her feet now. The calling card folded several times over, she extended a shaky hand.

Shannon eyed the note the way one looked at a mosquito before swatting it.

Still, Jennie rationalized, if she were able to look beyond her disdain once, Shannon might just do it again. Everyone had their soft spots, after all. Hit on the right one, the preverbal Achilles heel, and she'd win her over. Those catty girls had certainly brought out a fierce sense of loyalty by association. Jennie felt slightly guilty about exploiting something so profoundly personal, but what choice did she have?

Shannon huffed and started to walk around her. It was now or never.

Chin up, Jennie blocked her. She pressed the note in Shannon's palm, curling the other woman's fingers around it. "For him," she said solemnly.

A slight nod was her only reply, and Shannon dashed off.

The grandfather clock down the hall struck one. Jennie re-read her latest journal entry and closed the book, patting its leather cover before locking it back in her desk. Shoulders stiff, she returned to her bed and pulled a pillow onto her lap. What if Shannon changed her mind? Tore her note into teeny-tiny shreds and threw them into the ocean?

There was no doubt Danny's sister loved him dearly. Jennie replayed their short discussion over and over. All she kept coming back to was, *"I did it for him, not you."* His well-being meant a lot to Shannon, Jennie told herself. She'd deliver the message.

The hour grew late. Jennie strained her ears for the sound of his car, but all she could hear was the rushing surf. The possibility Danny received her note and ignored it never occurred to her. Once hatched, the terrible thought was all-consuming.

"O happy dagger!" Jennie never fully comprehended the magnitude of the statement until now. Despite lesson upon lesson, much to her governess's chagrin, she'd always thought Juliet over-dramatic. The play was a tragedy- it was all to get a rise from the audience. Of course, she hadn't understood it before. Danny's love was as constant as the North Star. Warm and bright. He was everything to her. That she could lose him left her broken, empty. Worse still was knowing it was of her own doing, his crestfallen face all she could see every time she closed her eyes. Destraught, Jennie stuffed her face in the pillow to muffle the sobs she could no longer contain. Shakespeare was right all along.

She rose from the bed and peered through her lace curtains. The sky was as dark as her heart. She squinted, holding her breath as she prayed.

The Model T was there as usual.

Jennie covered her mouth with her hands, chiding herself for ever doubting him. How long had he been out there? Her eyes were dewy again-joy was a much better reason to cry, but she hadn't time to let herself. Ever thankful for the wraparound porch, out the window she went, tiptoeing across its roof on the far side nearest the dunes. She shimmied down the pole while Danny cranked the engine.

He wouldn't even look at her. They rode in stone silence along the dark beach road. No head lamps- they couldn't chance it. Having traveled the route countless times, both knew it by heart. She wanted to tell him to slow down but managed to hold her tongue.

It wasn't long before they reached the lake on the island's far side, the Ford rolling to a stop on its gravel shore. The Spot. Craggy trees dotted its perimeter, down Signal Hill all the way to the bay, the thick scent of beach plum and honeysuckle blossoms clung in the mist coming off the water. Crickets and bullfrogs their only companions, a melody sweeter than any Jennie heard earlier in the evening.

Slam! Danny got out without a word. He stormed toward the willow tree a few yards off. Grabbing the blanket from the backseat, Jennie hurried after him.

"I'm sorry!" she called.

"That you're ashamed of me? You should be sorry, Jennie." His back toward her, he didn't budge.

Jennie blinked furiously. "Danny, it's not like that."

"Well how is it, then?"

She finally caught up to him, the tree's sweeping boughs dancing in the gentle sea breeze. Jennie reached for his arm, then stopped herself. If it were only up to her, it'd be different. They just needed more time.

"It's complicated. Please, if you'd just let me explain…." She choked back a sob. "God, I *hate* this."

Danny finally turned to face her. He slid a callous hand into hers and gave it a light squeeze.

"Forgive me?" he asked. "I'm an ass."

Overcome, she could only nod.

"We'll get through this. I love you, Jennie Martin." Cupping her cheeks, he wiped away the tears with his thumbs. "Complicated or not, nothin's gonna change that."

Jennie sniffled and shook her head resolutely. "I have a plan."

CHAPTER 3

Three days later, the Culligan siblings were in their bedroom, conspiring Danny's next move. Shannon eyed his reflection in the vanity mirror.

"*That's* her plan? Golfing with Daddy? Danny, you can't be serious."

"C'mon, Shannon," he pouted from his seat at the foot of the bed. "Give her a little credit."

She ignored him, turning her attention to her hair, yanking the horsehair brush root to tip. Each stroke was harder than the last. *Should'a never given him that note.* This was the thanks she got? Shannon rose from the bench and marched toward him. Arms akimbo, she stopped short, forcing him to look up.

Danny tilted his head. "It'll work."

"Oh, really? When did you last play, huh? That time you and Will Barkley snuck into the country club doesn't count."

His silence answered the question, and he crossed his arms against himself.

Shannon plopped down next to him. "Anyone we know caddying there this summer? They could at least help you choose the right club."

"None I can think of." Danny shook his head. "I'll just ask Hugh to give me some pointers beforehand."

"You're sure he's on board with this?"

"Yes."

"Good." At least she could feel secure about one thing. Hugh Callaway was a good friend to both of them. He certainly didn't take after his mother, it must've been the boarding schools. "Tell me more."

"Walter Martin's a self-made man. Emigrated here when he was a kid. Ended up working at some glassworks up in Gloucester. Learned the craft, now look at him."

She arched a brow. He sounded so smug. "If I didn't know better, I'd think *you* were the one who made all that money."

Danny bumped his shoulder against her. "He's a scrapper, alright. That's what Jennie says, anyway."

That grin. That stupid, lopsided grin. Every time he said her name.

"And? What, exactly? She thinks he'll see himself in you?"

Her brother nodded.

"Hmm."

"Now what?" he snapped.

"She looks down her nose at you and all you can do is smile?"

"You're doing it again, Shannon. Twistin' everything around." Danny put his hands on his knees and looked away from her.

He was so blind when it came to Jennie, Shannon thought bitterly. Always had been.

The girl had everything. Her father owned the largest cottage on the island. So big, in fact, the workers split it in half when they moved Juniper Grove closer to town from the beach. In two, it remained, the Martins summering on the east side, that dreadful aunt on the west.

Shannon perused her own shanty bedroom with a frown, wondering if Jennie knew her beloved slept on its grimy floor with little more than a well-worn secondhand quilt from the church and a pile of clothes for his pillow.

16

Probably not, she decided. Their world was a stage. She and Danny did their best to keep those outside from seeing behind the curtain. Sure, some locals might have suspicions, but nobody ever said anything outright. They knew John Culligan well enough to know what would happen if they did.

Her eyes fell on the doorframe, where the pale blue gown she'd borrowed from the eldest Barkley girl was waiting to be cleaned. *Add it to the list.* There was always something to do and never enough time to do it—cooking, mending, emptying the chamber pot, boiling the weekly bath. Meanwhile, Jennie had closets full of Worth dresses, each tailored to her personal specifications, never worn more than once. Never knew the word hunger, either—Martin's personal chef and staff ensured that their dinner parties were the talk of the town from the Main Line to the Cape.

Just thinking about it made Shannon's stomach rumble. They were out of flour again, but she made sure Danny and Pa got their eggs. Black coffee would have to suffice for now—it hadn't failed her yet. She tried to envision Jennie bargaining with the hucksters, tirelessly preserving what little damaged goods they offered, but Shannon couldn't. Why were some people born into one lot in life while others, another? And what had she ever done to deserve hers? Jennie Martin already had everything. Yet even that wasn't enough for the spoiled little bitch.

Assuming Walter Martin was agreeable to marrying his darling daughter to a fisherman's son, which was still a stretch in her mind, there was no way in hell Jennie's aunt would allow it. And then there was Pa to contend with. Shannon shivered at the thought of living alone with him, gazing with envy out the window as a pair of gulls glided by.

She glanced back at Danny, aching at the growing distance between them. Her intentions were good. Buried under fear and a healthy dose of envy, yes, but good nonetheless.

"I'm just trying to look out for you."

He let out a heavy sigh. "I wish you could see her the way I do. There's a lot more to her than you think."

"Look, I know she cares about you, Danny." Though her tongue bled, she was careful to leave out the "*in her own way*" her heart was screaming. "The plan has flaws. I don't want to see you get your heart broken."

"It won't."

"You sound awfully optimistic."

"Do you trust me?"

"What kind of question is that? You know I do."

"Then let me worry about the details, okay? This'll work out for the both of us, Shannon." Danny gestured their surroundings. "I'm not gonna leave you in this dump." He took her hands in his. "There's tons of jobs in Philadelphia. And I don't mean the factories. Think of the possibilities. You could take a typing class— work in one of them big offices on Market Street. Or a shop girl, maybe, at one of the department stores." Danny smiled. "Lit Brothers? *John Wanamaker's*? Whaddaya say?"

The smile she returned was for his benefit only. Three was always a crowd. "And where would I live? Or do you have that all figured out, too?"

Before he could answer, Pa's voice bellowed up the stairwell. "Danny! Get your ass down here, boy!"

Shannon grabbed her brother's hand. "Thought he was sleepin' one off," she shuddered.

"Think he overheard?"

"I dunno."

"You know the drill- just play dumb."

He started to rise, and she followed. Together, they tramped downstairs into the kitchen.

Pa's beady eyes gleamed. Usually able to read him, Shannon didn't know what to make of it. She folded her arms behind herself while he addressed Danny.

"You're not gonna believe what's happening up north. Gruesome." Pa shook his head. "Unthinkable. Right there in the surf."

"Not another U-boat!" she blurted despite herself.

"No one's talkin' to you, girl." He waved her off and went back to pretending she didn't exist. Unfolding the paper he held under his shoulder, Pa read the headline aloud, "Man-Eating Shark of Variety Infests Atlantic." A wide smile crossed his face as he handed the *Philadelphia Inquirer* to her brother.

"Two dead," Danny summarized. "One in Beach Haven, the other Spring Lake... *Christ*- it bit him right in half!"

"What?" Shannon gasped.

Pa snarled, looking very much like a man-eating shark himself at the moment. "Either you shut that hole in your face or I'll shut it for you. Understand?"

"Sorry Pa," Shannon muttered.

"Sorry Pa," he mocked in a feminine voice. "Sorry- pfft. You're always sorry about somethin'. Wouldn't have to be if you just listened for once." He turned to Danny. "Didja see how much prize money they're offering?"

"A small fortune," Danny murmured.

"Ha-ha! 'Bout time my ship came in. Git upstairs and pack, boy."

Danny silently obeyed, but Shannon didn't dare move. She held her breath, every muscle constrained, waiting to see what Pa's next move would be. The belt was his favorite. Buckle-side down. Her lower lip trembled, and she bit down hard- it would only last longer if she cried.

"We'll need provisions," he barked.

Shannon gulped. Not only was the flour gone, but they were running dangerously low on just about everything else. "Pa?"

"What, dammit?"

"We, um...you see..." she cocked her head at the pantry.

Pa opened its lid and grimaced. "Why didn'tcha tell me before?"

"I...uh."

"Never mind." He nodded at the kitchen door. "Tell Old Man Kennedy to put it on our charge. Be able to pay him back soon enough."

Shannon unhooked her market satchel from the counter. "How long do you think you'll be away?"

"As long it takes."

CHAPTER 4

Hugh stretched and groaned. He rolled to his right and found himself falling.

Thud.

Wide awake now, he chewed his cotton mouth and squinted. *The Crusader?* Glued to the floor, he massaged an aching temple with his index finger, racking his brain to remember just how and when he returned to the yacht. It took him a few seconds to realize he'd never actually left.

He'd win it all back, he told himself. He always did eventually.

There was a minor upside, though. Still wearing yesterday's clothes, he rummaged through his trouser pockets for a much-needed morning cigarette. Hugh lit one, took a satisfying drag, and rolled onto his back. If only he had a strong cup of coffee to go with it.

He stretched again, cracked his stiff back, and pushed himself into a stand. Squinting, he frowned. The poker table mocked him- its lush green top still littered with chips and empty glasses. Most of them were, anyway. Hugh licked his lips- the surest cure to a hangover was to drink some more. It was the first lesson he'd learned in Cambridge and one he'd not soon forget. Smoke in hand, he padded his way over to the corner.

Hugh grabbed the highball glass, knocked it back, and promptly spit it out. Someone-mostly likely himself- had dropped a cigarette butt in the scotch. Gagging, he ground his current one in the ashtray (which was right there on the damn table in the first place) and ran toward the stairs.

He just about made it to the deck when he threw up over the side. White knuckled, he gripped the railing to steady himself and vomited again.

"Awful waste," called a man from the dock next to him.

Hugh scowled and wiped his mouth with his thumb. "Huh?"

He was in no mood for jokes. Apparently, the fisherman wasn't kidding. He held up a chum bucket and jiggled it back and forth.

"Said 'it's an awful waste'!"

What in God's name is this fool talking about? The thought no sooner left his mind, and Hugh immediately regretted it. At least he managed not to say it aloud. That had to count for something, right? He was too young to sound like his father. Despised the man, for that matter, which made it even worse.

With the Navy commandeering his slip at Corinthian Yacht Club, Hugh was still adjusting to sharing the harbor on the east side of the Cape. Some cottagers minded, but he was never one to turn his nose down on the working class. To him, people were people.

And now, as his head started to clear, Hugh realized there were people just about everywhere. He'd never seen the port so busy. Men assessed their sails. Boys of every age ran up and down the docks. Some carried buckets of bait. Others helped with the ropes if a sloop or schooner were ready to cast off. Everyone talked all at once- probably what woke him up.

He'd spent the whole of yesterday entertaining in the cabin. His cheeks hadn't seen a razor in two days. Had Wilson finally taken a stand? Hugh's thoughts sprang to his uncle before bouncing to Jennie. Concerns for their safety brought forth a fresh round of nausea. He heaved until there was nothing left in his stomach. The acid burned his throat- like he'd swallowed fire.

"You alright, son?" his neighbor asked.

Hugh offered a weak smile. "Must've been something I ate," he coughed, then looked around again. "What's all the hubbub?"

"Why, the shark, o'course," replied the angler. "Somebody'll git the son-of-a-bitch." He wagged a finger, "you better believe it!"

Confused, Hugh blinked.

"Don'tcha read the papers, boy?" He held up a copy of the *Star and Wave*. "Gotta get 'em before he ruins the whole tourist season."

"Ah yes, the shark."

"I expect all of Schellenger's to be empty by lunchtime. Hope to cast off, myself, within the hour."

"Every fisherman?"

The old man nodded. "Can't nobody turn down that much reward money." He smiled through his eyes, jutting his chin at the *Crusader's* helm. "Present company excluded, if ya don't mind my sayin'. Real beaute you got there."

"She is," Hugh murmured.

Under different circumstances, he would've gone on at length about his ship's attributes, probably offering his neighbor a tour and a stiff drink. But not now. Mirth tipping the side of his mouth, Hugh's eyes darted to his left. A stout man wheeling a barrel up the gangplank blocked his view. He craned his neck as far as he could (which was rather far considering his six-foot frame). There. Better.

He counted the boat slips. One, two, three slips in on the right. Empty.

"Here." The old man was at his side now, a tin mug in his massive, weathered hand. "Water. You're lookin' a little green in the gills."

Hugh accepted and brought the cup to his chapped lips. He was cautious not to gulp for fear he wouldn't be able to hold it down.

"Thank you," he said and took another sip. "Did you happen to see the *Molly Elizabeth* this morning?"

His new friend nodded. "Culligans left oh, I dunno, 'bout an hour ago."

Hugh returned the mug and squeezed the old man's hand. "Thank you, again, sir, for your kindness. Best of luck to you," he said before jogging off.

There was one benefit to sleeping in his clothes. If his smokes were in one pocket, his keys were in the other. He grasped them with fervor as he made his way to the roadster. Hungover or not, he had to get to Juniper Grove as soon as he could.

Hugh kept the top-down as he zigged and zagged across town. The cool, salty air caressed his cheeks, and he found himself wondering what Cook would be serving for breakfast. A quick glance at his watch told him that he hadn't yet missed it. Which was good because, head-splitting now, he still hadn't had any coffee.

The twin houses loomed large, and he parked in the back. Rutherford was outside buffing Uncle's Rolls, and raised a bushy gray brow when Hugh handed him the coupe's keys. He groaned internally- Mother must still be in the Breakfast Room. Hugh pulled out his money clip, thanked the butler adequately, and hastily tucked in his crumpled shirt.

The east wing buzzed with the usual flurry. A maid was polishing an armoire in the hall, and Hugh inhaled the lemony-sweet scent of the oil as he passed her. Another was feather dusting the ornate scrollwork along the grand staircase when he turned into the parlor.

Mother's voice resounded against the mahogany paneling, the shrill indicating she was- for the moment, at least- in good spirits. Hugh stopped short of the oaken door, hoping to catch an inkling about whom or what he owed this stroke of luck.

"The problem's practically resolved itself," she said in a blithe tone. "Why, everyone's all but forgotten the war! Of course, it's only temporary so we'll have to keep our guard up. As soon as the beast is caught the press will be right on to the next as always. But, *for now*, it's splendid just the same."

"Aunt Gertrude," Jennie replied. "Forgive me, but I hardly think 'splendid' is the operative word. People are dead."

"Not my concern. Nor should it be yours."

"I disagree."

Atta girl, Jen. His cousin had a backbone, after all. Hugh beamed, wishing he could see Mother's face. She'd kept Jennie on a shorter leash than her prized bichon for years. Trained her like a damn dog, too. Maybe things were finally changing. Or, maybe not...

"Jennie, darling, listen to me. Very carefully. You should be grateful that shark showed up when it did."

"But—"

"No buts. Now finish your toast so we can head to the promenade. Cook, could you please—" Mother glanced over her shoulder and locked eyes with him. Her expression quickly changed from astonishment to concern. "Darling, you look affright! What happened?"

Making sure his dimples showed, Hugh flashed a winning smile and shrugged. "Hit a rough current on our way in. Nothing I couldn't handle, though."

"Oh," she softened. "Well, come," she waved and gestured to the seat next to her. "Do sit down."

Hugh sank into his chair. Throat still raw from earlier, he hoped his voice didn't sound too raspy. Ever dutiful old dear that she was, Cook poured him a fresh cup of coffee. He savored the bitterness of that delightful first sip.

"Thank you," he sighed.

She backed away silently, but he caught a glimpse of a slight smile on her plump face. *There's no fooling you, is there?*

"Jennie and I were just discussing the shark attacks." Mother dabbed a napkin to the corner of her mouth. "Which I'm sure you already know. Skulking in doorways and such."

Ah- there was the rub he'd been waiting for. Not two minutes in, a new record for her. He peeked at Jennie before responding. Eyes down, she was buttering her toast.

"Lotta traffic on the water." The first lie he hadn't told all morning.

"Hugh Callaway, what's gotten into you this morning? You know I don't care for slang." Aghast, she shook her head. "So *vulgar*. I hope you don't speak that way to your professors, young man."

Hugh drained his cup and wished it was Irish coffee. "A lot of."

"Better."

The brass mantel clock across the room announced the quarter-hour.

"Right," Mother nodded at it. "Jennie, finish up, dear. There's a good chance of a crowd along the promenade with this fine weather. We'll want to use that to our advantage."

"Mind if I join you?" Hugh asked. Jennie's head shot up. Before Mother could shoot him down, he added, "I'll change first. Rest assured."

"Wouldn't you rather go to the club?"

He shook his head.

"I think it's a great idea," Jennie interjected. She looked at Hugh first for confirmation, then back at her aunt. "Maybe we can even get Father to go. A show of solidarity."

"Well—"

"And Samuel," Hugh added of his younger brother.

"Nanny took him to the beach to look for shells."

Hugh sat back in his chair and tilted his head. "Come now, Mother, that's a poor excuse even by your standards. Jennie's right. There's safety in numbers." He paused for emphasis. "Perhaps even a photo opportunity."

Mother took the bait, drawing a hand to her mouth in consideration.

"Jennie and I can walk down and fetch him," he offered.

His cousin beamed. "It'd be no trouble."

"Oh," Mother huffed. "Well, I suppose. Don't forget your parasol. Can't have you browning up."

⊷⟹⟸⊶

Twenty minutes later, Hugh and Jennie were strolling down Ocean Avenue on their way to the beach. The air was thick and warm, and he took advantage of rolling up his shirtsleeves while it was just the two of them. It was a wide, quiet street. Except for a neighbor walking his bulldog, there wasn't a soul in sight. The perfect place for a discreet conversation.

But how to tell her? The headache powder he'd taken while in his room was starting to take effect, but Hugh still wasn't at his best.

"Did you catch anything?" Jennie asked.

"What?"

"Seabass."

Oh, right.

"Nope. Guess it wasn't my day."

They reached the corner of Beach Avenue and stopped to check for traffic. Samuel and Nanny were somewhere on the other side- the boy likely to be overjoyed at the prospect of a family excursion. Knowing Samuel, he wouldn't let them get a word in edgewise on the walk back either.

Jennie tilted her head reassuringly. "Well, I'm sure they'll be other—"

"Jen, listen," Hugh put a hand on her shoulder before she could cross. "We gotta talk."

CHAPTER 5

J ennie loved everything about the boardwalk. A symphonic rhapsody of carousel music, vendors shouting from their game tents, and the roar of the coaster all competing against the whoosh of the surf. Swimming was closed, but that didn't stop people from enjoying the beach below.

The air was filled with the delectable aroma of roasted peanuts, fresh popcorn, and cotton candy. Jennie inhaled but was quick to use her painted fan to cover her mouth- a lady never smiled. She wished she could bottle it up, take in the heavenly scent on cold winter nights, a warm sable muff for her insides. What a magical atmosphere. A place where nothing bad could ever happen.

She was on Father's arm while her aunt and cousins walked ahead. Hugh was right. With such a backdrop, she could have her heart-to-heart with Father out in the open, and Gertrude would be none the wiser.

Head held high, Jennie was glad she changed dresses upon returning from the beach. Still a tea gown, of course- the July mercury was furious- she now donned a lace dress of pale, buttery yellow, Father's favorite color. The royal blue velvet sash around her waist might look outdated to some, but she didn't care. It had been her mother's, and Jennie needed her presence today.

However, now that she had her golden opportunity, Jennie found she had no idea what to say to the man. She peered at him through the side of her parasol, knowing all too well the prickly heat at the nape of her neck had little to do with the temperature.

He was always so busy. Like most men of his stature, Father left the island for Philadelphia every Sunday evening. He'd attend to his affairs- the glassworks, various boards and committees, philanthropy- and return to the seaside on Fridays. However, even down the shore, there always seemed to be a meeting, luncheon, or ceremony.

Why she hardly knew him; was only aware of her parent's courtship from the stories Cook told her as a girl. *So romantic.* Her headstrong mother declined a viscount in favor of a man twice her age. An industrialist, to boot. Those weren't the only strikes against Father. With a lineage dating back to the Revolution, her grandparents were mortified to learn he was also an immigrant.

Mother gave it all up. Her reputation, her inheritance, her family. She followed her heart and married the man she truly desired. The elopement sent shockwaves up and down the Eastern Seaboard. But, and this was the part where Cook always smiled- deep-set crow's feet on her ruddy cheeks- she'd never seen two people more in love.

A rise of laughter from the beach caught her ear. Jennie couldn't bring herself to look for fear she'd lose what little nerve she had. Somewhere on the horizon, her Perseus was hunting real-live sea monsters. Jennie refused to allow herself to be chained to the rocks. She was her mother's daughter. If Danny could fight the carnivorous savage, she could fight for their relationship. And if they had to run away together? Well, so be it.

"This is nice, Father." Finally finding her voice, Jennie allowed herself to smile. "It's so rare we're alone together."

He patted her glove in agreement. "*Schatz.*"

Jennie looked down at the boards, all hope dashed. Their moment was lost before it even began.

"Father," she whispered, "perhaps...."

"What is it?"

She drew a deep, calming breath before looking at him again. "Perhaps... well, please understand. The papers...."

The old man nodded. "'Darling' it is, then."

"Unless we're at home," Jennie added, hating the thought she'd hurt him.

"Of course."

The group continued along the promenade toward the Iron Pier, where a group of children was gathered outside the window of Roth's Candy Land. Noses pressed to the glass, they watched the taffy stretch. Samuel ran ahead to join them, and Jennie felt her own mouth water. This is where she took after Father- the man had a terrible sweet tooth.

"Daddy?"

He gave her a warm smile along with an extra dime. "Get some for the little ones, too."

"Walter," Gertrude admonished. "It'll *ruin* their teeth."

Both Martins, for once, ignored her. Jennie scurried into the store, pleased to have won back Father's good humor. She purchased a box of taffy for them to share, another for Samuel, and several individual pieces. The youngsters were delighted as she passed them out, and her cousin wasted no time tearing into his.

"Can we go on the amusements after this?" Samuel asked between chews.

"Oh, I don't know," Gertrude postured. "I don't want you to get a belly ache." She cocked a brow at her brother-in-law. "Especially after eating so much sugar."

"We can take him," Hugh jutted his chin at the Martins. "Besides, I thought I saw one of your acquaintances back by the pavilion."

"Really? Whom?"

Her cousin drew a hand to his chin.

"Miss Parmentier," Jennie piped up.

"You're quite sure it was Emilie?"

Jennie nodded.

Gertrude's nostrils flared. "Hugh, why on Earth didn't you say something when we passed her?"

"Wasn't sure. I tipped my hat, of course, on account o' both of us. Wouldn't want to be rude."

"Now she'll think *I'm* rude."

"All the more reason you should let us take Samuel."

Jennie could see the wheels turning. "It's really no trouble, Aunt Gertrude. Perhaps she'll accept an invitation to tea? You know how it is with the Old Guard."

"Yes," Gertrude quipped. "Once one is swayed, the rest fall in line. Very good, Jennie." To Samuel, she added, "Behave."

"I will, Mama."

Gertrude smoothed her skirts and bid them adieu.

"Whaddaya say, pal?" Hugh tickled his brother's ribs. "You wanna go on the Ferris wheel first? Or the carousel?"

"Ferris wheel!" Samuel cheered through his giggles.

"Done."

Hugh grabbed the boy by his hand and started toward the amusements. Jennie retook Father's elbow and began following after.

Her cousin turned around. "Don't rush on our account." Hands in his pockets, he walked backward. "Enjoy your taffy."

"Thank you," she said.

"Don't mention it," Hugh grinned. "He's off to boarding school in the fall. Nice spending time with him while I can." He whirled back around and tousled Samuel's chestnut hair.

"Nice young man," Father mused as the Callaways faded into the crowd.

Jennie silently agreed. She certainly owed him one. Again. Hopefully Hugh wasn't keeping a running tally. Eyeing an empty bench, she led Father in its direction. A little girl with a balloon skipped by just as they were about to sit down. Her strawberry curls sprang more with each stride, and she was humming to herself without a care in the world.

"Not so long ago you were that small. And now? A vision."

Jennie blushed.

"You know, your mother was about your age when we met."

A smile ruffling her lips, she choose her words carefully. She wasn't a little girl- that much was true. Now a young woman, Jennie knew her heart as well as the curve of Danny's face when he smiled. Would Father take her seriously? Or call it puppy love and insist she be sensible?

"Darling, what's on your mind? Is it those blasted headlines?"

Jennie shook her head and summoned her most mature tone. This was it.

"Father, do you remember the Culligans?"

Brow furrowed, he drew a hand to his chin. "I wondered when we'd have this conversation."

"Pardon?"

"Jennie," he took her hands in his. "You've always loved him, haven't you?"

Still perplexed, she nodded.

"Thought I didn't notice," Father chuckled. "The watermelon parties and hayrides all those years ago. How the two of you partnered for the three-legged race then attempted to wander off unchaperoned." He shook his head in mock reproach. "You gave poor Nanny more than a few gray hairs, my pet."

Jennie laughed at the recollection. Inwardly, she hoped him unaware of her current late-night antics.

"You know your aunt—"

She cringed.

"She means well, Jennie. In her own way, I suppose." He smiled. "Poor Gertie. She thought Paris would cure you of him. I always knew better."

"You did?"

"You have your mother's heart."

Right now, that heart was about to burst. "So you approve?"

"I just want you to be happy."

Jennie threw her arms around him. "Oh, Daddy, I will be."

Though years of etiquette training taught her otherwise, she didn't even bother to mask the tears of joy threatening her composure. The discussion had gone far more smoothly than anything she had anticipated. In a dreamlike state, she almost couldn't believe it.

That was one obstacle overcome. The other, Jennie thought, as she cast her eyes on the sea, was out of all their hands.

Keep him safe, Mother. Bring him home.

CHAPTER 6

Danny baited another eel on the line and cast out over the stern. A week into the hunt and they hadn't caught a single shark. Striper, yes. A few skates and rays, too. He eyed the hull and stifled a sigh- at least the bluefish and tuna they'd pulled in could be sold.

Pa, strangely, didn't seem to mind. The man was in better spirits than he'd been in years, even whistling sometimes. Danny enjoyed working with him. He found himself increasingly eager to please him, basking in the glow of whatever crumbs of praise were thrown his way. They shared a quiet comradery, the two of them against the ocean. Sails full, the *Molly Elizabeth* held her own with the swells. He only wished Shannon got to see this side of their father.

"Today's the day," Pa said for probably the fifth time that morning. He smiled, chipped front tooth peeking out from his black mustache. "I can feel it, boy."

"Yeah, Pa," Danny agreed.

Inside, he hoped not. He did a mental recalculation of the animal's supposed size compared to the eighteen-foot boat. It didn't add up, could throw off *Molly's* buoyancy entirely. Sure, there was a lot of money at stake- more than they'd earn over several years- but they'd need to make it back to shore to be able to spend it.

Danny knit his brows. There was no doubt what Pa would do first- a round for everyone at the Pilot House. And that was just for starters. Forget that the bungalow needed a new roof (*"and indoor plumbing!"* Shannon's voice rang in his ear).

It didn't matter. He'd use whatever small percentage Pa allotted to get them both out of there. Rent a tiny apartment in Philadelphia like he'd told her. Hopefully, he'd have some leftover to eventually put toward a rowhome of his own. From what he read, new neighborhoods were springing up every day. Overbrook, in particular, had a nice ring to it. Located on the west, it put him just a trolley ride away from the Martin's Germantown section. Jennie *would* want to be close to her father, after all...

"She pretty?" Pa asked.

"Huh?"

"I know that look, boy." Pa crossed his arms against himself and casually leaned on the mast. "Been a long time. But I know it."

Danny avoided his father's eye. He wasn't prepared for this discussion. Not in a calm, playful manner. Ideally, he'd rather not tell Pa about Jennie at all. The situation would go one of two ways- either Pa would chastise him for "putting on airs" or, more likely, come up with a scheme to shake down Mr. Martin.

His current escape plan, if he could even call it that, involved him and Shannon taking one of the late trains east while Pa was off on a bender, ending the vicious cycle they'd been locked in since they lost Ma. *We were so young.* The mosquitos were horrible that year and malaria ravaged the island, an indiscriminate, silent killer. Shannon stopped speaking for a month afterward. Thought it was her fault which, of course, Pa indulged. Poor kid would draw pictures on scraps of newspaper and leave them all over the shack. *"Pleez com bak* or *I luv u."* Sometimes both. Danny could still see them in his mind's eye; crooked little stick figures with distorted faces. One was always taller than the other two. Its circle mouth constantly open, triangle eyes traced over and blackened in like a jack-o-lantern.

Haunted, they were right to be afraid. They tried to stay out of his way but never quite could. Sure, it was a little easier now that they were older- until Pa went to the dark place, and the bottom dropped out all over again.

The way Danny figured, Philadelphia was so large they could easily hide out until his eighteenth birthday. It was only a few months away. He didn't even feel guilty about it, not in the slightest; he only wished they'd run away sooner. Pa misread his silence.

"No use denyin' it. You got it bad, son," he chuckled. "Plain as the nose on your face."

"Pa—"

"The way you creep around at night she must be a real dish."

Danny sucked in a deep breath.

"It's alright, boy. I was young once." Pa stroked the end of his mustache. "Make sure you pull out first. Y'know what I mean, right? Some girls'll try and trap you that way." He shook his head. "Your sister, on the other hand. *Pfft.* I can tell she's a virgin the way she crosses her legs."

Danny tried his best not to cringe. Failing, he bent his head down and pinched the bridge of his nose. "C'mon, Pa. Can't we talk about somethin' else?"

The older man shrugged. "Just doing my fatherly duty."

For once. All of a sudden, Pa wanted to offer advice? Act like they were close? Teeth clenched, Danny steadied his breathing as best he could. One thing was clear- he needed to get Shannon the hell outta there sooner than he thought.

"Look, Pa. It's not like that. Jennie's—"

Shit. It was too late to take it back now. Leave it to Pa to know which buttons to push and exactly how hard to push them. He threw a glance at his fishing pole- still straight as an arrow- he was the one who'd been hooked.

"Jennie, huh? Pretty name for a pretty girl."

Head cocked, Danny glared at the man.

"Don't tell me you love her."

"Why not?" he shot back. "You loved Ma."

Pa sneered. "Look how that turned out." He thundered across the deck to the bow. Back to his son, arms akimbo, he stared into the infinite cobalt.

"She *died*, Pa."

"You think I forgot?" He pounded the wooden rail. "I wish she'd taken me with her. Every goddamn day."

Suddenly, Pa rounded. Black eyes cold and flinty, it was a look Danny knew all too well, and his body braced itself. Jaw set, stomach firm, back-rim rod. He should've kept his mouth shut. Still, Pa needed him- there was no way either of them could bring in the shark alone. It wouldn't be that bad this time. It couldn't.

Danny met his eye, ready for whatever came his way first. Usually a left hook, there was a chance Pa might change it up to account for the rolling swells.

Pa leered forward. Quick as a rabbit, his right hand went low. Danny flinched and tightened his stomach, but the blow never landed. Instead, Pa seized the watch from his pocket.

Danny tried to grab it back, and- *wham*- there came an uppercut. Wincing, he wiped the corner of his mouth and tried again.

Pa backed away from him to the port side. He held the watch high over his head.

"Don't!" Danny pleaded, his own arm extended.

"Love?" Pa chuckled, deep and low. He made a show of winding up like a pitcher and launched the watch into the ocean. "There's your love, boy."

Another week passed, and still no shark. They'd lost the wind, too. From what Danny could tell by the charts, the *Molly Elizabeth* drifted closer to the shipping lanes. He wanted to drop anchor, but Pa disagreed, the older man insisting they'd have better luck with the creature if the bait kept moving.

Exhausted, Danny kneaded a sore shoulder muscle. He didn't know how much longer they'd last. He drew a deep breathe only to be disgusted by the stench coming off his body. Had July always been this hot? Rations running low, he'd long stopped sweating. He felt himself dizzying but didn't dare complain about it. His skin was leathered, his hands; raw. But it was his mouth that bothered him the most. The lower lip still hadn't healed from Pa's outburst, and the sun only made it worse until both were so cracked and dry they bled.

Sitting cross-legged on the starboard side, Pa looked just as grisly. However, judging by the half-empty bottle of Jack in his hand, he felt no pain. Probably had no clue his odor rivaled that of the fish rotting away in the hull, either. Ice chests and summer simply weren't friends.

"Where is it?" he slurred. "Hmph- it's like he knew we were comin'."

Well, I didn't tell it, that's for damn sure.

Too weak to argue, Danny swallowed what little saliva he could muster in hopes to trick his body into thinking it was actual water.

"This was s'posed to be yours," Pa continued, patting the deck. "Was gonna git me another one with that there prize money."

"Geez, Pa. I don't…I dunno know what to say."

Pa waved his free hand. "Ya don't hafta thank me."

Gratitude wasn't exactly what Danny had in mind. Numb was more like it. He didn't want this life. Never had.

There was nothing wrong with being a mariner. It was hard work and an honest living. But all his memories of the profession were tied in with Pa. He was so close to finally breaking free of the man, to starting his *own* life under his *own* terms. Danny looked down at his boots, their rubber bottoms so hot he thought they'd melt right onto the deck. And here he was- just as stuck.

"You're lucky, ya know that, boy? You and your sis'er."

Lucky? Pa was drunker than he thought.

Danny offered a limp nod.

"I mean it. My old man didn't teach me nothin'. Wouldn't let me get away with half o' what you and Shannon do neither." Pa put the bottle down, positioning his fists into a boxer's stance in front of his face. "See these?" he said of his hands. "Only way he knew how to talk." He picked the whisky back up, took a long pull, and clicked his tongue. "Man had a lot to say."

"Sorry Pa. I...I didn't know."

"How wouldja? Never even told your Ma." Pa motioned for Danny to sit beside him and, when he did, passed him the bottle. "You look like shit. Here. It'll take the edge of."

Parched, Danny lifted the rim to his mouth and stopped- the immediate sting of a hundred bees assaulting his lips. He forced the whimper in his throat into a grimace, eyes too dry to allow even the slightest tear.

"G'head now." Pa tipped it back. "Down the hatch."

Danny had drank before. Too many times, in fact, no thanks to Hugh. He already felt wretched enough. He tried to push it away, but Pa held firm.

The amber liquid burned as it went down. Danny tried to swallow as much as he could without spilling it out the side of his mouth. Breathing through his nose, he gulped. Once. Twice. Then once more. Just when he thought he couldn't drink anymore, Pa slapped him on the back and yanked the bottle away.

"Atta boy," he cackled and took his own swig.

Danny panted and placed his hands next to his hips. It felt like the *Molly* hit a swell, but he wasn't sure. His stomach was warm. Tingly. Everything else was, too.

Pa raised the whisky in a toast. "To you and me, boy." The pirate smiled, glugged, and offered it back to his son, this time only shrugging when Danny waved it off. "Eh-more for me. To the future!"

An hour later, the man was passed out cold, his sonorous wheeze echoing on the water. Noodle-legged, Danny crawled to his satchel and pulled out what remained of the bread. The first crunchy bite scratched his throat. Far from satisfying, at least it would sop up some of the booze. The stench wafting from the hull was unbearable, and Danny gagged. He took another dry mouthful to quell the nausea.

Poseidon mocked him. Miles of open ocean as far as the eye could see; none of it drinkable. Oh, but it was probably cold. So, so cold and delightfully refreshing. If it weren't for the damn shark, he would've jumped in to cool off hours ago. Frantic, he drained the few drops left in his canteen only to have them turn to ash on his tongue.

Danny clapped a hand over his forehead and slid it down the bridge of his nose. So much for his great escape. He scowled at the reeking hull. They'd have to dump the dead fish anyway. He clawed his way up the side of the bow and gripped the rail. The sooner it was gone, the better.

He scraped the first ice chest as far as he could push it, disturbing the greenhead flies and gnats feasting on the carcasses in the process. Furious, the gnats swarmed Danny's sweaty hairline while the flies went straight for the sweet spot— his ankles.

Ouch! He swatted and slapped the first fly, but there were too many, and he was too tired. Better he finishes the task at hand. Danny held his breath, grabbed a tuna by what remained of its tail fin, and chucked it overboard. Then another, two-by-two. Plop, plop, plop.

Now half empty, he might be able to dump it. Grunting, Danny gripped the sides of the wooden chest. Slick with melted ice and fish guts, he lifted it a quarter way up and fumbled. The chest slammed against the deck, just missing his feet. Danny glanced at Pa, but the man didn't even bat an eye.

I just wanna go home.

Danny had no idea how far they'd drifted, and it wouldn't be dark for hours. At the rate he was going, the stars might decide not to show up at all. He reopened the chest's lid and yanked a bluefish over the side.

"Here!" he shouted to the god of the sea. "Take 'em back! Take 'em all back!"

A rancid ticker-tape parade of fish flew over the bow. Finished with the first chest, Danny heaved the remaining two from the festering hull. He didn't know where this sudden burst of energy came from, but he didn't care. The entire trip was a waste. No shark. No watch. He gulped and glared down at his father. No Jennie if Pa had anything to say about it. *He'll never let me go.*

Every muscle ached. Pain shot through his shoulder blades with each twist and turn. Danny hadn't grown used to the stench, not by any means, but he was too focused now to allow himself to be overcome.

Seabirds flocked and dove into the surf. Every now and then, an occasional splash hit his cheek, and he relished what little relief it gave him. The scavengers gorged themselves. They laughed and cawed, fighting each other for every last scrap until the surface was white as snow, seafoam and seagull an undiscernible swirl.

At last, Danny hurled the final carcass into the water. Hands on his hips, he struggled to catch his breath when his eyes fell on the anchor's thick chain. Mustering every bit of strength he had left, Danny threw that overboard, too. Drained, he slid down the side of the vessel, and his bottom sloshed on the chummy planks. Danny leaned his head on a shoulder and closed his swollen eyes.

Thump.

"Pa?"

Thump.

Didn't sound like boots. Danny squinted. He didn't know how long he'd been asleep. Judging by the sun, it was probably about an hour or so. Something was off. The *Molly* was eerily still, Pa's snoring the only sound for miles. Where were the birds? There'd been hundreds of them.

Thump— there it was again.

Cape May was founded by whalers, and Danny had grown up on stories by Ahabs from all walks of life. *Dammit.* They were out here for shark. There was no money in whale anymore. He crawled to the helm, grabbing the harpoon beside it. Better he try to scare the Goliath than end up in the deep with him. A few pokes might just do the job.

Danny crept back to the bow, and his jaw dropped. The sea before him was red, its surface splattered with white and gray feathers. Some were fluffy, others, still connected to the remains of their bodies. He scanned the horizon to no avail. Flabbergasted, Danny covered his mouth and shook his head. Should he wake Pa? No, he resolved. That would accomplish nothing more than a fresh shiner.

He searched the starboard side. Nothing. Not even a ripple.

Only when his eyes returned to port that he saw it— a small black triangle about fifty yards out.

Better late than never. Maybe he'd been right about dropping anchor, after all.

The shark turned, almost as if it knew it was being watched. Up came the tailfin now, Danny's only point of reference as it approached the *Molly*, the rest of its sleek body blending perfectly with the brine.

It circled the monstrous flotsam and opened its bloodstained mouth to reveal rows and rows of wedge-shaped teeth. Danny watched with a mixture of awe and horror as they detached from its snout to chomp on one of few brazen gulls that remained, thrashing and gnawing the bird to pieces in only a few bites. Try as he may, he couldn't tear his eyes from the sheer power of the jaws. Muscular and strong, it was a hauntingly beautiful creature, unafraid of anyone or anything. Satisfied, the shark disappeared into the fathoms, and Danny found himself disappointed.

Two weeks. Two weeks baking under the merciless sun, and that was it? That was *it*? Surely, this couldn't be the same animal the papers warned of.

Thump.

Danny looked down. The shark was in throwing range now. Not two feet away. That money was as good as his. His grip on the harpoon tightened, and Danny raised it over his head. Would serve the sonuvabitch right for taunting him.

It turned on its side, white belly in stark contrast with the rest of its dark body. Magnificent as it was, the creature was nowhere near its reported size. At best, he'd put it at about six feet. Danny gazed from the shark to feathers and back, locking eyes with the animal as it meandered the *Molly's* length, seemingly just as curious about him.

It was a juvenile.

Danny frowned. Prize or not, he couldn't go through with it.

"Git!" he called as if shooing a stray. Danny lowered the harpoon to his side. "Go on, now. Get outta here!"

The shark, in response, looped itself in a circle and glided back to the stern. Danny kept pace with it, nearly tripping over Pa's outstretched leg in the process. The animal blinked and began gnashing on what appeared to be a seagull wing.

This was no savage beast. Gruesome, yes, but acting on primal instinct. It only did what it had to do to survive.

Monsters did exist, of course. Danny knew that all too well. Pa was an omnipresent voice inside him, always shouting how he was worthless or that he'd never amount to anything. He didn't want to give Danny the *Molly* out of kindness. The man didn't know the meaning of the word. No, Pa only ever did what was best for Pa. Having two boats meant more earnings, which, undoubtedly, would end up at the bottom of a bottle. Danny slid his thumb along his lips, still feeling the excruciating pain of earlier. The effects of the whisky had worn off, and he was even more dehydrated than before. Images of his treasured watch sailing through the air juxtaposed with those of Shannon crossing her legs at the breakfast table flashed before him. What kind of man eyeballs his own daughter? A monster— that's who.

White-knuckled, Danny raised the harpoon and held it perpendicular.

His free hand rose to meet it, forming an equally vice grip. He glanced at the ocean where the shark was now swimming away. It was free. Crack! Danny snapped the rod over his knee. *That makes one of us.*

CHAPTER 7

Shannon finished sweeping the kitchen and smiled. She tucked a flyaway behind her ear and hooked the broom back up on the pantry door. The place never looked so good. A small vase of wildflowers sat in the center of the table. She'd even managed to scrub away the grimy ring in the corner where they kept the tub.

That was one way to use up her nervous energy. It gave her a sense of pride. Accomplishment. A part of her hoped Pa would be pleased. Their tiny house was immaculate— she was a good girl. Another part, a larger one by far, fantasized about how her life would look away from here. Free. The possibilities were endless. She'd take the city by storm and never look back; relish this same gratification when cleaning her new home, or at least her part of the apartment. Despite what Danny said, there was no way they'd manage without a roommate.

And just like that, her temperament soured. Shannon promised herself not to think of him. Fear dictated her life for so long she'd become a master at shutting out her emotions. She controlled them, not the other way around. Swallowed whole, Shannon buried her feelings deep inside herself, locked away forever. It was as natural as breathing— she didn't know any other way to live. This one broke through, and she hated herself for it. *You're better than this. Get it together.*

Still, they'd been gone a long time, and she had no idea when they were coming home. Not even an inkling as to which course they'd set. The buzz in the papers was the shark made its way further north. It even swam up one of the rivers. *A river.* A chill ran through her, and Shannon clenched her fists. She took a deep breath in, held it, and then released— a process she'd repeat as many times as necessary for the fear to pass. It always did. Eventually.

Her stomach growled, bringing her back to reality. While she rose with the sun, Shannon hadn't eaten. Outside, linens danced in the seaside breeze, and an oystercatcher yeeped from its nest in the dunes. She, at least, was safe on dry land. Safe and voraciously hungry.

Shannon palmed her forehead— the milk. Good thing the morning was still young. She glided to the front door to retrieve the day's canister, already tasting it on her tongue. Thick and creamy, and all to herself. She opened the door and scowled.

There, parked along the curb, was a shiny maroon roadster.

She yanked the milk off the stoop and marched back into the house. *How dare he?* It was one thing for Hugh to know she was poor, to have some semblance of her station and never mention it out of respect. It was quite another for him to bear witness to her deprivation.

Sure, he'd driven Danny home more times than she could count. The shanty was practically invisible under a midnight coverlet. Here, in the stark light of day, it was amazing the ramshackle door was still even on its hinges. One of the front shutters was snapped in half, another missing entirely. To say nothing of the poorly patched roof. If, for some Godforsaken reason, they were still here come winter, she prayed for fair weather.

And that was just the outside. Shannon could've spent a month cleaning. Scoured the place top to bottom. Scrubbed until her nails were cracked and raw. Didn't matter. No amount of cleansing would ever wash away the sins that occurred indoors.

Never knowing what they were coming home to after school, she and Danny rarely had friends over when they were younger. The oft chance one stopped by set off sheer panic; empty bottles kicked under Pa's chair, his overflowing ashtray dumped haphazardly out the window. Poor excuses were given, time and again, until people stopped coming altogether. Hurtful, yes, both she and Danny probably lost some friendships in the process, but it was better than the truth. No one could ever see how they really lived. Isolation was the only way to cope with the shame of their predicament, a tiny self-contained isle of their very own within the larger cape peninsula.

Dammit. Who did Hugh think he was? Showing up out of nowhere. She didn't need a babysitter. She didn't need *anyone,* got along just fine on her own the last few weeks. Shannon slammed the canister in the icebox then stomped back outside.

She peered through the passenger side window. Hugh was sleeping in the driver's seat, slick black hair glistening as the Brilliantine caught in the sunshine. His tie was undone, as were the top two buttons of his shirt, and he cuffed the sleeves up to his elbows. Hugh's mouth was slightly agape, and when Shannon found her eyes drawn to the stubble along his strong jaw, she promptly reminded herself that she wasn't here to look. She tapped an open palm on the glass.

"Wake up!"

He stirred, brown eyes blinking under his long, dark lashes.

Shannon knocked again. "I said *wake up.*"

Hugh stretched and smiled. He made a hand-visor to shield his eyes and leaned across the console to unlock her door.

She jerked it open. "Whaddaya think you're doin', huh?"

"Geez, Shannon. Good morning to you, too. Just thought I'd check in on ya. Don't get so bent outta shape."

"Did my brother ask you?"

"No, but—"

"But nuthin'," she crossed her arms against herself. "I can take care of myself."

"I never said you couldn't."

"You didn't have to."

"Been almost three weeks." Hugh shrugged. "If it were Jennie, I'd want Danny to look in on her. I'm just trying to do the right thing."

Jennie. The only upside to this nonsensical hunt was it gave Shannon a reprieve from hearing her name. Hugh may as well have thrown a bucket of cold water in her face.

"For *once*."

The blow hurt him. She could see it in his eyes. But Shannon didn't stop there.

"Where were you this time? The Blue Pig?"

"Jackson's Club House," he mumbled, unable to look at her. "Came here straight after. Didn't want to go home."

She softened, a tsunami of guilt cresting as she drank him in. He had the broad, athletic shoulders of a man but the spirit of a child. Right now, he wore the look of a puppy on its way to the pound.

"Well," she cleared her throat, "thank you for your honesty." Shannon held her head as high as she could. "As for watching the house, perhaps I misjudged you."

"Perhaps?" Hugh grinned, dimples prominently pronounced.

Shannon arched a brow.

"Say, I'm starvin'," he continued, dragging a hand through his hair. "How 'bout we go to Kennedy's? My treat."

Shannon smoothed her apron. Having cleaned all morning, she was suddenly aware she looked like it, too. Her long locks were pinned under a kerchief, and there were sweat stains on the armpits of her paisley housedress.

"I don't want your money."

"Go Dutch, I don't care."

That was one thing she appreciated about him. Hugh never pretended to be the gentleman he was supposed to be. She was about to come up with another excuse when her stomach grumbled loud enough for him to hear. Shannon looked down and wrung her hands. Even at Kennedy's Pharmacy, eating out was a luxury she simply couldn't afford.

"Hugh, I…"

"It's just breakfast, Shannon. What kinda jerk do you think I am? You really think I'd let you pay?" Hugh waved his hand. "Y'know what— don't answer that. Just go get changed, wouldja?" he smiled. "I'll wait."

Twenty minutes later, they were sitting opposite in a booth at Kennedy's. The store's black and white parkay floors were freshly polished, and the scent of fresh pine tickled Shannon's nose.

Hugh spread his menu across the table. "What looks good?"

"Besides everything?"

"Get whatever you what. I mean it."

Shannon took a sip of coffee, wishing she could disappear into the mug. She knew he was just trying to be kind. Unused to benevolence from anyone but Danny, she didn't know how to respond. Hadn't she insulted him earlier?

Mr. Kennedy strode to the table, his pale blue eyes twinkling under their bushy white brows. He always reminded Shannon of Santa Claus, minus the beard, and had the heart of the jolly old elf, too. Knowing Pa often didn't settle his charge account timely, some months not at all, they had a secret, standing agreement she would sweep the floors and re-stock the shelves to make up any differences.

"Mornin' kids," he smiled. "What can I get for you?"

They both ordered the scrapple and eggs with an extra side of toast for dipping. Outside on Washington Street, a newsboy hawked the latest *Star and Wave*. Hugh got up to buy a copy.

"It's good to see you out, Shannon," Mr. Kennedy mused while wiping down the counter.

"Thank you."

"I had the missus throw an extra piece of meat on for you."

"You *didn't*?"

"Already done, lass." He winked. "Frying up as we speak."

"Entirely unnecessary."

"If you don't finish it, we can always wrap it up."

The bell on the door chimed as Hugh walked back into the store. "Wrap what up?"

Shannon waved a hand. "Oh, nothing."

Inside, however, her cheeks were burning. She wasn't a charity case. Is that how everyone saw her? Pride wounded yet again, she stared vacantly out the window.

"You alright?" Hugh asked a few minutes later.

"Hmm?"

He reached across the table and squeezed the top of her hand. Shannon fought against the knee-jerk instinct to pull it away, only to find she didn't really want to. The touch was gentle, his eyes; earnest.

"He'll be back any day now."

Shannon trained her eyes to the ceiling, praying Hugh was right. "The U-boats…"

"They're not after small craft."

"But…the minefields."

Hugh circled his fingertips over her knuckles. "I wish Samuel and I were that close."

"How many years apart are you?"

"Ten."

"I suppose that does make quite a difference."

She finally allowed herself to look at him, his gaze intent, almost as if he wanted to say more. Hugh hadn't moved his hand, either. What kind of game was he playing? Shannon pulled hers back slowly and smoothed the napkin on her lap.

"You like crossword puzzles?"

Shannon took a sip of coffee. "Doesn't everyone?"

"Not Mother." He grinned. "Though, unless it's from Tiffany's, there's not much she does like."

He turned the paper around to show her what he'd been working on. "Eight across," he pointed. "Nine letter word for 'loved one.' Starts with 'b'."

Shannon squinted. She chewed her lip, silently counting out letters on her fingers.

"Buttercup?" she giggled.

Hugh chuckled and traced the column in question. "Ends in 'd' though. Sorry. Shoulda mentioned that."

She leaned over the table to get a better look. They were so close she could smell his aftershave, or what was left of yesterday's, anyway. Clean yet spicy, she allowed herself another heavenly whiff. Heads together, they went through the remaining possibilities.

"Beloved?" he suggested.

"Only seven letters."

"Right."

"How'd you get into Harvard?"

"Don't be cheeky."

"I'm not. Just stating the obvious."

"Which is?"

"You can't spell to save your life. Try 'betrothed'."

Hugh wrote it out and shook his head. "Nope. See, look at four down. I'm pretty sure that's..." he solved the riddle. "Yes. 'Carpenter.' Which means—"

"It can't end with 'ed'."

"Exactly."

"Boyfriend," Mr. Kennedy announced as he brought their plates over. He plopped a bottle of Heinz on the table.

Shannon recounted the letters while Hugh scribbled them down. It fit.

Mr. Kennedy smiled. "What I tell ya?"

"Boyfriend," Shannon repeated, slowly seating her back against the booth.

Hugh mimicked the movement and reached for his silverware. "How 'bout that."

Mr. Kennedy gestured to the heavens and padded back to the counter. "Why is it always wasted on the young?"

Doggy bag in hand, Shannon's feet never felt so light. The car was just a few steps away; she reached it before Hugh. Her hand lingered on the door handle. Taking a deep breath, she spun around just as he leaned over to open it for her.

Face to face, her heart slammed in her chest. He must've felt it, too, because he gulped.

"Oof! Sorry I...just wanted to say, um," she struggled. "Thank you. For, uh..."

"Breakfast."

"Right," she nodded. "And dragging me out of the house."

"What are friends for?"

"Friends. Of course. Friends eat out together all the time."

"All the time."

"Well, I...I had fun."

"Me too."

He hadn't moved. Not even an inch. Neither did Shannon.

Transfixed, Hugh cocked his head, and a black wave dropped down next to his right eye. Shannon reached up and smoothed it back in place, her hand lingering longer than it should have as she traced his temple.

Friends didn't do that, right?

Her eyes fell to his mouth, and she wondered why she'd never noticed the small cleft in his chin before. Or the slight freckles dotting the bridge of his nose. Is this how Danny felt when he was with Jennie? Dreamy. The whole world could collapse around them, and it wouldn't matter. It was nice. Warm and…safe.

Something dull scraped along the sidewalk. A slow lurch. One foot, then, with some effort, the other. She paid it little mind, probably just one of the merchants wheeling in a crate of inventory, and returned her attentions to Hugh and those big brown eyes.

Scrape, scrape, scrape.

Distracted now, Shannon caught the image in her peripheral. Thinking it was a figment of her imagination, she blinked and checked the rearview mirror. Unmistakable now, she pushed Hugh aside and sprinted up the pavement.

"Danny!" She flew to his side, practically tackling him in the process.

"Hey," he forced a smile.

"You're back. Thank goodness! I was so worried, Danny. I missed you so much."

She'd never let the world see her cry. Not even now— sheer joy overtaking her. Unaccustomed to the patchy beard he'd grown at sea, Shannon kept her touch feather-light, beaming as she traced his cheeks.

"Oh my God," she clutched him tighter, palming his forehead, then rechecking it with the back of her hand. "You're burning up."

"I'm okay, Shannon."

"You're not."

She gulped. *Ma had a fever, too.*

"It's not the same," Danny said, reading her thoughts the way only he could do. His voice was barely audible. "Too much sun is all. Just need a little sleep."

Hugh joined them now, the lines on his face showing the same concern as Shannon. He pat Danny's shoulder. "You alright, pal?"

"What a ridiculous thing to say! Does he look alright, Hugh? Does he?"

Danny grimaced. "Been better."

Shannon looped Danny's arm over her shoulders. Hugh took the hint and supported him from the other side. Slowly, the trio made their way to the roadster.

Hugh opened the passenger side door and pushed the seat up. Shannon crawled in the back, cradling her brother against her torso.

"Mace Hospital?" Hugh asked from the driver's seat.

"*No*," both Culligans said simultaneously. There was no way they could afford any additional expenses right now.

"Home it is, then."

A nickelodeon of summer scenes whirled by as they sped toward Beach Avenue; seaside artists capturing the lighthouse, ladies in finery out on the promenade, a peppermint beach of red and white umbrellas. Shannon missed them all. She grazed her thumb along Danny's puffy lip, the ache in his eyes confirming this was more than mere sunburn.

"What happened out there?"

"I don't wanna talk about it."

"Where's Pa?"

"Tore off in the car." He drew a raspy breath. "Soon as we docked."

She stroked his greasy hair. "I should've never let you go."

"Like you coulda stopped him?"

"I should've tried."

Drowning in a sea of guilt and shame, Shannon didn't realize the car had stopped moving. Until that moment, she'd also forgotten they weren't alone in the vehicle. How much had Hugh heard? Danny could all but whisper. She thought she kept her own voice down but was so shaken she couldn't remember.

Hugh opened the door. She got out on the driver's side while he leaned in to give her brother a hand. Again, they kept a careful pace. She was much shorter than Hugh and not nearly as strong. Danny was so weak his legs buckled, and it took both of them to get him up across the yard.

They reached the steps to the front door, and she stopped. This was her fortress. Regardless of circumstance, she couldn't allow Hugh entrance.

"I'll take it from here."

"Are you crazy?"

"I've got it, Hugh."

"I'm not leaving you."

"I *said* I can handle it. Thank you for breakfast," Shannon was so agitated she was jabbering now. "And for the ride. But we can manage on our own."

"Let him help," Danny croaked. He drew his head up and gave her a slight nod. "It's okay."

They managed to make it through the threshold with effort before proceeding to the narrow staircase leading upstairs. Shannon went up first. Walking backward, she held Danny's hand. He braced himself with the other, gripping the splintered rail. Hugh was behind both, his physique enough to block the way should either lose their footing.

Finally, they reached the closet of a room she and Danny shared. She motioned the bed, and they laid him out on the threadbare blanket. Shannon got the water basin and poured her brother a small amount. He took a delicate sip, then another, tiny fractures of her heart shattering every which way as she watched him sigh in sweet satisfaction. He struggled to push himself up, ready to take his usual spot on the floor.

"Oh no you don't." She pressed a gentle hand on his shoulder. "You need to rest."

"She's right, buddy," Hugh said from the doorway. "Better get your beauty sleep if we're gonna hit the driving range. You just let me know when you're up to it."

Danny smiled as best he could. "That'd be swell."

"I'll be in touch."

He laid back down, eyes fluttering closed as Shannon pressed a wet cloth to his forehead. She laid another across his collarbone, and he emitted a soft groan. It wasn't long before his breathing regulated— the steady rise and fall of slumber.

Sleep held him in a chrysalis, Shannon; her heart. What had Pa done this time? Hours passed yet she couldn't tear herself away. She laid rag after rag along Danny's pressure points, and the pitcher was almost empty.

Shannon padded down the stairs to pump some more and stopped in her tracks.

"You're still here?"

Hugh rose from the armchair in the corner and moved to face her. Bathed in ribbons of sunlight thanks to the windows she'd so carefully washed only hours earlier, he took the basin and gently placed it on the side table, then withdrew a handkerchief from his pocket.

Shannon let it drop to the floor when he tried to hand it to her. How could she let her guard down? What a fool she'd been, allowing herself to feel—what—normal? Relaxed? *Desired?* She wasn't sure. One thing Shannon did know was that Hugh had seen too much. Overheard things he had no right to hear. He may not have been sitting in Pa's shabby wingback anymore, but he was just as much an enemy.

Shannon narrowed her eyes. "I asked you a question Mr. Callaway."

Jaw agape, he picked up the hanky and shoved it back in his pocket.

"Why, huh?" she crossed her arms. "I don't recall asking you to stay."

"He's my friend, Shannon."

"Your *friend?* You like that word a lot, don't you?"

"You are, too." He took a step toward her, but she jerked away.

"You can leave now."

"Shannon, I—"

"Don't."

One hand on her hip, she pointed at the front door with the other. Hugh lowered his head and did as he was told. Magnetized, she followed. Hand on the knob, he gave her one last look over his shoulder.

"For what it's worth," he began, "whatever I said, whatever I did, Shannon...." His Addams apple bobbed, and Hugh set his jaw. "I didn't mean it."

He closed the door behind him, and she heard the squeal of tires a few seconds later.

It's what you didn't say. What could never come to pass between them.

Shannon's lips spread into a drooping line. She should've felt triumphant—shutting him down, practically tossing him out. Instead, her whole insides hurt, and a heaviness shot through her chest. The dreadful sensation was unnerving. She'd taken her share of blows, but nothing physical—not even the damn belt—had left her so distressed.

Alone, at last, she pressed her forehead against the wood. One trembling hand on the oaken door, she covered her mouth with the other. It was better this way. It had to be.

CHAPTER 8

Three weeks later, Danny put on the clothes Hugh lent him for golf. With Mr. Martin's schedule being so complicated, it had taken a while to find a free day. Summer was almost over, and there wasn't much time left to get to know him before Jennie and her family returned to the city. Everything was riding on today.

He squinted in the vanity, struggling with the buttons on the argyle vest.

"Let me," Shannon insisted. "My fingers are smaller."

Chin up, Danny let her loop it through.

Shannon brushed her hands along his shoulders before stepping back to admire her work. "Not bad," she grinned.

"Almost like a real, swell, huh?"

"Almost? Danny, you do know you'll be required to carry yourself a certain way."

"I know."

"Let's go over your talking points again," Shannon insisted.

Danny frowned. It wasn't complicated. Stay away from politics and anything involving the war. Follow Hugh's cues to keep the conversation sounding natural yet focused on the commonalities between himself and Mr. Martin. Hard work. Determination. Ambition.

Shannon heaved a sigh, and he knew she wasn't satisfied.

"Look," he said, wetting a comb in the basin and running it through his hair, "I appreciate what you're trying to do."

"Theirs is a different world. I just want you to be prepared."

Danny set the comb down and turned to face her again. He glanced out the window, unsure how to relay his suspicions about Pa's ill intent. No one had seen or heard from the man since they'd docked. Both siblings knew the cycle all too well; their father got blind drunk, flying into a rage and disappearing for days on end only to return and pretend as if nothing ever happened. Sometimes Pa even came home bearing gifts.

"Shannon," he said, tone serious now as he guided her to the bed and sat down. "There's somethin' else we gotta talk about."

She crossed her arms against her chest. "Like how you've been watching me like a hawk ever since you got back from the hunt?" Shannon grumbled. "Insisting I go to all your little pow-wows. Accompanying you down at the docks. Did Hugh put you up to it?"

"What? No."

She cocked her head.

"He'll be here in about five minutes, you know."

"Your point?"

Danny fought the urge to lecture her. She could be so stubborn sometimes. The tension between his sister and his best friend was obvious. Palpable. While some brothers might feel territorial, overprotective even, Danny stood on the precipice of getting his heart's desire- Jennie's hand. Who was he to stand in the way? Especially if the connection was between two of his favorite people.

"It's not so bad having someone care about you."

"You care about me."

"That's not what I meant." Danny took a deep breath and put a hand on her knee. "Guess I tried to hide it but," he offered a half-smile, "you're right. I don't like leaving you alone. Even for somethin' as important as today."

"I'm a big girl, Danny. Got plenty to keep me busy."

"Who knows where Pa's holed up this time? Or when he'll come back."

Shannon shook her head. "You don't have to worry about me."

"I'd feel better if we dropped you off at the Barkley's."

She poked his bicep. "Oh, so now you're trying to push me off on Will? Stop playing Cupid, wouldja?"

Danny wanted to return her playful smile. He had every reason to be happy. Excited. Even absent, Pa poisoned the air inside the house; his shadow lurked in every corner.

"Listen, Danny, say Pa does come home. So what? I've covered for you before."

"Yeah, but this is different."

"What aren't you telling me?"

They heard the sound of tires along the dirt road outside. Slowly, they crunched to a halt on the drive.

"Nuthin'." He stood, checked his reflection one last time, and popped his head out the window to acknowledge Hugh's arrival. Danny looked back at his sister, still sitting at the foot of the bed. "This should only take a couple o'hours. Hugh said somethin' about getting lunch after, but I'll have him bring me straight back."

"Why? If things go well with Martin won't he be offended if you decline?"

Danny swallowed hard. "I'll be back by dinner. I promise."

"Go," she urged him. "And Danny? Good luck."

"Thanks," he mouthed from the bedroom doorway.

They had about an hour before tee time, and the morning passed uneventfully. Hugh brought a Dewar flask of coffee for them and some biscuits and jam. They parked by the lighthouse, munching as the sun shone over the water.

Danny took a gulp from the thermos. "Thanks. For all of this, Hugh."

"We go back long enough."

"That we do," Danny agreed, passing the coffee back to him.

"Surprised you need this though," Hugh said as he replaced the lid. "Thought you were used to being out all hours."

Danny raised an eyebrow.

"Davey's Lake?"

"A gentleman doesn't tell," Danny smirked.

"Who said you were a gentleman?"

"Who said you were?" They shared a laugh, and Danny grew serious again. He thought they'd been more careful. "How'd you know?"

Hugh shrugged. "The servants talk." Seeing his friend flush, he quickly added, "I'm teasing, pal. You forget I'm out all hours myself. Caught her on her way up the lattice once. She was so surprised I thought she'd nearly fall off."

"I never touched her, Hugh. Not like that," Danny assured.

He wanted to. It killed him, but he valued Jennie's integrity too much. The lake was the only place they could be alone together. Still feeling Hugh's eyes on him, Danny finally settled on the half-truth that Jennie read to him.

Hoping he remembered it correctly, Danny offered, "*She walks in beauty, like the night.*"

"That she does, old friend. That she does." Hugh lit a cigarette, shaking out the match. "I envy you," he said, exhaling out the side of his mouth.

Danny shot him a questioning look, lighting his own smoke.

The other man took a deep drag and nodded, leaving Danny confused. It was unlike his friend to sound so morose, and he wondered if Shannon had anything to do with it. *What the hell happened while I was away?* The eldest son of a shipping magnate, the world was Hugh's oyster, and indulge he did. His friend was usually full of life, constantly regaling their card games with stories of his campus mixers and football team. He had his toys, of course— the roadster they currently occupied, his yacht, and the ponies. Yet, despite the money, Hugh remained unaffected, just as Jennie was. It was one of the reasons they got along so well.

Hugh retrieved a postcard from the pocket of his trousers, thumbing absentmindedly over the stamp. "At least you have choices. Freedom. My whole life's been planned out since before I was born."

Danny wanted to tell him the truth. That living under John Culligan's roof, he was just as trapped.

"You really think your uncle will accept me?"

"Walter?" Hugh shrugged, cigarette dangling from the side of his mouth, "He's never been like us. He loves Jennie. Jennie loves you. Simple as that." He tossed the postcard onto the dashboard. "My father's in Newport with his mistress right now."

"Hugh, I'm sorry."

"It's alright. They all do it. Hell, I probably will too." Hugh threw what remained of his cigarette out the window, turning to his friend and clapping a hand on his shoulder. "Jennie? She'll be spared of all that."

Danny ground his own butt in the ashtray. A solemn nod was his only response. They'd move in different circles than she was used to, but they'd have each other, and somehow he'd make it all work.

The old Hugh returned when they reached the Cape May Country Club, casually pointing out some of its more notable patrons while they freshened up. There was Ned Stotesbury, the prominent Philadelphia investment banker, and John Wanamaker. Wait 'til Shannon heard, she loved his department store catalogs. The man had more money than he knew what to do with. Actually proposed the United States buy Belgium from the

Germans to stop the blood bath overseas. *Buy it.* For the bargain price of a hundred billion dollars. Money was nothing to men of that caliber. Danny shook his head despite himself as he recalled the talk along the harbor after the story broke last year.

Around them, lockers were opening and slamming shut. Members chatted about everything from the Phillies' odds at another pennant to Wilson's chances at a second term. Danny felt a tightness rising in his chest and plunked himself on a bench. Hands on his knees, he gulped in a thick musk of smoke, after-shave, and shoe shine. What was he thinking? He didn't belong here. Shannon was right, he should've rehearsed more.

Hugh summoned a caddy to take their bags upstairs. "Drink?" he asked, cocking his head toward the bar across the room.

"Sounds good," Danny replied. Anything to take the edge off.

It was already crowded as everyone relished the last days of the summer. Danny stuffed his hands in his pockets while they waited for the bartender. He reached for his watch only to feel sick when he remembered it wasn't there. It would never be there again. *Dammit, Pa.*

That lit a fire in him. He'd be out from under his father's thumb soon enough. Shannon, too. And Jennie? Jennie depended on him to unlock the door of her gilded cage. He'd free them. He'd free them all.

Mr. Martin would be there any minute. Danny could do this. Win him over. Show him that, while he might be young, he was a good person. He could see it all in his mind's eye now. Laughing at one of the older man's jokes. Shaking hands at the end of their round. Making plans for him to call on Jennie at Juniper Grove and write her in the city. He'd wait for Jennie. However long it took, he'd wait for her. Do whatever Walter Martin wanted.

Danny gazed at the flickering light streaming through a window at his right. The stained glass took up a wall the size of his room. A shadow was forming against the crimson carpeting. He cleared his throat, hoping to greet Mr. Martin in a smooth baritone, not the staccato he was sure would slip out if he didn't. He was about to turn to shake his hand when an unfamiliar voice stopped him dead on.

"Hugh Callaway? You old devil!"

Danny looked over his shoulder, what little resolve he had left wavering. Joseph York— Jennie's escort on the Fourth of July.

The bartender finally made his way over. "What'll it be boys?"

Turning back to the bar, Danny stared him straight in the eyes. "Bourbon. Make it a double."

By the time the foursome made it to the first tee, Danny was already feeling sick. Snake oil salesman that he was, York weaseled his way in at the last minute. Happened so fast Danny's head was still spinning. He knew that the second round was a mistake, but Joseph insisted on it. A toast to new acquaintances or some other malarkey.

His brow was drenched. The liner of the wool cap he borrowed was stained in sticky sweat. Danny dabbed it with his handkerchief and surveyed the links while the others chose their clubs. No way could he return it to Hugh now.

The first hole was a dogleg left, and he shanked it. Between the liquor, the heat, and his nerves, he wasn't sure he'd be able to make it through the first nine, let alone the whole course.

"Tough break," said York.

"Happens to the best of us," offered Hugh, picking up on the other man's lack of sincerity. "Mulligan?"

Mr. Martin, for his part, gave a nod of encouragement.

Danny was mortified. He came here for Mr. Martin's approval, not his sympathy. He didn't need a do-over of the drive; he needed a do-over of the last thirty minutes.

The afternoon dragged on. Danny spent most of it in the rough. If that weren't bad enough, York monopolized all conversation as they walked the greens. He peppered Walter about which baseball team he preferred, the Athletics or the Phillies, hardly letting even Hugh get a word in edgewise.

Mr. Martin only shrugged. "I keep boxes at both Shibe Park and the Baker Bowl. Though, they're mainly for business purposes."

"Danny likes baseball," Hugh interjected, jutting his chin at his friend. "Got quite an arm, too."

"Do you play for your school?" Joseph asked with a hint of sarcasm.

"No," Danny admitted, resisting the urge to clench his jaw. "Just neighborhood games." *Remember your commonalities.* Grit. Sheer will. "Teams and games are for children," he said. "I have my future to consider."

"Children?" York cocked his head and laughed. "Hugh, did I hear him correctly?"

Hugh waved his hand and shrugged.

"The athletic department at Harvard, at any of the Ivies, would seem to disagree with you. And I have a job, too. At least, I will after graduation. An entire corporation, actually, but let's not split hairs."

Joseph chuckled. Danny felt his cheeks warm. *Let it go. Be the bigger man here.* He trudged along in silence, trying to think of a better strategy and praying he'd be on par for at least one hole.

"Wilson threw the first pitch of the World Series last year," Joseph was saying now. "No doubt he'll do the same again. Man loves to have his photo taken."

Politics. Better to let York step in that one.

Hugh must've thought the same.

"Shaping up to be a tight race," his friend was quick to add.

"Do you miss the campaign trail, sir?" Joseph asked Walter. "You were a spokesperson for Roosevelt in '12, correct?"

"I see you've done your homework," the older man replied. "Yes, I represented German Americans. But I don't miss it. Not for the faint of heart, as they say."

"True," said Joseph, lighting a pipe as they strolled toward the back nine.

"Wilson's on a slippery-slope. Alleging pacifism but committing funding and supplies to the Allies. My father doesn't like him." He took a puff, claiming Hugh with a pat on the back. "Mostly because he's a Princeton man."

First politics, now war. Joseph should've had Shannon tutor *him*. Danny trudged behind them, curious to see what his rival would say next.

Walter merely turned his attention to his clubs, ignoring his caddy and selecting a seven iron from the bag.

Joseph bit the pipe, stretching as the older man teed up. "Not that we'll have anything to worry about if Wilson changes his position."

Hugh was busy tying his shoe. He mumbled something in response, and Danny noticed his face clouding over for the second time that day.

"At least the papers have finally quieted down about those shark attacks," York remarked. "Four dead. Unbelievable."

Mr. Martin returned to the group. "Did I hear you were on one of the hunts?" he asked Danny.

A direct inquiry. One York couldn't speak to. A chance to bond, maybe even shine. Danny opened his mouth—

"My goodness!" Joseph puffed. "How is it already three thirty?"

He shoved his watch at his caddy for further proof, its gold glimmering in the afternoon sun.

"You were about to say?" Mr. Martin prodded encouragingly.

Danny's eyes never moved from the watch, the splash of his own ringing in his ears. "I, um. Nothing, sir. I," he shrugged. "I didn't catch anything."

By the time they finished the last hole, Danny thought he'd nearly pass out. A game that normally took four hours lagged on eternally. What had he accomplished outside of nothing? The only thing Mr. Martin learned about him was just how terrible he was at the sport.

What am I going to tell Jennie?

Danny reached in his wallet for his caddy's tip. The boy looked glumly at the dime he received compared to his companions' dollars, and Danny's heart sank.

"I'm sorry, pal," he muttered. He wished he could've given him more. He owed the kid that much after such a long day. Still, lugging clubs around was a better job than he had at his age. It was better work than Danny had now.

He fished in his pocket for his cigarettes, indulging in a long first drag. His feet ached from walking, and he couldn't wait to get changed.

Joseph had Walter's ear again. Danny couldn't tell what they were talking about now, but it didn't matter. He couldn't keep up. Sure, he read the papers but mainly for the tide reports or the occasional sports page. Where Joseph was smooth and polished, he was all rough edges.

"Nineteenth hole?" Hugh interrupted his thoughts, coming up alongside him.

"Thought there were only eighteen?" Danny asked wearily.

"Lucky for you there are." He glanced in his uncle's direction. "Let's go to dinner at the club."

Danny followed Hugh's gaze. Mr. Martin was smiling, Joseph nodding at whatever he'd just said. "I don't know…."

Though he was hungry, Danny promised Shannon he wouldn't be out late. His stomach rumbled, and Hugh shot him a look.

"You know I heard that."

Finished with his cigarette, Danny crushed it underfoot. "Alright."

"Good, 'cause I'm starving," Hugh said as Joseph and Mr. Martin returned to the group. "We were just talking about going to dinner. Care to join us?"

Joseph checked his watch. "I'd love to but I'm afraid I have a prior engagement." He looked apologetically at Walter. "Another time, perhaps?"

"Of course, my boy."

Danny flinched. *My boy.*

"Hoping I'll see you again before Labor Day," Joseph said to Hugh. "If not, drinks once we're back in Cambridge." He turned to Danny, a triumphant grin as he shook his hand. "Better luck next time."

A few minutes later, the trio approached the locker room when Joseph drove by in his coupe. He waved as he passed them.

"Arrogant wind bag," Mr. Martin said through his smile, waving back in return.

"Uncle!" Hugh scoffed.

"I don't know how you put up with him, but better you than me." Walter pulled out a gold cigar case. Clipping the Robusto, he turned to Danny. "I believe you and I have some catching up to do."

CHAPTER 9

Prized bichon on her lap, Gertrude Browne Callaway sat in her balcony box at the Iron Pier's opera house reviewing the proposed program for the Labor Day Gala. She finished a sip of tea when the pup's ears perked.

"Well?" she asked.

"It's done."

So her son's valet had been correct. She pet the dog, making a mental note to increase the servant's weekly wages.

Her associate sat down beside her. "Thanks for the tip off."

"You left me little choice." Gertrude clenched her jaw. She couldn't believe the audacity of this man. Quickly scanning the music hall, she spat, "What are you doing? You know we shouldn't be seen alone together."

"Why my dear Mrs. Callaway," replied a smug Joseph York, "there's no need to get upset."

She stiffened in her corset. Posture ramrod straight, she held her head so high she could no longer see over the wide brim of her hat. A backbone of steel, her mother would say.

"Come now, Gertie. Your family doesn't need any more scandal now does it? If this marriage works out, we all win."

"Hugh doesn't."

"His secret will be safe."

"Until you need another favor."

"Perhaps you should take your son's life choices up with him." Joseph rose, walking backward to the balcony entrance. "I expect a dinner invitation by week's end."

CHAPTER 10

Across town, another woman was struggling with her own family obligations.

Shannon peered through the kitchen curtains for the umpteenth time and frowned. The sun was getting low in the sky, most of the beachgoers were long gone, and her brother still wasn't home. *Danny, where are you?* The stench of soon-to-be burnt biscuits in the oven demanded her attention. Cursing the old stove, she pulled them out just in time, slamming the pan on the top burner in the process.

"Quit making so much racket!"

She jumped.

"Yes Pa," she chirped, chancing a look at her father in the other room.

He strolled in about an hour ago. Boots off, feet up, and already through half a bottle of whisky.

"So sorry to disturb you. Dinner will be ready shortly."

Pa waved her off, much to her relief. When he'd initially asked after her brother, Shannon told him Danny was helping the Barkley's with their harvest. The lie didn't seem like too much of a stretch at the time; working on the farm was typical for this time of year, but if Danny showed up fresh from the locker room, they'd both be in for a world of hurt.

She gulped, trying to decide whether or not to set the table for three and ultimately deciding against it. Piling the biscuits on a platter, she placed them next to the flounder Pa brought home and straightened the crease in his napkin.

They ate in stony silence for a few minutes. Shannon was glad for it. No telling how long it would last, though.

"More peas," he barked.

She was up in a flash, spooning them onto his plate. "Glad you like them, Pa."

"Picked this morning," he said between bites while she returned to her seat beside him. "Couldn't decide between these or lima beans. Good thing I ran into Matthew Barkley at the market."

She froze.

"Where is he, girl?"

Shannon stared vacantly at her plate. "I don't know, Pa."

"You look at me when you're speaking," He growled, clamping her jaw on both sides, his massive hand squeezing her cheeks as he forced her chin up. "Don't you lie to me."

"I'm not," she whimpered. She tried to jerk away, but he tightened his grip, her lips puckering like the sea bass he caught daily. Just another worm on his hook. "I'm sorry," she choked, hot tears streaming down her face. "I really don't know."

Surprisingly, Pa let her go. "Got the house all to ourselves, do we?"

The answer abundantly clear, Shannon wasn't sure how to respond. Avoiding his eye, she nodded.

He pushed his chair back, patting the top of his legs. "Why don't you come over here and sit on my lap."

"Pa," Shannon laughed nervously, "I'm not a child anymore."

He looked her up and down, blackened eyes finally settling in the vicinity of her breasts. "No. No you're certainly not."

Pa grabbed her wrist and yanked. She tried to brace her free arm against the table but couldn't find her footing. Her knees crashed against the hard wooden floor, and she let out a yelp. Pa rooted his long fingers in her hair. Jiggling her head like a ragdoll, he lifted Shannon off the ground and planted her firmly on top of him.

Shannon thrashed, but he wrapped his arm around her torso and covered her mouth with the other. *Yeah, but this is different.* Was this what Danny meant?

The hand around her waist slowly snaked its way down and groped her right thigh. Bile rose in her mouth. This couldn't be happening.

"You lied to me, girl," Pa snarled in her ear. "And I know just how you can make it up to me. Settle down now." He uncovered her mouth. "Be good."

Panting, Shannon tried to force herself to stop shaking. She eyed the tin plates on the table. If only she could reach one. With her arms pinned like this, it was impossible.

"Here Pa," said a voice almost like hers.

She ground her body down against his, and he grunted.

"You like that?" asked the voice (not her voice-who was this person?). "Lemme go and I'll help you with that belt."

"You little slut," he chuckled, stroking her hair. "You want this just as much, don't you?"

"I do," Shannon agreed. She rubbed against him again, sliding her free hand along the table until she felt the edge of a plate and gripped its rim. "I've wanted to do this for a long time," she said as she swung the dish up, slamming her father across the face.

"You bitch!" He cursed her as he let go, the metal plate landing with a clank.

Shannon threw her chair in front of him and darted out the kitchen door. Lungs burning, she sprinted up Beach Avenue, rounding the left on Decatur before slowing to catch her breath. Her knees ached, and she rubbed the tenderness along her jaw. Hopefully, it wouldn't swell too much before she got to the telephone at Kennedy's. Shannon was grateful the older man was generous with their use of it. Escaping with only the clothes on her back, she didn't have money for any of the booths in the hotel lobbies.

⟡

The maître d' was annoyed. "Male or female caller?"

"Female, sir," the new waiter replied. He covered the receiver with his hand, following his boss's stare to Table 33, where an older gentleman and his two young companions were just about to start dessert.

"Must we go over this again?"

"Sir, she says it's urgent."

"With women it's always an emergency," he huffed. "Lewis, our members come here to escape. They want to relax. Get away from all that nagging. Understand?"

"Yes." The younger man lifted the phone's mouthpiece. "I'm sorry, miss. Mr. Callaway left hours ago."

⟡

Shannon hung up the phone. She slouched on her stool at the soda counter while Mr. Kennedy silently slid her an icepack. Shamefully avoiding his eye, she pressed the cheesecloth against her face.

"Thank you," she whispered.

The pharmacist tilted his head in acknowledgment, turning his back toward her as he readied the usual items in a white paper bag. In went cotton balls, gauze, antiseptic, and a small bottle of laudanum. It grew dark outside. He folded the bag closed and slid that across the counter, too.

"Do you need a ride, Shannon?"

"No." The less he knew, the better. "Thank you again, Mr. Kennedy."

"Anytime, lass. Anytime."

Bag in hand, she rose from the stool, eyeing the clock on the wall above him one last time before venturing out into the night.

CHAPTER 11

"How is it already eight o'clock?" Danny laughed, a loose tendril of his blonde hair sliding down over his eye.

"Time flies, my friend," Hugh replied as the host ushered them into the parlor for a nightcap.

Danny couldn't believe it. He never had a meal like that in his entire life. Steak and lobster, gobs of butter, a plate piled high with roasted potatoes. The meat was so tender he could slice it with his fork. That was after the oysters and bisque. Then out came dessert, the beach plum tarte second only to the jam Ma used to make with the fruit. He felt like a king; all earlier thoughts of his interloper status vanished, floating away in the sea breeze blowing through the window. It kissed his cheeks, and he almost felt like he was in a dream.

He sank into his chair, the leather glossy against the roaring fireplace across the room. Brandy promptly served; Mr. Martin put a hand on his shoulder, puffing away on his cigar like they'd known each other for years. There was an easiness about him, and Danny could see where Jennie and Hugh got their unpretentious nature.

Danny tried his own cigar, wincing when he inhaled too much. It was nothing like the Lucky's he was used to. The older man only smiled, a glint in his olive eyes.

"Can't believe I have to go back to school next week," Hugh complained.

"Hugh, my boy," Mr. Martin started, "you know if you were mine I wouldn't push you one way or the other. I've probably already said too much, but," he chuckled, "when has that ever stopped me?"

Hugh grinned back.

"You know, you'd save your father a lot of money if you could just be honest with him."

"Uncle, I—"

Mr. Martin took a sip of brandy and waved his hand. He turned to Danny. "How about you, son? Any plans for the fall?"

Danny placed his cigar in the crystal ashtray beside him. "Well, Mr. Martin—"

"Walter," the older man insisted.

Danny fought the urge to grin and lost; the edges of his mouth had a will of their own. "Walter," he repeated stupidly before clearing his throat. "Looking to make a move," he began, hoping his tone was even. "I'd like to come to the city."

"Really?"

Danny nodded.

"Which section?"

"Haven't started looking yet, but...uh, heard Overbrook's real nice." Danny bit his lip. "Really nice, I mean, sir."

"Enough with this 'sir' business, too."

"Okay."

Walter stroked the whiskers along his chin. "Do you think you'll stay in the fishing industry? There's plenty of docks on the Delaware."

Danny took a sip from his decanter. "Well," he sighed, "not exactly. Don't get me wrong, I love being on the water. I just..." All he could see was Pa. Head back, mouth open, passed out cold. "I want to chart my own course, you know?"

"I do. My father was a shoemaker."

"I never knew," Hugh said.

Walter nodded. "Had a nice little shop for the longest time. But," his eyes clouded over, "as industry grew, no one wanted to go to the cobbler anymore." He shrugged. "Why wait for boots when you can get them," he snapped his fingers, "like that?"

"Was he angry?" Hugh asked. "That you didn't want to follow in his footsteps?"

"Probably at first. He never let on. Couldn't. Not with all the mouths he had to feed." Walter took a long pull on his cigar, looking from Hugh to Danny. "You see, boys, everyone has their own path. Some are paved with gravel. Others, gold. Neither matters if you don't take the first step."

He twisted in his seat, stretching his lower back. "Last word of advice: don't get old."

The boys chuckled. Walter eyed the clock on the wall and rose.

"Must you leave, Uncle?"

"'Fraid so. Early meeting with the Cottager's Association."

Danny stood to shake his hand, pleasantly surprised when Walter pulled him into a bear hug.

"Feel free to call at the house anytime. Here or in the city."

"Thank you," Danny smiled.

Hugh wasn't ready to go home just yet.

"Jackson's Club House?" he asked after the doors closed behind his uncle.

"Haven't you had enough fun for one day?"

It was rhetorical, of course. Danny wasn't so sure he wanted to leave, either. His thoughts drifted to Shannon. She'd be miffed he missed supper. But hadn't he insisted she find something to occupy herself? *Got plenty to keep me busy.* He could see her now, sewing or ironing, and felt a bit better about it. He'd make it up to her.

They drove through the city, recalling the days' events. Hugh joked how he hoped Danny's triumph over Joseph would rub off on him and bring some luck at the roulette wheel. Climbing the stairs of what appeared to be an ordinary house, they were received by a servant upon reaching the porch on the second floor. She was perched in a rocker overlooking the street below, embroidery ring in hand.

"Mr. Callaway," she said, returning to her work.

Hugh flung open the door, cheers erupting throughout the bustling casino.

"Ladies," he grinned, his arms outstretched.

The girls happily obliged. Oozing sex, they flocked to each of his sides. He lapped up the attention, throwing his head back, laughing after one of the call girls whispered in his ear. Hugh pulled out his money clip, its gold shining against the cut glass of the chandelier while he purposefully counted out several bills and handed them to the proprietor for chips.

"C'mon!" Hugh shoved a tumbler in Danny's hand and dragged him by the other one to the spinning machines.

Dice. Cards. Jackson's had something for everyone. *What's a round or two?* Danny decided. He was entitled to a bit of celebration. After the morning he had, he certainly earned it. Hell, he might even win enough to get Jennie something extraordinary. Hugh offered to spot him for the night. It wasn't the first time, so what difference did it make? He knocked back his drink and joined his friend at the card table.

One poker game blurred into another, with liquor flowing every time they lost. And lost, they did.

The room was hot and thick with smoke. Hugh loosened his necktie and rolled his shirt sleeves to his elbows. He tilted his head toward the veranda where the servant was still outside sewing.

"She starts rocking and we're all in trouble."

Danny smiled at the dwindling chips in front of them. "I'd say we're already in trouble."

"She's a lookout," Hugh said, missing the rub. "That's the signal."

"I know." Of course, he knew. Everyone knew. Bess had been a staple in the city for years. Danny took another look at the chips. Then at the dealer, as he reshuffled the cards. "We should get going."

The redhead leaning on Hugh's shoulder pouted at the suggestion.

"Don't worry, doll," he assured her, "I'm not going anywhere. It's only midnight."

"Midnight?" Danny grimaced, pinching the bridge of his nose. "Shit."

"Careful going home," Hugh called after him, but Danny was already halfway down the stairs.

He tripped at the bottom and grabbed the railing. His tie was suddenly choking him, so he undid it. He wobbled along until he reached Gurney Street, where Button's dollhouses stretched down the block. Danny steadied himself against their wrought iron fences. He passed garden after garden, careful not to tear Hugh's suit jacket or, worse yet, impale himself on one of the spikes.

Finally, he reached Beach Avenue. How he made it, he wasn't sure, grinning despite himself. It wasn't much further now, and he kept to the dunes as he headed south.

The house was eerily still when he got there, something that would've alerted him immediately were he not shitfaced. Why hadn't Shannon left the light on? *She must be really pissed.*

The kitchen door creaked when he opened it, and he paused. Bloodshot eyes adjusting to the shadows, Danny peered around the room.

Tidy. Not a thing out of place.

He walked through the house as quietly as he could. No need to wake her. He'd clear things up in the morning. Danny was so busy concentrating he never saw it coming.

The poker struck him from behind with a sickening crack. Pain shot down his spine, radiating across his back as he slammed face-first on the floor. The first of many blows to his midsection.

Danny couldn't breathe. Heaving, he choked on his own blood and spat at the taste. He slid his tongue along the inside of his mouth to see if he still had all of his teeth, and when he couldn't tell, he spit again.

His father towered over him. Silent yet dangerous, circling him.

"Get up, boy," he snarled.

Panting, Danny struggled to push himself up. His forearms shook and he slumped back down.

"I said get up!"

His father leaned down a swift backhand to the left side of his face. Danny's head jerked over his right shoulder as more blood splattered on the floor. Dizzy and disoriented, he still couldn't breathe. Everything hurt, but he had to obey, somehow mustering the strength to try again.

On all fours now, the room spun around him. He felt his head bobbing yet managed to look up at his father.

"Pa, please," he begged, his face caked in blood.

The other man was relentless. He kicked Danny in the stomach and splayed him on his backside.

Danny clutched his abdomen. He scrambled toward the corner, curling into himself. His teeth chattered, and his whole body shook. He sucked in air, his lungs refusing to cooperate. Terrified and exhausted, he cowered on the hard floor, praying it would stop but knowing damn well that Pa wasn't through with him yet.

CHAPTER 12

Shannon gulped. Cattycorner from where she stood was the island's most notorious house of ill repute. Having looked for Danny everywhere else short of Juniper Grove itself, she had to at least give it a try.

She didn't need to feel along her jaw to know it was still swollen, and undid her hair to try to cover it. A resolute nod, and she crossed the street.

An older woman greeted her at the top of the steps, her brown face frowning as she set down her sewing.

"If you're looking for work, you'll have to come back tomorrow afternoon. Boss is otherwise occupied."

"Me?" Shannon looked over her shoulder. Was Pa right? Did she really look like a whore?

"Nobody else out here, child."

"No, I'm not…." She blew a flyaway out of her face. "I'm…sorry."

The woman squinted, and Shannon felt her cheeks flush— her chin must've looked worse than she thought.

"I'm looking for my brother."

Her companion snickered. "They're all somebody's 'brother'. I'm afraid

I can't give out any information."

"What if I describe him?" Shannon blabbered. "Blonde, late teens." Her tongue had a mind of its own. "Was probably wearing golf clothes."

"Word of advice, hon? If he's coming in here, he ain't worth the trouble."

Shannon put her hands on her hips. "He really is my brother. And I have to tell him something important. Please. Its life or death."

"*Mm*-hmm."

"I'm sure he's been here before. Our friend comes here all the time to gam—"

She'd no sooner thought of Hugh when she saw him through the window. Except he wasn't just gambling. Nor was he alone.

No. No, it couldn't be. Shannon blinked, but he was still there, clear as day, not fifty feet from her. A girl with long strawberry ringlets was perched on his lap; Hugh's hand rested on her milky leg in the same place Pa had grabbed her earlier. Shannon could still feel it, the ghost of his grubby fingers, and she shuddered.

Simultaneously, hot pain shot through her chest. She thought she was special. Hadn't Danny told her as much just this morning?

Shannon scrambled backward and slammed her back into the gingerbread railing.

Concerned, the servant stood. "You okay, child?"

"I'm *fine*," Shannon spat. "You were right," she called as she flew down the stairs. "I should never have come here."

CHAPTER 13

Jennie woke up with the sun. She rang for her maid earlier than usual. If she wanted to speak with her cousin alone, she knew her best bet was to catch him on his way to breakfast. Hugh never missed a meal. The last curls pinned into place, Jennie glanced at her reflection in the looking glass and pinched her cheekbones. A little color would do her good.

"There," she said triumphantly. "That will be all, Bridget."

Jennie tiptoed down the stairs, lying in wait for him in a nook between a large potted plant and the grandfather clock. It wasn't long before he emerged from the garden path connecting their houses.

"Hugh," she hissed as he hung his bowler hat on the coat tree.

Index finger over her mouth, she waved him over. After scanning the corridor for staff, Jennie led him into the music room and shut the door.

"How did it go?" she grinned.

Everything went sideways after that, trapping Jennie in a hazy fog. Someone shrieked. No, no— they were crying. Someone was hysterical, sobbing uncontrollably. *Poor dear.*

Cold.

So cold.

Hard.

Smooth.

The marble? Why was she on the floor?

Jennie couldn't feel her limbs. Couldn't see anything but shadows.

Clammy hands pawed at her. Many hands. Too many hands. Everyone talking all at once, yet she didn't understand any of it. *Daddy? Daddy, I'm scared.*

She felt as if she were flying, floating weightless on her back. Wait— her backside? No. She should be on her stomach, arms wide like Wendy in Peter Pan. Her arms were bound. This was wrong. All wrong. Try as she might, Jennie was stuck in a vice. She just couldn't rollover.

Up, up, up. Sharp turn. Up, up, up again.

Floating. Floating.

Down.

Soft.

Teddy bear? Yes. *Danny.*

Darkness.

"She's coming to, ma'am."

"Bridget?" Jennie winced, her throat dry.

"It's alright, miss."

The girl helped her sit up and stuffed a pillow behind her shoulders.

"How did I?" She gazed about her bedroom. Shutters drawn, Jennie had no concept of time. "What...what happened?"

"This little infatuation has gone on long enough." Aunt Gertrude stepped out of the corner. She held something in her hand, and Jennie squinted to get a better look.

It was a tranquilizer.

"No!" Her long hair swung wildly as she shook her head.

"You cried yourself to sleep," her aunt reprimanded. "Refused to eat a thing yesterday."

Jennie sprang out of bed. But her knees were weak, and she grabbed the side post to steady herself. Bridget took her by the elbow. Cook appeared in the door and hastily latched her other arm.

"*Please*," Jennie begged the older servant. "Please don't let her do this to me."

"Come now, miss," Cook's emerald eyes glistened. "I hate to see you like this. 'Tis breakin' my heart."

Her aunt crossed the room, readying the needle. Meanwhile, both servants pinned Jennie against the mattress so she could administer the shot.

Gertrude caressed her cheek as the medication set in. "This is for your own good, Jennie. One day you'll thank me."

"I highly doubt that," she growled, hot, angry tears streaming down her face.

"Rest, child. We're hosting a dinner party tomorrow and have the gala the following evening. You need to look your best," her aunt demanded. "Forget about that boy. He's not good enough for you."

"You don't know him like I do."

"Your father's guest at the club and he leaves in a stupor? I know he disgraced this family. That he's in the hospital on account of his own reckless behavior." Gertrude crossed her arms and looked down at the bed. "Do tell, Jennie, is there anything else I should know?"

The following two days passed in a blur. Her aunt watched her every move. She couldn't get Father or Hugh alone to ask for help. Even Cook refused to relay her messages.

"I don't like it any more than you do, miss. I'm under strict orders."

Joseph York, on the other hand, Gertrude ensured they had ample opportunity to get to know each other better. Morning walks along the promenade, their guest for supper, her escort to the opera; Jennie watched it all play out like scenes in a film. She was merely Lillian Gish.

CHAPTER 14

Danny awoke to a bright white flash. He tried to peel his eyelids open but saw only blackness on his left. Sawdust mouth, splitting headache, he struggled to focus. He tried to lift his head to gain a better perspective but was too weak to do so, moaning in frustration.

"Shh," whispered a hazy shadow. She swept her fingertips across his forehead and gently thumbed his aching temples.

"Shannon," he murmured, feebly reaching out.

She took his hand and gave it a squeeze before lifting a glass to his chapped lips. "Drink," she instructed, tilting it ever so slightly that he got just the right amount of water.

Danny blinked with his good eye and finally got a better look at his sister. Her cheeks were sallow with dark circles aging her well beyond her youth, and she had the greenish-yellow remnants of a bruise on her chin. She trained her eyes to the ceiling and bit her lip in a vain attempt to hide she was crying. Shannon leaned over him and cupped his cheek.

"I thought he killed you," she croaked.

Danny tried to speak, flinching at the pain in his chest. His breath hitched.

"Hold still. I'll let Dr. Mace know you're up."

A few minutes later, he was greeted by a petite middle-aged woman in a doctor's coat. He looked around the room. It had crisp white walls and smelled of bleach, but other than that had the feeling of an ordinary bedroom. He leaned back against the pillows while she checked his vitals.

Danny was soon horrified to learn the extent of his own injuries. His left eye was swollen shut, requiring several stitches where his brow met his temple. His bottom lip was split. Yet, by some miracle, he still had all of his teeth.

Most painful, however, were the multiple fractures along his ribcage. His torso was covered in deep purple bruises, as were his forearms from where he'd tried to shield himself. Dr. Mace told him it would be better if he slept upright when he got home and not to be alarmed if he saw blood in his urine for at least a week or so.

She started to explain what he could expect in terms of recovery from his head wound, but Danny stopped listening after she relayed he'd been asleep for four days.

Four whole days.

He did the math. Labor Day was tomorrow. *Shit.* His pulse quickened. Jennie would be heading home to Philadelphia. He had to see her before she was gone. There was so much left unsaid. Danny sprang up, instantly regretting it and holding his left side.

"Easy now, young man," Dr. Mace helped him right himself before turning to Shannon. "Not much we can do for his ribs. You'll have to keep them wrapped tight. Remember how I showed you?"

His sister nodded.

"Alright then," the older woman smiled sympathetically, touching Shannon on her shoulder. "We'll get some soup in him. If all goes well he can be released within the next few days. In the meantime, my dear, why don't you go home and get some rest yourself?"

"Just a few more minutes?" Shannon asked. "Please?"

"Of course, dear."

Dr. Mace left them to check on other patients, and Shannon sat down on the bed.

"Four days?"

She hung her head. "Yeah. It was bad, Danny."

"Pa?"

"He's gone." Her shoulders tensed. "For now."

They took their share of licks over the years, thankful Kennedy's was in such close proximity, but this was the first time either of them ended up in the hospital.

Danny threw back the blankets, pushing himself upright despite his discomfort. "I can't stay here," he wheezed. "Jennie—"

"Is not expecting you."

"What?"

"I told Hugh that you fell down the stairs."

"Why?"

"What was I supposed to do, Danny?" she shot back. "Tell him the truth?" Shannon crossed her arms against herself and looked away. "Also gave him an earful for keeping you out so late in the first place. Jackson's? *Really?* What would your precious Jennie think?"

"Shannon, I'm sorry. We got carried away. I…I lost track o'time."

Guilty as he felt, Danny was still determined to leave. He braced himself against the bed, attempting to swing his legs over the side.

"What do you think you're doing?"

"I can't stay here," he paused to catch his breath. "She's probably worried."

"She's worried? That's real swell. What about me, huh? I tried to warn you, Danny. I searched for hours." She swallowed back the lump in her throat. "And when I found you…"

His good eye focused on the tell-tale marks on her jawline. Bruises that wouldn't have been there if he'd been home. *I did that.* Hurt her just as much as Pa. What else had their father done? How far did he take it?

Danny grabbed her hand, entwining their fingers together. "It's over now."

"Is it?"

"As I live and breathe."

He felt drained. Head heavy on his shoulders, he stifled a yawn.

"You just focus on getting well, ok?" Shannon tucked him in, remembering to add an extra pillow behind his back. "I'll get a message to her," she promised, pressing a kiss to his forehead. "Tell her you'll write when you're up to it."

CHAPTER 15

Shannon rushed down Atlantic Avenue. The trolleys stopped running an hour ago, and she had to hurry if she were going to catch the last southbound train for the evening. She was hungry and exhausted, but she didn't care. Danny was awake. He came back to her, and that was all that mattered right now.

Reaching the station, she bought her ticket and sank onto a bench. Shannon looked over the platform, crinkling her nose at the stench drifting across Otten's Harbor. Danny explained it to her once— how having the fisheries and ice house next to the railroad made for fresher shipping. The smell reminded her of Pa, and she wanted to vomit. Shannon wouldn't care if she never saw him again. The man was a lunatic. Still, she knew he'd come home eventually, and there was no telling what he'd do next time. She looked down at her hands, absentmindedly picking away at a hangnail.

Lost in her thoughts, Shannon failed to realize she wasn't alone.

"What's a dame like you doing out all by herself?"

"Wouldn't you love to know?"

"Mouthy. I like that."

He approached from the pole he leaned on, tossing the matchstick he used to pick his teeth onto the rails. The brim of his cap sat low on his head. Though she couldn't see his eyes, Shannon got the distinct impression he was envisioning what she looked like in only her corset.

She clutched the purse on her lap. It wasn't much, but it was all she had. After everything she'd been through the last few days, there was no way in hell she was giving any of it away. He inched closer, slowly reaching into his pocket, and she held her breath.

"There you are, darling! Sorry I'm late."

Shannon followed the voice, turning her head to see a well-dressed man in his mid-twenties waving at her from the street below. She raised an eyebrow, playing along.

"You know I don't like to be kept waiting."

"I'll make it up to you," he replied, taking the stairs two-by-two. Tossing the bum a quarter, he added, "Thanks for keeping her company."

The ruffian left them, polishing the coin between his fingers as he walked off.

"Shoobies," sneered the man in the suit as he sat down next to her.

Shannon smiled. She could hear Danny saying the exact same thing. Though initially a playground for the elite, the railroads made it easy for working-class Philadelphians to travel to the shore for a day trip. Many of them immigrants, they swam and played in the ocean but could afford little else, earning their name for the lunches they packed in their shoeboxes.

"Thank you," she said.

"Don't mention it," he extended his hand, and she shook it. "Frank Hilton."

"Shannon Culligan."

"Well, Miss Culligan, I don't mean to be rude but what *are* you doing out at this hour?"

"I could ask the same of you," she smirked.

Frank tilted his head toward the harbor. "My family owns a fishery.

Was just looking over the books for the day."

"On a Sunday night?"

"Labor Day weekend, doll. All the locals are working. No rest for the weary."

"True," she agreed, suddenly aware she looked affright. Shannon tucked a stray tendril behind her ear. "I have a relative at Mace Hospital."

"I'm sorry to hear."

She couldn't meet his eye. There was kindness in his voice. And the way he was looking at her, almost like he really cared. Shannon shifted in her seat. She hadn't eaten since breakfast, barely finishing her toast. It was already late, and she still had to find Hugh. *Damn him.* She couldn't think of him without thinking of that redhead. Bone tired, her emotions were finally catching up to her.

"Me too," she sniffed.

"Hey, it's alright kid." Frank handed her his handkerchief. "Dr. Mace is the best. Really cares about her patients, you know? Even makes house calls."

Shannon dabbed her eyes. Was she really crying in front of this guy? "Swell," she whispered.

"It is," he agreed. "One time, she rode horseback through a snowstorm to deliver a baby."

"Yeah?"

Frank nodded. "Another—and this story was all over the docks, let me tell ya—she saved the arm of some fella that got bit by a shark."

She scrunched her nose.

"I know, sounds pretty bad, huh? Wasn't one of our employees though," he was quick to add as if that somehow made a difference. "Worked over at Union Pound Company."

"Well," she offered a weak smile, "it's good to know my brother is in such capable hands."

Frank tipped his hat. "Glad I could be of assistance. Say, where you headed? I'll give you a lift."

She twisted her hands in her lap. "Oh, I don't know. I hate to impose on you anymore than I already have."

"I insist."

"Cape May."

✦⇒◎⇐✦

Recalling her last conversation with Hugh, Shannon had Frank drop her off across the street from Jackson's.

"I can wait for you if you'd like," Hilton offered.

"Thank you, Frank. But that's not really necessary."

"I understand. Well, how 'bout this, you can give me a signal to let me know you've found your friend? That way, if he's not here, you don't have to walk all the way home. Wherever home is, of course. Sound good?"

"Ok."

Shannon drug herself up the steps, praying Hugh wasn't with his girl-friend again. She didn't know how much more she could take. The same servant from earlier that week eyed her skeptically when she reached the top.

"You again."

"I'm looking for Hugh Callaway. And don't give me that bullshit about confidentiality."

"On the nest, hon?"

"No," Shannon snapped. "Tell him it's Shannon. Shannon Culligan."

"Culligan?" The servant frowned in recognition. "He really was your brother, huh? We were all real sorry to hear about what happened. How is Danny?"

"Alive."

The woman poked her head in the casino, ushering Hugh onto the veranda. He pulled Shannon into a hug. God, he smelled good. It felt good, too, being in his arms. Until she remembered how he'd probably held *her* that way.

Shannon pulled away. She threw a quick glance at Frank's sedan and winked. Hilton waved out the window and drove off.

"Who the hell was that?" Hugh glared.

Hurts, doesn't it?

Shannon cocked her head. "None of your business."

"I've never seen that car before."

"Yeah, well, he's not from around here."

"Where's he from?"

"Why do you care?"

"I *don't*."

"*Good*."

The servant let out a low whistle. "Anymore sparks and I'll have to get the water hose."

"Enough, Bess," Hugh warned.

"Sorry," she grinned, "couldn't resist."

Shannon filled him in on Danny's status. Hugh insisted he at least drive her home for her troubles. Too exhausted to argue, she agreed, and they left the club a few minutes later.

The roadster crunched on the gravel driveway. The tiny house was just as dark as it was when she'd left days ago, and she didn't want to get out yet. Hugh offered her a cigarette, but she silently declined.

"Hey, what happened to your chin?"

He couldn't find out. No one could. Not even Danny.

"It's nothing." Shannon tried to laugh it off, hoping Hugh would buy it. "Walked into the door."

"You gotta slow down."

"I know," she shrugged. "Danny's always telling me that, too."

They fell into an awkward silence, the rhythmic waves of the incoming tide the only sound for miles.

"I go back to school Wednesday," he said, seemingly out of nowhere.

"You don't sound too excited."

He frowned. "It's expected. My father—"

"Wants what's best for you? God, Hugh. Do you hear yourself sometimes?"

Hugh snorted smoke through his nose. "Do you ever listen?"

"I can't do this right now." Shannon reached for the door handle, but he grabbed her free hand. A warm jolt radiated through her, and she trembled.

"Please don't go."

"Why?"

"Because," he looked out his window. "Because we're friends."

Friends. Not this shit again.

Hugh was making the damn puppy eyes, too. "I could really use one right now."

"You? *You?*" Shannon bit her lower lip. "*I'm* the one who just spent the last four days at the hospital because *someone* got my brother so drunk he couldn't even see straight. But *you* need a friend?"

"I'm sorry, Shannon. About that whole night, I really am. I had no idea—"

"Oh, I'm sure you didn't. Not the way that little strawberry tart was distracting you."

"What?"

Shit. Shit, shit, shit.

"Did you..." Hugh cupped his mouth. "Did you come to the club?"

Well, now she'd stepped in it. Unsure how to backpedal, Shannon could only look down.

"Shannon," he tightened his grip on her hand, "it's not whatcha think."

"We're friends, Hugh," she said, refusing to meet his eye. "Doesn't really matter what I think, now does it?" Shannon opened the door, and he let her go. "Good luck with your semester."

Once in the bungalow, Shannon poured all her pain into barricading herself in. She pushed Pa's favorite chair against the front door and locked every window. From there, she moved back to the kitchen. Groaning, she slid the table against the back entrance. She grabbed the poker as she left the room and climbed into bed with it. Eyes bloodshot, Shannon's mind played tricks on her, and she jumped at the slightest sound. There would be no sleep tonight.

CHAPTER 16

Alone in her room, Jennie scribbled away in her journal, the only outlet where she could be honest. She replayed the scene on a loop, jotting down all the main points, yet she still didn't understand exactly what happened after Father left the country club.

What am I missing?

She went over them again, counting them out on her fingers. Father came back to Juniper Grove in high spirits. They drank lemonade on the back porch overlooking the sea. He told her he understood why she was so fond of Danny. Called him a 'fine young man.' Father recalled how the three of them laughed over dinner, retiring to the smoking-room for a brandy afterward.

One drink. That was it.

This was where she always got stuck. Jennie just couldn't see how Danny got falling down drunk after a single cordial. Especially if they just ate. She asked herself over and over, unable to make sense of it all. Even if she did have the whole story, it wouldn't change the outcome. Her Danny all alone, face down at the foot of the steps in a pool of blood.

Jennie shuddered. The only person who could fill in the missing blanks was Hugh. She eyed the pink daybreak streaming through her window. Maybe she could catch him pulling into the garage. It was risk— she hadn't snuck out in weeks— but it just might be worth it. She put her pen down and tiptoed across the room.

She no sooner dropped off the lattice when she heard a rustling by the hydrangea.

"Psst-Jen," Hugh whispered from his crouched position next to the bush.

"What in the world?"

"I was coming to see you when I saw you on the roof."

"Oh," she blushed, remembering the last time he'd caught her. "You're just the person I wanted to see, too. How is he, Hugh?" Her eyes searched him. "Please tell me you have news."

"He's awake."

"He *is?*" Jennie covered her mouth as relief surged through her.

"Last night." Hugh hugged her.

"Thank God," she whimpered into his shoulder. "Oh, thank God."

"Won't come home for a couple o'days though."

"Days? How many days? We're leaving tomorrow."

"Shannon wasn't sure. Said he'd write you soon as he's able."

"She said that?"

He sighed and let her go. "She came through for you before, didn't she? She'll do it again. Loves him too much not to."

"I didn't mean…" Jennie grimaced and tucked a hair behind her ear. "I'm sorry. I know you two are friends."

"I hate that word."

Something had been off about her cousin since before Danny's accident. His eyes drooped, and he wasn't nearly as jovial. Hers wasn't the only fragile heart in the garden.

"Does she know?"

"Hmm?"

"Shannon," Jennie smiled. "Have you told her how you feel?"

Hugh looked down and picked his thumbnail.

"C'mon Hugh." She nudged him. "You're not exactly shy."

"Leave it alone, Jen. You don't know what you're asking." Hugh shuffled from one foot to the other. "Besides, it would never work. I'd only hurt her more."

"More?"

Exasperated, he held his arms out. "I messed up, okay? That what you want to hear?"

"No, Hugh—"

"She wants nothing to do with me." He shook his head in defeat. "And I don't blame her. I don't blame her one bit."

A rooster crowed from a neighboring yard, and Jennie cautiously looked around them.

"Better get going." She squeezed his hand. "See you at breakfast?"

"Yeah." He walked her back to the lattice. "Here, I'll give ya a boost."

CHAPTER 17

Perched at her desk later that evening, Gertrude drummed her fingertips on the mahogany. Another summer had come to a close. Hugh was due in Massachusetts later in the week, and she was wrestling with her desire to keep him home entirely. Things appeared to be going well between her niece and York, but she wasn't sure if that were enough to keep him satisfied until Jennie made her official debut in December. She certainly hoped so anyway, for all their sakes.

There was a tap on the bedroom door.

"Come in," she commanded.

Rutherford bowed upon entry. Bridget followed him in with a curtsey of her own, closing the door tightly behind her.

"You wanted to see us, ma'am?" the butler asked.

"Yes," Gertrude replied without looking up. She slid Jennie's journal across the desk, addressing the maid. "You've done well."

"Thank you, ma'am," the girl replied, a lilt of brogue in her voice.

Gertrude opened the top drawer. She took out her checkbook and began writing. "I assume you have family?" she asked.

"Waterville, ma'am. County Kerry."

Finally lifting her head, Gertrude glared. She never heard of it, nor did she care. Ireland was a backward country full of papists. She ripped off the check, dangling it in front of the maid before eyeing the journal again.

"I want to see this weekly."

"Of course," Bridget promised, placing her earnings in the pocket of her apron.

Gertrude moved on to Rutherford. "As for you," she said, "I'll need her correspondence."

"All of it, ma'am?"

"Yes, all of it," she snapped. "Nothing comes in or out of the house unless I see it." She fanned herself with the checkbook and raised an eyebrow. "Understood?"

The butler gave a resolute nod. Gertrude jutted her chin toward the door, and they bid her good evening.

Alone again, she leaned back in her seat. Framed miniatures of her parents and plump babies stared back at her. Gertrude sighed. If Mother could see her now, she'd be so disappointed; her sister's disastrous elopement still left a ripple effect decades later.

Following the union, the Browne's were tossed out of The 400, immediately elevating her status as a daughter to that of the family savior. New York was no longer an option, and The Continent entirely out of the question, Mother was reduced to parading her around Boston, Washington, and Baltimore. Failing to be received by any of the better families, they reluctantly circled back to where Louisa and Walter settled along the Main Line.

She finally met her husband at a regatta along the Schuylkill. The youngest son of a shipping magnate, Edmund favored her dowry over her family's reputation. She was traded like stock with absolutely no say in the matter. Her parents, meanwhile, spared no expense for the wedding. They still had a pew at St. Thomas', after all, Mother angling for even a brief mention in *Town Topics*. There was never any love between them, nor would there ever be. Still, she managed to produce the obligatory heir.

Gertrude would never forget the moment they told her she'd had a son.

"You'll love me," she murmured as the midwife placed Hugh in her arms.

"All little boys do," the nurse replied, wiping her brow.

He was all she had in this world until Samuel arrived ten years later, the byproduct of an evening of drunken debauchery on her husband's part.

Her boys. They meant everything to her. Even more than the deathbed promise she made Louisa swearing to look after Jennie. Gertrude loved her niece, but she saw no other option. She spent most of her life trying to rebuild what her sister besmirched. Unfortunately for all of them, Hugh took after his father. She reached for his christening picture, lovingly glossing over his chubby cheeks.

Jennie would have her own children someday. Then she'd understand. Maybe even forgive her.

CHAPTER 18

September came and went. Danny slept through most of it, his heart as broken as his ribs. There were days he couldn't even get out of bed. Others, he fought against the urge to drive to Camden, hop the ferry, and tell Jennie everything. But the truth? It would change how she looked at him, and Danny couldn't give that up. However, by late October, it was beginning to dawn on him that he might not have much choice in the matter.

Meanwhile, Shannon never left his side. Sometimes he awoke to her curled up beside him. Her eyes were full of concern, looking at him as if it might be the last time. He worried about her.

That night she made soup again for dinner. Danny couldn't tell whether it was potato or onion. Either way, it was mostly hot water. Paper-thin, his sister always made sure he ate first.

"You have to keep your strength up," she insisted.

"What's the point?"

"Don't say that." Shannon placed the tray on his bedside table and cozied up next to him, resting her head on his shoulder. "She needs you well, Danny. We both do."

He slouched against the pillows.

"Maybe you could write Hugh?" she suggested. "Or try calling? A walk into town would do you good."

"You could write him yourself, you know." Danny pet the top of her head.

"Pretty sure he wouldn't want to hear from me."

Shannon pushed herself back up and measured out another even spoonful of soup. He blew on the steam before opening his mouth. What a hopeless pair they made.

CHAPTER 19

Frank sauntered into the hospital lobby and stopped at the front desk. He flashed the clerk a winning smile.

"Morning, doll. Dr. Mace in yet?"

The girl nodded to her left. "In her office, sir." She held up a clipboard. "May I take your name, please?"

"Oh, I'm not a patient." He smoothed the lapels on his suit. "Just got a question for her."

"Regarding?"

"That's kinda between me and the good doctor."

"She's very busy, sir. If I'm to interrupt her, she'll want to know why."

Frank tilted his head back. "You don't know who I am, do you?"

Unfazed, the brunette blinked behind her coke-bottle glasses.

"Let's just say I'd like to make a charitable donation."

"Mr. Hilton," Dr. Mace offered a warm smile as the clerk showed him five minutes later. She rose from her worn leather chair and shook his hand.

"Thank you, Judy," she told her staff. "You may close the door on your way out."

The doctor folded her hands on the desktop. Her office was tidy, the tang of bleach lingering in the air. A wall of dark green medical books lined the shelving behind her, while another held several rows of walnut cabinets.

"I assume you're here about the children's Christmas donations?"

That time of year already? Yes, now that he peeked at her desk calendar. November 1st. Frank squared his jaw, chiding himself for feeling like a schoolboy. Two months later and he still found himself thinking about the gorgeous blonde from the train station. He'd even casually put out some inquiries. The father was a deadbeat—they didn't have a pot to piss in. The brother, gravely injured but doing better under her care. If he could take this one thing off her plate, maybe he'd be able to forget her.

"Mr. Hilton?"

"Yeah," he brought a fist to his mouth and cleared his throat. "Thank you for seeing me on such short notice. Actually here about one of your patients. Kid was in around Labor Day. Had a sister about the same age. Fairhaired."

"I don't feel comfortable giving out particulars. A matter of privacy." She sat back in her chair, obviously trying to appear taller in stature. "You understand, of course."

"I don't want particulars. And I don't give a shit about privacy. I just wanna take care of their bill."

"I see." Dr. Mace furrowed her gray brow. "How generous."

He cocked his head and tapped an index finger on the table. "And another thing. Not a word of this to anyone. I want to remain anonymous."

"Oh, I don't know...."

"I'll triple the contributions to the children's fund."

Seeing she was flabbergasted, Frank stood up. He jerked his head in the direction of the receptionist as he opened the door. "Have your girl send the paperwork to Consolidated Fisheries."

CHAPTER 20

J ennie cried into her pillow night after night. Maybe she never really knew him at all. Everything they shared together. All their plans for the future. It wasn't real. Just a twisted fantasy she created. If Danny truly loved her, how could he ignore her? Why would he hurt her like this?

She cornered Hugh at Thanksgiving to ask if they'd had any contact, but her cousin didn't seem himself.

"Not everything's about you, Jen," he snapped.

She was about to follow him into the library when he held up his hands, glaring at her.

The following morning, he left on the early train while she was still asleep, a chicken scratched note about upcoming exams his only excuse.

Between the Christmas rush and her upcoming debut, Jennie spent the next three weeks in a whirlwind. Father gave her aunt carte blanche. There was shopping, teas, and parties to attend, lists to check and re-check, all with fittings in between. Her gown was ordered from Worth shortly after their return from Juniper Grove; Gertrude was unrelenting in her insistence she be present at every appointment with the seamstress.

"Twenty inches?" her aunt stormed into the kitchen after their last session, her long shirts swooshing as she rounded the butcher block island. She glowered as Jennie entered the doorway. "It needs to be eighteen. Seventeen would be ideal—you'll thank me after you've had children—but eighteen will have to do."

Jennie shrugged in apology. She was happy with her figure.

Gertrude huffed. "You have your father's sweet tooth."

"Did someone say sweets?" Cook grinned as she came out of the basement pantry, brawny arms piled high with root vegetables for the evening's dinner. No doubt one of her famous roasts and Jennie resisted the urge to lick her lips.

"You," her aunt pointed at the housekeeper. "She gets nothing but bone broth until the ball."

"Ma'am?"

Jennie stomped her foot. "That's not fair!"

"Don't question me. Either of you." She sneered at her niece. "Bone broth and water."

Still reeling from Gertrude's viciousness earlier, Jennie tried to process her feelings in her journal. The ball. The stupid dress. The attention. She didn't want any of it. She only wanted Danny, wishing he were here to dry her tears. That he didn't care for her was clear by this point, his silence deafening.

A telephone rang down the hall, and Jennie blew her nose. Probably about another appointment, they still had the flowers to consider. It rang again, and she sighed. Where was Rutherford? If it was the florist, she'd prefer to get it over with than have the hassle of calling him back. By the third ring, she closed the hutch on her secretary desk and flung open the bedroom door, hoping to catch whoever it was before they hung up. Jennie picked up the extension only to realize her father must've answered the downstairs line.

"*Guten Tag!*" he returned the caller's German greeting.

The two men wasted no time sputtering back and forth in rapid succession. Fluent in four languages, Jennie rubbed a temple, cursing herself that none of them were Father's native tongue. What were they saying? And, more importantly, why weren't they saying it in English? The papers had finally given them some repose— seemingly every story was about Wilson's recent re-election— but this was still no time to be idle. Hearing footsteps on the staircase, she glided the mouthpiece back onto its receiver and hurried back to her room.

CHAPTER 21

Gertrude could never sleep in hotels. Tonight was no different, even if it was the Bellevue- Stratford. She threw back the duvet while her dog groaned in protest from the foot of the bed. Though significantly smaller than her room at home, the noise echoed back against the suite's vaulted ceiling.

"Quiet Sasha."

She gave her a pat between the ears, and slipped into her kimono. The silk was cold against her skin as she relit the fireplace.

Gertrude crossed the room and removed the false bottom from her trunk. Out came two small stacks of paper neatly tied in string. Why she saved them, she really didn't know. Perhaps a part of her hoped it wouldn't come to this. She couldn't even bring herself to read Jennie's messages in their entirety. The journal told her everything she needed to know. Her niece would get over it in due time.

The boy, on the other hand. He was persistent; she'd give him that. Loyal, too— accepting full responsibility for his actions and begging for forgiveness. In fact, he didn't mention Hugh in any of his letters.

There was a sweetness to him. Quoting Tennyson and Byron. So unexpected from someone of his station. Under different circumstances, she could almost understand what Jennie saw in him. The situation being as it was, though, she couldn't take the risk.

According to Joseph, her son's behavior grew worse with every report. Apparently, he owed a staggering amount, and his marks were so bad the Dean was considering expulsion. York took care of the debt, but only a parent could deal with the Admission's Office.

Edmund. She frowned. An alumnus himself, Gertrude hoped she'd have an opportunity to speak with her husband before the ball, but he brought his whore with him and checked into the Ritz Carlton a few blocks down. It was only a matter of time before her interloper daughter sunk her claws into Hugh.

Gertrude stared into the fire. Crouching low, she blew on the embers. In went letters, and she rubbed her hands together as the flames engulfed them. Jennie's debut was this evening. What was done was done.

Lavish orchids were brought in from the hothouses, each centerpiece grander than the next depending on which guest was seated where. A garland of white roses and gardenia hung from the stairwell where Jennie would be announced, while majesty palms made for focal points near the balcony on the far end of the ballroom.

The best orchestra in the tristate area. A menu fit for royalty. Five hundred invitations, all bearing the name 'Browne' to err on the side of caution. And why not? She'd brought the name back to its original glory, hadn't she? It had all come down to this.

Gertrude unlocked her safe and retrieved the family heirloom she'd brought for Jennie to wear. It was the most beautiful tiara she'd ever seen, and she could still envision it atop Mother's curls at their dinners in Saratoga. Diamonds and sapphires, intricate scrollwork— the craftsmanship was unparalleled. She carefully placed it on a black velvet pillow and opened the adjoining door.

Her niece sat at the vanity, the gown even more spectacular than Gertrude could have ever imagined. Pure white, the cap sleeves accentuated Jennie's delicate arms, the whale-bone corset underneath producing just the right amount of cleavage from the empire waist. Thank heavens the awful 'S' shapes of her day were out of fashion. One could hardly move, let alone sit down with the bustle to contend with.

She set the pillow on the glass tabletop and signaled Bridget to leave them. Delicately, she traced one of the longer ruffles cascading from Jennie's torso. Thousands of hand-sewn crystals glittered against the soft light of the chandelier. Satisfied, Gertrude allowed herself to smile and gestured the headpiece.

"This belonged to your great-grandmother."

"It's magnificent," Jennie said.

"It is," Gertrude beamed. "She had the foresight to hide it under the floorboards after Lincoln was inaugurated. You come from a long line of strong women, Jennie. Women who've overcome insurmountable odds. Lived through things that would break your heart."

She grabbed Jennie's gloved hand, but the younger woman pulled it away.

"In case you haven't noticed, my heart's already broken. And I don't want to be strong. I never asked to be."

"Nor I. But it's our duty. We do what we must. There's a name for unmarried women and it isn't kind."

"You *know* who I want to marry," Jennie blinked furiously. "It's my life. Why are you doing this? Don't you want me to be happy?"

"Of course. It's not that simple."

"Why not?"

Gertrude caught her own reflection in the mirror. This wasn't the person she wanted to be. Today didn't hold a candle to the one she'd dreamed of for Jennie ever since her niece was a baby. Hopefully, the girl would bear sons and never have to deal with this torture. Still, she had a right to know the truth.

"Jennie," she began gently. "I know the last few months have been difficult."

"How very astute."

Gertrude ignored the girl's eye roll. Perhaps this called for a different approach.

"May I ask you something?"

"We both know you're going to anyway...."

"Fair enough." Gertrude plucked a copy of the *Philadelphia Inquirer* from the magazine rack on the floor beside them and tapped her fingers along its edge. "Did you notice the headlines have quieted down? Significantly, I might add."

"Well...yes, now that you mention it. I just thought with everything about the re-election—"

"Wrong."

"Wrong? What do you mean, wrong?"

"Do you know who Mr. York's grandfather is?"

Jennie tapped the corner of her mouth. "A steel tycoon?"

"On his father's side, yes. His mother is an Archibald. As in, Cornelius Archibald."

"Doesn't he own most of Manhattan?"

Gertrude nodded. "He's also a silent partner in the *Times*. Holds sway over the Associated Press." She dropped the newspaper back in the bin. "Whoever controls the media...."

"...controls the headlines," Jennie finished, her hazel eyes wide. The girl's hands shook, and she folded them on her lap.

"Fear sells, Jennie. And he's losing a lot of money right now." Gertrude finessed the ringlets framing her niece's face—a face that was now as sheet white as the gown she wore. "You're part-German. Your father's an immigrant."

"I know," she whispered.

"Then you know what you have to do. What you *must* do to protect him."

Her lip trembled. "There's no other way?"

Gertrude shook her head. "I wish things could be different."

Jennie stared vacantly at the large windows to their right.

"You're brave, child. It's in your blood. For that you'll be rewarded." Gertrude lifted the tiara from its pillow. "Someday, years from now, you'll pass this on to your own descendants."

The girl drew a deep breath while Gertrude pinned the tiara in place. She stepped back to admire her work.

"Come now. Your guests are waiting."

CHAPTER 22

Hugh took another glass of champagne from the waiter passing by. If he'd been to one debutante ball, he'd been to a hundred. Except Father made the trip down from Fifth Avenue for this one, his paramour Minnie Blackwell and her daughter in tow. He'd known about Minnie since the first time Father took him to Delmonico's, suddenly all the solo yachting voyages making sense. At the tender age of thirteen, he was strictly forbidden to say anything. Disgusted, Hugh carried the secret alone for years; his vices his only escape.

And escape he did, his guilt about Danny's accident a ghost in the night. He could still see the fury in Shannon's eyes. Feel the cut of her sharp tongue.

He *had* to go to Jackson's. *Just one hand.* That's how it always started, didn't it? The cards were a call he couldn't ignore. An itch he had to scratch, even if it meant hurting the people he cared about. Hugh wanted to write them—Danny was, he hoped, still, someone who'd call him a friend—but couldn't bring himself to do so. What would he even say?

Not to mention how it impacted poor Jennie. She tried to talk to him the last time he was home on a break, but he blew her off. He couldn't face her. He couldn't even face himself. His grades were plummeting, and his loan shark in Boston had just doubled the interest on what he owed.

Hugh looked at his surroundings. Vapid conversations, enormous floral arrangements, a sea of beluga and bubbly; none of this would be happening if it weren't for him. It didn't matter how large the ballroom was, the walls were closing in on him.

He drained the flute and walked out to the balcony. Lighting a cigarette, he looked over the river at New Jersey. *Shannon.* He wondered what she was doing right now. That they still shared the same sky was of little comfort.

Joseph joined him a few minutes later with a glass of champagne in each hand. "To new beginnings," he toasted.

Hugh took a gulp and set the glass down on the ledge. He loosened his tie.

"Glass and steel...." Joseph said. "My family will be pleased. Especially with the war on. Lots of money to be made." Pleased with himself, he took another sip.

"Money? Is that all you can think about?" A sarcastic snort. "Have you seen some of the reports? Men our age. Some are even younger. Maimed. Slaughtered. Blown to bits."

"It's a party, Hugh. Lighten up." The other man put his drink down, resting his hands in his pockets. "We won't serve, if that's what you're worried about."

"Wilson's still straddling the fence."

"For now, he is." Joseph shrugged. "Who knows what the New Year will bring?"

Hugh finished the rest of his champagne, sorry he hadn't remembered to bring his flask. "After the flamethrowers and poisoned gas? Pretty sure I don't wanna know."

"Worst case, they'll make us officers. And that's *after* the draft. We're untouchable." He grinned and drained his own flute. "Stop being so testy, huh? I've never known you to turn down a good time. Anyway, what I was *going* to say before you started bringing up carnage was thank you."

"You're welcome?"

"For the connection?" York cocked his head and cupped Hugh's shoulder. "I might not be here tonight if it wasn't for you. Teammates. Pledge brothers. And now practically family."

Hugh met the other man's eye, his best poker face yet. "Glad I could be of assistance."

"Your next, pal." Joseph chuckled low and deep. "Pretty sure I saw Cornelia Blackwell earlier. Word has it she's headed to Radcliffe next fall. Awfully convenient for you."

Hugh sucked in a long drag. "Don't know about that."

"All wild oats and brooding," he smiled in a way that made Hugh's blood run cold. "You'll fall in line soon enough. They all do. Just look at your cousin."

As if on cue, Jennie appeared in the doorway.

"Darling," Joseph crooned. "We were just talking about you."

"All good things, I hope."

"Of course."

Jennie flashed a smile, batting her eyelids. Hugh recognized the distress signal. He ground his cigarette out, flicking the butt over the balcony as he strode toward her. "May I have a dance with my favorite cousin?"

"I'm your only cousin, Hugh."

"Precisely," he smirked.

They made their way across the marble floor, stopping in a somewhat secluded area where there weren't as many couples.

"What is it?" He asked as they assumed the waltz position.

Jennie was close to tears. She threw a glance at Joseph, still outside. "This is a nightmare. I keep trying to wake up, Hugh, and I can't."

He pulled her closer so she could collect herself.

"He's awful," she breathed.

"I know. I know he is. I'm sorry."

Hugh was sorry. They should be fireside at Juniper Grove right now. Toasting wassail while Jennie plunked out carols on the piano. Shannon bobbing her head to the melody while he and Danny played billiards. Directly or not, he did this. Now everything was falling apart.

"What about your father? He know how you really feel?"

"My duty supersedes that." She replied as he twirled her.

"Your duty? You sound like Mother."

"You should give her more credit."

Hugh sighed. He wasn't up for a lecture.

"Besides," Jennie continued, "Father's not around much. Even when he is, he's distracted."

"Is it work? Manufacturing's booming right now."

"He never talks about the factory. Never did, really. Always left it to his managers," Jennie shrugged.

The orchestra intoned its last notes before starting another song, so they sat down at an empty table. She made sure no one was watching, lowering her voice to a whisper.

"I heard him on the telephone recently with some other man. Speaking German." An older woman walked past them, smiling at Jennie. His cousin gave a friendly wave back before continuing.

"I wasn't snooping, Hugh, I swear."

"Anyone else know?"

"I don't think so." Jennie bit her lip. "But I'm not sure."

He nodded, pulling out his Chesterfields again. Better to keep it quiet.

"Any idea who it might have been?"

"No." Jennie frowned. "I'm scared, Hugh. People can be so hateful. Some families in the neighborhood are considering changing their names to sound more American. The city doesn't feel safe anymore."

Only fifty years out from the last war, and there they were on the precipice of another. Hugh reached across the table for the ashtray. He put the butt down, taking Jennie by the hands. He wanted to protect her. Not only from York, but the upheaval sure to rain down around them in the months to come.

From the corner of his eye, he saw Minnie whisper in Father's ear. They weren't even being discreet anymore. He felt nauseous, hoping Mother didn't see it, too. Hugh was finishing his cigarette when Cornelia appeared behind them.

"Jennie," she gushed, "you look amazing! *Town Topics* has been dropping tidbits about your gown. Well, if you ask me, they didn't do it any justice." She winked at Hugh and popped her shoulder. "Hi handsome."

"Cornelia," he replied in an even tone.

"Mind if I borrow him?" she asked Jennie while already reaching for his hand.

"Enjoy the party," his cousin replied.

A waiter approached with another tray of champagne, handing them each a glass. Hugh made quick work of his, replacing the empty and grabbing another before Cornelia swept him away.

CHAPTER 23

S hannon was freezing. The calendar said it was spring, but it certainly didn't feel like it. She nestled closer to Danny in the sneak box. He put an index finger to his lips and pulled her in nonetheless. Warmth radiated off his body. He was finally looking well again. His weight returned, as did the light to his eyes. Grateful for every moment since he came out of the coma, she snuggled up, almost forgetting for a moment that Will Barkley was in his own boat beside them.

For months she'd watch Danny scribble away, agonizing over every word. It gutted her. Rejection was a friend she knew all too well. Worthless. Unlovable. Never good enough. Shannon wouldn't wish those feelings on anyone, let alone her own brother.

She and Hugh—they were different. Nothing was ever established. She pushed and pushed and pushed until he was finally gone. How do you mourn a might have been? You don't. Shannon got exactly what she wanted. Strangely, it didn't feel anywhere near as good as it should have. It only made her feel more lonesome.

Danny had given his heart openly. Wore it on his sleeve for the world to see. He and Jennie made plans. Dammit, Shannon had even started to warm to the idea of sharing him. Allowed herself to dream of a future outside the hell she'd grown up in. Not visiting her brother while he was hospitalized? Shannon would own that decision, it was for everyone's good. But abandoning Danny when he needed her the most? Heartless. Not a single response. He seemed to die a little more inside with each passing day, and she practically had to force-feed him. It was awful.

That was all over now. Through sheer grit and determination, Shannon managed to turn him around. The only consolation was the notion she wouldn't have to hear the name Jennie Martin ever again.

Theirs was a quiet, cozy existence. The two of them shared cigarettes while snuggled up near the stove when the storms came in January. The ocean was angry, winter winds flattened the grass dunes outside, and frost caked against the window. The whole world could've disappeared under the snow, and it wouldn't have mattered. Shannon already had everything she loved most right there in that tiny room.

There were rumors Pa was shacked up on the mainland, but she didn't let them keep her up anymore. If he hadn't come home by now, he wasn't likely to. And if he did? Shannon was ready for him.

The decoy sounded. Shannon swung the Winchester up. One eye closed, she lined up the mallard, and the bird landed in the water with a plop.

"Nice shot," Will called from his boat.

"Thanks," Shannon beamed at her brother. "I had a good teacher."

Why had she never learned to shoot before? She and Danny practiced for hours by the bay, setting up bottles along the fence by the old Higgins estate. Finally back to his old self, he showed her how to load and aim, swelling with pride as she hit mark after mark. Now that she knew what she was capable of, she wasn't afraid anymore.

It was great being out on the lake. The cattails whistling on the shoals. The brisk morning air in her lungs.

They bagged a few ducks each and walked back to the Ford. Shannon got out the sandwiches Ma Barkley packed for lunch and sank her teeth into one.

"You see the *Star and Wave*?" Will asked them. "Zimmerman admitted everything."

"What exactly are we talking about?" Normally up to date with current events, Shannon had been too absorbed in her own affairs recently to care about anything outside the cocoon.

"The Zimmerman Telegram," her brother explained. "Came across the wire last month and the Brits decoded it. Germany wants an alliance. Claim they're gonna help Mexico recover lands they lost in the Southwest." He took a swig from his canteen. "Finance the whole thing. Guess they figure if we're at war over here, we won't be able to help the Allies over there."

Danny reached for a second helping. "Not only that," he said between bites, "the Huns began unrestricted submarine warfare back in February."

Her jaw dropped. "Why didn't you say something before?"

"Didn't want to scare you."

She scowled.

"Careful, your face'll stick like that," Will teased. He glanced at Danny and puffed out his chest. "We can take 'em, right? Don't you worry, little lady."

Shannon leaned against the car. She held up her sack of ducks and cocked her head. "Maybe the Germans should worry about me."

Will grinned, holding his stare longer than she felt comfortable.

Her brother noticed too. He took the bag from her. "Better get these back to the farm for culling," Danny suggested and loaded it into the trunk with the others.

They dined with the Barkley's, staying well beyond the plum pie Mrs. Barkley served for dessert. It was delicious, every bite reminding her of Ma.

She even sent them home with a care package.

"Just little odds and ends," the older woman insisted when Danny began to protest.

Shannon was grateful for it. She tried not to let on, but there was only so much she could do with the supplies they had on hand. The weather would be turning soon, bringing the tourists with it. This would help them through the next month.

They pulled up to the bungalow to a shadow on the doorstep. Danny reached protectively over her in the passenger seat, his brow furrowed as he squinted to make out who it was. The figure stood, offering a friendly wave and her brother's face froze.

"Hugh!" Danny sprinted, Shannon right behind him. "Jennie—"

"She's fine," Hugh assured him. "Far as I know."

Wearing only a school sweater, his voice sounded broken. He shook Danny's hand before tugging her towards him. Hugh gave her a tight squeeze, and she could feel him shivering. Pulse racing, Shannon felt a quiver as her stomach flip-flopped. How did he still do this to her? She thought of all the things her heart was afraid to tell him. How he meant more to her than just a friend. So much more. She looked around their property but didn't see the roadster.

"I took the train," he explained as he released her. Hunched, Hugh crossed his arms against himself. "Sorry to just show up. I…I didn't know where else to go."

"Let's get you inside," she said as Danny opened the front door.

Shannon made them warm milk, and the trio sat down in the kitchen. Elbows on the table, Hugh put his head in his hands, fumbling for his words.

"I fucked up. I fucked everything up."

Danny put his hand on Hugh's shoulder. "What happened?"

Hugh cupped his hands around his mug. He blew on the steam, gazing at the bottom of the cup for several minutes. "Got kicked out of school," he finally said in a hollow tone. "My family doesn't know. Not yet. And when they find out...."

He covered his mouth.

"Stay here as long as you like," Danny offered. "You can have Pa's old room."

"You sure?" His chocolate eyes shone with gratitude as he looked from one sibling to another. "After what I did?"

Shannon caught her brother's eye and knew exactly what the slight lilt in the corner of his mouth meant. She went too far—shifting the guilt to Hugh's influence when it fell squarely with their father. No one would've believed her brother tripped were he sober. She'd been so shocked and terrified at the time she didn't know what else to say. Pa accosted her, she'd caught Hugh with another woman, and came home to find what she thought was Danny's bludgeoned corpse. She had no time to really think it through. Only did what she thought was best. It just slipped out. She never thought he'd pay the hospital bill.

Hugh's face was pained. His eyes; bloodshot. Shannon wanted to hold him. Wanted to scoop him up and tell him she was sorry for being so distant last summer. That she hadn't meant to hurt him. That whatever he'd done to warrant expulsion couldn't be that bad. Then again, everything paled in comparison to what she'd almost done with Pa.

"I insist," Danny said. "I'm sure my sister would agree. Isn't that right, Shannon?"

"Of course," Shannon added as she stood up. "I'll go make up the bed."

CHAPTER 24

Hugh trudged into the tiny back bedroom, Danny's footsteps as he went upstairs slowly fading. Save for the soft glow of an oil lamp, the room was dark, his eyes still adjusting to the new surroundings. The window on the sidewall was spider-webbed, and his breath came out in white wisps. The bed was neatly made, with a single pillow and a well-worn patchwork quilt. The mattress creaked as he sat down, and he gazed at the barren beach outside, subconsciously crossing his arms.

There was a light tap, and he turned his head to see Shannon outside the door.

"It's frigid for March." She gestured the blanket folded over her right arm. "Thought this might come in handy."

"Thanks." All these months apart, and that was all he could come up with? *Smooth.*

"May I?"

He nodded, and she sat down beside him. Neither seemed to know what to say. Silver moonlight streamed through the cracked pane. Shannon held the quilt tight on her lap while he looked stupidly at a knot on the floor.

After a few minutes, she glanced over, a shy smile dancing across her face, and draped the blanket over his shoulders. No touch could've been gentler. Delicate, like she was handling the finest lace. Hugh had never known such a touch, and he shivered with delight.

"You're trembling," she whispered, her breath warm against his cheek.

Hugh suppressed a smile. "I'll be alright."

He'd feasted on the flesh before, the clubs full of eager girls looking to earn their keep. Then there was Cambridge, townies hoping to stake their claim on the promising football star. Every so often, he snuck one into his fraternity house. Had a pledge serve as look-out if old Mrs. Schumacher were making her rounds. His body missed the feeling of being inside a woman's folds, that feverish rush of release. It wasn't until now that he wished he'd waited.

Shannon was his best friend's sister, for Christ's sake. She shouldn't even be in here. Already feeling the swell in his pants, Hugh inhaled deeply in hopes to keep it at bay, only to be further enraptured by the scents swirling around him.

Clean. Pure. With slight hints of pine.

He squeezed his eyes closed. This wasn't a family that had extra anything. Shannon hadn't given him a spare blanket. She'd given him *hers*. Hugh grabbed a tattered corner to pull it off, but she stopped him, her tiny hand resting firmly on his knuckles.

Shannon traced a figure eight across the top of his palm. Lips parted, her sapphire eyes flickered with apprehension. Or was it something more? God, he hoped so. Hugh tilted his head back, urgency flooding through him. *Don't stop.*

"Your hands are like ice. How long were you waiting for us?"

"Couple hours. No big deal," he lied.

"Wanna talk about it? What happened at school?"

Heart pounding, Hugh couldn't escape the visions swimming around his head: the Dean's bloated, ruddy cheeks; Coach shaking his head in disappointment; the broad shoulders of the bookie's enforcers when they came to collect. He gulped.

"No."

"Let me help you. Please?"

Hugh grimaced. He hated letting her see him like this. Weak. Emotional. Everything a Callaway shouldn't be according to his parents. "I let everybody down."

"Not everyone." Shannon's other hand found his back, applying the perfect amount of pressure as she massaged his shoulder. "Not me."

He leaned into it, needing her touch as much as he needed air. She never looked more beautiful, alabaster skin glowing in the silver moonlight. The yearning was too intense now, and he reached for her despite himself. Her returned embrace brought a tear to his eye. She pulled him close, resting his head on her bosom while she stroked his hair.

Hugh grew up in a Fifth Avenue mansion. Sailed the *Crusader* across two oceans. Before the war, he'd stayed at the finest hotels in London and Paris and, up until that afternoon, anyway, attended one of the most prestigious universities in the country. Never had he felt he belonged. But here, in this frost-bitten shanty, blustery winter winds squeaking through the broken window, Hugh wasn't lost anymore. He was home.

"Paying Dr. Mace's charges," Shannon cooed. "That was so generous."

What is she talking about? Hugh was glad she couldn't see the confusion that must've been all over his face.

She held him tighter. "Danny told me. I don't know how to thank you.

Gratitude? That's what this was? Hugh trained his eyes on the foot post. He should've known better. She'd never see him as anything more than her brother's buddy. Still, unrequited or not, he couldn't exploit her. Never.

He pulled back, fisting his mouth in an exaggerated yawn. "Should probably turn in," he added while stretching his arm. He slid the blanket off his shoulders and started to refold it.

"What are you doing?" she asked, tucking a stray behind her ear.

"I can't," he sighed, and a puff of vapor escaped.

She put her hand on the quilt. "Keep it. I'm used to the cold."

"Shannon..." Hugh stopped himself, his heart aching for her. How could anyone grow used to these temperatures?

"I'll sleep better knowing you're comfortable."

"You're sure?"

Unable to look at him, she nodded as she stood. "G'night, Hugh," Shannon murmured when she'd reached the door.

"Goodnight, Shannon."

Hugh's bones ached when he awoke the following morning, his muscles screaming like it was the first week of practice all over again. But those weren't the only parts of him in pain. Flinching, he adjusted his groin and stood up, stomach grumbling at the sweet aroma wafting in from the kitchen. Trying not to waddle, he slowly walked from one room to the other.

Shannon was busy at the stove while Danny sat at the table, coffee in one hand, cigarette in the other.

Hugh wiped the sleep from his eyes and gingerly lowered himself on the chair next to his friend. "Mornin'."

Danny smirked. "Sleep well?"

"Yeah. Thanks again for putting me up."

"No problem."

"Can I get you coffee?" Shannon chirped. "Just put on a fresh pot."

"That'd be swell," Hugh replied.

Carrying a steamy mug in one hand, she placed a plate piled high with hotcakes in front of him with the other. "Honey's in the jar," she mentioned before returning to the burner to prepare her brother's portion.

Hugh didn't realize how hungry he'd been until he started eating. Cook was distinguished in her profession, but these? These pancakes were spectacular. Light and fluffy, perfectly shaped and browned on each side.

Shannon stood to clear his empty dish a few minutes later. "Didn't like 'em, didja?"

He chuckled. "My compliments to the chef."

"Want some more?"

He waved a hand, patting his full stomach. "Nah, I'm good."

"I'll take some," Danny chimed in, but his sister only raised an eyebrow. "What? Am I invisible or somethin'?"

"Or somethin'," she grinned.

He turned to Hugh. "Wanna come into town with me later? Thought I'd swing by the hardware store. Get that window fixed for ya."

Still sore, Hugh put his hand in his pocket, discretely rearranging himself. "Yeah. Think a walk would do me some good."

They set out an hour later. The early spring air was just as biting as the previous day. Hugh buried his hands in his pockets, rubbing his fists to keep the circulation going. He was both thankful for the scarf Danny lent him yet sorry to see the upturned collar on his friend's thin jacket.

Danny told me.... What was the best way to approach this? Uncle would say head-on, but Hugh wasn't so sure. Part of him kicked himself for not thinking to take care of the bill. It was the least he could've done. Still, the conversation could turn just as quickly, opening up a can of worms he wasn't ready to deal with. Maybe if he paid for the window repairs...

"It's good to see you, pal," Danny said as they rounded onto Perry Street. "She might be prickly sometimes, but, I know Shannon's happy about it, too."

Hugh coughed nervously, wondering just how much about the previous evening his friend was privy to.

"She never makes pancakes."

"Never?"

Danny shot him a side-eye. "Nope."

Hugh couldn't let this go on. Couldn't accept their hospitality under false pretenses. Now was as good a time as any.

"Danny," he started. "There's somethin' I gotta talk to you about."

"Shoot."

"The bill. The one from the doctor's office."

"Yeah? What about it?"

Hugh stopped on the sidewalk. He looked down at his feet, then forced himself to meet his friend's eye. "Wasn't me that paid it."

Danny looked just as perplexed. "Never said you did."

"Shannon know that?"

"Don't know where she'd get that idea. Hospital said it was anonymous when I called 'em." He furrowed his brow. "Only told her we didn't owe anything. Just lucky, I guess? Prolly would've been higher than the value of the house and boat put together. What exactly did my sister say?"

Despite the cold, Hugh felt beads of sweat along the back of his neck. "She said, 'thank you'."

Danny cocked his head. "That all?"

Hugh held his hands up in surrender. "I would never take advantage of her. I care about her, alright? She's all I think about."

"Yeah, well, you could try tellin' her."

"What's that s'posed to mean?"

Danny squared his jaw. "We might not be perfect but at least Jennie knows how I feel."

"You sure?" Hugh crossed his arms, still seeing his cousin's tearful face at her debut three months earlier. "When was the last time you wrote her, huh?"

"Last week." He reached in his pocket and pulled out a small white envelope. "Was gonna drop this at the post office on our way home." Danny put the letter back and pinched the bridge of his nose. "I write her every week, Hugh."

Hugh drew his fist to his mouth and bit the knuckle of his index finger. "Every week?"

"Every. Week."

There was only one person with both means and motive to squash the hospital charges and the letters. Why hadn't he thought of it before?

"Look Danny," Hugh sighed and began walking again. "I'll speak with Shannon. Set things straight. I just…I gotta take care of somethin' first."

"I don't like lyin' to her."

"You didn't. She made an assumption."

Danny tilted his head in acknowledgment as they trudged toward Washington Street.

"Hey, mind if I meet you at Swain's?" Hugh jutted his head at Kennedy's. "Gonna pick up some toiletries."

His friend nodded, and the two parted ways.

Hugh strolled the cobblestone path to the pharmacy. He did a quick run-through of the balance in his wallet, glad he closed his college bank account before leaving Massachusetts. It should last him a little while, hopefully until summer. Then maybe he could find work on the docks.

The older merchant welcomed him with a smile and made quick work of the list of necessities Hugh requested. A toothbrush, comb, Brilliantine, soap. Hugh eyed the candy counter. Yes, sweets. Sweets would be a treat for her. Maybe soften the blow. So, he picked up a small bag of bonbons. A pound of sugar, butter, and coffee; commodities that were already in short supply given the high demand overseas.

"That all, son?" Mr. Kennedy asked before making his way to the register.

"For now," Hugh confirmed. He paid the bill but left the goods on the counter. "Can I trouble you to keep an eye on these while I use the phone booth?"

"No problem at'all."

Alone in the booth, Hugh placed his hand on the receiver and braced himself. "Philadelphia please," he asked the operator.

CHAPTER 25

"Hughie?" Gertrude exhaled into the mouthpiece. "Oh, thank goodness! Darling, I've been so worried—"

"Save it, Mother," he snapped. "What kind of game do you think you're playing?"

Gertrude blinked. Thankful to have taken the call in Walter's study, she cradled the telephone and walked to the massive paneled double doors. Confirming they were locked, she drew a sharp breath.

"Just *who* do you think you're speaking to, young man?"

"What do you want from me?" Hugh hissed. "Some sniveling apology? Fine. I screwed up, okay? Satisfied?"

"No, I'm not. Hugh Callaway, I will not tolerate such insolence."

"What are you gonna do about it, huh? Force me into some loveless marriage like you're trying to do to Jennie?"

"I beg your pardon?"

"Stop the charade. Please. It's unbecoming."

Gertrude sank onto the leather sofa. Nauseous, she felt cold. What had York told him? *Double-crossing little snake.* She'd gone to such great lengths.

Done things that made her skin crawl. And for what? Hugh's reputation lay in shambles.

"Alright, Hugh," she began calmly. "Kindly tell me what this is all about."

"Danny Culligan."

"The fisherman?"

"My *friend*."

"Your friend." That was hard to stomach. "My apologies."

"I'm not the one who needs to hear that, Mother. He does. Jennie, too."

They were interrupted by the operator with the request Hugh enter more change. If she could just find out where he was staying, she could be on the next train and settle this in person. York was undoubtedly responsible. Still, she needed to tread lightly. Better to deny than reveal too much. Hearing the coins deposited, she took charge of the conversation.

"Speak plainly, dear. We haven't much time."

"I know about the letters. He writes her. Weekly, Mother. I saw one myself. She never writes back."

He saw one. He *saw* one. Gertrude's heart skipped. *He's down the shore.*

"Your cousin is an adult. Unlike *some people*, she takes her responsibility to this family very seriously. Further, contrary to what you might think, I can't *force* her to do anything. If Jennie hasn't written him, he might consider checking with the post to ensure he has her correct address."

"He might consider...." Hugh snorted. "Why pay his medical bills then? Feeling guilty?"

This was most unexpected. "I...I didn't."

"You didn't?"

"No." The truth felt good, however fleeting, and she didn't care for his silence on the other end of the line. "Hugh? Darling, are you still there?"

"You really didn't, Mother?"

"I'm sorry, Hugh." She put Jennie through hell; that much was certain. Gertrude even felt a twinge of sympathy for the Culligan boy. Her heart was in the right place. Yet she also knew she wasn't the first person to do the wrong thing for the seemingly right reason. "I wish I'd thought to. Especially considering the amount was likely astronomical. He is your friend, as you say; an act of philanthropy and Good Will were certainly warranted. In that respect, I failed you and I'm sorry. Truly I am."

"I should go, Mother."

"Wait. Please." She coiled a hand around the telephone wire, squeezing it in place of holding him.

"Know that I'm somewhere safe. And—"

The switchboard cut in again.

"I'm happy. Finally." He let out a long breath. "Don't try to contact me. It's time I live my own life."

The line went dead. Gertrude tapped the receiver, but it was no use. He was gone.

An ache filled her heart unlike any she'd ever known. Hollow and deep, it crushed her. What happened to her little boy? Where had she gone so wrong? Debt, loose women, marks so poor he'd been suspended indefinitely from the team. It was only a matter of time before word got to Mann in New York. Oh, how she loathed *Town Topics*.

There was only one woman who'd want to marry him now. That should soothe Edmund's ruffled feathers, at least. Minnie would happily procure Cornelia. All she had to do was acquiesce to a divorce. She'd put it off for years, holding her goals for the boys in higher esteem than she held her pride.

Maybe it was time. York's proposal was imminent. Samuel was young enough to rebound. And Hugh? Happy or not, there was no way he could take care of himself. Cornelia could guide him. She'd been bred for it. Of course, there was the small task of getting back on his good side, but she was confident in her ability to convince him she had his best interests at heart.

Gertrude sauntered back to Walter's desk and returned the telephone to its place. She eyed his wet bar in the corner. The afternoon called for brandy, and no one needed to know about it. She poured some into a tumbler, her reflection in the sterling silver decanter spurring her on. *When have you ever shrank from a challenge?* She swirled her glass, savoring that first sip. *Never.*

CHAPTER 27

A month later, Shannon could still feel the humiliating sting of Hugh's rejection. Every moment they were together was like walking barefoot on cut glass. She knew he had experience, she'd seen it with her own eyes. He just didn't want *her*. She knew why, of course. Not because she wasn't pretty or smart enough, although they were probably factors. *You're poor white trash. Who would ever want you?* Pa did, she reminded herself in disgust.

Hugh wasn't unkind. Quite the contrary, he was the perfect houseguest. Shannon almost wished he wasn't so nice to her. She didn't deserve it. It was this over-politeness that shook her; how he'd speak past her during their short, casual conversations. A comment or two about the weather. Or, he went out of his way to do things like open doors for her or pull out her chair.

Worst, however, was when he complimented her cooking. It was absurd—no one liked boiled cabbage that much. Short of starvation, she didn't even care for it.

He and Danny got along like champs, and Shannon resigned herself to the fact that she would rather have Hugh in her life as a friend than not in her life at all. He was clearly making an effort, and so could she.

Hugh proved himself to be quite helpful on their hunts as well, putting his skeet shooting to good use.

"Shannon and her boys," Ma Barkley would joke when they picked up Will while his sister Sarah glared down from her bedroom window.

One Saturday, he treated them all to lunch at Kennedy's in a show of thanks. He received a telegram from New York, and Shannon got the impression he didn't want to be alone when he read it. She stole a glance at Hugh across the table, recalling the last time they'd shared this booth, painfully aware that whatever his father wanted didn't bode well.

She wished she could freeze this moment in time. Danny and their friends joking around. The biggest decision they faced was what flavor of ice cream to have Mr. Kennedy use in their milkshakes.

Will stared at the yellow envelope. "Well, you gonna open it or not?"

"Will!" Shannon jabbed him with her elbow. Good-natured, he could be so uncouth sometimes.

Hugh lit a cigarette while they waited for their order. "No, he's right." He tore across the top. "Better to get it over with." Seconds later, he slammed the telegram on the counter and swore under his breath. "They're cutting me off."

"Can they do that?" Shannon asked.

"Already done."

Danny sighed. "I'm sorry pal." He gestured at the plates Mr. Kennedy had just brought out. "You don't have to do this."

Hugh blew a stream of smoke out his nose. "I want to."

"That's rough," Will chimed in. "What are you gonna do?"

"Give him a minute," Shannon remanded.

Hugh shrugged. He took a drag and reached for the ketchup bottle. "I'm honestly not sure."

"There's always the Navy," Will suggested, taking a hefty bite of his hamburger. He swallowed hard, washing it down with a swig of soda. "My Pop said they're looking to build a base. Acquired the Ford property and the old Fun Factory over on Sewell's point."

"I miss that place," Shannon murmured of the abandoned amusement park. Closed two years earlier, it was a shell of its former self. The windows were broken, and Nor'easters swept sand all over the floor of what was previously a roller skating rink.

"Something to think about," Will was saying. "Three squares plus pay. Not a bad way to go. Me? I'm an Army guy myself."

"You're not even old enough to enlist," Danny grinned.

"Be sixteen in the fall. Older than some of those Tommies."

Shannon lost her appetite, picking at the food on her plate. Though she felt older than sixteen herself, the fact remained that they were all still kids. This wasn't their fight. She'd never heard of Franz Ferdinand, archduke of where-ever. So he died? Everyone did eventually. Damn the Germans, with their spies and secret alliances. Targeting civilians. Their world was rapidly changing whether she liked it or not, and Shannon hated them for it.

"Would you like me to wrap that for you?" Mr. Kennedy asked, bringing her back to reality.

She nodded and slid him her plate.

The following week, she was busy ironing in the kitchen. They had an invitation to dine at the Barkley's Easter Sunday, the gracious farmer opening his home to Hugh as well. Knowing they couldn't show up empty-handed, Shannon sent the boys to pick up supplies she needed for a side dish and dessert. Her best dress already hung in the entryway to the parlor, and she was about to move onto Danny's trousers when she heard car doors slamming and raised voices outside.

Shannon put the iron on the stove. She almost reached the door when it flung open, and her brother stormed in. Newspaper in one hand, bourbon in the other.

Hugh was right on heels. "Danny, please!"

"Jesus Christ, Hugh! Leave me alone."

Shannon put her hands on her hips. "Language," she admonished. "Today especially. It's Good Friday."

"Good?" Danny took a long pull from the bottle. "What's good about it, huh?" he choked.

Lips thin, she looked from one man to the other. "Will somebody please tell me what's going on?"

Danny threw the paper on the table. Shannon's heart stopped as she read the headline.

U. S. AT WAR

She clapped her hands over her mouth and scanned the rest of the article. The House passed the resolution by an overwhelming majority... They were seizing German ships... Wilson was set to unveil his plans for the military... More than a million men needed the first year alone...

Shannon forced herself to stop reading. "No," she whispered.

She turned to Danny for confirmation she was wrong, but her brother had his back to her. Hands in his pockets, he stared out the window.

Hugh steadied her from behind, that old jolt of electricity still just as shocking. Hand on her shoulder, he flipped to the *Inquirer's* society column. Jennie was engaged.

CHAPTER 28

Jennie leaned against her pillow, clenching and unclenching her left hand. She wasn't sure she'd ever get used to the feeling of her engagement ring. The two-and-a-half-carat emerald cut was a York family heirloom and just as vulgar as the groom. It got stuck on everything from her silk stockings to her hair when she was sleeping.

Marrying Joseph was her duty. From what very little she understood of the family business, what started with windows and bottles grew exponentially. Martin Glass was now responsible for producing precision optical pieces used in gun sights and telescopes. The fervor against her kind being what it was, it only a matter of time before the military turned to other firms for its supply. An alliance between the two families' companies would ebb the bleeding, maybe even stop it entirely with the elder York at the helm.

Reconciling this logic with her heart was another story entirely. She felt dead inside. The sad truth was there were few girls in her class who enjoyed a loving partner. Still, Mr. Archibald had kept his word, with news outlets focusing primarily on U.S. mobilization efforts until this morning. Every paper in Philadelphia reported yesterday's explosion at Eddystone, a little town just outside the city, and the headlines were grim. Ring or no ring, Jennie had never been more terrified for her family or what the future might hold for them. Because someone did die. A lot of someones.

The numbers were horrifying—122 killed and another 150 workers injured. Worse, most victims were women and girls not much older than herself. The hospitals were inundated, with shrapnel trapping some survivors for hours after the blast. Some of the bodies were so badly mangled they were unidentifiable. Sabotage was suspected, and the Department of Justice was already investigating the attack.

Father's secret ate away at her. Now, more than ever, she had to protect him.

And then there was Hugh. Knowing his whereabouts inflicted just as much pain as it did relief. Staying with the Culligans. How could he be so selfish? It was no different than the nursery games they played as children, her fingers tangled in a proverbial string from the intricate web her cousin weaved.

The purple sky outside her window told her she was late for tea, and Jennie sighed. She gathered her skirts for the walk downstairs, hoping the puffiness under her eyes had subsided. Her aunt hated to be kept waiting.

"So glad you decided to join me." The older woman was smiling, but Jennie knew she wasn't 'glad' at all from her tone.

She plastered on one of her own. "Must've lost track of time."

Gertrude rose and patted her thigh, scooping her small dog up when Sasha trotted over.

"You're done already?"

"I have correspondence to catch up on."

Both relieved and alarmed, Jennie curtsied. "I see."

"Do try to keep a better calendar."

Her aunt swept out of the room before Jennie could respond. The thought of returning to her own room and crawling back into bed was all too welcoming. At the same time, she salivated at the quiche Cook set out.

"Don't mind her, *Schatz*. Took another call from New York earlier."

Jennie squinted but couldn't place where her father was sitting until she saw his head pop up from the back of the couch on the opposite end of the room.

"You startled me! Hiding like that."

"Hiding?" He chuckled. "Can't a man read a book in his own house nowadays? Or is that illegal too?"

Jennie wanted to laugh back, but there wasn't anything funny about his remarks. She wanted to hide too. Feeling the blood rush to her cheeks, she sank into the nearest chair. Concerned, her father put the book down and pulled up the wingback next to her.

"You look troubled," he said.

Jennie gulped. He knew her so well, yet she couldn't say the same. Sometimes it took all her energy just to work up the courage to get him alone to ask about what she'd overheard. And when she did? Her emotions got the best of her, and she made up some excuse to escape the truth. It was time they finally cleared the air.

"Daddy?" she asked, her voice just above a whisper.

"Yes?"

Shoulders drooped, Jennie hung her head. "I have to ask you something. But I don't know how."

"I can't stand to see you upset."

"Promise…" She took a deep breath. "Promise you won't be angry with me."

He nodded.

"A while back…before my debut…." Jennie drew her eyes up shamefully and tried again. "I heard you on the telephone. I…I didn't mean to. I thought it was about the ball when I picked up the extension. But I heard you, Father." She lowered her voice with a side-eye to the door in case the servants were lurking. "Speaking German. I couldn't make any of it out, so…I'm asking you now: with the war on, do we have anything to worry about?"

Father sat back in his seat, arms crossed against himself, digesting the information. "So," he said finally, "you think I'm a spy?"

Her breath caught, and he reached for her hands.

"No, my love. I'm not."

"Do you even recall the conversation? What were you saying? Daddy, don't you *know* what they can do to you?"

"Slow down, Jennie," he said. "I'm well aware of the consequences." He cupped his chin with one hand, scratching his white whiskers. "This discussion occurred before your ball, you said?"

"Yes. Early December."

His eyes twinkled.

"So you remember?"

"Of course, darling. Not every day we get a request for a stained glass window. It was Fritz Reinheimer." Father smiled. "He didn't have the measurements when he came to the warehouse so I told him to ring me."

"Our neighbor?" she furrowed her brow. "He speaks perfect English."

"It was a Christmas present for Mrs. Reinheimer. He didn't want to chance her or one of the children picking up the upstairs extension and ruining the surprise."

Jennie blushed.

"So you see, *Schatz*, you have nothing to worry about."

She wished she could share his optimism. Dread filled the back of her mind; its razor-sharp teeth sunk in deep, feasting on every moment of happiness, including this one. Cold, dark hands twisted her thoughts like a pretzel while a tiny voice whispered how things would get worse before they ever got better.

Joseph came to call the following day, yet again confirming how obnoxious he could be. Jennie stared out the window, breath shallow as April rain pattered against the pane. She would've likened it to Bridget lacing her up too tight were it not for the fact her aunt wore the same expression. Dog on her lap, Gertrude stroked the pooch absentmindedly with one hand and took a sip of claret with the other. Sasha's diamond collar sparkled against the library's massive fireplace.

"Come now, ladies," her fiancé said. He leaned against the entryway between the library and the hall, immaculately dressed as usual. "The war hasn't started yet. Besides, we're in good hands."

Jennie forced her lips into a thin smile while Gertrude groaned. She wished Father would come down for dinner already. Though Joseph might claim otherwise, Jennie knew there were two things he would always love more than her— money and the sound of his own voice.

"Why's that, darling?" She played her part.

"Old Black Jack Pershing," Joseph said.

Jennie gave an encouraging nod and mentally braced herself.

"Experience, of course. Cuba, the Philippines. They put him with the darkies. That's how he got his nickname."

"What a terrible thing to say," Jennie interjected. There was no need to slur. Comments like that were over the line.

Even Gertrude spoke up. "Really Joseph," her aunt said, "this isn't the football locker room."

"My apologies," he bowed.

Jennie stood from the divan, her voice curt. "I think I'd like some claret after all. Can I refill your glass while I'm up?" she asked her aunt.

"Thank you, dear."

She strode over to the wine cart, her cheeks burning as she poured two generous amounts from the decanter.

"Shame what happened to his poor family, though," Gertrude murmured as Jennie handed her the wine.

"Ah, the fire," Joseph agreed. "Terrible."

"What fire?" Jennie asked as she returned to the chaise lounge.

"Smoke inhalation. Lost his wife and three little girls." he explained with about as much compassion as a rattlesnake.

Jennie set her glass on the side table, hands over her heart. "How awful."

Gertrude took a hefty gulp from her glass.

The reptile tilted his head. "Was in Texas at the time. Found out via telegram."

"I can't imagine," Jennie said, still trying to make sense of it. "Not only to lose your loved ones, but to be so far away from them when it happened. And a telegram no less? I just can't imagine." She shook her head, looking from her fiancé to her aunt. "Family is everything."

"Yes, Jennie," Gertrude met her stare, gray eyes gleaming. "Yes it is."

CHAPTER 29

Danny unleashed his fury on the barnacles. He scrubbed the hull with all his might, taking his pocket knife to any stubborn husks. He sanded, and he painted. Then he sanded some more. Taking a step back to admire his efforts, one foot landed in the paint tray.

"Just my luck," he muttered as he hurled his brush across the beach. "What?" he asked the seagull who was watching him. The bird cocked its head and flew away.

He plopped down in the sand and lit a cigarette. Cupping his chin with one hand, Danny stared at the horizon. A month went by, and it hadn't gotten any easier. He lost her. Then again, maybe she was never really his, to begin with.

The island, on the other hand, seemed to change overnight. Patriotism was at an all-time high, and businesses were booming. The city was building a convention hall. The Hotel Cape May was turned into a hospital, and Bethlehem Steel continued cranking out its munitions production.

Will turned out to be right about the Navy's plans, with preparations for Section Base Number 9 underway on Sewell's Point. Danny read it would include an aviation field too, support for the submarine chasers and minesweepers already in the area. Over on Henry Ford's property, they were working on Wissahickon Naval Training Barracks.

Sailors converged on the city by the thousands. Hugh joined their ranks but hadn't received his orders yet, while Shannon took a job with the barracks' kitchen staff.

All around him, the world was moving on. But Danny just wanted to stay on his little spot in the sand.

"Lunch!" Shannon called from the window.

Danny buried what remained of his smoke and pushed himself up. Whatever she made smelled wonderful.

"Just a quiche," she said nonchalantly, handing out their utensils. "Nice of Will to bring over those eggs yesterday."

"Nice," Hugh echoed with a grin.

"What's that supposed to mean?" She tilted her head.

Hugh held up his hands in mock surrender. "Just agreeing with you."

"Sure you were," Shannon teased as she doled out their plates. She took a telegram out of her apron and handed it to Hugh before sitting down. "This arrived for you this morning."

"It's from Mother," he frowned.

"Open it," Danny said, taking a hefty bite.

"They're arriving the Friday before Decoration Day. She's throwing Jennie an engagement party." He sighed. "She'd like me to come."

They ate in silence for a few minutes. Shannon grabbed his hand under the table and gave it a squeeze.

"Do you think you'll go?" she asked Hugh.

"Is it wrong I don't want to?"

Danny thought of his own relationship with Pa, recalling his great escape plan. Until Hugh arrived, he'd still hoped to relocate. Philadelphia wasn't the only city where they could hide. But he was eighteen now, and it seemed a moot point. Who knew what the war would bring? Shannon seemed to like her job, and plenty of places were hiring. Maybe he'd even join the Navy, too. He had enough experience on the water. Hugh's eyes were on him, anxious for his opinion.

"No. It's not wrong. Families can be complicated."

"You're more family to me than Mother ever was. Father, too, for that matter." Hugh looked from one sibling to the other. "Been so good to me these last few months."

"I'd hate to see you refrain on our account," Shannon quipped. "You needn't worry about hurting our feelings."

Why are you so thick-headed?

"What about Jennie?" she asked. There was that hand squeeze again, too. "You were always close."

Hugh swallowed hard. "I thought so, too." He pouted. "Danny, I'm sorry things didn't work out between you. If you don't want me to go, just say the word."

Danny sat back in his chair, crossing his arms against himself. He tilted his head, and a flyaway dangled down next to the scar Pa gave him on his left eye. "Jennie made her choice, Hugh. I gotta respect that."

Her choice. Respecting it was one thing. But understanding it? That killed him. "*Why?*" he wanted to scream. *What about us?* He'd give anything to know what he'd done. When? When had she stopped loving him? What exact moment? Not that Danny could go back and change it, but he would if he could. There were stories of Second Sight. Tarot card readings up and down the boardwalk. He drew a hand to his mouth, swallowing the lump in his throat.

"I don't wanna make things weird."

"You won't," Danny fibbed.

"You sure?"

"I'm not gonna keep you from seeing your family, Hugh." Now it was his turn to squeeze Shannon's hand. "Do they even know you enlisted?"

Their friend shook his head.

"Then you hafta go." He glanced at his sister, but she was staring at her plate. "You do. You have to. There might not be a next time."

CHAPTER 30

Gertrude paced the corridor outside the Iron Pier's ballroom. Hugh agreed to meet her for lunch. She hadn't seen him since Christmas and wasn't sure how her nerves would hold up. Meanwhile, Samuel, freshly home from boarding school for the summer, was testing what little remained of her patience.

"Mother," the boy whined, "we'll get cotton candy on the way home, won't we?"

"Yes. I've already told you that, Samuel. Please don't ask again," she snapped, immediately regretting it.

"Did someone say 'cotton candy'?" Hugh bounded up the steps, extending a ball of pink fluff.

"Hugh!" Samuel hugged him before eagerly gobbling away.

"Before lunch?" Gertrude grimaced.

"It's his favorite."

"I'm sorry. I didn't mean that," she pulled him close. "Hughie. I've missed you so much."

"Mother."

"You look well," she said, stepping back. A bit on the thin side, but she kept that to herself. "I'll let the host know you're here."

Gertrude picked at her boiled sea bass while Hugh inhaled his lamb and mint jelly. To no one's surprise, Samuel had only a few bites of his clam chowder before insisting he was saving room for dessert. More interested at the moment in what her oldest was saying, she nodded to placate the boy.

Hugh assumed Edmund paid his debts, and she was too ashamed to admit otherwise. He was sorry about his grades. That she could forgive as well. Life's best lessons were learned outside of the classroom. But the Navy?

"Darling, what were you thinking?"

"That I found a way to support myself. You know, being how you disowned me."

"That was your father's decision."

"Doesn't matter."

"How can you say that?"

"How could you let him?"

Gertrude struggled through the remainder of lunch. Her hands shook under the napkin on her lap. She watched Hugh's lips move but heard little of what he actually said, smiling when he smiled, giving Samuel a reproachful eyebrow when he slurped his ice cream.

They finally finished their meal, and Hugh stood to leave.

"We'll see you tomorrow night?" she asked for what was probably the third time that hour.

"Yes, Mother," Hugh smiled and bent down to kiss her.

"Until then, darling," she managed.

Hugh disappeared down the stairs, and she clutched her chest.

"Are you alright, Mommy?" Samuel asked, his brown eyes wide.

"Of course!" Gertrude flashed a smile while rummaging in her bag. Out came her change purse. "Here, Sammy," she said brightly, handing him some coins and glancing at the telephone booth across the hall. "Why don't you go play some games on the midway while Mommy makes a call?

I'll meet you at Roth's after and we'll get that fudge you like."

The boy no sooner left, and Gertrude locked herself in a booth. She pulled the brim of her hat low, looking down while waiting for the operator to connect the call and hoping no one would recognize her.

"Yes?" Edmund sounded bored.

Gertrude updated him on Hugh's enlistment.

"What would you have me do, Gertie? If you would've taken a firmer hand with him earlier he wouldn't be in this mess." There was whispering in the background. "Yes, kitten, I'm almost finished…."

"I'll grant you the divorce," she hissed into the receiver. "Do whatever you need to. Just, please, Edmund. Keep him State-side."

CHAPTER 31

Hands in his pockets, Danny looked around the wharf while waiting for Hugh. It being a holiday weekend, by his estimation, there had to be about triple the amount of people on the pier today compared to the week before. Kids ran all over in eager anticipation of the fishing nets being brought up. Neptune's Surprise was always a big draw, except for locals like him, who knew that fish like mackerel didn't swim so close to shore outside of spawning. He saw his friend exit the stairs and walked over to meet him. They strolled the side of the pier toward the promenade.

"How'd it go?"

"About as well as could be expected," Hugh replied. "She was nervous. We both were."

"I'm sure she was glad to see you." Danny turned up the collar on his coat. The city considered the end of May as the start of the summer, but he never really agreed.

"She was. Samuel too," Hugh said, a wistful look in his eye. "I worry about that kid, sometimes. He's so innocent."

"Amazing how much he resembles you."

"I know. Like lookin' in a mirror."

Shrieks rang out from behind, and both men stopped. Danny was the first to turn around, sprinting back to the cries for help. Hugh was right behind him. A crowd was already gathered at the open center of the landing. A plump woman in a veil gripped her beaded necklace. Another frantically pointed at the water below where one of the children had fallen in.

The boy struggled to stay afloat, thrashing against the surf. It was only a matter of time before he either slammed into a piling or entangled himself in the wharf's netting.

"Help!" he shrieked, only to choke on a mouthful of water.

Hugh's face went white.

Danny, meanwhile, threw off his cap and dove into the murky water. The cold shocked him, piercing his skin. He kicked up to the surface, his breath visible as he exhaled.

Samuel continued flailing around. His brown eyes bulged as another crest began to form.

"Go under it," Danny urged.

Samuel did as he was told. His head bobbed up seconds later to cheers from the onlookers.

Just a few strokes to go now. There, Danny had him in his arms. The child clung to him, his added weight threatening to drag them both under.

Someone threw a buoy down from the pier. Danny used one arm for swimming and pulled Samuel with him. He gave the boy the life preserver. Gripping its sides from behind, Danny kicked with all his might. He tried to get them out in the open water, but the tide was coming in, and the undertow was strong.

Whistles sounded along the beach, and Danny knew they were readying the lifeboats. Samuel started to cry.

"Danny, I'm scared."

"It's alright, pal. I got you."

A few minutes passed. Every time they got close to the edge of the pier, the current pulled them back under it. Samuel shivered violently, and Danny wasn't sure how long the child would last against the frigid mercury. His own legs were on fire from kicking, but he was starting to lose feeling in his hands.

The lifeguards finally rowed into view. "Swim toward the boat!" one called through a megaphone.

Sure, why didn't I think of that?

The breakers refused compliance. Merciless, hell rained down one whitecap after another, tossing them around like a paper boat.

"We're trapped!" Samuel coughed up more bile. "We'll never make it." He grabbed Danny's collar, tears, and snot streaming down his red cheeks. "I don't wanna die."

Danny fought the urge to slap some sense into him. If he kept up these hysterics, there was no doubt they'd both succumb to the deep. But he wasn't Pa. And the thought of striking another person, a kid especially, made him feel sicker than the water swirling in his belly.

"Samuel," Danny shook the boy's shoulder, "listen—you're not gonna die, okay? I won't let that happen."

The child stared blankly, seafoam clinging to his waist.

"I got an idea. But I'm gonna need your help. Can you do that?"

Overwhelmed, the question brought a fresh round of tears. "I dunno."

"You like football?"

"What?"

"I know your brother does. That he's pretty good at it, too."

Samuel gulped.

"That boat over there," Danny jutted his chin at the lifeguards, "That's the touchdown line." He patted the buoy. "This here's the ball."

The boy was confused. "The waves though. There's so many."

"Pretend they're from Yale." That brought a smile, and Danny was a bit relieved. "On my count, you gotta kick as hard as you can, alright?"

Samuel gave a determined nod. "Yeah."

"One, two, three!"

They took their opponent head on, pushing the tiny float further and further from the pier. The guards rowed the craft to its starboard side and threw a rope with a second buoy over to them. Danny grabbed it twisted the line around himself several times.

"Almost there, kid."

Grunting, he hoisted Samuel over the extra raft.

The guards pulled them in with lightning speed. Cloaked in thick wool blankets, Samuel coughed up a sizable portion of the Atlantic on the way back to shore.

The beach was packed as the boat came aground. Groggy and freezing, Danny heard the crowd burst into foggy applause. Salt burned his eyes, and he squinted, making out a hazy outline of Hugh pushing his way through the sea of bodies as they readjusted to the light. Mrs. Callaway clung to his side, breaking away as soon as Samuel was lifted out of the boat.

She tore across the sand. "My baby!"

"Give us room, Ma'am," the medic cautioned, his distant voice echoing in Danny's ear as another guard checked him for signs of distress. Head rolling to its side, he felt like a ragdoll.

Hugh's mother paid no attention, swaddling the blanket tighter around Samuel's shoulders as she held and rocked him. Danny was glad. At least one of them was warming up. Meanwhile, his own teeth chattered. He felt so tired, lids fluttering as he huddled under the felt wrapping.

"Stay awake," the medic shook him. "Keep those eyes open." He poured Danny a lid full of water from his thermos. "Here, drink this."

Pa. Danny winced and shook his head. *No, please.*

"What happened, Hugh?"

That voice. He knew that voice. Damn, he must really be out of it.

"The neighbors called from the booth at Roth's. Said to get down here right away."

Jennie?

Danny felt as if he were watching the world through a picture. Black spots clouded his vision; the scenes around him just as distorted as the sounds. Head swimming, he couldn't tell what was real from what wasn't. She tossed him away like a plaything. Why would she be here now? She couldn't be.

"Head up, now," the lifeguard instructed. "We're gonna get outta the boat but you need to stand up. Can you do that for me?"

Stand? What?

"Okay," he mumbled.

Weak, Danny propped himself against the bow. The voices around him sounded closer now, but the world remained a blur.

"Samuel fell under the wharf," Hugh was saying.

"I'm sorry, Mommy," came the boy's high-pitched cry. "I was looking for submarines. Like Hugh will. That's when... that's when...."

The vague silhouette of Mrs. Callaway cupped Samuel's cheeks. "It's okay, darling. Everything's alright now."

She stood, floating toward Danny while the medic finished up his examination. "Thank you," her garbled acknowledgment reverberated in his ears. He thought he felt her hand on his. *Maybe I'm getting some feeling back.* That was a good sign, right?

"It was nothin'."

"Danny? *Oh, God.*"

Jennie's voice was crystal clear. Unmistakable. He loved her so much it would always ring true. But she belonged to someone else now. This was just an apparition. His eyes were playing tricks on him. That he could see her didn't matter—he saw her in his dreams every night.

She said nothing as she drank him in. Delicate fingers shook as they slowly reached for his face. She grazed it tenderly, stopping at the spider webbing on his left temple.

Jennie bit her lower lip hard and buried her face against his chest. His heart pounding now, Danny felt her back rise and fall. If someone told him yesterday he'd have Jennie in his arms, he wouldn't have believed them. Part of him still didn't believe it. He nestled closer, the delicate scent of her lavender soap lulling him back to reality.

She was real. This was real. Danny willed his cramped muscles to life. He poured himself over her, relishing the touch as if it were his last.

Jennie pulled back and looked up at him. Time stood still as they finally locked eyes. Hers were dewy, pink lips trembling. Something carnal took over. Danny caressed her cheeks, slowly sliding his hands back into her hair. Grabbing her curls, he locked his fingers and pulled her into a kiss.

The beachgoers whistled and cheered. But the couple neither noticed nor cared; Jennie's mouth devouring his with so much fervor their teeth gnashed.

Photography bulbs flashed. Then flashed again.

"Good heavens!" Mrs. Callaway bellowed.

"Shut up, Mother." Hugh scolded. "Let them have the moment."

CHAPTER 32

Shannon settled Danny by the stove, swaddling him up in practically every garment they owned. Hot steam floated from the tea she made, and she blew on it before handing him the mug.

"There's some honey in it for your throat."

"Swell."

She combed a hand through his soggy hair. "You just relax while I pump some water for your bath."

"Will do, doc."

"It's not funny, Danny." *Did he have a death wish?*

"Want some help?" Hugh offered.

Shannon ignored him, storming outside to refill the kettle. This was his fault. This was all his fault. She was glad he enlisted. Good. Go. Leave. The sooner, the better.

Hugh held open the kitchen door for her return. Again she brushed by him, pretending to focus on her task.

"You're upset."

Shannon lit the stove. "I'm *fine*."

"You're not, I can tell."

He took a step toward her, and she recoiled.

"You're angry with me."

Angry? *Angry?* She had every right to be angry. She practically threw herself at him, and he just waltzed around like she didn't exist. Shannon was tired of the pleasantries. Tired of hanging onto his every word, desperate for even a crumb, and hating herself at her foolishness when nothing changed.

She threw a glance at her brother, huddled close to the fire. There was no doctor this time. No bill with which Hugh could bribe her forgiveness. With nothing to hold over her head, Shannon had nothing to lose. She whirled on him.

"Samuel's your brother. Why didn't you jump in?"

"I couldn't move."

Shannon glared. "How convenient."

Danny stood and moved between them. "Shannon, stop. Everything happened so fast. You can't blame him. It's not fair."

"What's not fair is you almost died! Again!"

She felt Hugh's eyes on her, an all-encompassing shame mushrooming as her temper flared and greatest fears surfaced. Shannon threw herself against Danny, sobbing hysterically. He moved them back to his chair, pulling her down on his lap and rubbing her back.

"I don't want to be alone," she choked.

"You're not. I'm right here."

The kettle whistled, but Hugh must've picked it up because she heard the door open and shut. Much as she hated to admit it, her tears were as much for him as they were for Danny. Rumor had it the coast was full of mines. She tried to ignore them, but the barracks was buzzing nonetheless. Thank goodness Danny hadn't signed up.

She didn't really want Hugh to go. Didn't want things to change. Change was difficult.

Shannon had never handled it well, even when not resulting from something catastrophic. Now things were changing again. Hugh would get his orders and ship off to God-knows-where, quite possibly never to return. And Jennie? Kissing her brother like no one was watching? Insisting Mrs. Callaway invite them to tea at Juniper Grove to properly thank him for saving Samuel? Shannon was glad she hadn't gone with them this afternoon. She never would've agreed to it. Never in a million years. Cruel and callous, Jennie treated her brother like a puppet on a string.

She sucked in another ragged breath, Danny holding her all the while. *I'll always take care of you.* And he did, didn't he? He knew her better than anyone. Wasn't afraid to call her out when she was wrong. What if she turned the tables on Miss Martin? Sabotaged her ridiculous tea. What kind of a thank you was that, anyway? Why, it was just as bad as Hugh and the damn hospital bill. What made them think they could just throw money at a problem and hope it disappeared? Enough was enough. Shannon could feel her pulse regulating as the idea took hold. A few minutes later, she sat up, a haggard look on her face.

Danny pat her knee. "I can draw my own bath, ya know."

"I know," she pouted. "You don't mind?"

"Not at all." He gave her a rueful smile.

"I'm going to lay down. We have a big day tomorrow." Shannon said it in her most proper voice. The one she only used when she was furious. Danny tilted his head at the stairs in agreement.

"I'll take care of the rest of the water," Hugh offered.

"Yes," she agreed. "That's the least you can do."

Shannon had never been inside Juniper Grove. She watched in awe as a child when the house was moved. Teams of local farmers and their livestock pulled it on massive logs away from the encroaching ocean. The Martins originally intended on piecing the two halves of the cottage back together, but spring rains that year meant both men and animals were needed back on their own properties without further delay. The best they could do was to wall up the open sides.

Heavily turreted and gabled, they looked like twin dollhouses from the curb. Mr. Martin had them repainted in what she could only assume were Jennie's favorite colors—the siding pale pink while the shutters were done in a royal purple with white gingerbread trim all around.

Hugh offered her his arm as she stepped out of the Ford.

"I'm so sorry about yesterday," he whispered as he led her up the brick walkway. "I feel terrible."

"I'm afraid I'm the one who should be apologizing," she said evenly. "I overreacted."

"Friends?"

A knife to the heart, Shannon faked a smile. "Always."

Young Samuel was only about ten or eleven. It was bad enough his mother sent him off to school for months on end. That the woman could care less about letting him run around a working fishing operation shouldn't have surprised her. Not after the way Mrs. Callaway cut Hugh off without a second thought. Not a single cent in weeks. Meanwhile, Shannon was left stretching their meager budget so far she was afraid it would break.

They reached the porch. Shannon took a deep breath to calm herself as Hugh held the door for her. Into the lion's den, she went.

An Irish girl greeted her upon entry. "May I take your cloak, Miss Culligan?"

The maid appeared close to her own age. Unaccustomed to being waited on, it was hard to meet the girl's eye. Reluctantly, she took off her jacket and handed it over.

"Shannon will do," she said, hoping her tone evoked authority.

The servant nodded and scurried off while Hugh led them down a long, heavily paneled hall. Shannon stole a glance at her brother, wondering if he were as nervous as she was. Sure, Danny got along with Mr. Martin, but that was one afternoon, and he'd never been here either.

Her brother cleaned up well; there was no denying that. His golden hair was slick with petroleum and parted down the center, and he wore the tie Shannon got him last Christmas, the mix of blues in its hexagon pattern perfectly complimenting their shared eye color. At least he looked the part.

That makes one of us.

In her rush to get ready, Shannon forgot her gloves. A lady's hands she had not. Hours of scrubbing and chopping in the barracks galley made sure of that. Her cuticles were cracked and dry; the nails were clean but certainly in need of a good filing. She folded them along the sides of her skirt and hoped no one would notice.

Hugh bowed upon entry to the parlor, and her brother followed suit. Mrs. Callaway and Jennie rose to meet them, the latter blushing at Danny.

Jennie smiled shyly. "We're so glad you could join us. Please, do come in."

"Thank you for having us," Danny replied.

Shannon felt queasy. She envied how at ease he felt in this mausoleum. Did Danny not notice how grossly different their lifestyle was from these cottagers? Or had he swallowed so much water yesterday he just didn't care?

The room was just as garishly paneled. Any space not covered in oak trim was done in ornate floral wallpaper or adorned by large portraits in gilt frames. Some of the paintings were as large as Hugh was tall and wider than her kitchen table. Thick-cut glass lamps gave off a soft glow; fractals of light glimmered everywhere, from the brass detailing on the mantel mirror to the silver teacart in the opposite corner. If Juniper Grove was the Martin's summer retreat, Shannon wondered what their home in Philadelphia looked like.

Reluctant to touch anything for fear it would break, she inched toward a chaise lounge and sat at the foot.

"Move up, dear," Hugh's mother directed, the chair's arm being closer to the set of Queen Anne's she and her niece occupied.

Shannon complied while Danny and Hugh took their places on a leather sofa facing all three.

"My father should be down shortly," Jennie announced. "He's usually the last one ready. We've sent Rutherford to let him know you've arrived."

Hugh leaned forward slightly. "The butler," he muttered just loudly enough for Shannon to hear.

The room fell silent as they each considered what to say next. Shannon looked down at her lap. Last night she'd felt so confident in her scheme to ruin the get-together, but now she wasn't so sure. She was out of her league. These people weren't her peers, and she didn't know their ways. It could just as easily backfire and end up hurting Danny even more. She caught him smiling in her peripheral— the happiest she'd seen him in months.

The maid brought around a platter of tiny sandwiches, handing out gold-rimmed plates to the group.

"How do you take your tea Miss—" the Irish girl caught herself, "Shannon?"

"I don't." It slipped out before Shannon really thought about it. Only kept it on hand for medicinal purposes. She quickly looked away, her cheeks competing with the rouge draperies.

"Some claret, perhaps?" Jennie offered. "I know I'd like a glass."

The maid attended to her duties.

"How is Samuel?" Danny inquired.

"Resting," Gertrude replied. "Still has a bit of a cough. Dr. Mace was here and advised that's to be expected."

The good doctor was a Godsend to the county. Shannon would never forget her gentle manner when she came to remove Danny's stitches. She sipped her claret, savoring the smooth, earthy flavor. She'd never tried it before and liked the warmth it brought to her insides.

"Daniel," a voice boomed from the foyer. "Good to see you, my boy," Walter smiled as he entered the room. The men stood to shake his hand, but Mr. Martin gave them each a hearty squeeze instead. "Hugh," he said. "Welcome home."

"Uncle, I…"

The older man held up his hand. "What's done is done. Today is about celebrating."

He snapped his fingers, and a footman in livery promptly gave him a glass of wine. He turned to Danny again, and the servant handed him a goblet as well.

"What you did was very brave, son. We're all grateful." Mr. Martin raised a toast. "To Daniel."

The others lifted their glasses in turn.

"To Daniel."

Shannon didn't recognize the sound of her own voice. She was losing him. It felt no different than if the tide succeeded in carrying him away. That Jennie was engaged to another clearly didn't matter to the girl. Eyes sparkling, she beamed at Danny; his eyes equally locked on her as if they'd never been apart. What of the letters? Danny might be able to ignore her silence, but Shannon couldn't. It didn't make sense. She forced down the wine, nearly draining her glass.

They were interrupted by a disturbance in the hallway. The front door slammed so hard it shook the teardrops on the crystal wall sconces. Shannon heard yelling and instinctively sat lower in her heat while the men rose from theirs. She saw the color drain from Jennie's face as the voice became more apparent.

Just then, a stout man in a tuxedo backed into the room. He held his arms outstretched before him attempting to block the door.

"I'm sorry, sir," he said firmly. "This is a private gathering."

The intruder paid no attention. He thrust the servant aside and stormed into the parlor, shaking a newspaper over his head.

"You little tramp!" He shoved the paper in Jennie's face. "What is the meaning of this?"

Shannon squinted to get a better look, but all she could make out from where she sat was a large photograph of a couple embracing splashed across the front page. It didn't take a genius to put two and two together. Jennie started to cry, and Shannon almost felt sorry for her. *Almost.*

"Leave her alone!" Danny growled.

Mr. Martin put a hand to his chest, holding him back. He rounded on the man.

"Joseph! How dare you speak to my daughter in that manner."

The servant reappeared, closing in on Jennie's fiancé from behind. York elbowed him in the stomach.

"Rutherford," Mrs. Callaway gasped as he doubled over.

"You," Joseph spat at her. "We had a deal!"

Hugh's mother squared her shoulders. "I daresay you reneged long before me."

"What the hell are you talking about?"

"You were supposed to keep an eye on Hugh. Keep him out of trouble."

"I did my part, Gertie, but I'm not a babysitter. Do you know how much I paid that bookie? Do you?"

Now it was Mrs. Callaway's turn to shift uncomfortably.

"You? You paid off my loan?" Hugh ran his hands through his hair. "Mother?" he asked in a small voice. "I thought Father...."

The older woman shamefully shook her head.

Hugh's red face was pained, and Shannon felt her heart constrict. He was so hard on himself. Always so concerned about letting his parents down. She wanted to go to him. Grab his hand and run for the door. But he didn't want her hand, the rejection returning with a vengeance.

Joseph, meanwhile, surveyed the parlor. He sneered from Jennie to Danny, then back at Mrs. Callaway. "You're hardly innocent. Would you like to tell the happy couple?" he said with a wicked grin. "Or shall I?"

Mrs. Callaway gulped.

"She burned your letters," he said bluntly.

Danny clapped a hand over his mouth, and Jennie sank back in her chair. Shannon resisted the urge to hurl her empty glass at the woman, all previous thoughts of sabotaging the tea flying right out the window.

"Gertie, why?" Mr. Martin looked desperate, but his sister-in-law could say the same.

"I never wanted it," the woman whispered. She stared at her gloves. "Not any of it...I only did what I thought was best for the family."

"By separating two people who love each other?" Jennie snapped.

"Love?" Joseph scoffed. "You really are a whore. I won't stand for this behavior, Jennie Martin. Do you hear me? Not now and certainly not when we're married."

Shannon watched in awe as Jennie yanked what could only be described as an ice burg from her left hand.

"Jennie, no! Don't—" Mrs. Callaway reached for her niece, but Jennie pushed her away, hurling the engagement ring across the room. It struck the paneling with a thud before bouncing to the floor.

York shook his head sideways, searing his black eyes at Danny. Shannon felt a pit in her stomach. Her brother could hold his own with the best of them, but he was still weak from yesterday. Thank goodness Hugh was here. She looked at him, then, just at the same time as his mother.

"I had to," Mrs. Callaway whimpered, imploring her son for mercy. "He knows about Minnie."

Well, that did it. Hugh leaped over the coffee table. Danny was on his heels but couldn't get there quickly enough. The offensive tackle pushed his uncle aside as if Mr. Martin were made of straw. Jennie shrieked and hid her face in a pillow as her cousin wound up.

The right hook sent Joseph stumbling backward, a crimson tide pouring out his nostrils as he glared at Hugh. And that was just the beginning.

"Blackmail my mother?" Hugh continued his pursuit, landing a jab in the ribcage. "You son-of-a-bitch!"

Joseph spit out the blood dripping into his mouth. "You cretin. If it weren't for me you'd have two broken kneecaps."

Panting, Hugh shook out his hand.

Danny stood behind Jennie's chair, hands resting protectively on her shoulders.

Rutherford returned, this time with a small army of uniformed servants. He pointed at Joseph, busy blotting his nose with a handkerchief. The men grabbed his arms.

"This isn't over!" he shouted as they carted him away.

Mrs. Callaway openly wept into her hands. "I'm so ashamed," she murmured.

You should be. This woman was just as toxic as Pa.

Hugh walked to his mother. He squeezed her hands, and she looked up at him gratefully. Mrs. Callaway took a moment to compose herself, glancing around at everyone but Shannon before further explaining herself.

"It was all for nothing," she swallowed. "You're not in school anymore and Edmund's divorcing me."

This brought a fresh round of gasps. Hugh bit his fist. Mrs. Callaway shot a knowing look at Jennie, and something passed between them. *What are you up to now?* Shannon reached across the coffee table for what remained of Danny's claret and knocked it back.

"I'll summer at the Browne lodge in the Adirondacks. As soon as Samuel's well...."

"Slow down, Gertrude," Mr. Martin cautioned. "No one's asking you to leave."

The older woman cast her eyes down.

"Indeed. Well," Jennie's father stroked his beard and looked about the room, "I hate to cut our gathering short but I think we've all had enough excitement for one evening."

He jutted his head at the maid, and Shannon realized for the first time that the girl witnessed the incident from her place in the corner. It was astonishing, really, how she seemed to blend into the backdrop. The servant understood Mr. Martin's unspoken command and left the room.

"May I call on your daughter tomorrow?" Danny asked.

Walter Martin smiled through his cheeks. "I was hoping you'd ask."

Jennie beamed. Shannon knew she should be happy for them. But something, she couldn't exactly put her finger on what, wouldn't let her. It wasn't jealousy this time. Or even fear of Danny abandoning her. He made it clear he'd never do so. He *promised*, and her heart trusted that promise; she trusted him.

The maid reappeared at the doorway with their belongings. A few minutes later, Shannon was waiting on the porch with Hugh while Danny and Jennie confirmed their plans for the following day. Unused to wine, her legs were weak, and she clutched Hugh's coat.

"Easy there," he grinned.

Their eyes locked, Shannon holding her breath as Hugh held her steady. Unable to breathe, she shifted her gaze to his mouth and slowly tilted her head back. When nothing happened, she broke away and cleared her throat.

"My family…" Hugh started.

"You never met Pa," she said ruefully.

They walked in silence to the Model T, and she leaned against the side. Danny jogged down the walkway.

"Can't go anywhere without these." He jingled the keys and smiled.

"Not now, Danny," Shannon quipped. "Let's just go home, okay?"

CHAPTER 33

The trio spent much of the drive home from Juniper Grove in silence, but Danny didn't mind. The afternoon brought about as much pleasure as it did heartache, and he wasn't sure how to process it all. From the rearview mirror, he glanced at Hugh; his friend peered absentmindedly out the window. Shannon propped her chin up to his left and stared in the opposite direction. *These two.* Danny thought about locking them into a room alone until they worked out their complicated feelings. Still high from the hug Jennie gave him before he left, he wished everyone could feel such affection.

At the same time, he worried about what she went through when they were apart. Why she'd agreed to marry such a man like York in the first place. True, Mrs. Callaway withheld their communications, but she didn't force Jennie to accept the proposal, did she? That was the part that gutted him; how Jennie agreed to spend the rest of her life with a man that she obviously couldn't stand.

Hopefully, after tomorrow, he'd have at least somewhat of a better understanding as to why. 'Course he wouldn't bring it up right away. Why ruin the mood? Danny couldn't wait to be alone with her. Jennie wanted a picnic and a picnic she would get. He'd give the best damn picnic this side of paradise.

The kitchen light was on when they pulled up to the house. Danny turned off the car but didn't move.

"That from earlier?" he asked his sister.

"Nope." Shannon patted the back of her head. "Too busy upstairs fighting with these pins."

"Pretty sure we left through the front," Hugh remembered.

"Yeah," Danny agreed. "We definitely did."

They proceeded with caution to the rear entrance. Danny went first and slowly opened the door.

"Pa. You're back."

Shannon's breath hitched behind him, and his own voice sounded far away. Hugh said nothing, and he was glad for it.

Danny had little recollection of his last beating, almost as if it'd happened to someone else. His mind left his body, hovering on another plane; there but not really there, watching it all happen and powerless to stop it. He and Shannon never really talked about what she came home to that night. The truth was, Danny didn't really want to know.

Now, the dam burst, and it all came flooding back. He heard himself scream. He begged for mercy, his cries unanswered or met with a grunt when Pa kicked him. Danny could still feel the pain of his bones cracking. Excruciating and all-encompassing, it stalked him like a phantom.

Cold sweat beading on the back of his neck, Danny gulped as the trio entered the kitchen. Pa sat at the table with a copy of the *Star and Wave* off to the side of him. The man's pupils were so blown his eyes looked black.

"Daniel, my boy." Pa smiled.

My boy.

A shiver ran down Danny's spine, the contrast of Mr. Martin's same statement hours earlier reverberating in his ear. He opened his mouth to speak, but his throat was dry— tight— and no words would come.

"Our brave hero returns," Pa continued with a glance at Hugh. "And with a friend."

Hugh extended his hand. "Nice to meet you, Mr. Culligan."

"John's fine." Pa refused to shake. "I guess this is 'Who's been sleeping in my bed'?" He chuckled at his poor impression of Papa Bear.

"Pa…" Shannon interjected.

"C'mon, girl. Would it kill ya to smile? Goldilocks used to be your favorite. On account of, you know, your hair." He touched his head and gestured at her. "Now, git over here and give your Ol' Pa a hug."

Danny could feel his sister's haunted eyes on him. He tilted his chin in the slightest of nods, and she ran to the table, embracing their father and kissing both of his cheeks.

Pa leaned back in his seat and rubbed his stomach. "Been staying with the Widow Peterson over in the Courthouse. Good eatin'."

"Wish we could say the same," Shannon muttered.

"What was that now?"

"Nothing," she apologized. "I'll make us some coffee."

His sister tied on an apron and hurried around the room. Cabinets opened and slammed shut as she took out the mugs. The pleasant aroma soon filled the darkness bubbling under the surface.

Meanwhile, Hugh looked as if he wasn't sure whether to sit down or not. Still standing, Danny took his seat, motioning for his friend to follow. Hugh plopped down beside him.

Pa patted the newspaper. "Well done. Didn't think you had it in you."

"I'm not even sure why they covered the rescue." Danny shrugged, unable to accept the compliment, however backhanded. Of course, Pa didn't think so. He probably didn't think Danny would've lived after that fateful night. Part of him relished the idea of proving the man wrong while another was justifiably terrified of the consequences should he be brazen enough to get too cocky about it. "Must be a slow day."

"This your lady friend?"

Danny wasn't sure how to respond. He didn't really know the answer himself. All he knew, all he cared about, was that she loved him. She said so. Right there in front of everyone. And she wasn't engaged anymore. He fought the urge to smile at the recollection being that the man next to him liked to throw things, too. Still, they had a lot to work out, and he was looking forward to their date. With Pa home now, would he still be able to go?

Pa cocked his head, speaking to Danny as if they were the only two people in the room. "She's a looker, alright." He let out a low whistle.

"I think so," Danny offered a half-grin olive branch.

"You never mentioned she was rich."

"You never asked."

Pa bit the inside of his cheek and inspected his fingernails. "Just an observation."

An observation. Danny squeezed his eyes closed, wondering what kind of hustle the man had in store. He couldn't dwell on it now, though. Shannon brought their coffee over along with a plate of cookies.

"Fancy," Pa remarked, biting into one. He dunked the shortbread in his cup.

"Just left over from this afternoon." she explained. To Hugh, Shannon added, "That was so kind. Sending us home with these."

"Yeah. Cook's pretty swell."

"Cook?" Pa snickered. There were some crumbs stuck in his mustache, but no one dared tell him. "You people don't even use her real name?"

Hugh cleared his throat, and Danny threw him a cautious side-eye. He felt a toe tap on his leg in response, their code undetected by the others.

"She prefers it, sir," Hugh said.

"Sure she does." Pa took a sip of coffee and promptly spit it back in the mug. "Tastes like piss water. Shannon!"

"Sorry, Pa. I'll make you more."

His sister was up in an instant, ready to dump it into the sink when

Pa grabbed her hair. "Don't bother."

Shannon whelped as Pa tightened his grip and rang her head side to side like a bell.

Danny and Hugh were both on their feet. Pa's glare told them not to move even a fraction of an inch, forcing them to watch in horror lest he snap her neck.

"Stupid girl. Can't do anything right."

Desperate to free herself, Shannon clawed at him. She scratched his cheek, and Pa wheeled her into the door jamb, sending her crashing to the floor. He bent down and slapped her hard across the mouth.

"Don't you ever!" Pa pointed in her face. He stormed into his room, slamming the door behind him.

Shannon tucked her head in her knees.

"Dear *God*. Should we…" Frozen, Hugh stood absolutely dumbfounded beside him. "Should we contact the police?"

"Don't," she sobbed. "Please. It'll only make things worse after they're gone."

Danny scooped his sister up, and Shannon buried her face in his chest. He moved slowly, methodically, like he'd done so many times before, and gently set her down on the couch. He bent down beside her, stroking the top of her head while she curled into herself.

"I'm gonna getcha an icepack."

Shannon gripped his collar. "Don't leave me."

"Be right back, I promise."

"I'll get it," Hugh said from behind him.

Danny looked back at his friend, the other man's eyes brimming with tears. "Thanks," he mouthed.

At the sound of Pa's boots stomping around the kitchen, Danny instinctively held Shannon tighter. How was it already morning? Neck cramped, he sat up, looking around for Hugh, and relieved to see his friend smoking outside. The icebox clicked.

"Want bacon?" Pa called from the other room.

"Yeah, sounds good."

And so began their game. Only this time, the stakes were higher. Danny wondered what, if anything, his father remembered about the previous night.

Hugh came in from the front steps. He looked at Shannon with concern, whispering so as not to wake her.

"How is she?"

Danny stroked her shoulder. "She'll be okay." He glanced at the kitchen, pork crackling, and spitting. "Just go with it," he urged.

"Whatever you need."

Shannon stretched beside him. She opened her mouth for a yawn and flinched. Danny leaned over and grazed her swollen lower lip with his thumb.

"Come and git it!" their father hollered.

Into the kitchen they went. The table was neatly set for three.

"Who's your friend?" Pa asked. Fryer in hand, he served the bacon and eggs as the toast popped from the counter.

Danny winked at Hugh while Pa's back was turned.

"Hugh Callaway, sir. Pleased to meet you." He tried the handshake again, and this time Pa accepted.

"John Culligan. Here, sit down. I'll grab another plate."

"Thank you, sir."

Pa placed a dish full of toast at the center of the table. He was about to take his seat at the head but stopped, frowning at his daughter. "What the hell happened to you?" he asked of her face.

"Tripped." Shannon hung her head. "Clumsy me."

"You gotta be more careful, girl," Pa said and stuffed his fork in his mouth.

The last twenty-four hours were sheer chaos, a cyclone sweeping a path of destruction impacting everyone Danny held dear. No matter how many times he tried to convince himself otherwise, how hopelessly optimistic he felt about Jennie's return to his life, Danny couldn't shake the doomsday feeling this was the beginning of the end for all of them.

CHAPTER 34

"This isn't the end," Joseph snapped into the telephone.

He unwrapped the steak room service brought up with his breakfast and gingerly placed it over his cheek.

Joseph looked out the window at his surfside view. The sky was on fire. A vibrant swirl of orange and deep pink stained the sea red.

"I mean it, Grandfather. She needs to pay for what she did. One way or another," he clenched the cord, "Martin Glass will be ours."

CHAPTER 35

"I'm fine."

Shannon tucked her work blouse into her skirt. She smoothed her hips and reached for the sash on the bureau. That tied on, she opened her box of hairpins and pulled several out. Danny wouldn't let up.

"I'll drop you at the gate," he was saying. "Hugh will meet you there afterward and walk you home. What time does your shift end, again?"

She cocked her head. "Six o'clock."

"Got it. Meetcha downstairs."

Alone, at last, Shannon sat on the side of her bed. Her hands hadn't stopped shaking all morning. She took a few deep breaths, rocking herself back and forth.

Pa wasn't happy that she now worked outside of the home, but Shannon didn't care. She liked earning her own money. She was finally able to contribute, and he wanted to take that away from her, just like everything else. He only agreed to let her go to the barracks if she handed over her wages at the end of the week.

She'd pay him, alright. Make sure he got exactly what he deserved for what he did. In front of Hugh, no less. Shannon cupped her mouth, choking back a sob. There was no hiding it now— this hell she was raised in, he'd seen it with his own two eyes. Shannon didn't think she'd ever be able to face him again, layering on another wave of emotion she didn't fully understand. That ache. That strange feeling she refused to put a name to. Naming it would make it real. Hugh was leaving her life, so why go to the trouble.

She wasn't thinking only of herself. Pa's presence practically signed Danny's death certificate. Cringing, she could still see her brother's lifeless body. Caked in blood, it haunted her dreams. What if he was here to finish the job?

Shannon tiptoed over to the bedroom door and locked it. From there, she opened the closet where they kept the hunting supplies. She took out the fixed blade and tucked the sheath into her garter. If Pa ever tried to touch her there again, he'd be in for a rude awakening.

The Winchester leaned against the inner wall. Shannon slid her index finger across her fat lip and glared at her reflection in the barrel. "Never again," she said to herself as she hid it under her bed.

"Almost ready?" Danny called.

"Be right down!"

CHAPTER 36

Jennie floated down the stairs. Danny would be picking her up soon. At the front door. *Her* front door, like they'd always talked about. Giddy, she grinned at her reflection in the looking glass and twirled around.

"Here you are, Miss."

She stopped spinning and blushed at Cook, who held out a large basket. "Where would you like it?"

Jennie absentmindedly traced the bare skin on her left hand and nodded at the table in the corner. Freed from the shackles of the York family ring, she'd taken the liberty of having it sent back to the hotel first thing that morning. She knew Joseph was rotten before but was still reeling from yesterday's events.

Her aunt took breakfast alone in her room. *Just as well.* Jennie couldn't stand the sight of her. Trading her life, her freedom, for Hugh's. Manipulating her into thinking, she had to 'save' Father; that duty and honor superseded love. Rubbish! Not to mention her letters. Had her aunt read them? There were things she'd written for his eyes only. Pieces of her heart bled onto those pages. And poor Danny. It was a miracle he didn't despise her. His love for her gave her strength. He hadn't said it yet—*that word*—but she felt it.

Jennie sighed dreamily, remembering their kiss. In all the times they'd kissed before, Danny never kissed her like that. She was still weak in the knees.

Lost in a cloud, she strode over to the music box. A crank of the dial, it filled the parlor with the sweet sounds of Bach. Jennie cupped her hands over her heart and closed her eyes, sashaying about like she used to do when she was a little girl. The music box had been her mother's, and Jennie never felt closer to her.

Thoughts of Mother softened her anger toward Gertrude. The divorce would indeed be difficult, turning her aunt into the social pariah she feared most. Her standing with Hugh remained shaky at best. Jennie was glad he'd be visiting while she was out. She hoped mother and son would be able to patch things up or, minimally, come to an understanding before Hugh shipped out.

The mere contemplation of the war threatened to sour her mood. Without Joseph, there was no telling what the papers would print now. She brushed it aside, bouncing right back when the doorbell rang.

Jennie smoothed the lace on her white tea dress and smiled her best smile as Rutherford announced her guests. Hugh murmured something to Danny before excusing himself. They were finally alone.

"You look beautiful," Danny said as he handed her a bouquet.

"Thank you," Jennie smiled, taking a whiff of the peonies. "Heavenly," she sighed and rang for Bridget to put them in water.

Their hands brushed when they both reached for the picnic basket simultaneously. Jennie giggled but didn't pull hers away. Danny hoisted their lunch and offered her his free arm. She gladly accepted, stopping only to grab her parasol from the coat tree on their way out the front door.

He held the door for her and made a grand gesture at the Model T. "Your chariot awaits."

They held hands down the walk, and he also opened that door for her.

"Where would you like to go?"

"Anywhere," she said breathlessly. "As long as it's with you."

Danny grinned. "Lake Lilly alright?" he asked. "The steel company is open seven days a week now, so The Spot's not so private anymore."

"I'd love that."

They drove down Beach Avenue toward Cape May Point. The lighthouse loomed largely the closer they got. He pulled in behind it.

"Not too far of a walk from here," Danny said, reaching for the basket in the back.

He was right. Behind a meadow of wildflowers lay a sight so magnificent it made Jennie regret not taking her art lessons more seriously when she was younger. Though a holiday weekend, the place was deserted, locals and shoobies alike heeding the ocean's siren call instead. She longed to unlace her boots and run barefoot through the sand.

Danny got right to work spreading out the eyelet blanket and setting up their lunch while she watched from the shade of the parasol. He held her hand as she sat down. Off came the shoes, her dainty feet now as free as her heartfelt. Unable to contain herself, she threw her head back and laughed at her silliness.

They fed each other canopies and finger sandwiches, washing them down with the champagne Cook chilled for them. Jennie reached for the plate of fresh strawberries and popped one into his mouth.

"They bring out the flavor," she said with an arched brow.

Powdered sugar from one of the crème puffs lingered on the outside of his mouth. Jennie took off her lace glove, smoothing a bare thumb along Danny's lower lip.

The spell was broken. He gulped and looked over at the water.

Jennie bit her lip. "What's wrong?"

"Nothin'." He took her hand in his. "Everything's fine, Jen. More than that. It's perfect."

She cocked her head and smiled, hoping Danny bought the façade.

Something was bothering him. She could hear the distance in his voice. His eyes looked at her, but he was somewhere else. While her movements were fluid, Danny's body was rigid, as if he were holding back. And why wouldn't he? There was so much unsaid between them. How foolish of her to think she could erase the pain of their past with a simple lunch.

She'd fantasized about this moment for months, the afternoon passing like something out of those novels her aunt was always telling her not to read. She would spin her parasol and laugh at Danny's awkward jokes. He'd procure an empty rowboat and float them to the middle of the lake, and every time he leaned forward with the oars, she'd grab his face and kiss him.

Jennie looked at that face now, his boyish looks fading away. There were traces of purple under his eyes she hadn't noticed before. Retrospectively, she wondered if she'd simply chosen to ignore them. She wanted to ask why he hadn't slept but was too afraid for fear the reason was tied into their painful separation. Where was the hopeful boy from earlier?

"Do you have the time?" he asked.

She glanced at her wrist. "Three-thirty. Day's still young."

"Yeah," Danny said, picking at a hangnail.

Jennie placed her hand on his knee. Danny was never without the pocket watch his mother left him, the object holding as much esteem as her beloved music box.

"Where's your watch?"

His lips twitched. "Lost it in the water."

"Rescuing Samuel?" She squeezed his leg. "I'm so sorry. I know how much it meant to you."

"It's gone," he said flatly. "No sense dwelling on it."

"What are you dwelling on, then?"

Danny shot her a questioning look.

"Please don't patronize me. I know that look." Jennie crossed her arms against her torso. "It's about yesterday, isn't it?"

"Jen c'mon," he tried to smile but failed, "let's not ruin the day, huh?"

"We have to talk about it at some point. No time like the present Father always says."

He picked up a pebble and tossed it into the lake.

"Did you hate me?"

"What? No, no...of course not." Danny frowned. "Him? Yes. 'Specially knowing what I know now. But you? Jennie, I could never hate you."

Her eyes brimmed with tears. She hadn't realized how much she needed to hear him say that. "I didn't love him," she choked, covering her mouth with a hand. "I didn't even *like* him."

"I know. I know that. I just..." Danny shook his head. "Why'd you accept?"

Jennie swallowed hard. "I thought you indifferent," she whispered. "It was wrong, so wrong. I should've never doubted you." She gazed at him hopefully, eyes imploring him for forgiveness.

"It wasn't your fault, Jen. Your aunt messed with your head."

Jennie looked down at her lap, wringing her hands. "There's more. I couldn't say so yesterday, I didn't want Father to think me ashamed of him."

Danny touched her cheek, brushing a fly away behind her ear.

"Joseph's family owns an interest in the media. It's not widely known. His grandfather is a silent partner."

"Did he threaten you?"

"Not...exactly. He offered his protection."

"From what?" Danny knit his brows. "Jen, I'm confused. Your father's a powerful man."

"A powerful *German* man," she corrected him, pretending not to notice Danny clench and unclench his fist. "You remember some of the headlines...."

"I could kill 'em."

"Don't talk like that."

"I *could.*" Danny punched the sand next to the blanket.

She knew he had a temper, but Jennie had never seen him so angry.

His face was red, the veins in his neck bulging, leaving her both frightened and aroused.

"Jennie, I love you. I never stopped, and I never will." Danny's eyes shone brightly. "You're the best thing that ever happened to me."

He loved her. He never stopped. Jennie knew it all along, yet she still cherished those three little words.

"I love you, too," she gushed.

He grabbed her hands, holding them against his heart. "Marry me."

"Wh—"

"I know it's soon. I know… a lot's happened. The whole world's gone crazy." He cocked his head, a loose tendril dropping down next to his left eye. "Let *me* do the worryin'. Let *me* deal with the papers." Danny was on his knee, now, her hands tightly in his. "Let me love you forever. I swear, Jennie Martin, I'll die before I let anyone hurt you or your family. I don't ever wanna lose you again."

"You won't."

Danny grinned. "Then say yes."

It was soon, but only in terms of their reunion. Jennie had loved him for as long as she could remember. Could still recall the first time she saw him at one of Father's hayrides. This was what she'd always wanted. What she dreamed of. What she cried about when she thought she'd lost him. Now, she wanted to run across the barren lakeshore and tell it to the world.

He loves me! We're getting married!

Inching herself close to him, Jennie wrapped her arms around his neck. The kiss was endless. She leaned back on the blanket and pulled him on top of her. He kissed her with an urgency she'd never known before. They were one, he and she, two souls colliding to form a single entity. His breath was hers, his life, her own. The world faded away, everything in their past leading up to this moment. Wrapped in love, Jennie had never been happier or more secure.

Danny broke away, his chest working hard. Jennie pushed the picnic basket off to the side, meeting his lustful stare with a hungry look in her eyes. She bit her lower lip and gave him a resolute nod.

"You sure?" he panted.

"Yes," she whispered. "Nevermore so."

Jennie took off his cap and ran her fingers through his lion's mane while Danny made quick work of the buttons on the back of her dress. The summer air was hot and thick all around. Jennie buried her face in the nook where his neck met the shoulder, peppering him with kisses. Each sweet, salty bite tasted more delicious than the last until there was practically no space between them. She traced her fingernails up and down his back and let out a low moan.

Shoulders taunt, Danny hovered over her. A few stray hairs dangled down next to his face. Jennie leaned up and softly grazed his scar. His Adam's apple bobbed, and she wondered if she'd crossed an invisible line. Instead, he kissed her hard on the mouth. She pulled him closer, so there was nothing but skin on skin.

Jennie whimpered when he entered her, and Danny looked at her with concern.

"Don't stop," she breathed.

The lake was empty. There wasn't a soul around for miles. And they'd waited their whole lives for this moment.

CHAPTER 37

Danny heard thunder rolling in the distance and blinked open his eyes. Jennie nestled beside him, head right on his heart. His fiancée. His soon-to-be-wife. The girl he'd loved for years. He pet her soft curls and watched as she peacefully slept.

The storm sounded like it was close. Careful not to wake her, Danny shifted and craned his neck. The sky changed dramatically in comparison to earlier that day. Dark clouds swirled as far as the eye could see. Meanwhile, a howling wind swept across the landscape, rustling the grassy dunes on either side of the lake.

Jennie started to stir. She grimaced and checked her wristwatch.

"Six thirty?"

"Shit."

The blanket was a flurry of activity. Clothing traded back and forth between the two as neither could find exactly what they were looking for when they needed it. He finished dressing first while Jennie continued to struggle with her corset.

"Turn around," he said, grabbing the laces. "Can't believe you girls hafta wear these contraptions every day. Don't know how you do it," he said, looping the knots in place.

"We still have some of Mother's crinoline gowns in the cedar closet," Jennie mused. "Trust me, these pale in comparison."

He moved onto the buttons on her dress. "Almost done."

Jennie smirked over her shoulder. "You're pretty good at that."

Danny pecked her cheek. "My first," he swore. "My only."

They nuzzled before sharing another kiss. Thunder crashed, and Jennie jumped. It was getting darker and darker outside.

Just then, a car swung around the bend and charged directly at them. Its headlamps were blinding. Something silver flickered, and they both squinted.

Jennie gasped. "It's Daddy!"

"Lemme handle this, okay?"

The limo screeched to halt, and Danny braced himself for the worst. The driver left the engine running and waved his arm out the window, flagging him over. *Turn off the damn lights.* Prepared to take full responsibility, he approached the car.

"Danny!"

"Hugh?"

"*What?*" Jennie asked from behind.

The wind was so strong it blew Danny's cap off.

"Shannon wasn't at the barracks when I went to get her," his friend panted. "One of the girls said she slipped out early."

"Okay..." Danny said, trying to stay calm.

"There was yelling when I got back to the house. From both of 'em, Danny."

Jennie joined them. She crossed her arms against herself to shield the sand flying everywhere.

"I was halfway up the steps when she came barreling out the front door," Hugh continued. "Wouldn't tell me what happened. Just took off into the dunes." Terrified, he glanced from one to the other. "I looked for her, Danny. I called her and called her. Even swung by the Barkley's on my way here but they hadn't seen her either."

Shelf clouds were forming over the ocean behind them. A thick blast of lightning crackled down into the raging surf.

"This one's gonna be a whopper," Hugh said. The desperation in his voice was unmistakable.

Beside him, Danny felt Jennie squeeze his shoulder. "Go," she urged. She pecked his cheek and ran around the front of the Rolls, taking a seat next to her cousin.

"Tell your uncle we got a flat tire and give him my apologies." Danny instructed. He patted the driver's side door.

"Got it." Hugh grabbed his hand. "I'll meet you at the bungalow right after."

CHAPTER 38

Shannon wore a sinister grin as the sky opened up. The storm was just as furious as she was. She cast her arms wide and threw her head back. The cold rain came down in sheets. Hair and clothing clung to her bodice. Soaked to the bone, she didn't feel a thing.

Turrets of water poured onto the sand, creating pockets of mini rivers from the dunes to the waterline. Meanwhile, the white caps rolled in one after the other. They feasted on the coast like starved children, each bite of sand larger than the last.

The laudanum she swapped out in Pa's whisky bottle should have taken effect by now. Having already forgotten she had a job, tonight he was upset dinner wasn't ready-and-waiting for him when he got home from the docks.

Shannon chewed the cuticle on her pinky finger. She hadn't counted on Hugh. It was bad enough he witnessed last night's debacle. He was getting too close, and that was a problem. What if he told someone? She would deal with him later. Right now, she had to focus on the task at hand.

She walked with purpose from her hiding place in between the dunes. Danny would've found her by now but, for probably the first time in her life, Shannon was grateful he was with Jennie. That would at least give him a solid alibi.

Just as suspected, Pa was in the wingback when she crept through the front door and gently latched it shut. Head back and mouth half-open, he snored away. *Sweet dreams.*

Shannon tiptoed up the steps to her room, heading straight for the bed before she lost her nerve. The rifle wasn't there. Her pulse quickened. Frantic, she got down on all fours. She groped deeper and deeper. It was no use. The gun was gone.

"Lose somethin'?"

Lightning crashed outside the window illuminating Pa's silhouette in her doorway.

Shannon couldn't breathe. She didn't know whether to crawl further under the bed or try to make a break for it. Given the amount of opium he had coursing through his veins, she should be able to easily get by him. She stood back up and leered at him as she found her footing.

Pa only laughed. He held up the Winchester he'd been hiding behind his back. She froze.

"You stupid bitch. You really think I don't know the difference between laudanum and Jack Daniel's?"

"Pa, I —"

"Save it!" He pointed the rifle and cocked the hammer.

Shannon dropped to her knees. Wet hair dripped into her eyes as she bowed her head. It was amazing how the Latin returned. She never fully understood what the words translated to aside from 'Saint Michael,' but she fervently uttered them just the same.

"*...be our protection against the wickedness and snares of the Devil...*"

Pa stomped across the tiny room, placing the barrel in the middle of her forehead. Shannon took a deep breath. Reaching up, she grabbed his testicles and twisted as hard as she could.

He doubled over, dropping the weapon. She scrambled to seize it for herself, but he kicked it out of reach. The gun went off as it slid across the floor, leaving a hole in the wall. The blast echoed the thunder from the relentless gale.

Shannon pushed herself up to try to escape. Pa clutched her ankle. She shook her leg, but his grip was too tight. He squeezed her Achilles tendon, and she let out a yelp as she crashed to the floor. Pa grunted as he succeeded in pinning her on her back.

"One of us isn't leaving this room alive," he sneered.

She spit in his face. "And that one of us is you!"

He grabbed her hair and slammed the back of her skull against the wooden floor. Woozy, Shannon thought she saw a figure as she glanced at the door, but it wasn't there anymore when she blinked.

Pa wreaked of garlic and tobacco. He used one of his massive hands to tether Shannon's arms above her head while the other balled into a fist. She squeezed her eyes closed, stiffening in anticipation. Just then, a second shot rang out from the gun.

"Enough!"

Danny swung the barrel away from the ceiling and aimed at Pa's head. The older man charged him, and the two wrestled to control the weapon.

Shannon watched in horror as Pa inched her brother closer toward the bedroom door, the top of the stairway only a few feet behind them. It was then she remembered the hunting knife under her skirt. Reaching for the blade, she bolted toward them. She plunged it deep in Pa's upper back, his spine arching as she twisted with all her might.

Pa staggered to the door. He braced himself against the frame as he tried to remove the dagger. Danny took mercy on him, groaning as he yanked it out. Blood squirted every which way, covering all three. Pa still didn't have his balance and stumbled back until he teetered on the top step. Still within reach, his leathery hands grabbed her by the neck.

Danny was there in an instant. He locked a free arm in his sister's and thrust the knife into Pa's side with the other.

Eyes popping, Pa gagged and released her.

Shannon clung to her brother. Throat sore, she struggled to catch her breath.

"You'll burn in Hell for this!" Pa hissed.

"Then make sure you save me a seat," she glared back.

He made a final lunge at her, and Danny kicked him in the stomach.

Their father sailed backward down the stairs. The only thing worse than the guttural scream he let out as he fell was the silence that followed.

Shannon stroked the tender muscles along her neck. Still holding the blade, Danny looked down at his shaking palms. His mouth twisted, and he shook his head in disbelief.

Pa's body bled out below them. A river of red gushed from his side, pooling thick under the corpse.

Danny grimaced and threw up. The bile splattered down his vest. Shannon reached to comfort him, but he recoiled.

"I killed him. I killed him. I killed him," he muttered before heaving again.

"No." She rubbed his back, and this time he let her. "*We* did." Tears streamed down her face, and she forced him to look at her. "I'd be down there with him if it weren't for you."

He sputtered, and Shannon laced her fingers through his. It took a few more minutes for him to compose himself.

Outside, gale-force winds continued to batter the home. The bedroom shutters unhinged. One of them crashed through the window, the chards of glass right at home amongst the destruction.

"Hugh," Danny whispered. "Shit. He'll be here soon."

"*Damn* him."

"He cares about you, Shannon. Almost as much as I do."

She softened, looking away as she picked a hangnail. Her brother looked over her shoulder at the steps.

"We can't just leave him there."

Shannon agreed. Destroying the evidence had been part of her plan all along. She just hadn't counted on being so pressed for time. "I have an idea."

Together they drug Pa's body into the kitchen then quickly changed into fresh clothing.

Shannon loaded half of their coal supply into the stove. She added their soiled belongings and lit the oven, scattering the remaining lumps around the corpse and into the far corners of the room.

Meanwhile, she sent Danny on a hunt to gather all of the kerosene lamps they had. When he returned, they wasted no time dousing the floor along with the wooden table and chairs. Shannon used the last of the fuel to drizzle a trail from the stove to their father. She looked at her brother, and he nodded in turn as they headed out the door.

Danny took out his cigarettes and removed a book of matches from the box. Using his hand as a shield, he struck one and then used it to ignite the rest before flicking them into the kitchen. He grabbed his sister's hand, and they raced toward the Ford.

The gates of Hell opened wide as the bungalow erupted. Black smoke billowed out the windows while long orange tongues licked the side of the building. The rain stopped, but the winds remained on their side as the flames spouted higher and higher. It wasn't long before the second floor was engulfed too.

Shannon looked up at the whirling clouds and squinted in the sand-storm. *We must be in the eye.* Her head was killing her. The fumes from the kerosene further agitated the damage done by their father.

The stench of burning flesh was nauseating. She covered her mouth, coughing until she gagged.

Danny pulled her close as they leaned against the side of the car. He lifted an arm out of his jacket and held it over their heads. Shannon rested her head on his shoulder.

They were safe. Overwhelmed, she finally allowed herself to succumb to what they'd done.

"We're free, Danny," Shannon whispered, collapsing in his arms. "We're finally free."

CHAPTER 39

Headlamps flashed through the lace curtains, and Jennie ran to the window. The Rolls parked on the curb, the Model T behind it.

"They're back!" she called over her shoulder.

Relief washed over her aunt's face. Father dropped the newspaper he was reading and hurried to the parlor door.

Hugh rushed in, carrying an unconscious Shannon bridal style. The poor thing was draped in his jacket to keep warm. Danny was right behind them, along with another boy Jennie had never met before. Judging by the dusty overalls, it must be Will.

"The divan," Gertrude instructed.

Hugh was already there. He steadied a pillow under Shannon's neck. "Give her space, you idiot!" he snapped at Will, who hovered on the other side of her.

Jennie focused on Danny. He looked like he aged a decade, and she reached for his hand. It fell limp inside hers.

"Thank God you found her. What happened?"

Shannon started to come to before he could answer. Hugh backed a few steps away, and Danny knelt on the floor next to her.

The girl looked so small. Outside of childhood, Jennie had only ever seen her in the high collar dresses of the day. It was only now, with her blouse semi undone to allow for air, that she noticed just how frail Shannon was. Her collarbone jutted out, as did her sharp cheekbones. She offered her brother a weak smile as he swept loose hair from her face.

"We're at Juniper Grove," he whispered.

Cook charged into the room, hot water bottle and teapot at the ready.

"Wait," Jennie said as the servant prepared to spoon out the tea leaves. "She doesn't care for it." She poured a small glass of claret and handed it over. "Here."

Shannon accepted it gratefully and took a few delicate sips.

"Get Mace on the line," Father ordered Rutherford.

"No, please," said the patient. Lips thin, Shannon shrunk into herself. "There's no need to fuss."

The farm boy leaned on the back of the chaise while Danny and Hugh flanked her sides.

That her cousin was looking at Shannon the way she'd looked at Danny only the day before on the beach wasn't lost on Jennie; gratitude juxtaposed with the horror of the Reaper. Hugh might crumble any second.

"Shannon, what happened?" he asked in a quiet voice.

She averted her eyes and cupped her hands around the wine glass.

"Let her be, boys," Gertrude said.

"It's alright, Mrs. Callaway," Shannon replied. She coughed, clearing her throat. "I did it. It was all my fault."

Danny's jaw dropped. "Whaddya mean?"

Shannon finally looked up, eyelashes fluttering at the slew of concerned faces around her.

"Well," she pouted, "I knew Pa wasn't happy about my working at the barracks so I asked one of the girls to cover for me toward the end of my shift. Thought I'd surprise him with supper. Turns out he beat me home."

Shannon turned to Hugh. "That's right around when you got there." She hung her head. "I was being disrespectful," she mumbled.

Hugh put his hand on her thigh. "I'm sure that's not true."

"It is." The girl drew her hands to her mouth. She shook her head shamefully. "I…I shouldn't have run off but …Well, I was just so upset I didn't know what else to do."

Jennie clutched her heart. Danny wasn't home because they were together at the lake. She tried to meet his eye, but his thoughts were clearly elsewhere.

"I'm terribly sorry, Shannon," she blurted. "We had car trouble."

"My brother told me. It's okay."

She sneezed. Hugh and Will dueled over handkerchiefs. Shannon accepted the one Gertrude held out and blew her nose.

"The fire," Will said. "You could see the flames all the way from Washington Street."

Shannon broke down, and her brother held her close. "Poor Pa!" she wailed. "He must've tried to make dinner himself." She clung to Danny, shoulders rolling as she sobbed against his chest.

Jennie wanted to go to them. To comfort him as he comforted his sister. Tell him just how awful she felt and that he didn't have to bear it alone. But, like the others in the room, she stood frozen in place. There was nothing she could say or do to change the tragic circumstances.

Rutherford whispered to Father, who announced the rooms had been readied upstairs. Danny slung his arm under Shannon's, and the two retired for the evening.

Gertrude sank into her chair. "Poor dears," she murmured as Sasha hopped onto her lap. "Dr. Mace is coming tomorrow to check on Samuel. I'll make sure to send her over afterward."

In the days that followed, Jennie was touched by how many people called at Juniper Grove to show their support. Will returned with his entire family. Mrs. Barkley was kind enough to bring the siblings several garments each. The pharmacist, meanwhile, arrived with a huge basket of fruit and sweets. The older gentleman inquired after the health of both Culligans on a first-name basis.

When the fire marshal showed up with a detective, Rutherford almost didn't let them cross the threshold. The butler relented seeing the paperwork and determining it was only a formality.

"Got nothin' to hide," Danny remarked upon meeting the officials. There was a darkness to his tone. Like he was somehow daring the other man to prove him wrong.

Jennie ignored the tiny voice inside her head. *It's just his grief.* Danny scarcely survived the wharf incident, only to be homeless and orphaned the following day. Of course, he wasn't himself. Still, when questioned about the timeline between the picnic and the Culligan's arrival at Juniper Grove, Jennie neglected to tell them Danny was wearing a different shirt.

CHAPTER 40

D anny paced his room in the east wing in what had become a nightly ritual. Sleep was for the living. He was a murderer. A zombie. So what was the difference? Still, there were times his body betrayed him, and Pa's beady eyes were right there every time staring back. He'd force himself awake, panting as he struggled to remember where he was.

He crouched along the side of the four-posted bed and pulled a bottle of bourbon out from underneath. Palms sweaty, he twisted off the cap. Danny licked his lips in sweet anticipation. He wished he could crawl down the neck and just float away. Like father, like son.

They got the death certificate that afternoon. The investigation deemed Pa's death as accidental by his own hand. Cigarettes in one hand, Jim Beam in the other, Danny slid down on the floor and leaned against the wall.

Somehow, Shannon had done it. She was frighteningly believable. Her tears were real. Soaked right through his shirt. She could be in the pictures with that performance. In one fell swoop, his sister won the sympathy of all. No one would dare question his involvement. Even Jennie chimed in.

Yet, he knew the truth. *What have I done?* Danny bit his fist. Shannon tried to convince him otherwise. Deep down, he knew she wasn't entirely wrong. There was no doubt in his mind she'd be dead too if he hadn't shown up when he did. That didn't even scratch the surface of the guilt consuming him. Danny's mind wandered back to the summer. He was late coming home then, too.

I can tell she's a virgin the way she crosses her legs. There could be no mistaking Pa's intentions. That the man wanted to take an act of love—something so pure and beautiful—and defile it was disgusting. Danny would retake the beating in a heartbeat if it meant Shannon was never alone with that pig. He'd never seen Pa so brazen, chastising her over, what, coffee of all things?

The slight taste of freedom they'd gotten while he was holed up on the mainland wasn't enough. Not with a lifetime of abuse and neglect bubbling under the surface. It was bound to come to a head sooner or later. And erupt it did their very own Vesuvius. Ashes to ashes, dust to dust.

Danny drained the bottle. Try as he might, there was no way to justify it. He was nothing but a murderer.

"Jennie," he cried into a pillow. He wasn't even worthy of her before. And now? He could wash his hands a thousand times, but they'd still have blood on them.

"Rough night?" Hugh asked when he came down to breakfast.

Danny squinted. His eyes were so bloodshot they hurt to open. It felt like someone took a hammer to his temples, and he welcomed the pain. That was the least he deserved. Shrugging, he sat down beside him.

"Eggs, Mr. Culligan?" offered a servant.

He cringed. That was Pa's name, not his. The footman tilted his head in confusion and held out a silver platter. Sunlight bounced off the serving spoon, and Danny looked away. Hugh took charge.

"Yes," he instructed. "Coffee and dry toast as well."

Danny couldn't hold anything down lately but tried to eat anyway. The funeral was that afternoon.

His sister sat at the other end of the table. If Shannon were even remotely upset, she did an excellent job hiding it. At the moment, she didn't appear to have a care in the world. *Must be nice.*

"Have you ever played chess?" Gertrude was asking as another servant poured them fresh tea.

Shannon mimicked the older woman, holding her pinky finger out as she took a sip. "No."

Mrs. Callaway leaned closer. "It's a game of queens, dear. I'll have to teach you."

His sister smiled. "I'd like that."

Her strange behavior continued throughout the morning. Mr. Martin was generous enough to have them each fitted for a new wardrobe, but it would take the tailor a few weeks to complete. Danny borrowed Will's Easter suit for the funeral while Shannon donned one of Jennie's mourning dresses.

"It's from last season," she said in true Gertrude-like fashion as they drove to St. Mary by-the-Sea. One of the maids styled her hair, piling it high under a wide-brimmed black hat. She jabbered away, explaining how the girl rolled her curls in "rats" to give it extra volume.

"Horsehair!" Shannon giggled. "Can you imagine? All this time I've been teasing and backcombing."

Danny didn't understand how she could joke at a time like this. They were on their way to their father's funeral. A man who would still be very much alive right now if not for their actions. He was worried about her. It was as if she'd left a piece of herself in the bungalow. The woman before him looked like his sister but had taken on another persona. Someone he didn't know and wasn't sure he wanted to.

"How about that," he muttered as they pulled into the parking lot.

The congregation was sparse. Martins and Callaways intermingled with mostly island folk. The Barkleys, of course, along with a few men from the harbor. Mr. Kennedy offered a solemn nod as they walked up the aisle.

The service was short. Father O'Brien was only a few breaths into the first reading when Shannon started crying. She clutched Danny's arm and hid her face as she moaned. He didn't know what to make of it. Was this real or for the audience?

He tried to be strong for both of them, but he was exhausted and nauseous. Danny looked up at the ceiling as the room started spinning. Hours later, he wasn't sure how they made it through the final procession, let alone the ride back to the cottage.

Mr. Martin arranged for the funeral luncheon to be served on the second-floor veranda overlooking the ocean. Danny broke away from the group afterward and leaned on the railing. He sipped his tonic water. God, he wished there was gin in it. Jennie ambled over. He'd been trying his best to avoid her, but, even in a house that size, it proved difficult.

She stood next to him, her dark veil blowing in the salty air. Jennie looked up at the turret on the third floor.

"They're called widow watchers," she said. "The men would go off to sea, sometimes never to return."

"I know."

Jennie looked at him and swallowed hard. She opened her mouth then shut it again. He knew his behavior must've been brutal on her. He couldn't help it. Overwhelmed, he furrowed his brows.

She reached in a hidden pouch deep in her gown and took out a shiny gold pocket watch. Jennie opened his left hand and gently placed it inside the palm. "To replace the one you lost."

Danny was speechless.

"Turn it over," she said.

A lump formed in his throat as he read the inscription. *"I'll love you until the end of time."*

"Wow, Jen," he swallowed. "This must've cost a fortune."

"Every moment with you is priceless to me."

"Don't say that."

"It's true, Danny." She put her hand over the watch. "I hope you don't think me inappropriate."

He started to shake his head, but she cut him off.

"Life is so fragile. Precious." Jennie's eyes were earnest. "We've lost so much, Danny. My parents didn't have nearly enough time together. Samuel's rallying, thank goodness, but your father...darling, I can't imagine how you must be feeling."

You don't wanna know.

"I know we haven't talked about it since..." she blushed, "that afternoon at the lake. Please don't think me selfish. With the war on, I'd rather not delay our nuptials." Jennie cast her eyes across the veranda at Hugh, and Danny followed her gaze. "I need him to be there. There are already too many empty seats."

Danny exhaled as the gravity of what she was saying finally hit him. Here she was, a vision even in her black gown, speaking of wearing a white one. Jennie would look beautiful in burlap, and he couldn't begin to fathom her in full bridal attire. They'd been close before to seeing their dream come to fruition, right there on the edge, and Danny glanced at Mr. Martin, remembering their dinner at the clubhouse. Had time and circumstance been kinder to them, Jennie would already have a ring on her finger. Though a simple band, paling in comparison to York's monstrosity, his would be given with love and received with love in turn.

Weddings and funerals weren't so different, he supposed. One a celebration of life, of love, the other an homage to a life well-lived. 'Cept Pa, of course. At that, Danny fought the urge to cringe. He wasn't the man she thought him to be. Like his sister, a part of him was gone, forever changed, a mere shell of his former self. Despite every instinct screaming he shouldn't, that he should mercifully break it off and let Jennie spend her life with someone who wasn't an executioner, Danny found himself nodding his head.

"I'll speak with your father."

Jennie beamed, and they sealed it with a kiss.

"Who knows?" she giggled as they walked to rejoin the group. "The way Aunt Gertrude's been getting along with your sister, maybe there'll be another wedding."

⋄⟶⊃ ⊂⟵⋄

Mr. Martin was only too happy to agree. Danny left the planning to his bride, secretly hoping it would be a much smaller affair than society dictated. To this, Jennie did not disappoint, arranging for an outdoor ceremony at the lighthouse in two weeks along with a brunch reception of only nearest and dearest at Juniper Grove.

Hugh and Will took him to Jackson's for one last hoorah the night before the wedding. Bess gave them her warmest welcome. They drank and played, then drank some more. Hugh even managed to win a few rounds. He crooked an elbow around Danny's neck, grinning like an imp.

"What would you say if I asked for Shannon's hand?"

Danny knocked back a shot. "Same thing I told Will when he asked yesterday."

They looked across the club where their friend was playing roulette and watched his face light up when it landed on red.

"Lucky bastard," Hugh shook his head.

"It's up to her," Danny smiled and ordered them another round. "But you won't hear me object."

"You mean it?"

He nodded. It would be nice keeping Shannon close, and he fantasized about the four of them becoming inseparable. Raising kids together, never spending a holiday apart, and starting new traditions. Surprisingly, Hugh grimaced.

"What?"

"I never told her the truth about that hospital bill. I wanted to. I swear. The timing just…never seemed right."

"Was a long time ago. She probably forgot all about it. Hell, I did."

"I dunno. Seems moot now, but…well, with everything Mother's done," Hugh sighed. "She lied about the letters when I asked her point blank. Obviously, she lied about the bill, too." He set his jaw, a flinty look in his eye. "I just don't want any more secrets hanging over our heads."

Danny stifled a cough. "Me neither."

"The way the two of them have been getting on…."

"I understand."

He smirked, feeling lighter-hearted than he had in days, even if it was just the cups. Hugh lit a cigarette as the waitress brought over their order.

"Got my orders this morning," his friend said, tipping back the glass. "Of all the places in all the world, the Navy stuck me right here in good ole' Cape May, New Jersey. What are the chances?"

Danny shrugged and looked around the casino. All around them, people were laughing, indulging in life's pleasures. Dark and smoky, the room was filled with the ragtime rhythm from the piano in the far corner. Will strolled toward them, the pockets of his pants pulled out and a glum expression on his boyish face— it was a good thing he didn't play poker. *Life's like that.* A game of chance. One day you're up; the next, you're down. On the surface, Danny was up, about to marry the girl of his dreams. Pa was gone. Mrs. Callaway seemed genuinely remorseful. And Joseph York? Heaven help the bastard if he ever came near Jennie again.

CHAPTER 41

A songbird chirped outside Jennie's open window. Her mouth played at smiling, she fluttered open her eyes. In all likelihood, she'd smiled the whole night through, her dreams filled with rapture. The warmth of Danny's touch. The tautness in his shoulders as he hovered over her. The way their bodies melded so perfectly together. They'd get to do that again tonight. They'd get to do that *every* night.

Jennie suppressed a giggle and sighed dreamily. Today was her wedding day, a day she'd waited seemingly ages for. She cared not what he did for a living or how her circumstances would change. Today, Danny was a prince, and she was a mermaid. How many times had she rewritten the story, changing the ending in her diary to the happily-ever-after Andersen so egregiously denied? It started with simple pictures during her childhood, not long after she came upon him one day at the beach. Then again, they were separated by an evil witch and a betrothal of convenience, were they not? Hadn't she given up her proverbial voice in exchange for Father's freedom from persecution? Danny would protect them now, her knight in shining armor. Pinching her arm, Jennie smiled. Her story was real. So too, was her fairytale ending.

Though not particularly hungry, she rang for breakfast anyway. Better to have some sustenance than none at all. A few minutes later, there was a tap on her door.

"Come in," she called from the bed. After finishing her last entry, Jennie closed the journal and held it tight against her chest.

Bridget entered carrying a tray, Cook immediately thereafter with another. Gertrude tapped lightly on the doorframe, and Jennie could see the top of Shannon's head peeping out behind her aunt.

"Do you mind if we join you, darling?"

"Of course not," Jennie beamed. She slid into her kimono and house slippers as the servants set up their feast adjacent to the fuchsia settee in the corner.

The three women nibbled quietly on warm, fresh blueberry muffins and slices of savory pork roll. Cook poured steaming cups of coffee and passed them around while Bridget stood quietly off to the side. They made small talk about the fine weather, especially considering the outdoor ceremony.

While Gertrude commented about the lighthouse metaphorically being a "beacon to guide them through life," only the happy couple knew the venue's *true* significance. Jennie couldn't imagine getting married anywhere else. As far as she was concerned, it was already consecrated. However, it was only now Jennie realized that, in stark contrast to her debut, her aunt played a minimal role in planning the nuptials. She hadn't completely forgiven her but could see the older woman was trying and knew it wouldn't be long before she could receive her aunt with an open heart.

How strange, this new freedom. This womanhood. Jennie felt she was floating on a cloud.

Pop!

"Mimosas, girls?" Gertrude nodded to Cook, who promptly filled three stems with orange juice and champagne. "They're delightful," she assured Shannon when the girl looked unsure.

"She's right," Jennie giggled as the bubbles tickled her tongue. Shannon took a large sip and licked her lips. "You're not kiddin'."

"Not so quickly, dear," Gertrude cautioned to which her soon-to-be-sister nodded.

Her aunt glanced at Bridget. The maid went into the hall, arms piled with golden wrapped packages when she returned.

"What is all this?" Jennie chided in a playful tone. "You didn't have to—"

"Tradition, darling." Gertrude's eyes were moist. "Please? I've made mistakes, I know, but I love you, Jennie. Truly. Like you were my own daughter. I know Louisa would want this for you," she bubbled. "I wish she could be here."

Jennie choked back a sob. "Me too."

"Maybe she can," Shannon said gently. She shrugged sheepishly, biting her lower lip as she picked up a long rectangular box. Handing it to Jennie, she added, "This is both 'borrowed,' and 'new'."

Jennie silently repeated the words as she untied the ribbon and opened the top. Her hands flew to her mouth, and she nearly dropped it. Quick as a jackrabbit, Cook grabbed the bottom. Inside the box lay a lace handkerchief. Slightly yellowed with age, it bore the letters 'JC' in intricate silver and gold embroidery. Holding the garment ever so delicately, she traced a finger over the elegant stitching.

"I gave that to your mother when I found out she was carrying you," Gertrude explained.

Jennie always knew she would wear Mother's wedding gown. Fashionable or not, it was the only thing she held firm to during her prior betrothal, and she treasured how nicely the dress was preserved in its cedar box. Father had saved some of her other favorites, and Jennie had fond memories of plodding around the nursery in too-big velveteen heels and one of Mother's merry widow hats. But she'd never seen this before.

"She used it at your christening, child."

Jennie could feel large tears pooling in her eyes. "She did?"

Her aunt nodded.

"I added the initials myself," Shannon said, her shy voice just above a whisper.

"It's exquisite. Why, this must've taken hours."

Shannon raised her shoulders. "Haven't been sleeping a lot. Might as well make use of my time."

Jennie's smile withered. The girl was in mourning, and here they were celebrating. Was she wrong to rush the ceremony? Father hadn't thought so. Not when she explained herself and her adamancy concerning her cousin. Still, she knew some families who mourned a full year before re-entering the world.

Then again, Shannon wasn't like other girls. Jennie was thrilled she'd agreed to stand as a witness despite their rocky history. Whether it was the champagne or her sheer bliss, Jennie didn't know. She couldn't help herself either. Today, love conquered all thought and reason.

"You do realize, Shannon," she giggled, "if I were to make one for you, your initials wouldn't change."

"Pardon?"

"Hugh," Jennie said earnestly. "He loves you so."

Something changed in Shannon's eyes, as if she'd flipped a light switch.

"Today is about you and my brother," she said. Her face wore a smile, but her voice was flat, devoid of any emotion.

Gertrude cleared her throat. "Well now," she eyed one of the smaller boxes, and Bridget obediently picked it up. "Time for my gift. 'Old' and 'blue.'"

Her aunt smiled through her eyes, nodding eagerly as Jennie opened it. She sucked in a deep breath. Sparkling in the band sunshine streaming through her lace curtains were a pair of diamond and sapphire teardrop earrings that perfectly matched the tiara from her debut.

"They were part of a set," Gertrude confirmed.

"I don't...I don't know what to say." Lips trembling, Jennie looked around at the other boxes Bridget brought in while they'd been occupied; even stacked tall, they took up a large portion of the floor beside her vanity. "Thank you," she gushed, bringing the older woman into a tight squeeze. "Thank you so much."

Gertrude blinked furiously, smoothing her skirts as they parted. "Oh my," she feigned a look at her wristlet, thumbing away a stray tear in the process. "Do look at the time."

At that, Cook and Bridget made quick work of piling the breakfast dishes on their respective trays. Shannon, meanwhile, stood statuesque, her solemn eyes cast on the sea outside. She looked like…a widow watcher.

Why, of course! Jennie knew she touched a nerve, but Shannon's icy reaction made perfect sense now. *She's afraid.* She had every reason to be. Somewhere, maybe even close by, the Kaiser's war machines raged below the surface. And Hugh was charged with patrolling the coast. Jennie shivered, grateful Danny hadn't enlisted with him. She pushed the dreadful thought away, refusing to let anything ruin this precious day. Today, she was a mermaid and her fisherman, a prince.

They took multiple cars to the lighthouse. Danny and Hugh left first in Father's silver touring vehicle while Gertrude and Shannon followed behind five minutes later. Eyes sparkling, Father held Jennie's gloved hand as he led her down the front path to the Rolls. Rutherford bowed, his own eyes dewy, and opened the door for them.

"Congratulations, miss," he said as she gathered her skirts to climb in.

"Thank you," Jennie blushed.

The cape rolled by in sweeping scenes of blue and green as they drove down Beach Avenue, not a cloud to be seen in the endless sky. It was no wonder why so many brides favored June. The weather was splendid, and Jennie turned her face to the window to bask in the sun's warm glow.

It wasn't long before they reached a certain beach road, passing Lake Lilly on the right. Jennie blushed but did not have regrets about that magical afternoon. Father remained silent throughout the ride, one large hand atop hers and a distant smile on his whiskered face.

Jennie couldn't predict the future. She knew not if the press would reinstitute hunting their people, though she suspected as much. But Jennie also knew Father wanted her to be happy. He'd been furious with her aunt for meddling. If a storm were brewing in the press, they'd weather it together, with her husband leading the charge.

Soon, they reached the light; Father and Rutherford both helped her out lest the long lace train catch on the seashell footpath. Father adjusted her veil, giving her one last peck on the cheek before covering Jennie's face.

"Ready, *Schatz?*"

Overcome, she could only nod. Rutherford offered her bouquet, a billowing arrangement of white roses and gardenia, and took a step back as father and daughter linked arms. A red velvet runner stood before them, leading to a floral trellis of the same varieties. Mixed with the salt air, the plumery cast an enchanting aroma sweeter than any Parisian eau de parfum. Off to the left stood a string quartet. At Father's indication, the first strands of Wagner's *Bridal March* soared in harmony with the rushing surf.

Jennie floated down the aisle. She could feel the kind eyes of the chosen few in attendance but could see only Danny. Her heart rattled, and she was never more thankful for her corset for fear it would burst right through her ribcage. He looked so handsome. His blonde hair was slick against his head. Sun-kissed, it appeared golden. And then there was his smile— so adoring and true; his piercing blue eyes a beacon of love pulling her forth, calling her home.

Reverend Gardner stepped forward. Jennie was touched he'd made the trip down from Philadelphia for the occasion. A friend of the family for years, she couldn't imagine anyone else performing the nuptials. Smiling at Father, he asked the necessary question. Soon the veil was lifting, Father squeezing her hand before taking his place in the front row.

Shannon rose from her seat beside Gertrude. She received Jennie's flowers, and the two took their place under the trellis with Danny and Hugh.

The ceremony was simple yet sweet. Though not in a church, Jennie chose a reading from Corinthians she'd always admired. The couple wrote their own vows, and Danny surprised her by incorporating Tennyson's *Marriage Morning* in his. How many times had they read poetry by moonlight? It was perfect, absolutely, incandescently perfect, more splendid than anything she could've ever dreamed.

They were kissing, his mouth on hers, those soft, supple lips. Drunk on his love, Jennie heard vague clapping and cheers. She smiled and took his hand, a hand that was hers now to hold forever.

Time warped into a blur. A flurry of handshakes, hugs, and photography. She'd lost her bouquet somewhere, and her heels kept sinking in the sand, but Jennie didn't care. Her cheeks hurt from smiling so much. One look at her husband, and he appeared the same.

Soon they were piling back into the cars. Sweating, Jennie itched the lace collar around her neck and rested her head on Danny's shoulder. This was the last time they'd be alone together for a few hours.

"Rutherford," she chirped.

"Mrs. Culligan?"

It took a moment to sink in. *Mrs. Culligan.* That was who she was now.

"Could you please take the long route home?"

The older man winked. "Of course."

Jennie knew something was wrong the minute they pulled up to the cottage. There was no one outside. No fanfare of rice or clanging of empty cans. She clutched Danny's hand.

"Samuel," she whispered. The boy hadn't even been strong enough to attend the ceremony.

"Stay here. I'll go check."

"No, I..." She creased the corner of her mouth. It was touching how much he cared for the boy. Still, Samuel was her cousin. They were a team now. Come what may, they'd face it together. "I'm coming too."

The newlyweds walked hand-in-hand up the brick path. Cook greeted them at the door. Where Jennie's heart fluttered earlier this morning, it now thumped. Where she couldn't breathe from bliss, she now choked on every breath. *Not today.* Selfish, yes, but it didn't seem fair. This was *her* day. Hers and Danny's.

"Everything alright?" Jennie asked, hating herself at her absurdity.

"Your father would like to see you in the parlor." Cook gulped and looked at Danny. "Both of you."

Jennie's mind scrambled. Maybe this wasn't about Samuel. Perhaps someone had seen them that day at the lake. Or Joseph caught wind of the ceremony and alerted his grandfather. She glanced at Danny that little voice in her head from two weeks ago suddenly not so little anymore. "*He wore different clothing,*" it shouted. Why had he worn different clothing? She squeezed her eyes closed, the staunch realization she didn't desire to know the answer hitting her like a sledgehammer.

Father stood by the mantel, a forlorn expression on his face. Gertrude and Shannon hovered near the Queen Anne's, while Hugh had already helped himself to a scotch from the wet bar.

"I'm sorry," Father began, pulling a stark white envelope from his inner jacket pocket. "I hate to do this, today of all days, but this was delivered while we were out." He turned to Danny, offering a nod of apology. "I believe matters such as these are time sensitive."

Jennie watched with bated breath as Danny opened the envelope, her eyes fixed on the shield insignia bearing stars and stripes on its upper right corner. Her husband read the document in silence and shook his head sideways. Brows knit, the letter in his hand began to shake as well.

"I don't…understand," Danny stammered. "I never…"

Shannon immediately flanked his other side, and Jennie grabbed her hand.

"There must be a mistake," he whispered. Danny swallowed hard, looking at Jennie before meeting his sister's eye. "I didn't register for the draft."

"No!" Jennie wailed, covering her face with her hands.

"Let me see," Shannon demanded, snatching the letter along with the yellow graph paper attached. Eyes wild, she skimmed the enclosures. "Danny," she pointed at a section on the second page. "This is dated before your eighteenth birthday."

"What?"

"Pa," she yelped, frantically waving the letter before pointing at it again. "That's his signature right there." She clung to him now, openly weeping as if no one else were in the room.

"Why would he…." Jennie's voice trailed off, suddenly hopeful. "It can't be valid then, can it?" She looked from Father to Hugh, trusting their learned opinions more than her own.

"I don't know, Jen," her cousin said gently. "It arrived Certified mail."

"Father?"

Eyes dewy, misery weighted the older man's lips.

"You can get him out of it, right Daddy?" she asked in a sing-song tone. "We'll just pay someone else. It'll be…it'll be fine. Everything will be just as it should."

The words no sooner left her lips, and Jennie knew they were wrong. That the government had, rightfully so, stopped the procedure of excusing drafted men for paid substitutes shortly after the Civil War. Still, the allies were in dire need of fresh men. Perhaps Wilson would reinstitute it? All the more reason for suffrage. These were husbands he was taking. Brothers, she thought, throwing a glance at the now inconsolable Shannon. Hugh thrust a crystal tumbler into her hand. Cousins. Sons. Nephews. What of the women? Where did that leave them? Voiceless yet again, Jennie could only scarcely hope where she wanted to scream. *Take someone else! Not him. Anyone but him!*

Jennie blinked. She was in her room, cocooned in layers of soft blankets. What a horrible dream.

It was a dream, wasn't it? Throat dry, she started to reach for the pitcher beside her and stopped halfway. She wasn't alone. The weight around her she'd assumed was that of an extra quilt was really her husband, and it all came ruthlessly flooding back. Instead of spending her wedding night in endless euphoria, she'd spent it in hysterics.

Shirtless, Danny looked so peaceful. His hair tousled, he lightly snored. *It's not fair.* None of it was. Her breath came in spurts as agony pierced her heart. He must have felt her watery eyes on him and began to stir.

"Mornin' Mrs. Culligan," he murmured, spooning her close.

It should have felt good. Right. But all Jennie could think about was how it wouldn't last, and she started to cry all over again.

Danny caressed her tear-stained face. "I'm here."

"For how long?"

"We went over this, Jen. I hafta go. You know I don't want to."

"Then why not fight it? Fight for us?" Jennie didn't have to look at him to know what her dutiful husband would say in response. Not when they'd gone round after round. Hoping his answer would change, she'd ask him again, too, until he relented.

"I'm not a slacker. How would that look, huh?"

"I don't care."

"Well I do. I love you."

"You sure don't act like it."

"Please just hear me out, okay?"

"Fine."

Danny released a rugged sigh. "It's not my own reputation I'm concerned about. You gotta know that. It's *yours.* Your father's by extension." He pet her hair. "If I stay? If I evade the draft, and someone like York gets wind of it, it'll only draw more unwanted attention. A helluva lot more. Fella's already got an axe to grind. I can't do that to you. I won't. I love you too much."

PART II

CHAPTER 42

H ugh shined the gold waist buttons on his jacket and straightened his bow tie. He looked down, making a mental note to stop at the florist on his way to get Shannon, and the reflection in his patent leather shoes grinned back.

Outside, the winter wind was biting. He shoved his hands in his pockets and turned up his collar. With minutes to spare before the next Liberty Special, he walked at a brisk pace toward the train station. "*Christmas Eve,*" Hugh thought as he looked out at the ocean paralleling the tracks, "*what a year....*"

One of his first assignments had been overseeing the reservists restoring the old seashore line to transport men and supplies from the Section Base to the Iron Pier. It was on time as usual, and he hopped on.

His parents' divorce would be finalized any day now. Only those closest to them knew ending the marriage was Father's choice. To keep the proceedings both as short and discreet as possible, Mother filed suit for legal separation on the grounds of adultery in July. She took her cue from the Astor affair nearly a decade before, with both Callaways opting to have the paperwork handled outside of New York City and the watchful eye of the press.

Hugh spoke with her earlier in the week, and she was thrilled to have been awarded custody of Samuel. His father also agreed to let her keep the Browne lodge upstate, an annual allowance of $75,000 and a settlement instead of alimony. The attorneys were still negotiating the amount, but Mother was confident it would be somewhere between $2 million to $3 million.

As for himself, Father put aside an undisclosed trust for him upon reaching his 25th birthday. Hugh suspected this was the older man's way of making up for having donated *The Crusader* to the Navy while still in the throes of anger over the Harvard debacle.

The trolley arrived at its destination.

"Merry Christmas, Lieutenant," said the seaman beside him as they stood up.

"Same to you," Hugh grinned.

One quick errand and Shannon would be his for the next two days. Not entirely; he was quick to remind himself as he strolled down Washington Street. Danny was granted a furlough as well, and they were set to meet him later that afternoon to spend the holiday in Philadelphia. As far as he was concerned, that was neither here nor there. They'd still have the whole train ride to and from the city alone together. As much as Hugh hated to admit it, he was eager for any precious crumbs she threw him. He was wearing her down, he knew, and hopeful their short trip would ease whatever underlying doubts she had.

The bells on the door handle jingled as he entered the shop. Hugh surveyed the rich array of evergreen and poinsettia arrangements, the place sparkling with a hope he usually only felt at the card tables. He settled on a nosegay of white baby roses accented with ivy.

Though a few minutes early, Shannon was waiting on the porch when he reached her rooming house. She looked exhausted, and he didn't regret bribing her coworker to pick up extra shifts so she could get a much-needed reprieve.

"The Rossini kids again?"

Pasquale Rossini was one of his men. Dreading to part from his family, he moved his wife and five children from their row home in South Philadelphia after he'd been called up. When not tending to the little ones, Mrs. Rossini somehow found the time to busy herself as one of the Section Base's many laundresses.

Shannon nodded. "The baby has colic." She squeezed her eyes closed. "Poor Marian. I don't know how she does it."

"I don't know how *you* do it, Shannon. Working all hours and still helping her out when you can."

"They're nice people," she popped a shoulder.

"Well, I'm sure Pat appreciates it." He handed her a small brown paper bag. "I know I do."

She poked his ribs. "Thought we said no presents."

"When have I ever listened to you?"

He pinned the corsage on the lapel of her coat, and they caught the trolley to the Reading station. They were no sooner off the island when Shannon dozed off. Chin on her hand, she leaned against the window as the locomotive sped east.

Hugh couldn't help himself. He put his left arm around her, gently rolling her neck, so Shannon's head rested on his shoulder. It was only then he felt how feather-light she was. He frowned. She didn't have to live this way. He was already earning enough to comfortably provide for both of them. Hell, in a few years, they'd never want for anything.

She shifted beside him, murmuring softly, and he wondered when she last had a full night's sleep. Her long lashes fluttered, reminding him of a butterfly and his mind wandered back to his first night at the bungalow. Hugh longed to stroke her cheek but stopped; the sharp pain of her apathy a knife to his heart.

Something changed in Shannon when Danny left. She worked herself into a tizzy at the going away party. Told both him and Will in no uncertain terms she didn't want or need anyone but herself. Mother came to his room later and recommended time and space. She reminded him that, having just lost her father, Shannon was probably terrified of losing her brother too. And Hugh had grown to know Mrs. Barkley well enough to surmise she likely had a similar discussion with her own son. Months later, to his chagrin, Shannon remained adamant about it.

The train reached Camden sooner than he would have liked. Hugh roused her for the exchange to the ferry that would carry them over the Delaware River. Shannon rubbed her eyes, and he was sorry to have interrupted her. Their bags loaded, he tucked her inside the vessel's second tier as the city of Philadelphia sprang up ahead. The Workshop of the World, grey smoke poured from hundreds of stacks along the waterfront. Meanwhile, chunks of dirty ice floated by.

It wasn't long before they reached Reading Terminal. Hugh carried both parcels on one arm and grabbed Shannon by the hand with the other. He led her down the platform to the street-level market. Massive, the place was booming. Hundreds of butchers and hucksters occupied aisles of stalls to the soundtrack of the railroad thundering above them. Shoppers pushed left and right, all vying for the finishing touches necessary for their Christmas Eve feasts later.

"Smelt! Baccala!" A boy called from his perch atop a wooden crate. Another rushed by, his tiny arms overflowing with deliveries.

The smell of fresh-baked bread made Hugh's stomach growl.

"You hungry?" he asked Shannon. Spotting a street cart a few feet away, he bought them a soft pretzel each.

"Mmm," she mused between bites. "Still warm."

Danny was standing right where he said he'd be, on the corner of 12th and Market Streets. Shannon flew into his arms. He lifted and twirled her, not hard to do considering her waifish state.

Hugh eyed the stripes on Danny's olive green coat. "Sergeant, huh?"

"Yeah," his friend replied. "We'll talk later."

Rutherford waved at them from across the street. The butler towered over the crowds. He loaded the Rolls for the short drive to Germantown.

Jennie was in the music room when they arrived. One look at her swollen torso, and it was clear why she hadn't met them at the train station herself. Hugh smiled widely. Mother hadn't mentioned anything. Come to think of it, neither had Danny.

Peripherally, Hugh saw Shannon shoot her brother a guarded look. They could only watch as the color drained from his face.

Jennie put a hand on her stomach and shyly bit her lip. Her husband bent down and kissed her cheek. Still in disbelief, Danny put his hand over hers, but she only nodded.

"Merry Christmas, darling," she cooed.

"Merry Christmas, Jen."

"Indeed!" Uncle Walter boomed from the hall.

The pitter-patter on the marble stairs told Hugh that Mother and Samuel weren't far behind him.

"Hugh!"

His brother raced across the room. The boy was winded despite the short distance. Their mother did her best to be cheerful.

"Oh, look at you," she prattled, hugging him. "So handsome in your white uniform. What happened to my little boy?"

Hugh raised his eyebrows. "*Mother.*"

Thankfully, she took the hint and moved on. "Shannon, dear. How was your trip to the city?"

The group settled into multiple conversations while Cook and Bridget served tea. Watching Shannon munch happily on cucumber sandwiches did Hugh's heart good. Samuel, on the other hand, gave him cause for concern.

His cough persisted through the end of the summer, much longer than

Dr. Mace anticipated initially. The spasms clearly took their toll. The boy's complexion was sallow, and he continued wheezing several minutes after they sat down. As with Jennie's apparent condition, Mother neglected to address his brother's health in the many times they'd spoken since his move to the base.

"What are you asking Santa for?" He was asking Shannon now.

"I hadn't thought about it. What about you?"

"Got my list right here." Samuel patted his pocket. "Hope it's not too late."

"Samuel, sweetheart," Mother interjected, "We've already been over this. I have to change for dinner, then again for church. I'm afraid we won't have time to get to Wanamaker's today."

The boy pouted. "You *promised*."

"I said no such thing."

He crisscrossed his arms as angry tears welled up.

"Darling," she backpedaled, her arms wide, "You've been a good boy. Santa knows that. I'm sure you'll get everything you asked for. Don't worry, my love."

"It's not for me, Mother," Samuel protested. "I can't say it out loud, or it won't come true. We gotta go downtown." He panted. "*Please.* I gotta give him my letter…."

Out of breath, the child trailed off. Bridget gave him a glass of water.

"I'll take him, Mother," Hugh offered. He turned to Shannon, "Would you care to join us?"

Her sapphire eyes sparkled. "I'd love to."

"Well, I suppose," Mother agreed. She glanced at the clock on the mantel. "But you'd better hurry. And bundle up or you'll catch your death." She shuddered. "It's unseasonably cold this year."

CHAPTER 43

Shannon's heart thumped as they piled back into the Rolls Royce, its twelve cylinders roaring to life as Hugh started the engine. She could feel him staring at her again and chanced a look back. Loving him would make life so much simpler were it not a lie. She'd done too much of that already. Friends since childhood and related through marriage, their lives would always be intertwined. And she did care for him. So much. She just couldn't risk her heart the way he wanted her to.

They raced up Market Street jockeying their way between the traffic and trollies. Samuel smuggled a cookie in his coat and chomped away in the backseat.

"Don't get any crumbs on the floor," Hugh chided. "Rutherford'll have a coronary."

"I won't," the boy replied.

Hugh was lucky enough to get a parking space close to the building. Shannon shielded her eyes, glancing up at the massive structure. The first of its kind, the department store towered several stories above the street.

Overjoyed, Samuel spun one too many times around the revolving door. He ran into the Grand Court, leaning on an enormous statue of an eagle while he caught his breath.

The store was just as busy, if not more so than the market was earlier. Awestruck, Shannon marveled at the sights around her. Having only seen the catalog, used ones at that, it was better than anything she'd imagined. Counter after counter of glass-encased jewels twinkled in the electric lighting. Swags of pine and holly were strewn around the perimeter of the court. Customers waited in line to the jangles of both the registers and the bells of carolers on parade.

Across the court, several floors up, was the largest pipe organ Shannon had ever seen.

"Wanamaker had it brought in from the World's Fair a few years back," Hugh explained as he followed her gaze.

"It's extraordinary," she breathed.

"Yup. Biggest one in the world. He even hired his own staff of builders to enhance it."

But Samuel was more interested in what was underneath the instrument.

"There he is!" Jumping up and down, he pointed at Santa. "We made it, Hugh. C'mon!"

Off he went again to secure a place in the seemingly endless line. Hugh groaned.

"I'll wait with him if you'd like," Shannon offered. The child was charming, and she didn't feel nearly as guilty spending time with him as she did his older brother.

"You're a doll."

"I know," she winked.

Hugh disappeared to do some last-minute shopping, leaving the two of them alone. Samuel looked down at his feet and fiddled with his letter.

"Thanks for coming with me," he mumbled.

"Sure," she said. "Always wanted to see this place. Heard cottagers talk about it for years."

"Pretty swell, huh?"

"Agreed." Shannon grinned at him.

Samuel smiled back with big, puppy-dog eyes. "Miss Shannon?" he asked in a quiet voice.

"Yes?"

Careful to ensure the pigtailed girl in front of them didn't hear, he whispered, "I know he's not the *real* Santa."

"I'm not sure what you mean."

He cocked his head. "I went to boarding school, I know how this works. Plus, I got an older brother."

Samuel put his hands on his hips. The boy was so serious. Shannon drew a hand to her mouth to cover the smile she could no longer contain and forcibly coughed out the chuckle threatening to give her away.

"Okay," she said. "This is obviously important to you."

"I *knew* you'd understand." He hugged her. "I tried to tell Mother but she won't listen. Do you wanna know what I wrote?"

"Only if you want to tell me."

Samuel nodded and took a deep breath. "I want the war to end."

She felt herself sharply inhale and hoped he didn't notice.

"Cousin Jennie, she cries herself to sleep every night. Thinks no one can hear her but we can," he sighed. "I just want everything to be the way it was before. Then Danny can come home. And Hugh." Samuel paused and looked at her thoughtfully. "And maybe you could even come live with us too. I mean, if you want."

Shannon squeezed him. "Sweet, sweet boy." She blinked back tears and tried to keep her tone level. "I hope you get your wish."

"This one's for you!" Samuel beamed from the floor.

"Me?" Shannon asked. Landing on the Nice List was the last thing she expected.

"Says so right here on the label." He grabbed a long red box trimmed in gold ribbon and gave it a shake. "Doesn't sound like much."

Hugh tousled the boy's hair. "I'll take it from here, kiddo."

Cheeks warm, Shannon tilted her head. "You didn't."

"Who else did you think I was shopping for yesterday?" he grinned, brown eyes warm with love as he gave it to her.

Truth be told, Shannon thought it might've been something for the baby, though after stealing a glance at her brother, she held her tongue. Accepting the gift, in front of everyone no less, was difficult enough.

Gingerly, she untied the bow and opened the top of the box to find a white sable muff. Shannon's pulse raced. She peeled back the tissue paper and caressed the soft fur. She caught Hugh's blush from the corner of her eye and loathed herself for giving him false hope.

"You like it, then?"

"Like it? Of course! Thank you," she managed with as demure a smile as she could muster. She struggled against the strong urge to hug him.

I don't deserve it. I don't deserve any of this.

"How lovely," Mrs. Callaway admired, hands over her heart. She nodded at a large box toward the back of the tree and winked. "It will look perfect with *my* gift."

Shannon's affections for the older woman warmed significantly in the months after the fire. She shouldered her divorce with a backbone of steel. A mother to all, her love for her boys shone through every action. *Including this one.* She didn't appreciate the added pressure, smiling graciously out of respect as she opened the present.

The gown was stunning. Shannon slid her fingers along the soft, midnight blue velvet and sucked in her breath. All eyes on her, she carefully pulled it out, noticing the collar and sleeves were trimmed in the same luxurious sable.

"For the Officer's Ball, perhaps?" Gertrude was saying.

Shannon could almost see herself gliding across the marble floor at the Iron Pier. One of *them*. Never having to worry about where her next meal was coming from ever again. If Hugh continued to allow his mother to make arrangements for him, she had no doubt what else she'd find herself acquiescing to. Only her pride and the fact that no one but Danny knew the dark depths of her soul held her back. The secret was theirs and theirs alone. It burned deep inside her, and she had no doubt it was tearing him to pieces too.

Gertrude motioned for her to hold it up, and Shannon obediently obeyed. A chorus of compliments echoed all around, but she forced herself not to listen. Bought and beholden, she'd never felt so filthy.

"Yes," she heard herself agree to the date. It sounded like someone else's voice. "Yes, that sounds wonderful."

Shannon reflected on the day's events that evening while a maid brushed out her hair. A part of her wanted the life Hugh could offer. It was practically hers for the taking. She'd awoken in his arms on the train yesterday, enveloped in warmth and security. How nice it would be to feel that every day. To give it freely in return. But, of course, she couldn't. Hugh could never find out.

There was no other way. Her contrition to a God she'd long stopped believing in. Or maybe he just didn't believe in her? So much for loving and merciful. He was neither when He took her mother, forcing her and Danny to endure Pa's wrath all those years. Still, inspired by Samuel's pure selflessness the day before, there might be something she *could* do as a small act of penance.

The Farmer's Almanac was calling for the coldest winter in twenty years. The back bays were nearly frozen over already. It didn't help that there was a coal shortage on the island and a nationwide call for Meatless Mondays and Wheatless Wednesdays to conserve for the war effort.

Folks on the mainland only worsened the matter. Despite their surplus, merchants increased prices in a vicious attempt to squeeze every penny from the already destitute locals. But some people, including the Rossinis, simply couldn't come up with the funds.

Shannon usually slept in layers, offering what little coal she could to the young mother across the hall. And now she'd be able to help them even more. A small sack would fit nicely in her trunk if she just rearranged a few items. If Hugh questioned its weight (though she suspected he wouldn't) she could merely explain it away as her Christmas presents.

She grinned to herself, envisioning the looks on the children's faces when they bit into the fresh fruit. Luscious citrus, shipped up from Florida. Quite the delicacy. Shannon sighed in contentment. She stuffed herself at dinner but might just have to keep at least one for later. And the pears. There was a lot Marian could do with them.

A tap on her shoulder brought her back to reality.

"Will you be needin' anything else, Miss?"

"Yes, actually. Some more coal for the fire, please. There's no need for you to stoke it though, I can do that myself."

"Of course."

"And..." Shannon paused. "I'm a little hungry. Can you please bring up some fruit? It looked divine."

The girl nodded, and Shannon perused the copy of *Vogue* Gertrude left on her bedside table. "You can leave everything on the chest next to the wardrobe."

The maid curtsied. "Merry Christmas, Miss."

"To you as well."

CHAPTER 44

Danny tossed and turned under the covers. This was, by far, the worst Christmas ever. And, God knows, he had some rough ones in the past.

Jennie snored lightly beside him. *Finally.* He thought she'd never stop crying. Part of him was furious with her for keeping such a large secret, while the other part rebuked his utter hypocrisy.

Young, rich, and beautiful, he made his peace months ago about the possibility of leaving her widowed. What could the papers write then? It'd be pretty hard to twist. How many Brits had gone over the top? Been plowed down at the Somme? He'd be a hero. It could even turn into being Jennie's only chance to have the life she deserved. The one he'd never be able to give her, even on his best day. But to leave her alone with a child? *His child?* Danny thought he couldn't hate himself any more than he already did. Apparently, he was wrong about that too.

A baby. It was bound to happen. What did surprise him, though, was how much he already loved it.

Danny gazed up at the copper ceiling and wondered what he or she would look like. Jennie's nose with maybe his eyes. He could almost see the little cherub. Tiny, chubby fingers wrapped around his thumb.

Pa would always be 'Pa' and, while it fits Walter perfectly, 'Father' was far too formal. 'Daddy'— now that had a nice ring to it.

The fantasy would never come to fruition. In another life, Danny could and would do better than his own father. But not in this one. Not after what he'd done.

Unable to sleep, he slipped downstairs for a nightcap. A candle was lit in the far corner of Walter's study, and he was glad to find Hugh in one of the leather wingbacks.

"Couldn't sleep either."

It was a statement, not a question. Brandy in hand, his friend filled a tumbler and handed it over. Danny sank down into the chair next to him.

"She still upset?" Hugh asked.

Danny shook his head. "Not now. Only cause she's asleep. Who knows what the morning will bring."

"Mother was a mess when she was carrying Samuel. In fact, I think those were Nanny's exact words after he was born."

Danny drained his glass and leaned his head against the back of the chair. Hugh topped him off.

"What am I gonna do?" A hand rested on his knee, and Danny was grateful for the quiet comfort of the man beside him.

"Why don't you tell me about those stripes, Sarge?"

"Not too much to say," Danny replied. He leaned over and pinched the bridge of his nose. "It's bad, Hugh. They're training us with wooden rifles. Some of the fellas never held a real weapon before."

"We have a lot of inexperience on our end too. Laborers. Broken English."

"Hell, at least they answered the call. Must be strange for some of 'em to fight against their own kind."

"Good point," Hugh said. He pulled out his cigarettes, and they both lit one. "Mother told me the Philadelphia school board just prohibited the teaching of German."

Danny took a drag. "That so?"

Hugh nodded.

"My kid's gonna be part-German. My *wife*. I—"

"I know. The generalizations are the worst." Hugh set his jaw. "Makes me so mad I could just...."

"Save it for training. Sure do enough of that, right?"

"Calisthenics?"

Danny grimaced. "Every. Morning." He tapped his ash into a crystal tray. "And we're timed on how fast we can put on our gas masks."

"You think it'll be enough?"

"Sure as hell hope so."

Hugh crushed out his cigarette. Danny freshened their glasses and sat back down; a silence thicker than stale smoke clung in the air between them. Something neither man wanted to admit aloud. They could try to make light of it all they wanted, but masks and exercises were nothing when stacked against a torpedo. The men of the *Jacob Jones* could attest to that. The Germans sank the Navy destroyer earlier that month, the incident fresh in everyone's minds over dinner and, no doubt, one of the reasons Jennie struggled to keep herself collected. There was a lot of ocean between here and France.

Danny cocked his head, and that pesky cowlick skimmed his left eye. "Hugh," his voice a haggard monotone, "if somethin' happens—"

"Of course."

He couldn't have finished the sentence even if he tried. What was there to say that hadn't already been said? They both knew the risks.

His friend laughed and stood up. "Better turn in."

"I'm right behind you."

But Danny stayed in the study until the early morning. He didn't need to be visited by any ghosts to see his future. He already knew where he was headed and why. There was no redemption in this story. No miracle.

He had to protect Jennie from himself. And now the baby. Distance. That was the only way to do it. If he survived the war, he'd re-enlist. Plain and simple. Lots of fellas made a career out of it.

The colors in the sky were changing when he finally went back to Jennie's bedroom. Giant red and white poinsettias lined both sides of the stairway. They looked like floral peppermint sticks, alternating in color every other step, culminating under a fir tree on the landing. Though not as imposing as the one in the music room, the Christmas tree was decorated with just as much care. Its candles long extinguished for the evening, Danny caught a whiff of the pleasant gingerbread ornaments when he made the turn for the second flight and stopped.

He smiled, remembering Jennie telling him about their trees of yesteryear. Walter brought the custom with him to America long before they appeared in other homes. He imagined her in the kitchen with Samuel, an apron covered in flour, rolling out the dough before cutting out the little men. She laughed and crinkled her nose, pretending that it tickled them when she added the icing for their buttons. The vision faded as it occurred to him she'd do all that and more with their own child, and he covered his mouth with his hands.

His legs felt like tree trunks as he continued his ascent. His mind was clear. It would be their first and only Christmas together, and he hoped Jennie was happy with the memory to pass on to their child. After the 26th, he'd never see her again.

CHAPTER 45

S hannon sat on the edge of the bed and stared up at the rickety ceiling. It was a rare moment of quiet she knew wouldn't last for very long, little Enzo Rossini still not sleeping through the night. She crossed her arms against herself, her tiny room chilly as usual, but it was worth it.

The children loved the fruit. She packaged it along with some leftover cookies in the stocking Mr. Martin gave her. Marian initially protested the coal, relenting only when Shannon agreed to join them for a month's worth of Sunday dinners. Her mouth was already watering at the thought. With supplies in short demand, she primarily relied on scraps from the barracks. A small price to pay for the greater good.

She looked across the room at her open closet and sighed. The muff would undoubtedly keep her hands warm right about now, yet she couldn't bring herself to put it on. And so it sat in its box on the shelf, her gown hanging directly on the rack beneath. Entirely out of place next to her work clothing, both were an inescapable weight on her back. The Officer's Ball was on New Year's Eve, less than a week away. Shannon had half a mind to lend the garments to Marian for a much-needed night away from her brood, but poor Pat was only a seaman. She just didn't see how she could get out of it.

Frowning, she turned out her light and tried to sleep, wishing Danny were there. She missed him more with each passing day. Would sell her soul if it ensured his safe return. Yet even if he did survive the war, she knew he'd have little time for her. Not with a family of his own to take care of. Nothing, nothing could fill the hole inside her.

She tossed and turned but couldn't get comfortable. Punching her pillow for what seemed the tenth time, Shannon heard a strange noise. She held herself very still, straining her ears. More a high-pitched howl than cry, it wasn't Enzo's usual wailing. The sound was definitely something—or someone—outside.

Shannon threw back her blanket, squinting through the window into the small courtyard. Its pane was smeared with dust, and she cursed herself for not taking better care of the place. The moonless winter sky did not help matters. Frustrated, she cracked the window, her arm already rippled in goosebumps.

She heard it again and looked down. Some ridiculous new law mandated the closing of all saloons within a radius of the naval station, yet the island somehow remained wetter than the Atlantic. Expecting yet another wayward sailor, Shannon was surprised to see something small and white thrashing in the bushes below. It looked up at her helplessly and moaned again.

"Poor thing," she gasped as she realized it was a kitten. Her overcoat on in the next instant, Shannon rushed outside to retrieve it. She did her best to soothe the animal; its tiny paw caught on a thorn. The cat was still and trusting as if it instinctively understood she was trying to help.

The kitten bumped its head on her chest as they entered her room, and she flicked on the light. Rubbing against her again, she noticed it had a left cauliflower ear, the same side as Danny's scar.

Shannon swallowed the lump in her throat. "Gonna hafta keep you now," she whispered, stroking the kitten's soft white back.

It purred gratefully in return, and she smiled through her tears. He was scrawny, far too young to have been weaned from his mother, with large green eyes. Four pink paws matched a wet pink nose, and his coat was as pure as freshly fallen snow.

"How does Snowball sound?" Shannon asked, deeming his head rub in reply as acceptable.

Carefully placing him on the bed, she retrieved the muff from her closet and laid it out next to her pillow. She put Snowball on top and grinned as his tiny paws took right to kneading. Safe and warm, he curled into a tight ball and went to sleep. Shannon climbed back into bed herself, giving him a pat on the head as she pulled up her blanket. She'd always wanted a pet but was surprised at how much happier she felt just knowing she wasn't alone anymore.

He greeted her at the door upon her return from work the next day. Shannon poured a splash of milk into a saucer and unwrapped her own dinner of a day-old roll and a hunk of cheese. She was two bites in when there was a knock at the door. Checking the peephole, she grinned at Will's disproportionate reflection staring back. She let him in, and Snowball protectively pounced at his ankles.

"Woah there. I come in peace, little fella."

Shannon nodded to the burlap sack Will carried over his shoulder. "Christmas is over, you know."

"Sure is," he replied and offered her the parcel. "But the Almanac's sayin' it's gonna be a long winter. Figure this'll come in handy."

The bag was so heavy she almost dropped it. Together they lowered it to the floor, and she untied the top. Filled with coal, the weight was no wonder.

"Will! Where did you get this?"

He stopped chewing the wad of gum in his mouth and stuck his hands proudly in his pockets. "Got me a job. Consolidated Fisheries up in Wildwood."

This wasn't exactly news. Still too young in his parents' eyes to join in the war effort, the Barkleys agreed to allow Will to look for work of his own after the fall harvest was cleared. The homely Sarah managed to snare a seaman, and Shannon supposed they knew it was only a matter of time before their son grew impatient with the monotony of his own life. Preferring he sew his oats on home soil rather than abroad, they reluctantly agreed to give him more freedom.

Will raised his eyebrows and pulled a thick green roll of cash from his overalls. Pa never earned that much in the summer months, let alone the off-season.

"I see business is good," Shannon said, trying to sound casual.

"Yep."

"Congratulations."

He crossed his arms against himself. "That all you can say?"

"No, actually." Shannon straightened her spine and tilted her head up. "If you're trying to compete with Hugh, you should know it's futile." She jutted her chin at the closet. "I won't be bought either way."

"Jeez, Shannon. You're so stubborn," Will shook his head. "Is it wrong I don't want you to freeze? Look atcha. Skin and bones." He gestured to the sack. "If I know you, you'll probably give half of this to the guinea across the hall. Stop punishing yourself."

Arms behind her back, she clenched her fists. "That how you think it is now?"

"I care about you. Be a liar if I stood here and even tried to deny it."

"I'd say you're already a liar." Shannon glared. If Will was going to call her out, she'd give it right back. "There's no way all that money came from working at a fishery. You have a good night at Jackson's? Don't play dumb. I've been there myself."

Will reddened and looked at his feet.

Feeling Snowball brush against her leg, she bent down and scooped him up. "What's the matter, Will? Cat got your tongue?"

"No," he mumbled.

"Well, then?"

"I don't think you know what you're askin'."

She angled her chin, a smidge of guilt getting the better of her. "I'm no porcelain doll. There's not much I can't handle. Did you steal this coal?"

"Heck no! I bought it on the mainland, fair and square."

Shannon raised an eyebrow, and he squirmed.

"The owner of the fishery has a nice little side business. Some of us help him out." He shrugged. "No big deal."

Will pulled out the chair at her kitchenette and plopped down. Still cradling her furry friend, Shannon sat across from him and nudged the cheese plate between them. He declined before proceeding to tell her more. Voice hushed, he explained how he and a few others had been making secret liquor deliveries all over the cape and neighboring Wildwoods to the north.

Located on Otten's Harbor, the fishery itself was a perfectly legitimate business. A refrigerated warehouse and access to both the rails and waterways kept Philadelphia area restaurants well stocked with fresh catches year-round. As for the alcohol, well, that was still legal everywhere offshore and easy enough to come by. Just a matter of supply and demand. No different in Will's eyes than seeing his father's crops to market.

Shannon listened attentively, her lips curling into a smirk. It was clear neither Will nor Hugh was willing to move on. While she wouldn't sell herself to either man in marriage, earning an income greater than the meager wages from the barracks would undoubtedly make her life easier. She put the cat down and leaned her chin on her hands.

"Your boss need any more help?"

His brows scrunched. "Don't think so. 'Sides, Shannon, you're a girl."

"Oh, you noticed, did you?" She leaned back and crossed her arms against her chest.

"Don't get all uppity. You sound like Sarah. Next you'll be telling me you wanna vote."

"I do, actually. But let's save that argument for another day. Fair enough?"

Will frowned in agreement.

"Well then, Will, as you already astutely pointed out, I'm female. What seems to have escaped you, my friend, is that I have direct access to Wissahickon. My sex—"

He turned beet red, and Shannon moved in for the kill.

"My *sex* plays to our advantage. No one would suspect a thing."

He fiddled with his hands on the table, refusing to look at her face. "I dunno, Shannon. It could be dangerous."

"You know I can shoot straight."

Will looked from her to the dress in the closet and back. Shoulders slumped, he sighed.

"Just get me a meeting, Will. I'll handle the rest."

"Alright."

Shannon beamed. "You won't regret it."

CHAPTER 46

Frank went over the year-end figures again. It was late, but he had to be sure. His fingers tapped methodically on the adding machine, a nuanced percussion to the soft lapping of the water against the bulkhead outside. And soon, he was smiling. Numbers didn't lie; 1917 was a banner year. Business was better than ever.

He closed the small leather book, locking it safely in the hidden compartment under his desk, and rose for a celebratory nightcap before heading home. The office was dim, only a few hours before the fleet went out for the day. They could haul in a school of mermaids for all he cared, and it still wouldn't compare to what the fishery was earning on the side.

Frank grinned. Efforts to keep the Wildwoods dry were futile. Pathetic, really. How long were they going to play this little game?

City officials tried to ban drinking near the boardwalk back in '12 and failed miserably. Blew right up in their face, speakeasies started operating out of bathhouses almost overnight. This was a tourist town, after all. Given the short season, success was paramount to giving people what they wanted. And, in this case, folks wanted a cold beer after spending hours on the beach. That was how Pop always explained it. Their customers decidedly wet, like all area hotels, the Hilton continued to offer alcohol every day.

The Drys took another swing the following year, this time arguing against booze on Sundays. Of course, Pop scoffed at that, too, not only ignoring the law but installing a few slot machines to boot. Who was going to stop him? He owned half the island, with interests in the electric company, building and loan association, volunteer fire department, even the Methodist church. A few bucks here and there, and the coppers looked the other way.

This new thing under the War Powers? *Liquid gold.*

Frank poured a second scotch. He swirled the amber liquid around his crystal tumbler a few times and knocked it back when there was a light tap on the door. His hand flew to his shoulder holster. The magazine full, he crept to the entryway. Back adjacent to the cinderblock wall, Frank readied the weapon.

"Who is it?" he called.

"Will. Will Barkley, sir."

The country bumpkin? What the hell was he doing out this time of night? Though practically harmless, Frank still held the Colt in full view in case Barkley wasn't alone and opened the door.

Will took off his cap, holding it in front of himself with both hands. "Thank you for seeing me, sir," he mumbled as Frank ushered him over to the desk.

Frank plopped down opposite, the leather still warm from before. "Drop the 'sir' shit, wouldja?"

"'Course."

"What brings you? Not trouble, I hope."

"No, sir." The farmhand shook his head, the side of his mouth playing at a smile. "Habit," he apologized.

"Good. Half the force is on-the-take. For what I'm payin', they better not be bothering ya."

Will nodded emphatically. He had so much to learn. It was hard to stomach, so Frank chuckled instead.

"Don't keep me in suspense, kid."

"Got us an in at the naval station." Barkley leaned across the desk. "Direct access."

"Direct, huh?" Frank folded his hands on the mahogany. "Tell me more."

CHAPTER 47

Hugh gave the cabby an extra dollar. It smelled of snow all day, and he wanted to make sure the heat was blasting when Shannon got in. "Keep it running," he instructed, exiting the vehicle.

"You got it."

His insides vibrating, Hugh bit down on a grin and knocked on the boardinghouse door, shoving his sweaty palms in his jacket when Marian answered.

"Mrs. Rossini," he nodded as she showed him in.

"Wait until you see her," his companion beamed. "My Josephina crowned the May Queen, and not even she looked so beautiful."

Marian jutted her chin at the stairwell, the thumping he heard confirming she'd sent one of her brood to fetch his date. The muscles in Hugh's legs twitched, something he hadn't experienced since he'd first stepped foot on the field for the Crimson. His mouth was suddenly dry, breath coming in short, quick spurts, and he wasn't quite sure where to look.

The petite brunette placed a gentle hand on his shoulder. "She's nervous, too."

Hugh snorted. "I don't know whatcha mean."

"Funny." Marian arched a brow. "She said the same thing."

At the click-clack of heels, Hugh felt a bit weak. Though glad for the full flask in his inner pocket, he regretted not taking a swig on the way over. A white-gloved hand appeared on the railing, and his pulse raced as the rest of her came into view.

Shannon looked like a goddess. Lips parted, he did nothing but stare. The midnight blue of her gown brought out flecks in her eyes he'd never noticed before. Tonight, they sparkled brighter than all the diamonds in Mother's vault put together.

"Hugh," she curtsied upon reaching the bottom of the stairwell.

"Shannon," he managed, cotton-mouthed. "You look…"

Giggling, Shannon twirled, patting her up-do. Her long blonde locks were secured in an elegant array of curls. A braided crown adorned the front, just beyond her hairline, a few soft tendrils accentuating her luminous face. Piled high like that, Hugh's eyes were drawn to her long, swan neck, and he felt that familiar pressure building inside him, a fervent need to touch and explore every inch of her. He imagined it loose, all those curls cascading down her bare back; his hands entangled as he carefully, *deliberately*, showed her just how much she was admired.

"You like it?" she asked, playfully grabbing her neighbor's hand. "Marian did it."

"Exquisite," he grinned. To Mrs. Rossini, he added, "What other talents are you keeping from us?"

Marian waved a hand as she walked back to the stairs. "Enjoy yourselves. And *Buon Anno!*"

The biting wind that greeted them outside wasn't in such good spirits. Mother may be cunning at times, but his finding the sable muff Christmas Eve was nothing short of serendipitous. An arctic blast whipped off the ocean, the kind of cold that made one's teeth hurt. Hugh opened the cab door, and Shannon held her skirt as she slid in. Soon they were huddled close as the small car pulled out onto Perry Street.

"So," he said softly.

"So," Shannon whispered with a slight flush of the cheek. Dipping her head, she looked out the window and didn't utter another single word the rest of the way.

The Iron Pier loomed bright over the frothy ocean. One look at the threatening clouds, and it was evident Mother Nature and Father Time had their own rendezvous planned.

"You think it'll snow?" Shannon mused as Hugh paid the cab driver. "Sure looks like it."

A wistful smile spread across her face. "I hope it does. It's magical, don't you think? I've always thought so, anyway."

Snow wasn't the only magical thing. This girl had bewitched him.

"I hope so, too," Hugh heard himself echo.

Hooking her arm, he led them up the stairs.

Though scaled back on account of the war, the ladies at the auxiliary managed to pull off an incredible array. Mother had given him explicit instructions to make mental notes of every scrupulous detail for the committees she oversaw in Philadelphia. Even miles away, he could still hear her shrill. *We simply can't be outdone, darling. Do I make myself clear?*

She'd be impressed. Round tables covered in ivory and gold damask were scattered in a U shape around the dancefloor, where a small ensemble was warming up. Instead of fresh flowers, they were topped in simple wreaths of greenery, columns, and tapers intermingling to cast a soft glow. The menu was limited, of course. Hugh had already taken the liberty of ordering their entrees of roast duck and chicken cordon bleu (and reported them to the Philadelphia caucus accordingly) when he accepted his invitation.

The only thing missing was the punch. What was New Year's without the bubbly? That was where the flask came in. And Hugh knew every other officer probably had one in their own jackets. Maybe even some of the girls. From what he remembered of Harvard, it was surprising what a garter or two could hold.

Those days seemed a lifetime ago. Looking at Shannon, Hugh had no regrets about his circumstances. He'd grown since then. Settled down. This was exactly where he was meant to be. A lucky man, he was proud to introduce her to his brethren.

Hugh spotted his roommate amongst a small group, and the pair strode over to say hello. A year or two older than himself, Charles Dutton had gone into the Navy right after high school, quickly working his way up the ranks. "Charles," he grinned as they approached.

"Hugh," the redhead replied, his freckled cheeks smiling widely in turn.

The conversation came easy; war and whisky, summaries of everyone's holidays. A few fellas offered mock resolutions to which their lady friends laughed and smiled as ladies often did. All but one. Arms at her sides, Shannon gripped the muff in one hand and periodically smoothed her skirt with the other. A closer look revealed her knuckles were almost as white as the fur. Hugh was trying to think of something clever to bring her into the fray when another couple joined their set.

"Gentlemen," piped the strong baritone of Tom Exton. He was a Main Line blue blood and one of Hugh's former teammates.

"Tom," Hugh shook his hand. "Good to see you, old friend. When did you join our cause?"

"Been here since September."

"Really?"

The blonde nodded. "Stuck in an office all day. You know how that goes."

Hugh cocked his head. "Can't say I do." He shoved his hands in his pockets. "Mostly out on the water myself."

"Does Cornelia know?" burst Exton's date. Petite with black hair and gray eyes, Hugh didn't recognize her. Nor did he care for her over-familiarity.

"Pardon?"

"Maddie," Tom playfully reproached. "Madeleine Darcy, Hugh Callaway."

"Shannon Culligan," Hugh was quick to add.

"Miss Culligan." Exton bowed, and Shannon offered a demure smile in response. "Maddie attended prep school with Cornelia."

"We *had* planned on rooming at Radcliffe together. But, with the engagement," she flashed her left hand, "there's really no need for schooling. And, *of course*, she stayed home, too."

"Congratulations," Hugh said.

"Yes, well," she sneered, looking his date top to bottom. "Bryn Mawr?"

Shannon ran her hand along her skirt again. "No."

Hugh puffed his chest. "Shannon works."

"Yeah," Charles added with equal pride. "Her cooking's almost as good as Ma's."

"I see," Madeleine chirped. "A sous chef. How impressive for someone so young."

"Oh no," Dutton corrected her. "Shannon's over at the barracks."

"The barracks?"

There was no need for clarification. Redundant questioning was one of Mother's favorite tactics, too. If she were a man, Hugh would've decked her. There was no shame in what Shannon did for a living. She worked hard, too hard for his liking, and practically gave most of it away.

"Excuse me," Shannon half-whispered. "I need to powder my nose."

She walked a little more quickly than Hugh cared to admit toward the facilities. He didn't want to further embarrass her by giving chase, but he also couldn't let Madeleine's viciousness go unacknowledged. Counting to sixty in his head, Hugh excused himself as well.

He lit a cigarette while waiting outside the hallway. Shannon returned about five minutes later, the puffiness under her eyes telling him all he needed to know.

"Ignore her," he urged, crushing the butt under his shoe.

"Easy for you to say."

The words cut, but she was absolutely right. That's what hurt the most. Shannon folded her arms against herself. "Who's Cornelia?"

"My stepsister. Soon-to-be, anyway."

"You never mentioned her."

Hugh chewed the inside of his cheek. "There's nothing to say."

"That's not how it sounded, Hugh."

"You're right," he acknowledged. "I'm sorry."

"I don't want your apology. You didn't do anything wrong." She sighed, narrowing her eyes. "If anything, I'm more upset with myself. I don't belong here. Should never have come in the first place."

"Don't say that."

"Why not? It's true."

The lights dimmed, and the band began to play. They should be dancing right now. In all the nights Hugh laid awake thinking about tonight, they were dancing, his arm on her tiny waist. She'd held her skirt off to the side, her eyes never leaving his as they glided about the room. This was all wrong.

"Want me to take you home?"

"And give her the satisfaction? Never!"

"What do you need, Shannon?" He wanted to reach out to her, to pull her close and block out the rest of the world, but the fierceness in her eyes held him back. "How can I fix this?"

"Fix it? I don't need fixing, Hugh."

"I didn't mean it like that...."

Shannon held up her hand, edging her way past him. She jutted her chin at the back balcony. "I need some air."

"Here," Hugh slipped out of his waistcoat and silently hung it over her shoulders. Even in fur and velvet, the temperature was so low it hurt to breathe.

Unable to bear watching her walk away, Hugh squeezed his eyes shut.

A few minutes later, he rejoined his friends but found himself speaking in broken sentences, sometimes entirely losing the thread of conversations altogether. His arms were heavy, shoulders; painfully tight. But it paled in comparison to the agony Shannon must've been feeling.

Fifteen minutes went by. Twenty. People began taking their seats as the staff served the first course. Bisque would do Shannon some good, Hugh told himself as he walked toward the French doors leading to the balcony. Warm her up. But it was up to him to warm her heart.

Shannon leaned on the railing, the Atlantic an endless void below. The surf was angry, too, sea and sky locked in fierce rivalry as the storm clouds churned.

"Prolly gonna get that snow you wanted," he said, cautious in his approach from behind so as to not frighten her.

"Hmm?"

"The snow," Hugh repeated as he joined her side. "Definitely cold enough for it."

"I don't feel anything." Eyes on the water, Shannon's voice sounded strange.

"Shannon, I know you're upset but look at me. Please? At least give me that."

She slid around, resting her elbows on the banister. "This better?"

Hugh could already smell the liquor on her breath and raked a hand through his hair. The flask. The goddamn flask. How could he have forgotten it was in his pocket?

"Where is it?" he asked, his hand extended.

She chuckled. "Where's what?"

"I think you know."

Shannon reached into the coat. "Oh, you mean this?" She laughed again, holding up the flask and giving it a jiggle.

"May I please have that back?"

"Take it." She thrust the vial in front of her. "S'no good empty."

"Empty?" Hugh grabbed it and turned it upside down, confirming the container was, indeed, completely drained. "Christ," he muttered.

"Oops."

"Forget it. Let's just get you home."

He reached for her, but she shrugged him off.

"Wouldn't want to embarrass you again in front of your *precious friends.*" She spat out the last two words with enough venom to take down an elephant.

"You could never," his own voice trembled.

Shannon took a step to face him and tripped over her other foot. Hugh caught her at the waist, and she locked her hands around his neck.

"No?" Tilting her back, she closed her eyes. "Prove it. Kiss me."

Hugh swallowed hard. He did want to kiss her. Hold her. Love her. But not like this.

"I'm waaaaiting," Shannon sang.

Hugh traced the back of his hand down her cheek. "I can't," he whispered, the knot in his stomach tightening.

She shoved him. "Why?"

"Please calm down."

"Why, huh?" Face red, she balled her fists at her side. "*What's wrong with me?*"

"You're drunk, Shannon. You don't know what you're saying."

"I know, alright." She glared. "I'm not an idiot, Hugh. I see the way you look at me. But I'm not some porcelain doll either." Her speech was slow, every syllable an exaggerated slur, and the veins in her neck throbbed. "You can't just dress me up and put me back on the shelf whenever it's convenient."

Hugh drew his eyebrows together. He leaned closer, trying his best to keep his voice soft and level. "Shannon, I care about you. I do. I have for a long time." He tilted his head, cognizant that not even the Puppy Face could save him now. "I'm not good at this. Feelings," he rang his hands.

"Expressing them. God, I wish I'd told you before. You have no idea how many times I've tried."

"You shoulda tried harder." She stamped her foot, angry tears streaking down her flushed cheeks. "I *hate* you! I never want to see you again. I hope your ship hits a mine. Or gets torpedoed. I hope...I hope..."

Shannon gulped for air. Shoulders rolling, she curled further into herself with each sob. Hugh pulled her close again, cradled like a child. He pet the curls he'd fantasized about the whole ride over. They were just as soft as he imagined, and she leaned into the touch, burying her face in his chest. His mind flew back to that night with her father. Oh, how he'd wanted to comfort her then, too, and he rubbed her back as he'd seen Danny do. After a few minutes, Hugh felt her breathing regulate, her small frame stiff in his arms. They walked in silence out the back exit and hailed a curbside cab.

She started to rouse close to dawn. A groan at first. Followed by the imminent gurgle. Mixing bowl in one hand, Hugh held her hair back with the other. Shannon coughed and spat, wiping her mouth with her knuckles as he placed the basin on the floor beside him. He gave her a glass of water, both hands shaking as she lifted it to her lips.

"Don't gulp," he cautioned. "It'll make it worse, trust me."

Shannon avoided his eyes but heeded the warning. She looked around her room, then down at her bare arms, scrambling to cover herself with the sheet. Mouth agape, she took him in from the ground up, her face a mixture of shame and astonishment when their eyes finally met.

"I don't..." she panted. "I don't remember...."

"We didn't."

"Oh."

"Corset was cutting into you. I slept on the floor."

She hung her head. "Sorry you had to see me like that."

"I've been where you are." Hugh felt his Adam's apple bob. "I'm sorry, too. I shouldn't be here. I just…"

There'd been a pledge in Cambridge. Not his year, or anyone else's that the team could remember, but Coach shared the story before every home game nevertheless. Midwest kid. New money and a strong arm. Found dead in the basement after a rush party. Flat on his back, he'd choked on his bile.

Bringing Shannon to the base was out of the question. Charles was a decent man, but the same couldn't be said of the wagging tongues on his floor. Still, she was a young woman who lived alone; family connection or not, there was no reasonable explanation that wouldn't compromise her reputation should he be seen on his way out.

"Your floor only has one water closet," Hugh mumbled, fixing his stare on the bowl. Her kitten sniffed it, lifting a paw and fanning his whiskers before hopping up on the bed. "I didn't want to leave you alone."

Shannon stroked the cat, her face just as ghostly white.

"Can I get you anything? Some toast perhaps?"

"No thank you." She picked a thumbnail, eyes watering over.

Hugh rose from his seat. He brought the bowl to the kitchen, rinsed it out, and then placed it on her side table.

Shoes in hand, he nodded toward the door. "Better get goin' while it's still somewhat dark."

"Right," she croaked.

January 1st, 1918. Day number one, and it was already the worst year of his life.

CHAPTER 48

J ennie stretched, gingerly kneading the small of her back with one hand while petting her extended stomach with the other. The baby was dancing again. Yet another activity Jennie found herself missing more than she ever thought she would.

She rang Cook for a glass of water, attempting to return to the book she was reading but couldn't concentrate at all. She never felt more uncomfortable in her life, sleep evading her night after night. Still, it prepared her for the little one's arrival and paled in comparison to anything her husband faced at the moment. Sighing, she looked wistfully at the bouquet Danny sent for Valentine's Day. The roses were wilting away a week later, but she refused to part with them. Not yet, anyway. Maybe tomorrow.

It was snowing again, so she waddled over to the window. The yard below was already covered from last week's storm, and she wondered how long it would take her aunt to return home from work this time.

Wilson's war machine was indiscriminate, stealing men from families all across the board with few exemptions. But it didn't end there. He also took mothers, wives, sisters, and daughters. After all, who else was left to carry the burden?

Philadelphia was no different, and women took up the cross all over the city. Be it clerical or manufacturing, they worked by the hundreds. The *Inquirer* touted production numbers in textile and clothing alone were the highest they'd ever been to meet the military's ever-growing demands.

On top of it, new civic groups popped up almost every other week. There was the Red Cross, of course, but Jennie read articles about the Women's Land Army and the Women's Battalion of Lit Brothers Department Store. The level of organization; the steadfast commitment of her sisters was amazing.

The Browne women proudly volunteered at the National League for Women's Service. It mainly consisted of various patriotic activities and assisting the Red Cross, but Jennie relished her time there. Not only did she secretly like the comfort of her dark blue uniform and sailor hat, but she enjoyed the conversations and bonding while they put together the comfort kits to be shipped overseas. But then she'd inevitably envision Danny receiving one of his own and excuse herself for a good cry.

With her lying in rapidly approaching, her aunt toed the line for both of them. Though she knew the other woman would never admit it, Jennie suspected she actually enjoyed the freedom of taking the El to and from the small office.

War effort aside, the calling cards stopped coming sometime in autumn. Whether a result of her own marriage or the end of Gertrude's, Jennie wasn't sure though she suspected a combination of both. Then, just as suddenly, they couldn't get reservations at the Bellevue for their weekly lunch. If a table were available, it was in a corner or hidden behind a column.

It was just as well. Jennie was aware this would happen. She hadn't cared about her social standing on her wedding day, and she scolded herself for mourning its demise now. The truth of it was pregnancy did not suit her, and she was horribly bored. Part of her envied those working women, at least they had a sense of purpose. With her father and aunt out, she had no one to talk to aside from Samuel, and he was only a child.

The boy's declining health kept him home from boarding school. Her aunt arranged for a private tutor, and he usually retired to his room after his daily lessons. Stamina-wise, he was unable to handle more.

Jennie checked in on him periodically, coaxing him out of whatever book he was enthralled in for a game of chess or her audience in the music room. But, like clockwork, his pallor would fade within an hour, and she'd see him back upstairs again. Worrying for him only made her feel more depressed.

There were far worse things in life than being alone in a mansion. Intellectually, she knew this but telling it to her heart was another story. She longed for the days of her carefree youth. Summers on the island. Barefoot on the beach, collecting shells while the warm sun caressed her cheeks. She could almost feel the delightful texture of the sand—spongey at the waterline, firmer a few feet up, soft as a blanket the closer one got to the dunes. Jennie closed her eyes, inhaling deeply through her nose, but it didn't help. Nothing did.

If only she had someone to talk to. A part of her wished Shannon would've stayed after the holidays. Hugh was head-over-heels, and even Gertrude seemed to genuinely approve. How lovely it would be if their children grew up together. Jennie glanced back out the window. In her mind's eye, they were already there—two little snow angels, clamoring all over the yard and pestering the servants for carrots and coal.

Cook appeared with her water and a small plate of crackers to nibble on. Jennie welcomed the distraction from her melancholy.

"Has the post been delivered?"

"Not yet, Ma'am. No doubt on account of the weather. I'll see to it you have it straight away. Will 'ye be needing anything else?"

Jennie opened her mouth to say no but acknowledged to herself that what she really needed was company. "Yes," she looked at the chair opposite her own. "Please sit."

"I beg your pardon, Mrs. Culligan?"

She offered a reassuring smile. "There's no trouble, Cook. I was just wondering if you had a moment to talk."

The servant sat down as told, her face wrought with confusion. "About what, Ma'am?"

"Oh, anything."

"A wee bit lonely?"

Jennie nodded. "Yes, I suppose I am."

"A lot on your mind. Mr. Culligan. The wee one."

"Exactly."

"T'will all work out in the end. The good Lord, He has a plan for all of us."

"You think the war is part of His plan?"

"I trust Him, if that's what you're askin'. Hasn't failed me yet. Nor you, if you don't mind me sayin' so."

"Of course. How right you are." Jennie gave a half-hearted shrug before resting a hand on her lap. "How right you are, indeed."

CHAPTER 49

Cape May Section Base No. 9
February 23, 1918

Dear Danny,
The enemy is gunning for anything coming in or out of the Delaware. I know this is what I signed up for. I fear not for myself but the safety of my men, many of whom have families...

Hugh crumpled the letter and covered his head in his hands. What the hell was he thinking? Like Danny didn't already have enough to worry about. Only weeks before, the Americans lost their first troopship, the *Tuscania*, to an enemy sub off the coast of Northern Ireland. Two hundred soldiers and crew. Gone. It was all over the press. If Jennie were fragile at Christmas, he could only guess as to how his cousin must be feeling now.

He couldn't believe his stupidity. There were spies everywhere. All military mail was being censored, and what did he do? Outright named the opponent right in the first line, that's what he did. His old literature professor would have a fit, not to mention what his superior officer would do to him. Hugh lit another Chesterfield and sucked in a long drag. He needed to be more careful.

Wilson's new Sedition Act carried stiff prison terms for anyone speaking or acting out against the war. The press warned daily how every German or Austrian in the country would be treated as a spy. The bar association went even further in Illinois, labeling attorneys defending draft resisters as unpatriotic or unprofessional. While Hugh might think the men cowards, he wasn't sure he'd go that far. Weren't there still two sides to every story? Hell, even John Adams defended the British officers following the Boston Massacre.

Of course, he knew better than to open his mouth about it on account of the American Vigilance Patrol. Citizen agents, they reported their own neighbors for the slightest infractions, though hoarding food and slacking seemed to be the most popular from what he could tell. Hugh was proud to serve his country, but he resented Wilson's iron will that the people bend to his every whim. That was tyranny, not the democracy they were fighting so hard to protect Over There.

Hugh tipped his ash and set the cigarette in the tray to his right. He feared for Jennie's safety in the city and Mother's by extension. He was even glad his cousin was housebound, however temporarily. The papers had taken to burning the Kaiser in effigy.

On the other hand, Uncle remained unperturbed and still went about his business the same as he'd always done. He doubled down on displays of patriotism, making a show of investing in large quantities of Liberty Bonds. According to Mother, Walter was also in negotiations with several other members of the Cottager's Association to host another 4th of July parade, the biggest one the cape ever saw.

As for Shannon, well, that was an entirely different kind of anguish. He'd sent the obligatory flowers by the dozen. Cards. Candies. He saw her practically every day at the mess, but she avoided all eye contact if she could help it. Conversation, too, uttering only what was required of her before moving on to the next seaman in line. Every time was like a knife to the heart. Pain so hot and raw the tray shook in his hands when he walked to his table; the food sawdust in his mouth.

Hugh didn't know what to do anymore. If his eating habits were poor, his sleeping was worse, awakening like clockwork shortly after the witching hour and wondering if she were alright, hoping she was thinking of him, too.

Maybe they were fated to live separate lives, after all. Or maybe, he thought, eyeing the blank sheet of paper before him, there was one person who just might be able to get through to her.

CHAPTER 50

Head cocked to the side, Danny sat back in his chair and reread Hugh's letter. Her armor up, one would never guess how vulnerable Shannon was on the inside. But he knew, his heart heavy in his chest.

They were wired the same, and her demons were just as bad as his. Chaos had been their norm for so long it was easier to just embrace it. And so they did, craving the discomfort the way others craved sweets; a thick wool sweater in the middle of July. He thought of involving himself—she'd listen to him before anyone else—but honestly hadn't the time.

Danny bit his lip in regret. The list of his regimental responsibilities grew longer each day. He huffed, staring up at the leaky roof. Hastily slapped together like practically every other Army camp, the building still miraculously stood after the harsh winter. Someway, somehow, most of his men survived the cold as well. Bunks crammed floor to ceiling; they huddled around a single barrel of fire for warmth every night until lights out. With little more than cotton blankets, Danny was grateful for the socks the women in his life knit him for Christmas. Some of the fellas weren't so lucky.

Though their marksmanship steadily improved, Danny held the private opinion the brutal Mid-Atlantic weather did more to prepare his men than any of the drills he oversaw. He glanced at the reports coming in from overseas. The mud was thick, knee-deep in some places along the Western Front. Stay on the duckboard, boy, or you'll be sorry; trench foot, dysentery, lice. To say nothing of the rodent infestation. He almost couldn't believe some of the things he read— rats everywhere, some as large as housecats.

After the spring thaw, they were moving onto bayonet training. Plans were already in place for his men to dig mock trenches for hand-to-hand combat. Danny frowned. He'd certainly earned his stripes in that department.

He was about to turn in for the night when a private rushed into the bunk.

"Sergeant Culligan," he saluted. "Telegram for you."

Danny's fingers trembled as he accepted it with bated breath.

"Sir?" asked the boy, awaiting his dismissal.

Danny looked up at him with a grin and a tear in his eye. Both mother and daughter were well and resting. *Daughter.* A girl! They had a girl.

"Molly," he croaked, but the private merely blinked in confusion. "That was my mother's name."

CHAPTER 51

"Take good care of her," Joseph winked.

He gave the valet a hefty tip, gently caressing the Marmon's driver's-side door one last time before stepping onto the cobblestone street. The stench caught him off guard, and he groaned internally. Philadelphia had a distinct smell, and it wasn't pleasant.

Unlike his beloved New York, where the poor were rightfully kept hidden in multistoried tenements, the City of Brotherly Love had a love affair with its working-class. These people had two-story *homes*. Each one connected to its neighbor, they stretched for miles from one end of town to the other.

Row after row after row. A city of neighborhoods, all made up of different immigrant groups who mostly preferred to keep to their own kind. Eastern European Jews, Irish, Italians, Poles, and Germans. A church on every other corner. Whether it was language or culture that bound them together, Joseph didn't care. Their presence alone was a living, breathing insult to everything his family strove so hard to protect for generations, and he despised each and every one of them.

The rabble dressed up in women's clothing every New Year. Inebriated, they'd parade up Broad Street to City Hall, leaving their filthy offspring to shoot marbles out on their front stoops.

Many still favored the horse yet failed to clean up after the animals. Curbside carts lined the streets; wagons carrying everything from produce to chicken to Italian meats and cheeses. In dialects thick as the garlic on their breath, the shoppers rejoiced in the allure of some semblance of the old country. *If only they'd stayed there.*

It was enough to turn his stomach. Waste mixing with the exhaust of automobiles and trolleys. At least he didn't have far to walk. Located at 13th and Walnut, the Philadelphia Club stood just catty-corner across the street.

One would never guess it was the oldest club in the United States by the building itself. The red brick was simple in design. Three stories high, it had green awnings on every window to provide the privacy its elitist clientele paid top dollar for. Men with names like du Pont and Biddle, although somehow William Vare and his cronies weaseled their way in. Greasing palms, no doubt. *Just like his construction contracts and runs for office.* Even Walter Martin held a membership, though not for much longer if he had anything to say about it.

Billiards, card rooms, smoking rooms, and dining rooms—the club offered a lavish respite from the grit outside. Richly furnished with no expense spared, each space epitomized its members' masculine and dominant status. Furness himself oversaw a renovation in the late 80s, and Theodore Roosevelt Jr. donated a collection of prized mounts. They were American Royalty. Masters of the universe. And this was their castle.

Joseph took the stairs to the bar on the second floor.

"Another round on me, Johnny," he overheard while checking his coat.

He grinned and slid his tongue over his teeth. Having courted Jennie as long as he did, he'd know that accent anywhere.

"Congratulations, Martin," another man was saying. "I'm sure she's beautiful."

"Thank you, Ned," Walter replied. "But, now don't tell my Jennie, she's even prettier. Never saw eyes so blue in my life!"

Ned. Joseph stiffened. No one referred to Stotesbury by his nickname. Not to his face anyway. He was so perturbed that it never occurred to him what they might be talking about until a waiter appeared to offer him a Robusto.

"Courtesy of Mr. Martin. To celebrate the new baby."

His nostrils flared as he accepted the token and stormed to a darkened corner in the back. Sliding the cigar into the breast pocket of his coat, Joseph sank into one of the leather chairs. Like most of the Republicans in the room, while he hadn't voted for Wilson, he'd come to appreciate some of the President's measures to return the country's balance of power to where it rightfully belonged—in the hands of the wealthy and the white.

All he had to do now was wait and listen. Martin would trip up eventually. And when he did? Joseph sneered and patted his coat pocket. *I'll save you for later.*

CHAPTER 52

Shannon carefully unscrewed the brass bed knob. It squeaked, waking Snowball from his nap. He'd grown more cat-like in their five short months together. Torso, legs and tail elongated, he now took up the foot of her bed when stretched out. She shot a cautious glance at her rooming house door and made a mental note to grease it with lard next time, she'd worked too hard for the precious contents stuffed inside the post. Thanks to her arrangement with Will, it was almost filled to the top. She smiled, pulling out a few dollars to put in her shoe before securing the knob back in place.

The Juniper Grove clan were returning for the season in a few weeks, and Shannon couldn't wait to meet little Molly. Jennie wrote her and Hugh separately, asking them to be godparents. Though raised Catholic and quite unsure if she believed in anything these days, Shannon couldn't say no to the Episcopalian ceremony. She was Danny's child. Her only connection to the beloved brother she may never see again. Shannon could transfer that love to the baby. Give Molly anything her little heart desired, just as she knew he would.

It would be odd, painful even, seeing Hugh again outside the barracks. Having to converse amongst the rest of the family. To be civil. Friendly.

Shannon tried not to think it. He was sorry, she knew. He'd apologized profusely. For what she still wasn't entirely sure, that awful night was a blur even months later. All she knew was he'd gotten too close. Again. It was too much for her risk. The bond needed to be severed, and that was that.

Finished pinning her hair back, she left early for her shift to window-shop along Washington Street. *What to get Molly?* A spoon or silver hairbrush. Perhaps a blanket. It was nice having the means to indulge. How she earned it wasn't anyone else's business as far as she was concerned.

She did her part, spreading the word among the men or helping unload crates from a *certain* farm truck, the bottles of golden hooch piled under the Barkley's winter crop ready and waiting for distribution. Still, on some level, it bothered her that everything went through Will. Communication, inventory, payment. Almost as if she didn't exist.

Shannon was still stewing about it when she clocked in. She looked over the lunch schedule, stopping halfway down the list. *1130— Yeoman (F).* That was a new one. She tied her apron on, soon forgetting all about it, the usual idle chit-chat during vegetable preparation taking precedence.

The morning flew by, and Shannon took her place on the serving line. She ladled out spoonful after spoonful, speaking in code all the while.

"Smells delicious, darlin'," grinned one of her regulars.

"Only the best for you, Bert." She winked. "Fresh off the farm. Gotta take good care of you boys."

"And that you do," Bert said nonchalantly and moved along.

Eleven thirty rolled around, and a hush went over the crowd. In walked a group of women officers. The place was so silent you could hear a pin drop. Shannon almost couldn't believe her eyes. Then she remembered the schedule from earlier- the "F" suddenly making sense. Female.

"I went to high school with her," hissed the girl beside her with a glare. She nodded to the redhead out in front. "Must be nice. Not smellin' like onions all the time. Of course, considering who her father is…" she patted her pocket as if it were full.

"Edith, don't you think you're being a bit harsh?" If these were the kind of remarks Molly would be subjected to, Shannon would need to start filling all four bed-posts now just to save for bail money.

The other woman shook her head. "Mayor of Wildwood, Commodore of the Holly Beach Yacht Club, a state senator. No doubt Daddy's little girl bought that brass."

By now, the women had their trays and worked their way down the line.

"Edith Smith?" smiled the redhead.

A false, toothy grin. "Joy Bright."

"Nice to see a familiar face," Joy said.

"I'll bet," the other woman lied. "I see you've been busy since graduation."

Joy gestured to their surroundings, now back to their usual humming. "Haven't we all?"

Edith shrugged in agreement.

"Don't be so modest, Joy," chimed the girl behind her. "I mean, *Chief* Yeoman," she corrected herself.

"I'm doing my part. No different than these fine ladies, Nancy." She proceeded along, leading the group to a table in the center of the mess hall.

Shannon was all ears as she bussed the surrounding area. It sounded like some of the girls went to business school together. From what she could gather, Chief Bright worked her way up. That she ranked higher than some of the reservists in the room clearly made some of the men uncomfortable.

"Just a skirt who thinks she's better than everyone," one sneered on his way to the trash can.

Joy let the comment go, holding her head high.

"You're right to ignore him," Nancy said pertly. "All those months as a courier up in Camden? You earned this, Joy."

The other woman nodded while Shannon scrubbed furiously at an imaginary spot on the table so she could hear more.

"What he thinks isn't important. I've known men like that my entire life. They chided my father for allowing me to mow the grass or empty the ashes. My grandfather Bright," she smiled at the memory, "he lived with us. Taught me all about tools, painting. Used to time me on how fast I could fix a flat on the Hupmobile."

"Sounds glamorous," said a brunette on her right.

Joy shrugged. "My father's always been a bit unconventional, I suppose. Unofficially deputized Mother when he was sheriff. Raised me and my sisters under the notion that girls could perform the same work just as well as our brothers."

"And, I, for one," Nancy raised a salute, "am glad he did."

Shannon was still thinking about them later that afternoon while sweeping the kitchen. Where others might have cowered, Joy Bright stood her ground. That was a girl who knew her worth.

Meanwhile, a blister formed against her ankle bone from the money in her shoe. She laid the broom against the counter with a sigh, shifting her feet and recalling how she'd gone toe-to-toe with her own brother right up until he reported for duty when a thought struck her. Why hadn't the female Yeomen been scheduled to dine with the other officers?

Shannon grimaced, massaging her tender foot. *Because they were women.* Nostrils flared, she took out the bills, squeezing them tight in the palm of her hand. According to Will, the barracks alone made up a hefty percentage of their earnings. If the Boss was "pleased," he had a funny way of showing it. Not a single acknowledgment. The same measly cut as when she started out even though, thanks to her, the business had doubled. Because she was a woman, too.

"Going out for a smoke," Edith said, interrupting her thoughts.

"Butt me," Shannon replied and slipped the cash discretely up her sleeve.

They sat on the back steps, smoking in silence the way they usually did near the end of their shift, hands raw, bones achy, hair and skin exuding a thick musk of sweat, grease, and anything that might've spilled on them during the day. Too tired to even think, let alone speak.

"You never told me you were from Wildwood," Shannon said finally.

"You never asked."

"True." Shannon exhaled through the side of her mouth. "Don't happen to know who owns Consolidated Fisheries, do you?"

Edith took a quick puff. "Hilton family."

"Hilton?"

Shannon's mind flew back to that night at the train station. She could still see Frank's knowing smile when he dropped her off at Jackson's. Cigarette between her teeth, she looked down at her cuticles. It couldn't be the same family, could it? What were the chances? Then again, the name was common enough. She might've easily seen it on any number of uniforms at the mess.

"Must be old home week," Edith mused. "Old Gus is in the yacht club, too."

Old.

"Oh," Shannon murmured. Disappointed, she picked at a hangnail.

Edith stubbed her cigarette out on the step, tossing the butt in the side yard. "Heard from your Lieutenant Callaway lately?"

"Edith," Shannon bumped her shoulder, "how many times I gotta tell ya? He's not *my* Lieutenant."

"Does he know that?" Her friend raised a playful brow. "Sure looks mighty handsome in that uniform of his." Giggling, she put her hands over her heart. "God bless America."

Arms akimbo, Shannon rolled her eyes.

"What?" Edith replied, feigning mock innocence. "It's my patriotic duty. Some of us actually like the idea of settling down, y'know."

"You've got it all wrong. We grew up together. My brother married his cousin. He's just looking out for me while Danny's away."

"Whatever you say, Juliet."

They heard the clanging of pots and pans from inside. Shannon took one last drag and crushed the butt under her heel. "C'mon," she nodded at the door. "Better help Lucy with those."

◆⟶◉⟵◆

The boutique on Washington Street was closed when Shannon got there an hour later. She frowned at the shabby image staring back in the window's reflection. The neon lights of the pharmacy flicked on behind her. Mr. Kennedy always brought a smile to her face. So did his candy counter.

Shannon fingered at the cash, burning a hole in her sleeve. "*No*," she told herself, but the idea had already taken hold. It was risky, but it just might work.

Twenty minutes later, she was knocking quietly on the Rossini's door. The eldest girl cracked it open.

"Is your mother in, Josephina?"

The girl nodded and undid the chain. A heavenly aroma wafted from the kitchen. *Perfect timing.*

"Shannon," Marian smiled. She pulled a pan from the oven and set it atop the stove. "Care to join us?"

"Oh, I couldn't impose." She held out the brown paper bag from Kennedy's. "Just a little something for the children."

"What is it, Mama?" squealed one of the boys.

Marian peeked inside. "You shouldn't have," she said of the oodles of sweets.

"All those Sunday suppers?" Shannon started. "This," she gestured at the place setting Josephina just added on her behalf. *So far, so good.* "It's the least I could do."

The other woman waved her hand as if it were nothing. "Wash up!" she called to the children. "And you," Marian added, still using her stern mother tone, "sit. You need to eat more."

Shannon smiled, neatly placing her napkin on her lap. "It smells delicious."

"Eggplant Parmigiana." The last word rolled elegantly off her tongue.

The kids piled in, and they all bowed their heads. Marian did the blessing, and Shannon passed around the breadbasket. A mere ten minutes later and there was hardly any left for Pat.

Shannon rose to clear the table, but her hostess stopped her.

"Theresa, your turn for the dishes," she barked. "Boys, take the trash and milk crate down. And grab Miss Culligan's too. Josephina, homework."

"You run a tight ship."

Marian cocked her head. "The responsibility. It's good for them."

"Gives you a break, too, I imagine." Shannon shot a glance in the corner. There. Just as she remembered. "Speaking of breaks, why don't you let me take care of that laundry for you?"

Hesitant, Marian glimpsed at the overflowing hamper.

"I was planning on doing my own washing tomorrow morning anyway. Really, it's no trouble."

The other woman bit her lip in consideration.

"Marian," Shannon said softly, "it's *me*. Pat's not here and the kids are occupied. You don't have to pretend." She reached across the table, giving her hand a gentle squeeze. "I know how many times you're up with the baby. You must be exhausted. Give yourself a rest, huh?"

"Alright. But just this once."

"It's settled. You're keeping all the earnings, too." With a triumphant smile, Shannon pointed her index finger. "I won't hear otherwise. Not even a penny."

Enzo cooed from his bassinet. Marian swallowed the grateful lump in her throat and went to pick him up. Meanwhile, Shannon rose to get the hamper, covertly tucking one of Pat's caps under the lid while her neighbor's back was turned.

"We're so lucky to have a friend like you,' Marian said. Cradling the baby in one arm, she opened the door with the other.

"I'm the lucky one."

Shannon lugged the basket across the corridor, where Snowball greeted her affectionately. "Missed you too. Won't be home too long, though."

She gave him some vittles along with a pat between the ears and began rummaging through the clothes. Out came a shirt of Pat's along with a pair of boy's trousers. They looked a bit short, but the waistline would definitely fit her better.

Shannon sniffed the button-down. Not too bad. If anything, the lingering aftershave was helpful whereas her soap was lavender. She'd have to bind her breasts, of course, but a part of her relished the idea of going without her corset. Dreadful contraptions. Even the War Industries Board said not to buy them anymore.

Humming to herself in the mirror, she tried on the cap. A near-perfect fit. Shannon pinned the last of her hair up and threw a quick glance at the clock. Still plenty of time to make the next train. If Mr. Hilton wouldn't come to her, she'd just pay him a little visit herself.

CHAPTER 53

F rank was locking up the office when he felt something hard press between his shoulder blades. *Fuck*. Pop had been on him about a bodyguard for months, and he hated when the old man was right.

"Keep your mouth shut and don't move," hissed the voice behind him.

Packing his own heat, Frank did as he was told. No need for things to get messy. Not yet, anyway.

The moon was low in the sky as they marched toward the lane between the warehouse and the icehouse. Rats scurried away from the tin trash cans lining the brick buildings, and a train whistled low in the distance.

"What's this about?" he asked.

"Did I say you could talk?"

They reached the dark alley, and the gunman kicked over a pile of empty crates.

"Sit down."

Frank turned one over with his foot but remained standing. Arms crossed against himself, he considered his options. This fella had alotta nerve. He was Frank Hilton, goddammit. His father practically built Anglesea. Fuming, he slid his right hand along the inside of his jacket until he reached the Colt.

"You deaf or somethin'? I said *sit down.*"

There was a pitch to the voice. The way it ebbed, nasal then scruffy. Almost sounded like the guy had a cold. Footsteps crunched on the shells as his assailant moved closer and Frank whipped around, his gun gleaming in what remained of the moonlight.

"I'll shoot," said the boy. "I swear I will."

The small .22 was no match for his own weapon. It was almost laughable.

"Go ahead, kid. I dare ya."

"I'm not a kid!" It came out an octave higher, and he gulped at the echo on the water.

A dame? Had to be by the way the clothes hung. This was too easy. Still, he felt a twinge of guilt. Moving slowly yet methodically, Frank placed the Colt on the ground and raised his hands in surrender.

"Alright, here's what you're gonna do," he said, keeping his tone diplomatic. "Gimme the gun and walk away." He cocked his head, "And I'll pretend none of this ever happened."

She glared, her blue eyes wild. Hypnotic, they were. Like he'd seen them somewhere before. Meanwhile, the little minx had the audacity to inch closer. He let her, waiting until she was just within reach before snatching the pistol and forcing her aim upward.

Frank squeezed her wrist, pushing her thumb back as far as he could. She let out a yelp as she lost her grip, and the gun landed with a clank. He pulled her tight and twisted her arm behind her back.

She was feisty, clawing at him with her free arm and stomping on his foot as she struggled to wriggle free. Grunting, he shoved her forward. She doubled over, her well-worn cap tumbling off to reveal a cascade of gold waves.

Her cover blown, he effortlessly drew her back around until they were face-to-face.

"Oh." A ghost of a smile played on his lips. "It's you."

"I gotta say, kid. Never thought I'd see you again." Frank poured a decent amount from the decanter and swirled his tumbler. "You want any?"

Seated opposite his desk, Shannon looked down at her lap. "No. Thank you."

He plopped in the leather wingback, a pointed look in his eyes. The sun was coming up. Golden beams broke through the blinds, glittering against the dust particles floating in the air— the only light in the office. Frank couldn't help but chuckle. *Of all the dames.*

"What's so funny?"

He traced a finger around the rim of his glass. "That brother of yours know what you're up to?"

She cast her eyes down.

Shit. He wasn't dead, was he?

"He's at boot camp."

Even worse. He'd be dead, soon enough. Though it did clarify her motives a bit.

Frank peered at the girl across from him. Still just as pretty as when they'd last met, there was an edge to her now. Her eyes were flinty. Impatient. Furious; tigers at a traveling circus, those magnificent beasts stalking from one end of their cage to the other, daring onlookers to get close—but not too close—to their wagon pen.

Though she referred to Barkley by his first name, Frank got the impression they weren't an item. Shannon's left hand bore no ring, and he found himself wondering where she'd procured her current attire. Filthy. His own cleaning lady didn't dress so shabby.

This was a woman in dire straits. Maybe her father was around, maybe he wasn't. From what Frank recalled, that lush didn't contribute much anyway.

There were other means for a girl in her situation to earn her keep, ways he was thankful she hadn't lowered herself to do. With so many sailors and soldiers on the cape, brothels took up a large portion of his distribution, and he found himself yearning to shelter her; take her away from whatever drove her to a life of crime. Hypocritical, yes, but this was *his* world, and it was dangerous. Spat out grown men like chewing tobacco. No place for a pretty little thing like her. He wanted to help her, just as he'd done before and lamented that she probably never even knew.

"What do you want, Shannon?"

"I told you, I only want what's owed to me."

Frank took a sip from his glass. "Not the money. I get that. How you gonna use it? What do you want for yourself?"

"No one's ever really asked me," she whispered.

"I'm askin'. What do you want?"

"I want…never mind." She shifted in her seat. "It's complicated. You wouldn't understand."

"Try me. You've come this far, kid. Might as well spill it." Frank leaned over the desk, careful to keep his voice soft. "What do you want?"

"Respect," she swallowed. "Freedom." Shannon's eyes met his with an intensity so bright they burned. "I want to be able to make my own choices. For people to look at me and *see me*, really see me. To listen when I speak. Value what I have to say."

"You're not gonna find that running hooch."

"Why?" She cupped her breasts. "Because of these?"

"Honestly? Yes." Her nostrils flared, but he continued anyway. "And you should know, carrying a gun makes no difference if you're not prepared to actually use it."

"Who says I'm not?" Shannon straightened her shoulders. "Maybe I've killed a man. What would you say to that?"

A thick silence hung in the air. Outside, the engines of the fleet roared to life, drowning out the call of gulls fighting for breakfast on the harbor.

She wasn't lying. Taking a life wasn't something anyone readily admitted. It was part of the job in his business, and those who acted were sworn to secrecy. Even the order was given in code.

Frank longed to reach for her. To press her body close against his own and tell her she'd never have to worry about anything—*anything*—ever again. But this wasn't the kind of woman who could be kept. If Shannon wanted comfort, she'd already have married. She wanted freedom; she'd said so herself. Respect, something he suspected few, if any, had ever shown her. That much he could give.

"I'd say you must've had a good reason."

Shannon looked at his half-empty glass. "I'll take that drink now."

The decanter needed a refill, too. Frank motioned her to wait and went to grab another bottle, silently counting the greenbacks in his pocket along the way. He poured her a decent amount and placed a thick wad of money next to it.

"We square?"

She placed a protective hand on the bills as if she were afraid he'd change his mind.

"You earned it. Barkley never gave you the full percentage. Makes me wonder what else he's ciphering. From now on, you deal with me directly. Keep doing what you're doing on the base and there's more where that came from."

White-knuckled, she tucked it in her bindings. "What's gonna happen to Will?"

"What do you think?"

"Don't hurt him."

The hint of concern in her voice bothered him. "He's a thief, Shannon. A liar. I can't let that slide."

"Forget I asked."

"Fair enough."

CHAPTER 54

H ugh was just finishing dinner when his superior officer tapped him
on the shoulder. He knew that stern look all too well, offering a
resolute nod in return and rising from his seat. Seconds later, the two men
were outside.

It was a bright June day, the sun kissing their faces as summer said
hello. Not a cloud in the sky, the harbor before them was calm. Inviting.
If not for the docked submarine chasers or the massive dirigible hangar to
their left, it almost seemed like there wasn't a war on.

But the other man seemed tense, his brow furrowed and lips thin as
they walked the grounds back to headquarters. It was a brisk pace, Hugh's
athletic build struggling to keep up without breaking into a jog while his
mind played out the possibilities.

Naval authorities received word last month of a German sub mining
ports in the Chesapeake just off Capes Henry and Charles. So far, the enemy
had fired at two British steamers in the shipping lanes, but no Americans
had directly been targeted.

In response, they upped their minesweeping efforts and flew more reconnaissance planes. Merchant ships were instructed to utilize blackout conditions at night. However, despite Hugh's recommendation, officials did not call for dim-outs on the shore communities as did their European counterparts.

"Captain?" He huffed as they reached the office.

"Assemble your men," his superior instructed. He handed Hugh some paperwork while continuing to brief him. "We received an SOS from a steamer, the *Carolina*. She's under attack by an enemy sub just off Barnegat." The Captain shook his head in frustration. "218 passengers. A crew of 117 and hold full of Puerto Rican sugar."

"Yes, sir."

Hugh stood on the bridge, eyes peeled on the horizon where thick clouds of dense smoke rose off the water. He wanted to close them. *We're too late.*

Barnegat was over seventy nautical miles from the base. They pushed the engines as hard as they could. Lit all the boilers, and it still wasn't enough. How many people were in the water right now because he hadn't gotten there in time? Black, frigid, North-Atlantic water. A year later, Samuel still hadn't fully recovered. *What a fucking disaster.* This was his mission, the failure his own, and he felt it more keenly than any other he'd known before. What was a loss to Yale compared to the loss of human life? He said a silent prayer for their souls when Pat tapped his shoulder.

"Lifeboats, sir," he panted. "Got a wire from a schooner. The *Eva B. Douglas*." Pat handed over the message. "Found 'em moored head to stern."

Hugh heaved a sigh of relief, immediately regretting it. He knew better than to show weakness, even if Rossini was a friend.

"Aye, sir." Pat agreed. "She's taking them back to inlet now."

"Good. Send a message back. We'll rendezvous at the lighthouse. If they rescued any crew, I'll have to interview them."

The *Eva* was a beaute, a worthy rival Hugh wished he'd encountered during those yacht club years. No doubt she would've given the *Crusader* a run for her money. It all seemed like a lifetime ago as he climbed the ladder to board.

"Lieutenant," her captain greeted him.

"Captain."

They walked to his cabin, where a few survivors were already waiting in the teak corridor. Wrapped in green felt blankets, they sat on the floor. One man met Hugh's eye as they passed. Gray, straggly hair plastered to his face, he cupped a tin mug.

"Tough old bird, she was," the man offered a practically toothless smile. "Her flags were flying as she went down."

"Everyone will have their chance to share their story, I assure you," Hugh replied.

What he really wanted to do was apologize.

The captain ushered in the first witness, a boy about a few years younger, his chestnut curls frizzy from the salt air, and the three of them sat down around a large, mahogany table. Hugh took out a small notepad and pencil. After obtaining the man's name and rank, he moved on to the pertinent details.

"Tell me everything you remember."

"Everything?"

"Everything."

"Well, sir...I mean Lieutenant...I mean..."

"Take your time."

Shoulders hunched, his companion drew a long breath. "It was just after six. I was in the crow's nest with Jimmy. We always got stuck with dinner watch." He shook his head ruefully. "A glass ocean, it was. Beautiful. Kinda day that makes you love this life, you know?"

Hugh bit down the smile threatening his composure and nodded.

"Jimmy saw it first. The periscope."

"Where is he, now?" he looked at the captain for confirmation. "I'll need to speak with him, too."

"Don't know," chimed the boy. "Got in a different lifeboat than me," he gulped. "Haven't seen him since."

Hugh offered him a cigarette for his nerves. "We'll find him."

The kid nodded, blowing smoke out the side of his mouth.

"Back to the periscope."

"Right. So, like I was sayin', Jimmy told me what he saw and I looked for myself with my own binoculars. Sure as shit, there she was. 'Bout a hundred yards starboard. We notified the bridge, o'course. Right away." He took another long drag, ash crumbling on the table. "Never been so scared before in all my life."

"I'm sure."

"Are you?" He narrowed his eyes. "Woulda been better if they outright torpedoed us. The waiting. The way they drew it out. Teasing us…"

From what Hugh could gather, the sub surfaced, trolling close enough for boarding. A small crew disembarked, each carrying two revolvers and a long knife. Every interviewee described the commanding officer the same. It was almost uncanny. He was in his mid-thirties, with a neatly trimmed brown beard and mustache. His cap and jacket were dark blue, as were those of his subordinates, and he wore khaki pants. Irritatingly polite, the officer's English was perfect. He asked for the *Carolina's* papers and began loading the lifeboats. All personnel boarded, the officer instructed the boats be strung together, just as the crew of the *Eva* had found them.

"They told us to pull westward," relayed the toothless man from earlier. "Tried to sink her with a torpedo, they did, and the sonsofbitches missed. They missed!"

"But she did sink?" Hugh hated the question as soon as it left his lips. Still, he needed to record every detail. It wouldn't bring back the *Carolina*, but maybe it would help other vessels as the war went on.

"She did," the old man confirmed. "They hit her with gunfire from the deck. Three rounds of it."

"Three rounds?"

"Toldja she put up a fight."

"She's from Jersey," Hugh allowed himself a slight grin. "Wouldn't expect anything less."

The war was here. In their home waters. The enemy was on a violent mission to sink and mine as much as she could, terrorizing the coast along the way. Hugh no sooner got back to base following the *Carolina* when they received another distress signal.

This time, it was from an oil tanker, the *Herbert L. Pratt*, beached after an encounter with one of the mines in the bay. Patrol boats were quickly dispatched from the base and Cape Henlopen in Delaware.

The crew safely conveyed to Lewes, Hugh's team still had to sail the bay again on their return trip. A bay that was riddled with mines and possibly another U-boat. Night had fallen, and Cape May softly glowed on the horizon, her lighthouse bright and steady.

Hugh took every necessary precaution, cutting their engines to avoid a wake and running the craft with no lights. Stealing a glance at Pat, he prayed they'd make it to port. *All those mouths to feed.* At least Rossini had someone to go home to. Someone who missed him; who'd be there when they docked, welcoming him with open arms and probably a steaming pot of her famous sauce on the stove.

He tried not to think of Shannon. To will his heart to forget, but it was futile. Looking out over the bay, her words came flooding back. She was drunk, he quickly reminded himself, but sometimes alcohol fueled the flames of truth.

The vessel rounded the light, and Hugh breathed a little easier. Crews swept this part of the coast regularly, and it was rare the blimp overlooked anything when it came to reconnaissance. Twenty minutes later, they were safely docked.

A small crowd gathered along the fence outside the base. Mostly wives and sweethearts, along with a few kids bundled up. Marian was there as suspected, and Hugh tipped his cap as he strode by. He was exhausted and paid no mind to the rest, marching to his office at a brisk pace to avoid the fanfare.

"Hugh?" called a voice behind him.

He stopped in his tracks. Was pretty sure his heart stopped, too.

"*Wait.* Please?"

He knew her enough to know she'd been crying. He could hear it, the break in her tone, even in those two simple syllables. Hugh held his breath. The clack of Shannon's boots against the concrete grew closer. Head tilted, he turned to face her.

"You came," he quavered.

Shannon nodded, eyes brimming with tears. "Charlie told me."

Hugh took a careful step toward her. There was a glint in those blue eyes, and he dared allow himself to hope.

"I..." she shrugged, wringing her hands. "I, um..."

He cupped her cheeks. "You're *here*. You don't have to say anything else."

She smiled gratefully, and a drop escaped from her right eye. Hugh brushed it away with his thumb and drew her into the kiss he'd been longing to give her for years. Softly, at first; gentle as a dove. Shannon looped her arms around his neck and opened her mouth. Fingers taunt, he held her face and slid his tongue inside. Part of him was afraid she wouldn't like it, but when he felt hers in return, he let out a low moan. Their tongues danced, eagerly exploring every nook. He savored hints of sweet peppermint and, for a moment, wondered what his own breath tasted like. Probably tobacco, he thought with a pang of regret.

Neither was inclined to break the embrace until someone whistled nearby. Hugh was still in uniform. On military property. *Too late now.* They were hardly alone, the entire Rossini clan forming semi-circle behind her. Charlie was there, too, a broad grin on his face; as well as Shannon's friend from the mess, little Enzo propped on her hip.

"'Bout time," Edith smirked, thrusting a flat palm in Charlie's direction. "You owe me a quarter."

CHAPTER 55

B aby Molly's first few months flew by in a blur. Nursing, rocking, changing, and then nursing again. Jennie loved every minute of it. Gertrude
insisted she use a nurse, but she just couldn't bring herself to. Molly was
her baby. Hers and Danny's. If Jennie couldn't have one, she wasn't about
to let the other out of her precious sight.

Holding Molly was holding a piece of *him*, and she longed for the
moment Danny could meet her himself. The best she could do now was
stare at the wedding portrait on her bedside table until her eyes closed each
night and pray she'd see him in her dreams.

Danny was a hero. He was fighting for their country. Their freedoms.
Their family. It was something she took great pride in, a story she was happy
to tell their baby girl and often did. She was lucky to have the affections
of such a man. But, oh, how she hoped that man would come back to her
in one piece.

Black Sunday. That was what the press called it. A chill ran down her
spine at the recollection, and Jennie clutched the baby closer to her bosom.
The enemy sank seven ships last week. Seven, all of them off the coast of

New Jersey. Poor Gertrude hadn't left her room in two days. Hugh was fine, thank God, but that didn't serve to quell anyone's anxieties, not with all the mines the U-boat planted.

Apparently, the submarine sank three schooners before that, the vessels having caught them carrying out their deadly mission. They kept the crews as prisoners, feeding them stale bread for days. *Days.* Jennie tried not to think of the horror those hostages must've felt. Cramped. Starving. Never knowing when or where they'd surface. She prayed for their loved ones, and, wrong as it was, Jennie also prayed she'd never be in their position.

Then the sub seemingly vanished. Was she returning to Germany for supplies? Headed North to New York harbor or up the river to Hog Island shipyard? It was anyone's guess, and her nerves were shot.

I really need to stop reading the newspapers.

When the press wasn't touting terror on the seas, it was turning on its own citizens. Selfish as it sounded, she couldn't help but wonder if the propaganda had anything to do with her. It wasn't farfetched, after all. Joseph felt wronged. Egregiously so. Had she brought this on the family? On her Germantown neighbors?

The support behind the Sedition Act was infuriating. Some days, Jennie just wanted to hide. To take everyone she loved and escape to the Browne lodge in upstate New York. Their own private oasis. Far from the ever-watchful eye of self-proclaimed patriots. Wasn't her husband a patriot? Wasn't Hugh?

She was born and raised in America. As for Father, well, he chose to come here. He left his family, his friends, *everything* to start over. Devoted his whole life to his work and his family. And how many other lives were better off because of it? How many other families were thriving off the respectable wages paid by Martin Glass? It didn't matter. The Philadelphia Club revoked his membership anyway. The first of many, she feared.

Someone apparently overheard something and repeated it to someone else. By the time the rumor reached the board, it was wild and blown out of proportion. Almost laughable. Her father, a long-lost cousin to the Kaiser and heir apparent. He was kidnapped at birth by a disgruntled servant who smuggled him to the States. His true identity revealed, Father swore allegiance to Germany and vowed to crush anyone and anything standing between him and the throne.

Jennie couldn't fathom how a reasonable person could believe such bile. Yet, the club maintained its position. Truth was sometimes stranger than fiction. They were quick to point out to the Martin attorneys that Father was, in fact, German. Cause enough for expulsion under the current circumstances as far as they were concerned.

She held Molly a little bit longer that night, caressing her chubby little cheek and watching in wonder as her dark lashes fluttered. What kind of world was this for her? For any child?

Jennie crept to the door, closing it behind her as quietly as she could. She looked at the hall clock and pouted, regretting her earlier promise to Samuel for a game of checkers. She straightened her skirt with a sigh and drug herself back down to the parlor.

"He went to bed half an hour ago, ma'am," Rutherford advised when she'd found the room empty.

"Oh. Thank you, Rutherford."

He bowed and bid her adieu.

Frustrated, she meandered to the secretary. Behind on her correspondence, now seemed as good a time as any to finally write her thank-yous for Molly's baby presents. She was two cards in when there was a tap on the parlor door.

"You're up late, *Schatz*," Father smiled from the entry, a small plate of black and white cookies in his hand.

"Amerikaners. My favorite."

"I know. Picked them up at Becker's on my way home."

"Thank you, Daddy."

He motioned the settee, and she followed. Jennie broke her cookie in half, nibbling away.

"This time next week we'll be back at Juniper Grove," Father mused. "You're looking forward to a change in scenery, I imagine?"

Jennie nodded. "I am. But…" she wrung her hands. "It'll feel different without him."

He looked thoughtful for a moment. "So much pressure. You've got a lot to shoulder. You're doing it beautifully but you don't have to go it alone."

"That means a lot," Jennie croaked, her eyes welling up.

He stroked her hair.

"I miss him, Daddy."

"I know."

"I'm worried," she started. "This insidious war is everywhere. When will it stop? And Molly, poor little dear. I want her to have this, too, what we have." Jennie sniffled, resting her head on his shoulder. "But I'm frightened. Father, I'm so scared. Everyone hates us."

He put the plate of cookies on the coffee table and took her hands in his. "Yours are the fears of every parent, *Schatz*, myself included. None of us know what will happen. Not now or when the war ends. But I can tell you this, the love I have for you is the same love you have for Molly. An indistinguishable light of hope, brighter than even Lady Liberty's torch."

Jennie swallowed hard. "If only they could hear you at the club now."

"Never mind them," he replied. "People will always be afraid of those different from them. I have an accent. I always will. But if I were young enough to fight beside your husband, Jennie, surely I would."

Jennie was in better spirits by the time Molly's christening rolled around.

She welcomed the sense of normalcy, however small. She even caught Hugh ogling at Shannon across the aisle and had to look away for fear her smile would betray her. As if on cue, Molly babbled, and Shannon raised the baby's tiny hand to wave at him. There could be no mistaking the electric look in her cousin's eyes. That her sister-in-law returned his feelings was equally evident; the radiant glow on her cheeks outshining the summer sun.

She opted to ride back to Juniper Grove with them in Hugh's recently acquired Dodge. She climbed in the back, fretting over the now crying Molly, while Shannon took her place in the passenger seat, her hand finding his along the console and entwining their fingers together. It was a sweet moment, one she wished Danny could've seen for himself. Molly apparently disagreed, her little face tomato red with tears.

"Someone's sleepy," Jennie apologized.

"It was a long morning for her," Shannon shrugged. "Nothing any of us haven't done before when we were that little."

Hugh beamed and gave her hand a light squeeze.

Thankfully, Molly slept straight through her luncheon, giving Jennie a needed reprieve. The happy couple was having lemonade in the garden courtyard when she popped her head out the side door.

"Hope I'm not intruding."

"Not at all, Jen."

"Hugh was just telling me your father's putting on quite the parade," Shannon added.

Jennie sat down in one of the wicker chairs and poured herself a tall glass. "Yes," she said between sips, "I just hope it isn't too much excitement for Molly."

"Nonsense. It'll be fun. The colors, the music." Hugh grinned, stealing a glance at Shannon. "Kids love that sorta thing."

"I'm not sure." Jennie cast her eyes down. "It feels wrong, celebrating without Danny. Even today."

Shannon softened her own gaze. "He'd be here if he could. You know that don't you?"

"I do."

They shared a smile while Hugh freshened everyone's glasses.

"How 'bout some gossip to cheer you up? Might not be newsworthy to you, but it was pretty big deal down here, wasn't it Shannon?"

"Was a nice break from the U-boats."

"Oh?" Jennie flicked her brows up. "Well, any distraction to this war a welcome one."

"You remember Will Barkley?" Hugh asked.

"That sweet farm boy?"

He nodded. "Not so sweet after all. Got himself arrested last week."

Jennie gasped. "What for?"

"Liquor's prohibited on the island. Falls under one of Wilson's new laws."

She groaned. "Another one?"

"Yup. Not as harsh as Sedition, but pretty damn annoying if you don't mind my sayin'." Hugh took a sip of lemonade, wincing at the sour aftertaste. "Will's involved in a rum ring. Been supplying the base right under our noses for months."

"How did he get caught?"

"One of the sentries tipped him off." Hugh lifted a hand as if counting money. "Kid was raking in a small fortune."

Jennie placed her glass on the table. "I'm confused," she said, motioning the house. "Father has a whole wine cellar inside."

"True," Hugh admitted, "but it's for private use."

She pondered it a moment then reached for a stalk of celery from the crudité. "Interesting. I imagine rationing is partially to blame?"

"Exactly," he confirmed. "Grain, corn, potatoes. Most distillers and brewers are only operating with half their supplies right now."

Jennie raised an eyebrow. "How's our grape supply?"

Shannon chuckled and leaned forward. "I'll have to introduce you to my neighbor. Her family makes their own dago red. Barefoot." She spread her arms wide. "Big wooden barrel. Skirts tied up to their knees."

"Sounds messy," she smiled.

"I'm sure it is. But the kids get a real kick out of squishing the grapes from what she tells me."

Rutherford appeared to announce lunch, and Jennie was sorry for it. She was finally among people her own age and relished the adult conversation. Her heart was lighter, too. Neither Hugh nor Shannon had spoken of their future, but it was clear they were an item now; that much was official. Jennie even found herself looking forward to the fireworks spectacular the following week. It would be a welcome change for all.

CHAPTER 56

"You're absolutely certain he gave all the servants the afternoon off?"

"Quite, sir. On account of the parade today."

"Good."

Joseph swiveled his chair around, drinking in the sight of the Irish girl standing opposite his desk. Ginger and freckles. Pert nose and pale skin. *Christ, they all looked alike.*

Gertrude's money trails easy enough to follow; he read the Pinkerton reports on the maid. One brother was killed in the Easter Rising, another while obediently serving the same crown at Verdun. Tenant farmer parents who bred year after year with a throng of little brats all dependent on her meager monthly stipend for their survival.

He got a notebook out of the drawer, wrote down a number, and slid it across the desk. Her eyes widened, and he felt the corners of his mouth curl.

"You can read, can't you?"

The girl nodded.

"Good." Opening a manila folder, Joseph retrieved a typed piece of paper and held it up. "Let's practice your statement, shall we?"

A hesitant gulp.

"Bridget, is it? May I call you by your first name?"

"Sir," she agreed.

"This is a matter of national security. It can't sound rehearsed." He glanced down at the notebook then back up at her. "There are a lot of zeroes in that figure. If you're not convincing enough rest assured I'll find someone else who is."

The girl averted her olive eyes, clasping and unclasping her ungloved hands on the desk. Joseph put the script down and cocked his head.

"Let me ask you something, Bridget. Do your parents know you work for the same Huns who killed Owen?"

She stiffened, a sucker punch to the kidney.

Joseph moved in for the knock-out. "Wonder how they'd feel if they found out? I know how important loyalty is to your family; how much it meant to Seamus at least."

The girl blinked furiously.

"Shame those Tommies had to bring in artillery. Would've proved to be of much better use to them in France than Dublin."

Lips trembling, she looked down at her feet. Joseph rose from his seat and walked around the desk. His touch feather-light, he placed his hands over hers and lowered his voice.

"I'm truly sorry for your losses."

Bridget squirmed before finally exhaling. "Thank you, Mr. York."

He lingered, circling a finger over her knuckles until he felt her relax. Drawing himself close to her ear, he asked, "Do you love your new country, Bridget?"

"Of course," she whispered.

"Good girl. You want to protect it, don't you?"

"Yes."

Joseph traced the nape of her neck, slowly trailing all the way down her spine and resting his palm on the small of her back. "Yes, what?"

"Yes, sir."

"Please," he urged, turning her to face him, "call me Joseph."

CHAPTER 57

D anny stood on the deck of the USS *Dakotan*, inhaling the last of the sweet-salty air he'd ever get this side of the Atlantic. The men around him hooted and hollered, waving frantically at their sweethearts below. Some fella from Temple paced above them on the bridge, shouting orders in a hopeless attempt to organize a regimental photograph for the university's library. Meanwhile, the band on the docks began a rousing rendition of *Over There,* and the crowd burst into song.

They were initially supposed to depart from New York, but the port was closed after last month's submarine strikes. The Navy did its best to put a positive spin on the situation but was thwarted by the press at every turn. One article featured the story of a young girl who took charge of her lifeboat after a storm. Separated from the rest of the boats, she insisted on taking her turn at the oars. One hour on, one hour off, she didn't stop until the tiny craft rowed into Little Egg inlet near Atlantic City.

Danny smiled despite himself. He knew a girl like that. Posted his letter to Shannon just yesterday.

Meanwhile, reports out of Washington continued to produce more information about the German vessel, *U-151*. Wilson praised the Navy's defensive actions, touting their use of flying boats, dirigibles, and submarine chasers. Still, Danny couldn't help to wonder about Hugh's thoughts on the attacks.

All around him, men hooted and hollered, waving frantically at their sweethearts below. Hands stuffed in his pockets, Danny backed away from the railing. Jennie wasn't there. He hadn't even told her he was shipping out. Their Christmas goodbye was brutal, and he couldn't put her through it again, not to mention with a baby. He already hated himself enough for missing the christening. One look at Molly now, and he might just go AWOL. Dive right into the Delaware and swim over to finally meet her. A German family sheltering a deserter? Where would that leave them?

Danny scowled, trying hard to think of something else when Connor O'Doyle strode up beside him. He looked every bit the mick he was, cupping one of those big Irish hands around his mouth to light a cigarette.

"Quite the send-off, huh?" Connor said as he shook out his match.

"It's the 4th of July in Philadelphia. Were you expecting anything less?"

"You're somethin' else, you know that?"

Danny fixed his eyes resolutely above the crowd, chewing hard on the gum in his mouth. "If you say so," he shrugged.

"Ah, c'mon. I was just kidding around." Connor shook his head, blowing a stream of gray smoke off to the side. "Why so glum, chum?"

"Still getting my sea legs."

"Bullshit," Connor said and pat his shoulder. "We'll be home soon enough."

"Dunno about that."

"I do." He leaned down and lowered his voice. "Got a cousin who works with codes. You didn't hear this from me but don't be surprised if there aren't any Germans left by the time we reach France."

Danny furrowed his brows. "The hell you talking about?"

"Heard about the grippe?"

"Yeah, so?"

"Word is the Huns lost a lot of men in Brest."

"From the flu?" Danny repeated, still not buying it.

Connor nodded and took a drag. "Think about the numbers. There's six thousand of us Doughboys right here on this ship. And that's just our regiment. Pershing's got seven divisions under him. Seven." He tipped his ash and smiled. "We're young. Fresh. Them kraut's been at this four years and still can't finish the job. We got 'em on the ropes, pal. Like Dempsey."

CHAPTER 58

G ertrude stood in the foyer at Juniper Grove, furiously rearranging the centerpiece on the entryway's circular table for the third time. She tucked in yet another plume of blue hydrangea and stepped back to admire her work. The job usually reserved for staff, today she found quiet comfort in the task. It gave her something to do while waiting for Jennie and the baby to come down.

Why that girl insisted on going without help, she'd never understand. At least her niece's temperament seemed to improve.

She stole a glance in the parlor where Samuel was reading. The doctors at the University of Pennsylvania said the sea air would be beneficial. She hadn't noticed any difference so far, but they were experts in their field, the best money could buy, and she trusted their opinions.

"Get out of the city," they urged.

Away from Philadelphia's sweltering heat and all it brought with it. Stench. Rats. Disease.

Gertrude shuddered, haunted by the disturbing rumor she heard whispered along the hospital corridors during Samuel's last check-up. It still troubled her even now, weeks later.

A new illness. Some pneumonia variant crept across the plains and left nothing but death in its wake. A person could wake up perfectly fine in the morning only to be dead by nightfall.

But that was miles away. Her family was safe in Cape May. From infection, at least. That submarine fiasco was too close for comfort. While her ex-husband pulled some strings to keep their son home, he apparently hadn't pulled the right ones. Hugh was supposed to be a paper pusher. It certainly wasn't the first time Edmund reneged on a promise.

Two could play at that game. Her mind flashed back to the night of Jennie's debut and the way Cornelia Blackwell practically dragged her son onto the dance floor. The girl laughed too loud, smiled too wide, and put her hands a little too close to places they didn't belong, not publicly and certainly not with a man she wasn't even courting. Nothing was official; her ex and that hag he now called a wife under the impression (per *her* suggestion, of course) it was prudent to wait until the war was over before making any formal engagement announcement. Still, correspondence from some of Gertrude's old acquaintances in the Knickerbocker set hinted Cornelia was not so discreet. Well, they'd be in for a rude awakening, wouldn't they?

Gertrude enjoyed watching the progression of Hugh's courtship with the Culligan girl. Though certainly not her first choice for him, the young lady possessed potential. Unlike Jennie, Shannon accepted Gertrude's advice with an earnest appreciation. She seemed eager to please, clay that could eventually be molded into the perfect wife.

She stared wistfully at her floral arrangement when Jennie's footsteps on the stairs called her back to attention.

Holding Molly on her hip, her niece waved a piece of stationery in her free hand. "Father wants us to meet him at the grandstand. I told Shannon we'd meet her there by noon."

Nodding, Gertrude popped her head in the parlor. "Samuel, honey, it's time to go."

The foyer was a flurry of activity as they gathered parasols and put on their lace gloves, trading the baby back and forth between them all the while. Molly was cutting a tooth, drool sliding down her dimpled double chin.

"Baby's first parade," Gertrude cooed as she wiped it away with her hanky. "How exciting."

It was the summer's biggest holiday weekend, and hotels across the cape were booked solid. Bunting hung along practically every porch and turret on the island; flags big and small waved proudly in the sea breeze.

The walk to Washington Street didn't take long, and the trio soon found themselves on the gazebo grandstand overlooking a swarm of people. Tourists and locals alike, the whole city had come out for the event. Everyone was clad in their Sunday Best, red, white, and blue as far as her eyes could see.

Gertrude spotted Shannon among the sea of people and waved. Like many of the women, herself included, the young lady was clad in white lace. A red satin sash accentuated her tiny waist, and the girl had been so bold as to paint her lips the same shade. She didn't wear make-up herself, but appreciated the nod to suffrage. Girls these days with their novelties. Going corset-less supposedly on account of the war. She wondered what it would feel like but dared not ask. *Next, they'll be cutting their hair.*

Miss Culligan joined their group, taking her place next to Jennie after they'd exchanged pleasantries.

"Do you know the line-up, Mrs. Callaway?" she asked.

"I have the roster in my satchel," Jennie offered.

"Thank you, dear."

Gertrude helped herself to the bag and perused the document. It was impressive. Walter had put together quite a show. Following the Grand Marshall was the baby parade, then the floats. Bethlehem Steel was rumored to have outdone themselves yet again. However, they were facing stiff competition from the Liberty Loan Drive, the details of which she'd already promised to report back to her own committee in Philadelphia.

There were Boy Scouts and Girl Scouts. Little League teams and Temperance League advocates. Duty to God and country was on display with a delegation from every church on the island proudly showing their support.

"When does Hugh march, Mama?" Samuel asked.

"Hmm, let's see." She knit her brows. "Looks like the Naval Color Guard is between the band from Wildwood Catholic High School and the Daughters of the American Revolution."

"I can't wait to see him." The boy smiled, and Gertrude eyed Shannon peripherally. He wasn't the only eager one.

"What time is it?" Jennie asked with a hint of impatience.

"Twelve fifteen," Shannon asked.

"Where's Father?" Her niece huffed. "It's not like him to be late."

"I'm sure he'll be along any moment now," Gertrude assured her. "These things take time, darling. With this many groups, the line probably stretches down Perry Street and back up Beach Avenue. He's probably just confirming everyone knows their place."

Jennie wasn't convinced, dabbing the back of her sweaty neck with a handkerchief. Frowning, she offered the baby her index finger to gnaw on.

"I think she's cutting a tooth."

"Poor little dear," Shannon remarked. She nodded in the direction of the carts lined up next to Swain's Hardware. "Want me to get her an Italian ice? Numb those gums a little."

"Would you mind?"

"Not at all."

"Can I have one too?" Samuel asked. "It's so hot out."

Gertrude raised a brow. *Manners.*

"Please?" he added hastily.

"Sure," Shannon smiled. "What flavor?"

"Cherry."

"You got it."

She watched as Shannon made her way back through the crowd. It would be a miracle if the girl returned without the treats being melted.

The sun was high, its rays fierce even from where they stood in the shade. "Hurry up, Daddy," Jennie muttered next to her.

CHAPTER 59

S hannon shifted her weight from foot to foot impatiently. There were a few people ahead of her in line, and she was anxious to return to the grandstand before the parade began. Meanwhile, a pair of children dressed up as Uncle Sam and Lady Liberty played tag. She tried to amuse herself watching them weave in and out around the small clusters of onlookers, but it was no use.

Oh, who am I kidding?

She couldn't wait to see Hugh. The rest of the parade could disappear for all she cared. She thought of him late at night, when she wasn't supposed to, the way that stark white of his uniform contrasted with those tanned, muscular arms of his, arms she wanted to be wrapped around her more than anything.

Shannon felt beads of perspiration along the nape of her neck even now. He'd worn the uniform before; Christmas, that horrible Officer's Ball, the christening only the week before. There was no denying Hugh was attractive. She'd always thought him handsome. His smile was warm and inviting, teeth pearly, brown eyes crinkling ever so slightly at the corners whenever he looked at her.

Now, everything felt different. Somehow, this boy, who she'd known for most of her life, was no longer a boy at all. He was a man she saw with an open heart, and Shannon's stomach fluttered with anticipation. The longer she stood in line, the weaker her knees felt beneath her. She may as well have been moving underwater and smiled to herself.

"Something funny?" said a voice beside her.

Will Barkley. Shannon groaned internally.

"Hello Will," she managed to say brightly. "You're looking well."

"For a jailbird you mean."

The line moved, and he inched nearer, standing so close she could smell the bourbon on his breath.

"I know it was you," he hissed.

"You're drunk, Will. Get away from me."

Swaying, he took a few steps back.

"You broke my heart, Shannon. The money I was saving? It was all for you. For us."

"There is no 'us', Will. There never was."

"My sis'er was right about you," he slurred. "Nothin' but a tease."

"Would you please lower your voice?"

They caught the eye of the Cape May police officer walking his beat along the parade route.

"Or what?" Will challenged her, jutting his chin at the cop. "You'll have me arrested? Wouldn't be the first time."

"There a problem here, miss?" the officer asked as he approached.

Shannon looked Will up and down. He was a sorry sight. Looked like days since he last bathed, overalls caked in soil at his knees. Complexion ruddy, there was a smudge of dirt across the bridge of his nose, and his brown hair was slick and oily.

She hadn't meant to hurt him. They were friends. Business partners, nothing more. She'd been honest with him from the start, yet he couldn't say the same.

This man stole from her. He knew she had practically next to nothing, but he did it anyway. Unacceptable from where she stood. No rationale or explanation on his part could ever negate that. Still, seeing him now, she felt a twinge of guilt.

"Miss?" the cop asked again over the noise.

Shannon smiled meekly. "No problem, officer. This fella's just leaving, isn't that right?"

Will accepted her mea culpa with a slight tilt of his head, and she lost him to the sea of people less than a minute later.

She returned to the grandstand with a smile despite the two cherry ices dripping down her arms. Passing one to Samuel, she spooned out a small portion of the other for Molly to suck on while Jennie squinted into the crowd.

Shannon looked up at the cloudless sky, the perfect shade of azure blue as if God himself agreed with their cause. She gave her sister-in-law an affectionate pat on the shoulder.

"I'm sure your father will get here shortly. Maybe he's with the Grand Marshal?"

Though her eyes shone with gratitude, Jennie said nothing in response, jostling Molly to her other hip as the orchestra began to play the *Star-Spangled Banner*. The crowd turned to face Old Glory, men and boys removing their hats.

BOOM!

The explosion rocked the island. Shannon had never heard anything so deafening.

She clapped a hand over her mouth, the air punched out of her lungs. *We're under attack.* She groped blindly for Gertrude, squeezing the other woman for strength when she found her. Jennie crouched beside them, Molly protectively cushioned in her mother's arms.

"Fire!" someone yelled from the crowd and pointed at the thick plumes of black smoke on the east end of the cape.

"Mama," Samuel asked, Italian ice splattered all across his seersucker jacket, "isn't that where the barracks is?"

"No," Shannon whimpered as she fought back the tears. "That's where the barracks *was*."

CHAPTER 60

The afternoon was a cyclone, and Jennie found herself swept right up the funnel. Chaos and pushing. Dust, smoke, debris. An unrelenting, merciless July sun.

Molly was inconsolable, her cries a melodic backdrop to the devastation unfolding around them. Gertrude and Shannon were on the verge of hysterics. Samuel was confused, too young to understand the ramifications of the explosion, and Father was still nowhere to be found.

Sirens replaced the orchestra's pomp and circumstance as the mob of people pushed their way to the barracks, searching for their loved ones. The once blue sky over the harbor was now awash in black, orange, and red.

"Was it the fireworks?" A woman in the crowd wondered.

"No! It's the damn Huns again!" replied a man behind them, and Jennie shuddered.

Sweat poured down her back, corset and undergarments thoroughly drenched, meanwhile, the high lace collar of the dress choked her.

Can't breathe, can't breathe, can't breathe.

Molly continued to fuss so much, so she eventually spit up her lunch, and Jennie's shoulder was now caked in sticky pink goop. It quickly seeped through the fabric and leaked down her arm. At some point, Shannon offered to hold her, but Jennie declined. Filthy as she was, with so much uncertainty, they'd have to pry the baby away from her.

She could feel her feet swelling in her boots. Heels clicked against the cobblestones, ankles twisting time and again when they got caught in between the bricks, yet she walked on.

Finally, they reached the scene. The police department set up a barricade around the perimeter so the firemen could work. From what Jennie could tell, it looked like every engine on the island was there. Some people held pocket photographs of their family members; others frantically rambled from person to person with vapid descriptions of those missing.

The battle was overseas, not here. It felt surreal. Like she was in the pictures, not standing in the middle of a neighborhood.

A mounted officer rode back and forth at the front of the mob, trying to get the peoples' attention. He informed them the naval barracks was empty at the time of the explosion, all of the men participating in the parade.

A collective sigh of relief washed over the crowd. Some women blessed themselves. Others broke down, tears of joy making trolley tracks down their dust-covered faces.

Shannon and Gertrude shared a meaningful hug.

"I wanna hug too," Samuel exclaimed, and he threw his arms around her. His mouth still red from the shaved ice, he looked up at Jennie with the wide-eyed curiosity that only comes with youth. "Why are we hugging again?"

She smiled at him affectionately, "Because your brother is alright."

"Alright?" Samuel scoffed. "Of course he's alright," the boy pointed over her shoulder, "he's standing right over there."

Her aunt nearly fainted, but Shannon held her up as Hugh emerged from the chaos, his once white jacket now the same dreary gray as everyone else's garments. He was missing his hat and the ends of his brown hair curled with perspiration.

They shared a solemn nod, and Jennie watched with a lump in her throat as he silently hugged his mother before moving on to Shannon.

The girl's whole countenance had changed. She looked down at her hands, then back up at him adoringly.

Jennie knew the feeling all too well. Knew exactly where it would lead, too. *We're really sisters now.*

Hugh explained the police wanted everyone to return to their cottages and hotels to wait it out. With fewer people on the streets, the missing, almost all of whom were parade participants, could be directed back to their respective residences. The crowd slowly dissipated as word spread, and they began the journey back to Juniper Grove.

It was nightfall by the time they got there, but every lamp in the cottage appeared to be lit, and the front door was wide open. Jennie cradled Molly against her chest. Having finally stopped crying, the child was now sleeping soundly, though for how much longer she couldn't be sure. Even from the porch, she could see the house was swarming with uniformed men.

Hugh told the ladies to remain outside, proceeding with caution as he entered the foyer of the east wing.

"What's the meaning of this?" she heard him ask in an authoritative tone.

One of the men held up a badge. "Agent Taylor, sir. With the Bureau of Investigation. Could you please identify yourself?"

"Lieutenant Hugh Callaway, United States Navy."

"What is your relationship to the owner of this property, Lieutenant?"

Hugh hesitated as a crash echoed from the parlor. He tried to move toward the noise, but Agent Taylor stopped him.

Jennie, meanwhile, peered through the open window only to find the room in shambles. The desk was open, the contents of its draws emptied all over the floor. Calling cards, bills, personal correspondence spilling every which direction. The couch and chairs were toppled, and agents sliced through the cushions. They pulled out the stuffing, feathers waltzing against the chandelier's glow.

Off in the far corner, an agent held her treasured music box upside down.

"Made in Austria," he squinted, while another jotted something down on a clipboard. They shared a sneer, and Jennie watched in horror as the man proceeded to lift the instrument high above his head.

"*Stop*," she begged, Molly promptly erupting in wails, "that was my mother's!"

It was too late. The wooden box landed with a resounding crack against the cherry flooring. The remains splintered like matchsticks while the cylinder rolled across the room and slammed against the bottom of the hearth.

Hearing the commotion outside, Agent Taylor emerged from the house with Hugh hot on his tail.

Jennie finally relinquished her daughter into Shannon's care. Face red, she whirled on the lead investigator, her voice unrecognizable.

"Get. Out. Of my house!"

"Jen, don't," Hugh cautioned.

"Mrs. Culligan?" Agent Taylor spoke over him.

"Go! Get out!" she insisted, flailing her arms toward the brick walkway. "Get out of here!"

By then, another agent appeared in the door frame. Taylor jutted his chin, and the man was suddenly next to her. Before she knew what was happening, he was handcuffing her.

"Jennie Culligan, you're under arrest for espionage."

Jennie couldn't stop shaking. Grubby, starving and exhausted, her lower lip quivered, sore eyes brimming with a fresh round of tears as the guard unlocked the cell door.

"No," she whimpered, but he only snickered.

"In you go, *kraut*."

The other women in her cell did not take kindly to allegations of treason, pinning her against the cold clay floor as soon as he was out of sight.

"Got a brother about to ship out," one sneered in her face.

"At least he's still alive," growled another. "Mine died of pneumonia at Camp Funston. 'Course he wouldn't've been in the Army in the first place if your precious Kaiser wasn't such a monster."

Jennie wanted to tell them she shared their anguish. How her own husband joined the fight. That she hadn't heard from him in months; didn't know if he even received the telegram about Molly. But she knew it was no use. That she, and Father too, had already been tried in the court of public opinion only to be found guilty based solely because they were German.

She tried twisting in protest, but the metal handcuffs dug into her back, and she cried out in pain. Two girls held her legs down, while another gripped Jennie's hair, yanking her back down as she struggled to sit up. They emptied the chamber pot on her, sewage seeping through the thin lace fabric of her tea dress, her corset soaking it up like a dirty scullery sponge. The stench unbearable, she vomited, the bile adding a greenish layer to the sludge.

God, she felt disgusting. Freezing, too. The holding cell was cold, *so cold*, and her saturated attire only made it worse. Sleep evaded her, teeth chattering so much the inside of her mouth was covered in tiny cuts and bite marks. If things were this bad for her, she could only imagine what Father must be going through.

CHAPTER 61

S hannon turned her key in the lock, thankful she took the time to make her bed.

"It's not much," she said casually over her shoulder while flicking on the lights, "but I hope it'll do. For tonight anyway. I'm sure you'll be back at Juniper Grove in no time."

The Callaways filed in behind her. Snowball pounced on the boy's feet, earning a rare chuckle that echoed against the plaster walls. Gertrude, meanwhile, shifted Molly from one arm to the other, her keen eye scrutinizing every detail of the tiny room from top to bottom. Shannon could already feel the heat rushing to her cheeks.

"It's..." Mrs. Callaway began.

"Small. I know."

"I was going to say quaint, dear."

Shannon offered a sheepish grin and pulled out a chair from the kitchenette. "Please, sit down. You must be exhausted."

"Hungry is more like it," Samuel replied, not realizing she spoke to his mother.

Shannon was too busy rummaging through the icebox to correct him. "There's some fruit on the table. Feel free to help yourself."

She grabbed a block of cheese, moving mechanically to the counter to slice it while considering the irony of the situation she now found herself faced with. Yes, the room was small, but it was hers. Paid for with her own money. Some acquired legitimately. The rest, well, that was debatable. She wasn't exactly innocent. Frank Hilton could certainly attest to that.

They played so perfectly off each other. Even that first night with the shoobie. It was easy, natural. He could've killed her in the alley. She'd pulled a gun on him, anyone else wouldn't have given it a second thought. But not Frank, who saw past her bravado, unthreatened by the ugly emotions she displayed. Instead, he not only let her talk, but he *listened*. Without judgment, without patronizing her.

That was just how he was. Frank never expected anything from her other than to hold up her end of their business transactions. He found her recommendations about moving the inventory insightful, implementing them where and when he could even though she was a girl. Shannon always felt at ease during their meetings.

She wasn't always proud of some of her actions, the falling out with Will when poor Mrs. Barkley had been nothing but nice to her for as long as she could remember. And Pa. That was a matter of self-preservation, but given a choice, she'd do it again in a heartbeat. Wouldn't even think twice.

Yet Jennie was the one currently sitting in a holding cell.

If someone told her two years ago that sweet, little, prim, and proper, picture-perfect Jennie Martin stained her spotless image, Shannon would've celebrated. But now? Hearing Molly's gurgle, she heaved a sigh of exhaustion, her tired eyes drawn to the baby they both loved so much.

Jennie was many things, but there was no way she was a traitor. Betray her country? The same one their beloved Danny was fighting for; would likely give his life for? She could never do that.

Shannon was no lawyer. She couldn't prove even an ounce of Jennie's innocence, but she knew it just the same. Could feel it right down to her core, the same dull ache that told her she'd never see her brother again.

Jennie wasn't a spy. Jennie was family.

CHAPTER 62

A thick fog rolled in off the Atlantic, shrouding the island in gray mist. *How fitting.* Hugh walked blindly through the streets. His head was just as clouded. Try as he might, he just couldn't reconcile the charges pending against the Martins.

Sedition. Such an ugly word.

He had no doubt Jennie was innocent. All the feds had on her, aside from bloodline, was the sheet music they found on the piano. So she liked Beethoven? When had that become a crime? Moreover, he fumed, who would've even reported her? It had to be someone close.

As for Walter, that was another matter entirely. Not only were they trying to link him to the explosion at the barracks, but the bureau also alleged his uncle was connected to the previous bombings in New York and eastern Pennsylvania. Claimed to have a witness statement but wouldn't tell him anything else. Both were being held without bail.

Hugh hadn't felt so helpless since the night he left Cambridge. He had so many obligations and people counting on him but didn't know what to tackle first. Concerns over the whereabouts and lodging of his men conflicted with his sense of urgency about getting in touch with the family attorneys. His chest tight, he undid his collar to no avail. Their office in Philadelphia wouldn't be open for hours.

At least he knew Mother and Samuel were safe, Shannon graciously opening her home yet again. God, he'd be lost without her. It was a small comfort knowing they were all together. One thing off his plate. Plus, Pat was right across the hall if they needed anything.

Overwhelmed, he stopped at the next corner and leaned against a curbside tree, the lamp post to his left illuminating Columbia Avenue. Just how he ended up at Jackson's, he wasn't sure. The cards beckoned to him like a siren on the shoals, their song a whisper in the smoky summer wind.

Hugh shoved his hands in his jacket. Palms clammy, his right fist closed tightly around the money clip in his pocket; cash he originally intended spending on the midway with Samuel before the fireworks celebration.

Just one hand.

He could control it. Hell, he hadn't gambled in months. He deserved this. A sweet escape, if only for a little while.

Bess greeted him at the top of the steps.

"Haven't seen you in a while," her smile alone a comfort already.

He stuck his thumbs on the filthy lapels of his officer's jacket. "Been busy."

"So I see," she nodded, granting him admittance. "Go on in. They'll be happy to see you."

Happy was an understatement. An hour later and Hugh was feeling more like his old self. Shoulders loose, he sat back in his chair, eyeing the pot-bellied man across from him.

"Well?" he asked, rolling his cigarette between his fingers.

His opponent bought the bluff and folded. Hugh continued to stay on top for a while, only to lose it all somewhere into hour three. Of course, by then, the bourbon had worked its magic, and he didn't care. Unable or willing to admit defeat, he just drank some more.

Inebriated and weary, his head bobbed so much Hugh was forced to prop it up. He leaned an elbow against the table, cupping his chin and already feeling the new stubble there, while attempting to persuade the dealer to give him a line of credit.

"One more hand, huh? *C'mon.* You know I'm good for it."

The employee firmly shook his head and raised an eyebrow toward the exit.

"I'll cover him," came a voice from one of the back bedrooms behind them.

Hugh swung his head around to offer his thanks, his smile quickly fading.

"York?" he squinted.

Joseph emerged from the shadows and shrugged. "That any way to greet an old friend?" He approached the table and sat himself opposite.

Hugh cocked his head. "Interesting choice of words, wouldn't you say?"

"In all our years, when have you known me to ever hold a grudge? As far as I'm concerned, last summer's ancient history. I've forgotten all about it."

"I haven't."

"Sorry to hear." Joseph pulled a money clip from his vest. "How much is he in the hole for this time?" he asked the dealer.

"You don't have to."

"I want to. For old time's sake. Think of it as a clean slate."

Hugh shrugged, not in the mood for any more surprises.

"You look like hell," Joseph said as the cards were being dealt.

"Thanks," he replied with more than a hint of sarcasm in his voice.

"Terrible what happened earlier. You lose any men?"

"No." *Thank God.*

Joseph nodded, then glanced at his hand. "Hit me."

The dealer complied, and the men were silent for a few minutes.

"I'm surprised you're not in Newport," Hugh finally said.

"Sorry to disappoint you," his companion replied. "But I happen to like this town."

"Really?"

"Really. Got a certain charm about it."

"A certain charm...."

"What are you, a parrot?"

"No," Hugh quipped. "Just not buying what you're selling."

"Hey, what happened to our clean slate?"

"She's my mother, York. I can't let it go that easily. Not to mention what you did to Jennie."

Joseph sipped his scotch. "Callaway, haven't you ever been in love?"

Hugh quickly looked down at his cards.

"Ah, you have. Must be *quite* a woman." This earned him a glare. "How would you feel if it was unrequited?"

"It's not, I assure you."

"But if it were," York pressed, considering his hand. "I'm no fool, Callaway. Sure the relationship with Jennie made perfect business sense, but it wasn't entirely mercenary." He paused, his full lips pouting at the memory. "I cared for her. Deeper than you'll ever know. I only did what I felt was necessary to win her affections in return."

"Are you really trying to blame your little blackmail scheme on Cupid's arrow?"

"What would you do? If your lady friend loved another?"

Hugh didn't answer right away, eyes fixed on the queen of hearts. His relationship with Shannon was still new, but he'd loved her long enough to know he couldn't live without her. Betraying her? That was something he could never do.

"There's no excuse, York."

"No," his companion replied in a quiet voice. "There's not." He folded the hand. Elbows on the table, he ran his fingers through his hair. "Look, I know she's married but...sometimes I still think about her. I can't help it." Joseph sighed, "How is she?"

"Jennie?"

Saying her name, Hugh was flooded by all the anxieties he came to the casino to forget. Pulse-pounding, he felt right back where he started when he left Agent Taylor hours before. It must've shown on his face.

"Callaway, what is it?"

"You really wanna know how Jennie is, huh?"

The other man nodded while pushing the chips from his loss across the table. Hugh picked one up, rubbing it between his thumb and index finger.

"She's in jail."

CHAPTER 63

Joseph looked across the table at Hugh in disbelief, all air punched out of his lungs. After a moment, he cleared his throat to compose himself.

"I'm sorry, I don't think I heard you correctly," he said in as casual a tone as he could muster. "Did you say jail?"

In a haggard monotone, Hugh proceeded to fill him in on the Bureau's raid at Juniper Grove that led to Jennie's arrest. He cashed out his chips and stood up.

"Got a long day ahead," he mumbled, staggering for the door.

Joseph, meanwhile, was glued to his seat. The thought of Jennie, alone and probably terrified, was so unsettling he couldn't move. He eventually forced himself up and retreated to the bordello, closing its red velvet curtain behind him. Bridget was coiled in sheets on the bed in the corner.

"Miss me?"

"No," he said firmly.

He put on a fresh shirt and tie and began combing his hair at the basin on the dresser.

"Goin' somewhere?" inquired the consort.

"How very astute. There may be hope for you yet." Joseph turned from the mirror to face her. "I have to go out for a few hours. You're not to leave this room, do you understand?"

"What if I have to use the facilities?"

"I'll see that you have a chamber pot before I leave."

Bridget pouted. He walked to the bed, leaning over as he tousled her curls.

"Be a good girl *now*, and you'll be rewarded *later*."

"I like the sound o'that," she purred.

But Joseph had already stormed back through the curtain. He took the secret passage out to the street, the keys to the Marmon jingling in his pocket as he jogged down the narrow stairs.

How could this happen? All those months of planning washed right out with the tide. His only consolation was that no one was injured in the blast. At least they had decent intel there. Fortunately, no stragglers lagged behind at the barracks.

He ducked into the phone booth at the corner of Washington Street on his way to the car. "The docks. Ten minutes," he commanded, slamming the receiver down.

Joseph was at the bar on the *Hercules'* lower deck nursing another scotch when Agent Taylor bounded down the stairs.

"Got here as soon as I could," he huffed, grabbing a tumbler and pouring a generous amount for himself. "I suppose you want to celebrate?"

"Celebrate? No, you imbecile."

"Something wrong, Mr. York?"

"Jennie Culligan."

"Martin's daughter?" Taylor blinked. "What about her?"

"She was never part of the plan," he growled.

"No," the agent acknowledged. "She wasn't. But her arrest certainly gives us another leg to stand on."

"We already have a witness. We don't need her."

"The federal prosecutor might not agree."

"Then we'll find one who does," Joseph insisted. "Let her go, Taylor."

"I'm afraid it's not that easy. We're talking about a conspiracy of unprecedented proportions here. Explosions at Black Tom, the Eddystone plant, and now the Wissahickon Barracks; each carried out by operatives with alleged ties to Germany. It's all in accordance with Wilson's mandate. We're simply doing our part Over Here to help our boys Over There. I know you have your sights set on Martin Glass, but this is far bigger."

"And Jennie?"

"She's collateral."

Joseph pounded his fist on the top of the bar. "Unacceptable."

"Put your feelings aside. This was a business arrangement, remember?"

"Remember? How could I forget?" Joseph puffed his chest, presence overshadowing the other man. "I'm the one who put the wheels in motion. Got the Pinkertons involved. Hell, I practically did your job for you. Fed you lead after lead."

"And the Bureau appreciates your efforts," Taylor replied, albeit too smug for his liking.

Joseph grabbed him by the throat. "Let her go."

The agent's hazel eyes bulged. He struggled to breathe and lifted his hands over Joseph's in a feeble effort to release himself.

But that only made him squeeze harder, both hands in a vice grip around Taylor's windpipe. Joseph lifted him off the ground, the other man's face purple while his legs kicked and flailed beneath him.

"It's simple," he explained. "Let her go, and I let you go."

Agent Taylor gurgled something construed as a yes, and Joseph dropped him. He panted, tears streaming down his ruddy cheeks while a dark stain spread across the groin of his trousers.

"I want an update by noon. Are we clear?"

"Y-Yes, Mr. York," Taylor stuttered while scrambling toward the stairs.

"Good."

CHAPTER 64

Gertrude awoke to a tantalizing aroma. The small of her back sore from the flimsy mattress, she peeled her eyes open, almost forgetting where she was until she saw Molly. The infant's tiny body was boxed snuggly against the wall with the room's only pillow to protect her from rolling.

Already up for the day, Shannon smiled from her place at the stove, mouthing a silent 'good morning' so as not to wake the baby. Gertrude nodded in acknowledgment before turning her attention to Samuel, seated cross-legged on the floor playing with the cat. She watched in amusement as he pulled a ribbon back and forth across the throw rug. The feisty pet gave chase, occasionally snatching it in his paws.

"Morning, Mama," her son smiled.

"Good morning, darling," she whispered.

"I think he likes me," Samuel said proudly as the animal rubbed up against him.

"It looks that way."

"Can we get a cat?"

Gertrude frowned. Didn't the boy understand they had far bigger concerns at the moment? *Of course, he doesn't.*

"We have Sasha," she said, trying to sound upbeat.

"*You* have Sasha," he corrected.

Samuel had a point, but she wasn't in the mood to acknowledge it. With the dog being left alone for so long, she didn't even want to think about what her bedroom looked like right now. The staff could take care of anything soiled, though she prayed her favorite duvet cover was spared. Head throbbing, her body screamed for caffeine after the arduous events of the previous day. Shannon seemed to read her thoughts.

"Would you like some coffee, Mrs. Callaway?" she asked.

"Yes, dear. That would be wonderful."

"Milk and sugar?"

Gertrude nodded wearily and walked over to the kitchenette. "Smells delicious," she remarked, slowly sinking into one of the two available chairs.

"Johnnycakes," Shannon shrugged and handed her a mug.

"Yummy," Samuel chimed in.

The trio devoured their breakfast in a matter of minutes. Shannon was busy cleaning the dishes when there was a knock on the door.

"Would you like me to get it?" Gertrude offered, her own hands dry.

"Sure."

She opened it to find a boy on the other side. He smiled at her, his missing front tooth indicating that, while on the taller side, he was slightly younger than Samuel. He wore knickers and a newsboy cap and held a glass baby bottle in his hands.

"Come on in, Sal," Shannon called.

Gertrude took the bottle and stepped aside, allowing him entrance.

"From my mother," he explained, addressing Shannon. "Said you might need it for the little girl."

"Please give her our thanks."

"Will do, Miss C," he smiled a crooked grin before turning his attention to Samuel. "You play stickball?"

Samuel squinted.

"You know, like baseball, but with a stick for the bat."

"Oh," he nodded. "Right."

"Got a game going soon in the courtyard. Me, my brothers, couple o' fellas from the neighborhood. Could use a shortstop."

Gertrude's heart swelled as Samuel's eyes lit up. With his illness keeping him from school, it had been so long since her son had been with boys his own age. She did what she could to occupy him. Jennie, Walter, and even the servants all shower him with attention where and when they could. Still, his was a lonely existence. Certainly not the boisterous childhood Hugh enjoyed at the same age.

"Can I, Mama?" he asked, those brown eyes now begging her to say yes.

In her heart of hearts, Gertrude wanted to allow it. But everything changed within the last twenty-four hours. She knew he couldn't have slept well, none of them did. He wasn't used to exercising. Or heat, for that matter—the July sun already raised the mercury in the room, and it was barely even nine o'clock.

"Please?" Samuel implored.

"Where is this courtyard?"

Sal cocked his head at the window. "Just outside."

Gertrude sighed. "Alright."

Samuel was already on his feet. "Thanks, Mama."

"But if you start to feel even the slightest bit winded…."

"I know, I know," her son pouted.

The women spent the next few hours making small talk. They tended to Molly, her dimpled chin bringing a smile to both their faces while awaiting the latest from Hugh. It was close to lunchtime when he knocked on the door, wearing the same soiled uniform as the day before. A five o'clock shadow dotted his usually clean-shaven face, and his eyes were bloodshot.

Gertrude set the baby in the make-shift bassinet on the bed and hugged him.

"Have you eaten?" Shannon asked.

"No."

He waved her off with one hand, clutching his stomach with the other, and began to tell them what he'd learned so far.

The Bureau agreed to release Jennie. Good news, yes, but they were freezing all of Walter's assets, including Juniper Grove and the Germantown mansion. The agency planned to move him to Eastern State Penitentiary pending trial. A preliminary hearing was already scheduled for later in the week. If convicted, which was highly likely given the anti-German sentiment, he'd be moved again, this time to a federal facility all the way in Georgia.

Shannon remained silent, pacing the apartment with a fussy Molly on her shoulder the entire time Hugh was speaking. Meanwhile, laughter from Samuel and the other boys outside echoed in from the open window, a stark contrast to the somber mood in the room. Gertrude attempted to process the information, careful to remain as collected as possible under the circumstances.

"Biddle really thinks they'll find him guilty?" she asked, fearing she already knew the answer.

"Mother," Hugh explained, "We're lucky he even agreed to take the case."

CHAPTER 65

B ouncing Molly on her knee, Shannon watched in awe as Gertrude barked orders to the staff who'd met them at the Stockton Hotel.

"She's a one-woman army," she murmured aloud.

"That she is," Cook agreed. She beamed with admiration, crow's feet gathering at the corners of her gray eyes. "Not her first crisis, dear. But," the older woman blessed herself, "God willing her last."

"Agreed."

The matriarch was a force to be reckoned with. Shannon certainly wouldn't want to be on the other end of her ferocity; that they were even able to get a room on such short notice was a miracle in and of itself, let alone a suite. Bombing or no bombing, it was still a holiday weekend.

The rooms were spacious with an oceanfront view. Their walls were royal blue from the chair rail to the dental crown molding lining the high ceilings. Lavishly furnished, an intricately carved vanity and matching wardrobe occupied the far corner outside the bathroom. While Shannon was thankful her own boardinghouse featured indoor plumbing, there was a big difference between a lukewarm shower in the floor's only water closet and a long, hot soak in a grand hotel's marble bathtub. Whether or not she'd ever find out that difference remained to be seen. Perhaps there was something to be said about the clout of the Browne name, after all.

The room's opulence stood in stark contrast to the chaos within it. In addition to Cook, Rutherford had joined them. So did Mrs. Callaway's personal maid. Citing budget cuts, Gertrude let the rest of the Martin's servants go, though not without letters of recommendation and a small severance from her own purse.

"It was the right thing to do," she explained to Samuel, who leaned against the side of the room's queen-sized bed.

Fresh off his team's victory, his was the only smile in the place.

"We'll go to the Browne lodge," Gertrude continued firmly. "You two will depart ahead of us," she instructed Rutherford and Cook. "Make sure the house is in order."

"Of course," the butler nodded.

She turned to the maid and continued. "You'll stay here with me. We'll need new wardrobes. Help with the baby."

The girl furiously took notes on a piece of hotel stationery.

Brow furrowed, Gertrude drew a gloved hand to her mouth in deep concentration. She charged from one end of the room to the other, Sasha tucked carefully under her left arm.

"Remind me to contact Alva."

"Alva?"

"Belmont. Write that down."

The maid did as she was told, and Gertrude moved on to Shannon.

"As for you," she instructed, "we'll have the engagement publicized in all the appropriate papers. I know a good photography studio in town, but we'll have to do something about that hair before your portrait." Gertrude turned back to the maid. "See if you can get Miss Culligan an appointment at the salon downstairs as soon as possible."

Her *engagement?* Maybe Shannon had given her too much credit, and

Mrs. Callaway really was cracking under all the stress.

"My engagement?" she repeated carefully, thinking she'd possibly heard wrong.

She hadn't.

"To Hugh, of course." Gertrude smiled.

"Mrs. Callaway," Shannon returned the smile, mimicking the politeness in the other woman's voice, "I'm very... *fond*... of your son. And, I'm flattered."

She looked at Molly, willing her to provide a wanton distraction. The baby merely drooled, the tooth she was cutting no doubt making her feel just as uncomfortable as her aunt. Forced to continue, Shannon chose her words with caution.

"But," she bit her lip and gave a slight shrug of her shoulder, "he hasn't exactly asked me."

"A formality, dear." Gertrude chuckled, waving her hand in good humor. "It'll be just the distraction we need," Mrs. Callaway gushed. "Won't she make a beautiful bride?" she asked her maid.

"Beautiful," the girl echoed dutifully.

"How lovely," Shannon chirped, smiling at Molly while praying she sounded even remotely convincing.

Though she didn't doubt his feelings for her, Shannon would've preferred a more intimate proposal. One from, for instance, the groom himself. However, looking at his mother, it was clear the subject was not up for debate.

Suddenly, there was a commotion at the door. *A minute too late.* Hugh swept into the room, Jennie staggering just behind him. She limped toward them, the heel of one of her boots broken off, arms outstretched for balance. Cook gasped, and Shannon instinctively clutched Molly tighter, glad, for the first time, that Danny was away. Seeing his bride like this would absolutely ruin him.

Her sister-in-law looked destroyed. The poor girl clearly hadn't slept a wink. Glassy and bloodshot, her eyes were sunken; bags upon bags darkening her normally porcelain complexion, she gave off an aura of the undead Shannon only read about in novels. Mary Shelley would've been in her glory. The family, however, was horrified.

Jennie's golden brown hair, usually swept up in a flawless array of curls, now hung limply around her waist. Spindles matted, the frayed ends jutted out in all directions, and her dress was a grimy, tattered mess. The left shoulder was splattered in what Shannon knew to be baby stains. As for the rest, well, she grimaced, remembering a long-ago time in her youth playing circus at the Barkleys; using the fence of the pigpen as the 'high wire' not one of her better ideas. Shannon sniffed and tried not to gag—Jennie smelled about the same, too.

Hugh trudged across the room, pulling her into a tight squeeze. Being in his arms never felt so good. He stroked Shannon's hair before moving on to their niece, thumbing across the baby's cheek.

"It'll be okay," he promised Molly. "I'll take care of everything."

CHAPTER 66

Gertrude frowned as she hung up the telephone. She wanted to scream, the only thing holding her back being Jennie and the baby napping in the next bedroom. Hugh was diligent in giving her updates from the attorneys, but there were some things she wished she didn't know about. Like the maid's affidavit. *I told Walter to fire that girl.* She knew, more than anyone, Bridget couldn't be trusted.

If only her brother-in-law had listened. But no. Instead, the little traitor found that soft spot of his, reminding Walter and anyone else who'd listen she'd emigrated alone, just as he had. The girl had moxie; Gertrude would give her that.

Samuel was out playing ball with his newfound friend, and Shannon ran errands. Alone, Gertrude thought of busying herself with some letters until she remembered her stationery was already packed away for their trip to the Adirondacks. Sasha pattered into the room and nudged her ankle. She scooped her up, stroking behind the pup's silken ears while considering her possibilities.

She still owed Alva a call of thanks for ensuring Hugh's engagement made the society pages. If there was one thing her old friend loved, it was going head-to-head with the Archibald family. The woman thrived on ruffling their feathers. Gertrude was glad to have her in their corner. In exchange for donations to the National Women's Party, of course. With the family's departure planned for tomorrow morning, Gertrude thought it best to make the call now, where she knew there was an adequate switchboard.

To her surprise, the phone rang again. Thinking it was Hugh again with more unsettling news, she reluctantly answered on the second ring.

"Gertrude," Edmund barked.

An impish grin spread across her cheeks. "Hello to you, too, darling."

"Don't be coy."

"Why, whatever do you mean?" She heard him sigh on the other end and inspected her freshly manicured nails. "Calling to offer your congratulations?"

"Minnie's beside herself."

"Oh, my. We can't have *that*."

"Dammit, Gertrude. Cornelia's refusing to eat," he stammered. "We had an understanding. You promised."

"Promises were made to be broken. Come now, Edmund. You practically wrote that rule."

"You spiteful witch."

"Sticks and stones, darling."

Her ex was launching into another tirade when she slid the receiver back in place. *God that felt good.* Let him be angry. Let *him* hurt, for once. As for the Blackwells, she couldn't care less. Hugh would be far better off marrying for love.

CHAPTER 67

F rank reread the headline and poured himself another scotch. That was her, alright. Her hair was different, her clothing, no question an improvement, too stuffy for his liking. But her smile? He'd know that look anywhere. It was the one he sometimes saw in his dreams, sheets stained the next day. He knocked back the shot, grabbing the bottle for a refill when his bodyguard wrapped on the door.

"Boss?"

Frank hissed through his teeth. "What?"

"Someone here to see you."

"Told you I'm not taking meetings, Bruno."

"Not even from me?"

Standing next to the beefy enforcer, Shannon looked even smaller than usual. Hands folded in front of her, she pouted. Frank cocked his head, filling the tumbler and raising it in a toast.

"Congratulations, doll."

She took a tentative step forward, and Bruno shut the office door behind her. "I wanted to tell you myself."

"Little late for that." He jutted his chin at the *Star and Wave*. "You look good."

Shannon did look good. She cleaned up well, just like he'd envisioned. Her blonde mane was pinned at the nape under a straw cloche. The hat's band matched her lace dress, tobacco brown, while large pearls adorned her neck and ears.

"That's not you, though."

"Excuse me?"

There. There was the fire he knew.

Frank took a swig and clanked the glass on his desk. "I get it. Read what happened to your sister-in-law, too. Shame. Looks like a set-up to me."

She met his eye. "Jennie's innocent. So's Mr. Martin. They're good people."

"I'm sure they are." He tilted his head at the wet bar, and she shook hers no in reply. "Doesn't mean you have to change who you are."

"Who says I'm changing anything?"

He knit his brows, deliberately looking her up and down. She swallowed.

"Bait-and-switch 101, doll. Tell me," Frank coughed to keep his voice calm, "do you even love the guy?"

Shannon glared. "What kind of a question is that?"

"Seems fair enough. What was it you wanted again? Freedom?" He snickered. "You're not free, Shannon. You're a puppet on a goddamn string."

"How dare you!" She crossed her arms against her chest. "You don't even know him."

"Enlighten me."

"He's a good man. Someone I've cared about for a long time." Shannon let out an exaggerated sigh. "He's kind. Generous."

"I'll bet he is."

"It's not like that, Frank."

"Oh, no?"

"No."

Shannon held her head high, and it took everything in him not to grab that pretty little face and kiss her hard on the mouth.

"How is it then?"

"He…well…"

"Go on. Ain't got all day."

"Do you remember the night we met?"

He remembered. Thought about it more than he cared to admit. Now he only wished he could forget.

"Hugh paid my brother's stay at the hospital."

A sharp pain spiked through him.

"*Did* he now?" Frank crooned.

Shannon nodded, primly folding her gloved hands on her lap. "In full."

"How 'bout that," he grinned.

"Frank, please. Don't make this difficult. I've liked working with you. Appreciate every opportunity you gave me. Truly."

"You don't think you'll regret it? Leavin' that is."

"I don't. I'd like to…." Shannon cleared her throat. "*We* hope to start a family."

"Well then." Frank rose methodically, filling a glass for Shannon despite her earlier protests. She accepted it hesitantly while he topped off his own. He lifted it, encouraging her to do the same. "To the bride," he smiled. "Sláinte."

Fifteen minutes later, she was gone. Walked right out that office door and out of his life forever. Frank raked a hand through his hair and took a long pull straight from the bottle. What a fucking nightmare.

CHAPTER 68

A nightmare, that's what it was. Hell on earth. No escape. No end in sight. Danny's unit arrived in France on July 18ᵗʰ, what would've been his mother's birthday. They were soon assigned to the front, supporting the French in a major offensive push by the Allies to crush the Germans once and for all.

They'd marched through Paris, her streets lined with women in black as if the whole city were in mourning. That should've been his first clue.

"Vive les Americains!" they waved from balconies, and for a moment, just a fleeting moment, Danny surged with pride for their cause. Hope. But that's all it was. A brief pause and the familiar dread returned.

Once outside the city limits, they moved under cover of darkness, crammed like sardines in trucks along the muddy roadways. No talking. Absolutely no cigarettes, the sound of the guns ever-present in the distance as they made their way through the French countryside. They crept along at a snail's pace, frequently stopping to refuel or fix (yet another) blown tire.

Days passed. Weeks. The weather refused to cooperate. The rain was relentless. Hard, driving winds pounded them around the clock for five days straight. The ground was so saturated the roads were impassable, forcing them to leave some of their tanks behind, the engines seized from the water. Food supplies, artillery, none of it could get through. Danny saw some fellas walking in mud as deep as their knees.

It was late September when they finally reached the little town of St. Mihiel, or what was left of it, anyway. Three days of hard fighting later, they had the Germans on the run. Danny still wasn't sure how, although the air support probably had something to do with it. Now they were marching north to Sedan; he and a private, Jones, sent ahead as scouts.

They found the mangy bitch cowering in a barn's ruins earlier that day. Merely a puppy, she whined, ducking her matted black-and-gray head as they approached.

"Had one just like that back home," Jones said.

"Feels like a lifetime ago, huh?"

Jones agreed. "You have any pets?"

"Nah. Always wanted one, though." Danny crouched down with his hand extended. "C'mere girl." He reached in his pocket when she didn't move and offered her some leftover crackers.

The dog limped forward, dragging the front paw on her left side. She looked shyly at Danny, taking the treat from him and devouring it. Poor thing. She didn't choose this. Damn the Kaiser.

Suddenly, Jones clubbed her over the head.

"What'cha do that for?"

"You see her leg?" Jones said. "Besides, she's not the only one hungry around here."

Back at base, it was Danny's job to skin and dismember her. *"No different than a rabbit,"* he muttered to himself as he laid her lifeless body across the make-shift table. Already salivating at the thought of fresh meat, he set his jaw, stroking her back one last time before setting to work.

Pinching the skin in the middle of her back, he plunged in his trench knife and made a small hole. Using two fingers from each hand, Danny reached inside and tugged her fur in opposite directions. The thin skin tore quickly, her blood oozing out. Slick and wet, it dripped all over.

He pulled and pulled, all the way down to her tail, grunting as he yanked the hide from her feet. He was covered in her, a river of red flowing off the table onto his boots.

Danny looked down at his hands, rotating the palms face up and turning them over again. *Pa. Shannon. Stop.* A wave of nausea crashed over him, and he felt dizzy, cold.

No, he resolved, gritting his teeth. This was different, she was dinner. The men were counting on him. And so it was on to her other half. He got all the way up her neck, tearing the skin off just behind her ears before throwing it over his shoulder.

With a cleaver, he chopped off her head, her tail, and her limbs. Whack, whack, whack!

He flipped her on her back. Out came her innards, and he made quick work of dividing the rest of her carcass into smaller pieces.

The whole unit ate stew that night. Sure, it was watered down, but it was still a hot supper, certainly a far cry from the canned garbage the Army deemed sufficient rations. Danny couldn't remember the last time he felt so full.

"Good thing we found the dog," Jones grunted while they walked back from the reserve line. He lit a cigarette and offered the pack to his friend.

Danny took a Lucky and tucked it behind his ear. "It's my turn for night patrol."

"Better you than me."

Weapons cleaned and face blackened with cork, Danny reported to his C.O. five minutes early. His partner, on the other hand, was late. Leave it to him to get stuck with a replacement for the mission.

Wide-eyed and innocent, Private Schmidt was fresh off the farm. Probably one of those kids duped into joining up thinking they'd get to see the world. Danny almost felt sorry for him. Smitty wasn't fit for guard duty, let alone reconnaissance.

"You're shaking like a leaf, kid," Danny said with disdain.

His companion puffed on his hands, fervently rubbing them together. "I can't feel them," the boy complained.

"You get used to it. Where you from, Private?"

"Oklahoma. You, Sir?"

"Jersey."

"Nice to be so close to the ocean. First time I ever saw it was when we left New York."

Danny had no time for small talk. They had a job to do, and it wasn't getting any earlier. "C'mon," he said, starting up the ladder.

Smitty hadn't tied one of his boots tightly enough. Tripping out of the parapet, he gave away their position.

The German machine gunners wasted no time. Bullets whipped toward them with frightening speed, their blasts echoing in the darkness. The smell of fresh gunpowder mixed with the acrid cordite of never-ending shelling.

"Get down!" Danny grabbed Smitty by the shoulder, thrusting them both into the mud. A sea of barbed wire stretched out before them. "We'll have to crawl from here."

They slid on bellies and elbows toward a nearby crater, ducking inside for shelter. Smitty vomited, remnants of their dinner splattered down the front of his muddy jacket.

"I can't do this," he choked.

Danny groaned. The kid was no use.

A grenade exploded in the distance. Smitty flinched, but Danny knew it was only a matter of time before more rained down around them.

"We gotta move," he commanded, inching toward the side of the hole facing the enemy.

"No," Smitty said, an air of defiance in his tone as prideful tears streamed down his cheeks. "I'm going back."

The boy looked at the American line, took a deep breath, and pushed himself upright.

"Wait—"

A sniper shot him not two seconds later. The back of Smitty's head in pieces, he dropped to the ground at Danny's feet.

Danny swallowed back the lump in his throat. He tried to warn him. It wasn't his fault the kid didn't listen. Hands deftly checking the body, he retrieved the private's weapons. No sense they both end up dead. Strapping the rifle to the shoulder opposite his own, he checked to ensure the Colt was loaded correctly, but it was too late.

The blast threw him at least fifteen feet, and he landed with a pop on his left side. Danny tried to roll over to crawl back to the trench, but he couldn't move his arm and plopped face down in the sludge. Gagging, he spat out the bile and began again. The more he struggled, the more he sank into the muck and mire.

No wonder they call it No Man's Land.

Four years of attrition. For what? Because a bunch of inbred Royals couldn't agree on how to split up their empires? It seemed so trivial to him.

Danny grimaced, gingerly grazing his shoulder. He knew why the U.S. really entered the War. Money. Power. A prime seat at the table whenever this hell came to an end.

The place was a living nightmare, destruction as far as the eye could see. Craters where there used to be trees. Rotting corpses of men strewn throughout, save for the decaying carcass of a horse here or there. Barbed wire zigzagged through the angry earth. Initially overpowering, Danny found he'd grown nose blind to the stench until now. Twisting himself onto his backside, he realized he was bleeding somewhere on his torso. Was it from the grenade? He wasn't even sure.

He saw movement through the haze. Gripping his bayonet with his good arm, he looked to his right where rats gorged themselves on what remained of Smitty.

An hour passed. Then another. Danny shivered from a spiking fever. He looked up at the night sky. Shells glowed as the guns raged in the distance. Suddenly he was somewhere else. Fourth of July. Fireworks. Jennie.

They were twelve, stopped at the top of the Giant Wheel no thanks to the quarter he'd slipped the amusement operator. Took him three weeks and several extra newspaper routes to earn it, but it was the best money he'd ever spent. He couldn't have timed it any better; the light show would be starting any moment.

Jennie crossed her arms against herself, holding tight to the stuffed bear he'd won her earlier. Goosebumps rippled over her alabaster skin. He put his arm around her, pulling her close.

God, she was beautiful. An angel on earth sent to him from his mother. Her honey-brown hair was pulled back off her face in a white bow, the ringlets he loved to play with cascading her back. She wore a pink short-sleeved dress, a white lace bib covering her neck and shoulders. White lace gloves matched her white stockings and shoes. It was her smile, though, he liked best.

Now she was looking at him in a way he'd never seen before, and Danny felt his cheeks flush. They were so close. His heart was pounding, and he cleared his throat.

Jennie closed her eyes, tilting her head back.

This is really happening.

His own lips parting, Danny leaned over. A thousand watts of electricity jolted through him. He felt his stomach flip flop and his toes curl. The sky erupted with fireworks, but they didn't hear a thing.

The guns grew quiet, the sky awash in the purple hues of a new day. Danny's head was heavy on his shoulders; what was left of this wretched world faded in and out of view. He wasn't cold anymore. His lashes fluttered, and he licked his chapped lips.

"I'm sorry," he murmured, giving in to the darkness.

CHAPTER 69

"It's alright," Jennie said in a nurturing voice. "Everything will be fine. Just fine."

Her reflection in the looking glass begged to differ; the dark circles just wouldn't seem to go away. Still, she'd been repeating the mantra to herself daily since Father's arrest, so why stop now? Three months later and she almost believed it.

Her time spent at the Browne camp did little to subdue her qualms. Thinking herself helpful, Gertrude hired a nurse and nanny for the baby, but that only worsened matters. She hadn't spent any real time with her daughter since. Were they feeding her enough? Was she sleeping?

Does she miss me? Will she even recognize me anymore?

Looking in the mirror again, Jennie hardly even recognized herself, her hand already resting on the tiny glass vile next to her powder. When she wasn't reliving her night of terror in jail, she obsessed about how Father was holding up at Eastern State. When she wasn't speculating Molly's whereabouts, her heart yearned for any information about Danny's.

The medicine would help. Just a sip. What was wrong with that?

Nothing. Laudanum had been around for centuries. They wouldn't have given it to her if it were harmful. Without it, Jennie just might be in an asylum right now.

It tasted awful, though. Bitter, so bitter, which was precisely why she'd been hoarding leftover sugar cubes. One here. Another there. Not so many Cook would notice. They were still rationing like everyone else, of course. Just enough to chase away the taste of what had become her daily dose.

The family returned to Philadelphia for the court proceedings, taking residence at her aunt's townhome in Rittenhouse Square. The lawyers were very upfront—there was no saving Father. They'd argue for lighter sentencing, but Jennie shouldn't disillusion herself.

That was hard enough to swallow, but it wasn't all they had planned in terms of defense. Her aunt was instrumental in the overall strategy, the chief goal to shift the press coverage off of "Mr. Martin" and shine the light on "Mrs. Daniel Culligan."

Jennie's schedule was soon so rigorous it was overwhelming. Smile and nod, smile and nod. Keep your emotions to yourself. Reporters from all over the city flocked to their neighborhood. Men with mustaches. Straw hats and tweed suits. They practically camped on the doorstep, angling for a bit of information they could squeeze out of her.

The oft chance she did get to see Molly was staged. A short walk around the fountain in the park, the pram draped in bunting. All for the cameras, of course. Jennie didn't even get a chance to hold her before Nurse swept her away.

An appearance at the National League for Women's Service? Not a problem. A luncheon at the Crystal Tea Room honoring the Red Cross volunteers? It was her pleasure. Her aunt did most of the talking, but Jennie's presence was paramount to their overall success. She did her best to put on a show, following the attorneys' instructions to the letter. She could manage as long as she had her Little Helper, giving scripted answers with ease.

"That's Culligan. C-U-" her aunt repeated the spelling to a gentleman from *The Inquirer*. "He's with Philadelphia's Own."

The reporter looked up. "79th Division?"

"Yes," Gertrude said, turning to Jennie for confirmation. "I believe that's correct."

"My neighbor's got a kid in that regiment. We were all there to see him off," he grinned at the recollection.

"What?" Jennie asked, suddenly sick to her stomach.

The man ignored her and continued taking notes. "You must be really proud. Your husband's a hero, ma'am. They all are."

Proud? Her husband hadn't written to her in months. Didn't even bother to acknowledge the birth of their child. Her husband, who apparently shipped out without even giving her a second thought. Danny knew nothing of the hell she'd been through. It was like he never cared at all. Jennie felt her hands shaking, diligently folding them behind her back as practiced time and again.

"Of course," she replied, her tone so well-rehearsed it sounded natural to the untrained ear. She flashed her pearly whites just as the bulbs burst.

"That's all for today," her aunt told the journalist. "I'm afraid we have another appointment to get to."

CHAPTER 70

Rutherford opened the door for them, and Gertrude folded her skirts as she slid into the backseat of the Packard. Jennie climbed in beside her. "Where to?" he asked.

"The townhouse, please."

He nodded and took his place at the wheel. *A Godsend.* With the men gone, the butler took it upon himself to look out for the family as if they were his own. He even refused the bonus she offered him. Loyalty like that was worth its weight in gold.

Not like that Biddy Bridget. Heaven help the girl when she gets through with her. Of course, they'd have to find her first, not that Gertrude didn't have plenty of resources poured into the effort. Still, the former maid seemingly disappeared without a trace.

She would be dealt with. All in due time.

Right now, Gertrude needed to focus on the Liberty Loan parade scheduled for tomorrow. There were rumblings in the planning committee the mayor was thinking of canceling for fear of Spanish influenza.

Preposterous. She didn't spend countless hours organizing to give up now, not when she'd been cajoling every official in the tristate area for weeks. Her publicity campaign was paying off, but they still had more ground to cover. She booked the marching bands and organized the military units who'd yet to ship out.

At last year's parade, the Liberty Bell itself was marched from its home at Independence Hall, the float pulled by none other than Uncle Sam himself. A hard act to follow, but Gertrude was not about to disappoint. Not when they were already expecting a crowd of nearly two hundred thousand. And those were the early projections.

This year, the committee planned to showcase the latest innovation—the floating biplanes they were building just down the river at the Philadelphia Navy Yard. Indeed, it was shaping up to be quite a spectacle. Even John Philip Sousa had agreed to delight the masses with a concert.

They needed to make those bond quotas. They *had* to. It was the ultimate gauge of patriotism. Sure the money would help the troops, but hers was the greater cause. Prosperity.

She had a family image to protect. She'd done it before, and she'd do it again, this time with Jennie in the forefront. They'd built the whole campaign around it.

Her niece was only a figurehead, of course. The girl couldn't be counted on for any actual decision-making, but she still had her looks, which was all they needed. Her niece's figure bounced back nicely after motherhood. As for her sullen complexion, well, that could be fixed with a bit of powder.

Yes, thanks to her hard work, Jennie was the face of the war effort. There were none more patriotic than she, with Gertrude ensuring she put her money (her *Browne* money, that is) where her mouth was. The papers touted her Knickerbocker lineage, centuries of steadfast loyalty, as well as her most heartfelt role, that being the dutiful wife of a Doughboy.

"Did you see the latest YMCA poster?" she asked as Rutherford turned the giant automobile onto Walnut Street.

"Hmm?" her niece responded distractedly.

"The poster, dear," Gertrude repeated with as much patience as possible. Sometimes she wasn't sure where that child's head was. "The one Mr. Brown designed?"

"Oh," Jennie said quietly. "Yes. *For Your Boy.*"

"He really captured Danny's likeness, don't you agree? And from your wedding portrait, no less." She patted her niece's hand. "I'm sure you miss him. Especially now, with everything that's happened with your father. But the war will be over before you know it and we'll make sure he gets the hero's welcome he deserves. Until then, we have to do our part to ensure that he, and the other boys, are equipped with everything they need to lead them to victory."

Jennie offered her a weak smile as they pulled up to the house.

"Aunt Gertrude?"

"Yes, dear?"

"Do you really think it's wise to proceed with the parade tomorrow?" She grimaced. "I mean, after the last one."

"Darling, that's precisely why we *do* have to go on with it." And, as much as Gertrude didn't mean to, out slipped a mirthless laugh. "What else could possibly go wrong?"

CHAPTER 71

Bridget leaned against the bed's metal frame, pouting when Joseph failed to acknowledge her. "You owe me money."

Wasn't it enough he saw she was fed and clothed? Had a goddamn room over her head and her pipes cleaned at least twice a week?

Martin should've already been in Georgia by now, but no one had counted on Biddle's office representing him through this mess. The trial had been over and done for two months, but Taylor recommended keeping her on hand for the appeal. It'd be squashed, of course, but they couldn't take any chances. It was frustrating as hell; the Board at Martin Glass was unable to move forward with naming him as new president until all the loose ends were tied up.

Bridget cupped her bare breasts and tried again. "Didn'tcha hear me?"

Joseph rolled his eyes, her brogue still just as repulsive as the first time she opened her mouth. Even the gardenia spray he'd given her had lost its allure.

He looked around the bordello she called home. Sheer scarfs draped the lamps on either side of the rickety bed while overflowing ashtrays added to the grotesque ambiance; the curtain where a door should've been allowing other johns to come and go as they pleased. Joseph felt his skin crawl, wanting nothing more than to never hear her voice again.

"I heard you," he groaned as he put his shoes back on. "What happened to the five I gave you last week?"

"Spent it," she shrugged. "Well, most of it, anyway."

"So use that."

"Can't."

"Why not, dammit?" Joseph looked up at her in a fury. If this were about those leeches she called parents, he wouldn't budge. About time they started supporting themselves.

Bridget slowly drew her hands from her bosom and slid them just under her belly button. She tilted her head, green eyes gazing down at her abdomen.

"Savin' it,' she smirked. "For the Wee One."

Joseph stood up and crossed his arms against his chest. This was the last thing he needed right now. "How do I know it's even mine?"

Her eyes widened. "How *dare* you?"

She marched across the room, winding up to slap him, but he grabbed her wrists and pinned them to her sides. Furious, she spat on his freshly shined shoe, black saliva adding a new stain to the already filthy floor.

The scenario itself wasn't so unusual; Joseph just never thought it would happen to him. He was a York, they were smarter than that. He wracked his brain while Bridget continued to wiggle in his grasp. There was a doctor back in Cambridge. Helped one of his fraternity brothers when he was in a similar jam. A couple of pills and done. Surely there were more such physicians. All he had to do was make a few discrete inquiries.

"Lemme go," she squirmed.

"You're not keeping it," he insisted, squeezing her harder.

"I won't put my baby in an orphanage!"

"Not exactly what I meant."

She craned her neck and bit down hard on his left shoulder. Stunned, Joseph faltered, and Bridget was able to free herself.

"That's murder," she hissed. Fists balled, she backed through the curtain.

He followed her into the casino, glad it was morning and empty of an audience.

"You little hypocrite. What exactly do you think Seamus was doing at the Post Office before he was blown to smithereens?"

"Don't bring my family into this!"

"Fine," he said, trying to remain calm. "Let's talk about you, then. Extortion, prostitution, perjury for Christ's sake."

The girl was so frantic she shook. Cocking her head, she scowled at him. "I read your letters while you were asleep. I know Mr. Martin plans on an appeal. I'll recant. Tell 'em everything, I will. How it was all a lie. That you paid me." Angry tears spilled down her cheeks. "I can't live like this anymore! Money or no money, I won't."

No, you won't.

It was about this time something in him snapped. This parasite and her bog Irish kin had been a drain on his resources for long enough. There would be no doctor. No pills. Nobody on this side of the pond to mourn her or her baby.

The casino echoed with Joseph's maniacal laughter.

"What's so funny?" she snarled.

"You, my dear," he smiled. "For thinking anyone will take the word of a two-faced whore."

She charged him—just the reaction he was hoping for—but Joseph quickly overpowered her, curling his right elbow around her throat. He pressed her against his chest and flexed his bicep.

Bridget gurgled. He gripped her tighter, watching her eyes roll back into her head as he crushed her windpipe. It wasn't long before she went limp in his arms. Only then did he let go, her half-naked body dropping to the floor with a thud. Not one of his finer moments but no one needed to know.

Joseph was straightening his lapels when he noticed the lipstick she'd left on his jacket and sneered. Leaving her still-warm corpse in the middle of the room, he walked over to the bar to look for some club soda to rub out the stain. There, behind the shelves, crouched a shaking teenage boy.

CHAPTER 72

"Barkley?" Hugh peered through the peephole in the apartment door. "What's he doing here?"

Shannon peeked up from her copy of *Hearst's*. "Haven't the slightest idea," she shrugged, motioning for him to open it.

Her fiancée hesitated, probably because he knew he shouldn't be there without a proper chaperone. The Rossinis looked the other way, and Hugh could usually slip in and out of the boarding house with Pat under the guise of picking up his laundry. On the other hand, Gertrude would have a coronary if she ever found out.

Still, Will shouldn't be calling on her alone either, and she wondered if there wasn't a hint of jealousy in Hugh's voice. He'd been occupied all summer. Too occupied to set a date, she thought with remorse. Between his monitoring the trial, overseeing the reconstruction of the sailors' quarters, and the never-ending paperwork, she hardly saw him. Maybe a little envy could be good for them.

Another knock. Shannon huffed.

"Alright," Hugh mouthed, smiling as he allowed the other man entrance.

"Will. It's been too long."

Their friend shuffled in. He looked like he'd just come from the farm, the front of his dungaree overalls covered in dirt, pant legs caked in mud up to his knees. Shannon tried to keep her surprise abated and rose from the kitchenette while Hugh gave him a friendly pat on the shoulder.

"Good to see you," she said graciously. She got a glass out of the cabinet. "Lemonade?"

Will hung his head and pulled a flask from his pocket. "Brought somethin' stronger. Think we're all gonna need it."

⋄⇒○⇐⋄

A week later, Shannon still couldn't believe it. Unable to sleep, she tossed and turned, Snowball glowering at her from the foot of the bed.

There was no telling what this York character was capable of doing next. Apparently, Will was at Jackson's making a delivery when he heard a couple arguing. Initially, he thought he'd be able to sneak back down the servant stairway but was found before he could make his escape. York forced him to help bury the body.

"We hid her under the crates in the farm truck," Will explained. "Same way it's done with the liquor."

He stopped at this point in the story, giving Shannon a knowing glance. She wondered if he were working for Frank again, realizing simultaneously that she, herself, missed doing so. Thankfully, Hugh didn't notice.

From there, Joseph had him drive to the bayside of the island, where they waded deep into the marshy low tide.

"Anybody driving by woulda guessed we was layin' crab traps." Will had scratched his head. "Suppose we were. Tying her limbs to the seagrass like that."

Will was beside himself, and Shannon felt for her friend. He gave Hugh the roll of bills York paid him to keep quiet.

"For Jennie," he'd said. "She don't deserve none of this."

Afraid York would renege and come after him, the trio agreed it would be best for Will to lay low, seeking refuge in the hayloft of his parents' barn until they could figure out their next move.

Hugh took the first train to Philadelphia to bring Biddle's office the update himself. Shannon had never seen him so angry. Her white knight. The family's great crusader rode off to clear his uncle's name. If only Danny were with him, they'd be unstoppable.

That was a week ago. Not a call or a telegram since.

The maid. Shannon punched her lumpy pillow, recalling her first introduction to the girl and the strange kinship she felt toward her. She was so young. Thousands of miles from family and all alone, probably doing the best she could. Plus, from Will's description, it didn't sound like York gave her much choice in the matter. After all, he'd blackmailed Gertrude before. Either way, the girl didn't deserve to die. Not like that.

But what was one less paddy? Nothing to those people; the same upper-crust she was about to marry into herself.

Frank had been right. She was a puppet. Stomach cramped, Shannon felt like such a fool. Just like she did reading Gertrude's letters, filled with so much flowery language, she needed a dictionary. Not having one on hand, she simply glossed over them, resenting each one more than the last, her inquiries after Samuel's health or Molly's latest tooth wholly ignored.

Instead, Mrs. Callaway carried on with her warped mission, thrusting Shannon into a world where she didn't belong. One where saying no wasn't an option; that would only be viewed as a declaration of war. Shannon knew she wasn't the only marionette—the matriarch paraded Jennie all over Philadelphia—but it didn't make her feel any better about being beholden.

Now Frank's words echoed in her ear, turning to dust as she choked on them in the dark, lonely room. She didn't want to see it at the time, was furious with him for even making the allegation, but he was right just the same. Deep down, she knew it. Which was probably why she had gotten so angry in the first place.

Frank Hilton never expected anything from her other than to hold up her end of their business transactions. Even though she was a woman, he treated her with equal respect. Shannon always felt at ease during their meetings, a fact which couldn't be any further from how she felt about herself leaving those wrenched committee meetings and ladies' luncheons she was now required to attend on the family's behalf.

Shannon might look the part, no thanks to the packages Gertrude sent seemingly every other day, but she wasn't blind. She saw the sneers from the Old Guard. Heard the snickering behind her back. She never knew what to say, which fork to use, or even why they had so many forks, to begin with. She was a local, not a cottager. They'd never accept her.

Which would be fine by Shannon if not for Molly. The whole situation was exasperating, and she longed to tell Hugh how she really felt. The pressure to perform was becoming too much. She loved him, she really did, but a part of her wished she'd rejected his proposal. Then again, he never really asked her in the first place. Gertrude made that decision, too.

Shannon knew better than to make him choose between herself and his mother. It was too risky; her opponent—too clever. If Hugh chose wrong, she'd lose access to the baby, the only blood relative she had left. The best she could do was bide her time and hope things would change once the war ended.

Tired of shuffling between her feet, Snowball crept up the side of the bed. He nudged his head against her shoulder and curled into a tight ball like he somehow knew she was sad. Shannon scratched him behind the ear, her thoughts settling on Danny as they always eventually did. His last letter was tantamount to the final goodbye. He didn't say much, the censors saw to that, but Shannon could read between the lines. They were sending his division to the front, and he wasn't sure how often he'd be able to write.

She could feel her heartbreaking. Living without him was supposed to have gotten easier, but it hadn't. It never would; it only got worse. He was the one person in the whole world who really knew her, *really* knew her; accepted her for who she was because they were one and the same. Faults and all, Danny loved her anyway. The best part of her was gone, never to return. Swallowing the lump in her throat, she rolled over yet again.

One o'clock turned into two and two to three. Still, sleep evaded her, memories churning as her brain refused to shut down. If only she could turn it off, like a key in a car.

Eventually, she must've drifted off because she had the strangest dream about Sal Rossini.

"Miss C! Miss C open up." He pounded on the door.

The banging continued, and Shannon groggily peeled open her eyes. "Coming," she groaned as she slipped into her robe.

"Good. You're up," the boy smiled.

"I am now," she mumbled, stifling a yawn. "Everything alright, Sal?"

"Call for you. The Lieutenant."

That woke her up. Shannon handed him a nickel for his troubles and headed to the communal lobby of the boardinghouse, where the only telephone was located.

Breathless, she picked up the receiver from the table. "Hello?"

"Hey, it's me," Hugh's voice sounded tired. "I know it's early. Did I wake you?"

"No," she lied. "Are you back in town? I'll fry up some breakfast."

"No."

She knew something was wrong by the way he said it. Dreadfully wrong. Shannon could feel it in her bones but dared not ask for fear of confirming her worst nightmare.

Jennie was next of kin. Of course, the Army would send the ghastly telegram to her.

Shannon gulped. White-knuckled, she gripped the edge of the side table, struggling to find the words.

"Hugh? Are you still there?"

"I am. God, it's good to hear your voice."

"What aren't you telling me?"

But there was only a rugged sigh on the other end of the line.

"Whatever it is, just say it. *Please*."

"I'm so sorry darling," Hugh said. "I wanted to tell you before you see it in the papers."

"See what? I don't…don't understand."

"I'm under quarantine."

"What?"

"Not just me, Shannon. The whole city."

CHAPTER 73

The Spanish Flu held Philadelphia in a death grip. It was terrifying. Unlike anything Jennie had experienced before. Every family was touched by the mysterious illness in one way or another. The city had over thirty hospitals and, within four days of her aunt's parade, every bed was filled. The *Inquirer's* morning addition claimed more than two thousand people already died from either the flu or its complications—a ferocious pneumonia—with predictions the death toll would be doubled by the following week.

The disease struck with a fury, and Death laughed at its harvest. It killed indiscriminately, winding carnage through the neighborhoods like spilled ink. A person could come down with a fever in the morning and be dead by dinnertime.

No household was safe, not even theirs. They lost poor Rutherford that morning. Right as rain one moment, on his deathbed the next. The butler's skin turned bluish-black. Blood seeped out his nose, eyes, and ears. He moaned, choking on it, and there was nothing, *nothing* they could do to help him.

"I'll notify his family," Gertrude said in a dry voice. "We'll send them a little something, of course."

"I think they deserve more than that," her cousin argued. "How long has he been with the family?"

"Years," Jennie croaked. "Ever since I was Molly's age."

The three of them were in the dining room. Cook was upstairs readying the third-floor nursery to seal off the children. Nanny fretted to and fro, her list of supplies and necessities longer and longer every time she appeared in the doorway. But it had to be done; there was no telling who would come down with it next or when.

The rest of the staff gave notice. Jennie couldn't blame them. They were either petrified (and who wasn't) or had families of their own to care for. In a few days, a week maybe, it wouldn't matter.

The hospitals were already overrun. With most medical staff assisting the military in some form or another, to say the city was ill-equipped was an understatement. Calls were going out all over for nurses. Any woman, even those without medical experience, was being pressed into service.

Gertrude took a sip of claret. "We should go by the hospital tomorrow."

"For the sick?" Jennie asked, her tone venomous. "Or for the press?"

"I beg your pardon?"

"You heard me. Rutherford's been gone less than twenty-four hours, the children are quarantined, yet you suddenly think it's a good idea to volunteer."

Tight-lipped, her aunt held firm. "It's for the greater good."

"The greater good? The *greater good?* After we've been exposed to this, this...thing?" Jennie shook her head sideways. "Did you know St. Louis cancelled their loan parade? Cancelled, Aunt Gertrude."

The older woman tilted her head. "I suppose they had different information."

"I'm fairly certain they had the same intelligence. Twelve thousand soldiers died at that base near Boston. And that was two weeks ago."

"What exactly are you insinuating?"

"You're a smart woman. I'm sure you can figure it out."

"My dear, you're forgetting I was merely part of the committee."

"Like you'd ever let me forget."

"Darling, we're all upset about Rutherford. But please," Gertrude patted the smock on Jennie's dress where she kept her vial, "do try to calm down."

Jennie took the laudanum from her pocket. She looked from the tiny bottle to her aunt and deliberately dropped it on the floor. Shards of glass splintered against the marble, liquid already pooling around the legs of her chair.

"Did you see him, Gertrude? He was blue. Blue!"

"Very unsettling, indeed."

"Is that all you can say?" Jennie blinked back tears. How could she be so cold? So selfish and conniving. Gertrude wouldn't really place social status above public safety, would she? Jennie didn't trust her own instincts. She wasn't sure of anything. "I'm so tired of this dog and pony show."

"Jennie," Hugh said in a gentle tone, "I'm sure Mother and the committee took every safety precaution into consideration before the parade. What happened today is a tragedy, I would never undercut that, but you can't go around making wild accusations."

She glared at him. "That's my daughter upstairs. My baby."

Hugh put a hand on her knee. "Samuel's up there, too."

"It's not the same. Danny's gone. I have no idea where he is or if... or if...."

"C'mere." He pulled her into a hug, and she cried on his shoulder. "I know it's been hard. I know. *Shh.* There's a big push going on right now. Might even lead to an armistice."

"Really?" She lisped.

Hugh nodded. "Why don't you go up and try to rest? Hmm? Just try." He pet the back of her head. "I'm afraid I agree with Mother on this. We're able bodied so we should help. It's our duty."

In her heart, Jennie knew he was right. She smoothed her skirts and rose.

"I'll drop you two off at Penn on my way to the Navy Yard in the morning."

⋖⋯⋯⋯⋯⋖

It was nonstop from the moment they arrived.

"Here." The head nurse thrust masks at them.

Gertrude held one up by the strings, eyeing it as if it were an insect. "I am *not* wearing that," she sneered.

The nurse rolled her eyes.

"I don't think they're for fashion," Jennie whispered loudly, tying the loops of her own mask and securing it behind her ears.

"Try to keep them comfortable," the nurse was saying now. "There's not much we can do. Cold compresses, kind words. Clean sheets on the bed after they've been brought down to the morgue."

"I was thinking more along the lines of administrative work," Gertrude said in her most condescending voice. She adjusted her hat, her look of triumph fading when it was apparent the other woman wouldn't budge.

The nurse let out an exasperated sigh. "We don't even have enough room for them all. There are cots up and down the hallway. Some people are just covered in blankets on the floor. I hate to turn you away but if you're not here to help you'll have to leave."

"I see," her aunt replied.

Jennie looped her by the elbow. "Come," she urged. "There's much to be done. Why don't you help me find some cloths?"

CHAPTER 74

Already in hot water for giving him a day's leave, Hugh's C.O. was none-too-pleased to hear he was unable to return to the cape. With most of the shipyard stricken, he was temporarily reassigned and given the grisly duty of transferring the dead to mass graves dug by some local seminarians.

As much as he tried not to dwell on it, he couldn't forget the horror-struck look on Jennie's face when he dropped them off at the University of Pennsylvania. Mostly, he agreed with her about Mother. The publicity stunts were becoming embarrassing. In the brief discussion he had with Biddle that much was clear. She needed to be reined in, and he kicked himself for not addressing it before the flu struck. Given the current state of affairs, Hugh didn't expect he'd be able to anytime soon. The body count rose higher by the hour.

The morgue couldn't keep up, and there weren't enough undertakers. Worse yet, the cost of coffins was skyrocketing as profiteers lined their pockets in a disgusting abuse of power. Corpses were stacked outside like cordwood. All of them the same sickening color Rutherford had been. Splotches of deep plum covered their faces like they'd never been human.

With only a thin mask covering his face, Hugh stacked body after body into the ambulance. One by one, like the wooden blocks he used to play within the nursery. He tried to be gentle, but some were heavier than others. The work was grueling, the smell unbearable, but there was no one else to do it. If they decayed any further, the city risked a rat infestation, which would only further compound the problem.

Hugh vomited on his way back from his first run. Pulled right over on the side of Broad Street and barely made it out the window. It seemed like there was more death on this side of the Atlantic than there was along the front, and he wondered if the stories were true—that the enemy released the virus as a calculated part of their war machine. The torpedoing proved they weren't above attacking civilians, and the Northeast region was pumping out quite an arsenal. If no one was well enough to work the factories, the Central Powers could gain the upper hand.

He couldn't let that happen. The city couldn't fall. Not if he had anything to say about it. And so he drove onward. Back and forth, back and forth, back and forth. Loading and unloading, helping the young priests dig at times. But he just couldn't get ahead. His hands shook, hunger and exhaustion taking their toll after hours of backbreaking work.

I'm coming down with it. No, he shivered. It can't be. He thought fleetingly of Shannon, regretting not taking her to the altar, or his bed, sooner.

Night fell, and Hugh could feel his weary eyes closing as he continued the route. He took a sip from his canteen, but it wasn't enough to quench the thirst of October's second summer. Throat dry, his breathing was labored from the sweaty mask stuck to his face. There was no other choice. He had to wear the damn thing or risk spreading the infection to others.

It was close to midnight when they sent him home. He had a splitting headache, but Hugh couldn't complain about an eighteen-hour shift. Not when he could hear the moans of his brethren coming through the portholes of the make-shift hospital ship. They sounded ungodly. Like wounded animals begging to be put down.

All he had to do now was make it to the townhouse. The drive wasn't far. He was almost there, just a few blocks ahead. He could see lights over the park, an iridescence gleaming over the long reflecting pool, and smiled to himself.

Cook would have something waiting for him. Such a doll, she was. A saint.

A nice full belly, and then he could sleep. Yes, that's all he needed. With a crackling fire in his room to shake off the chill that crept over him. So warm and toasty. Just a few hours, and he'd be fine. He had to be; they needed him back by first light.

Except he ached from his bones to his hair follicles. Everything, *everything* hurt. It felt like someone took an icepick to both of his eyes, a sharp, deep throbbing that only seemed to intensify as the night wore on. Hugh had his fair share of hangovers. He vaguely remembered getting the mumps in his youth. But never, never did he feel as bad as he felt right now.

He parked the Packard in the rear garage and forced himself up the kitchen steps, his grip tight against the iron railing. He flung open the door and staggered into the dark house.

It was so quiet. Too quiet. Mother and Jennie must've been sleeping, he knew, but Hugh's stomach was looking forward to that platter he'd been daydreaming about.

Crumpling the mask, he inhaled deeply for the first time in hours, hoping to catch a lingering whiff of whatever Cook made, but there was nothing. The room hadn't been used in hours.

He heard movement behind him on the servant stairs and turned, time itself standing still. The stout old woman hunched at the foot of the steps, tears flowing down her face as she wrung her hands.

"Thank God you're home." Cook managed between sobs. "The womenfolk are still at the hospital."

"They didn't walk home?"

She shook her head.

Hugh coughed into his elbow and reached for the door.

"I- I tried, sir. I tried but I couldn't—"

CHAPTER 75

J ennie pulled the sheet taut over the cot. She'd lost count of how many
died so far. This one was a woman, possibly about her age, but you'd
never know that looking at her now; the corpse a grotesque blue, her face
so swollen Jennie couldn't tell if she were Caucasian or Negro.

She'd writhed in pain, coughing so violently Jennie thought she was
going to snap a rib or two. Blood was everywhere, pouring out her every
hole. At least she wasn't suffering anymore. Jennie marked it down on her
clipboard and moved on to the next patient.

The day had flown by, with night promising much of the same. It
was horrific. All those people. People who, only a few days earlier, were
perfectly healthy. Mothers, fathers. Laborers, homemakers. Most of the
patients weren't even that old. These were people in their prime. It didn't
make sense to her. None of it made any sense.

Another corpse carted off on a stretcher, Jennie focused on remaking
the bed. She glanced up, strangely accustomed to the moaning around her,
and looked up at the sea of patients.

Bed after bed after bed. Neat little rows of white filled the ward.

She tried not to think of Danny, but she couldn't help it. Not when she overheard one of the other girls mention Camp Dix, her sweetheart's conscription delayed because so many soldiers there were sick. Jennie wasn't sure how long ago Danny's unit had left, but it now occurred to her that he might not have even gone with them. What if that was why he didn't write?

Something in her broke. Suddenly they were all Danny. The faces of her patients melted into his as she lifted precious water to their lips or dabbed at scalding foreheads.

"Jennie," she heard her name being called across the floor.

It was a man's voice.

I'm here, darling. I'm here.

She heard it again, looking longingly in its direction, ready to take flight. But this man was too tall, his hair; the wrong color.

Hugh waved at her from the doorway of the corridor. She forced a smile, feeling ridiculous because he wouldn't see it underneath her mask, but she didn't know what else to do, whether to laugh or to cry. She tucked in the girl she was tending to and hurried over.

"Where's Mother?"

Jennie looked up into his droopy, glassy eyes. The same eyes she'd seen in others for hours now. "Come," she said gently, taking him by the elbow. "Let's get you a bed."

"I'm fine," he grimaced. "Where is she, Jen? I'm taking you home."

"Nonsense."

"The trolleys aren't running." His voice was hoarse. "Public health department shut 'em down. Shut. Everything. Down." Shoulders hunched, he succumbed to a fit of coughing. "Schools, churches, movie houses...." He wheezed. "Everything."

"Dear God."

They found Gertrude boiling blankets in the laundry room. Hugh somehow managed to drive, and Jennie kicked herself for not taking him up on his earlier offers to teach her. Aside from her cousin's coughing spells, the streets of Philadelphia were hauntingly silent as they made their way down Market Street. His chest rattled, and Jennie rolled down her window.

When they finally got to the townhouse, Hugh shot her a look with those big brown eyes of his. Usually able to read him, Jennie wasn't sure what he was trying to convey and a pit formed in her stomach.

Molly? No, she told herself. It couldn't be. Hugh wouldn't do that to her, would he? He was clearly ill. What if, perhaps, he wasn't thinking straight?

Her baby. Her precious little baby. She couldn't lose Molly. Not now. She'd already lost too much.

Up the front steps, she went. Slowly, dreading whatever was on the other side of that door. She opened it with caution, Hugh holding his mother's hand behind her. Jennie heard her heels click against the marble flooring. What she heard next was a sound she'd never forget.

Gertrude's high-pitched howl reverberated through the foyer.

Dear Samuel was laid out in the parlor off to their left. A simple oil lamp lit the space, where her young cousin was dressed in his best church suit, his little hands folded neatly on his lap. If Jennie didn't know better, she'd think he was sleeping.

But she *did* know better, her own hands covering her mouth as she choked back a silent cry of her own. It wouldn't come; why wouldn't it come? Was it because she was relieved it was Samuel and not Molly? Glad, even?

What kind of person does that make me?

Her aunt flew to the boy, and Jennie felt increasingly guilty about her remarks the previous day. Gertrude threw herself over his body, the sounds coming out of her like nothing any of them had ever heard before. It was a cry so lonely, so desperately lonely, yet somehow angry at the same time.

No parent should have to outlive their child. It just wasn't right. It wasn't. None of this was right. It felt like they were living on an alternate plane. This couldn't be real. It hurt too much.

"I'm sorry, Mother. I didn't know...." Eyes bulging, he panted. Hugh heaved a deep breath and tried again. "...how to tell you."

His skin was gray, and Jennie's pulse quickened. God wouldn't take both Gertrude's sons the same day, would he? Why was he punishing them so?

Cook appeared seemingly out of nowhere. She could've been standing there the entire time for all Jennie knew.

"Where's Molly?"

"With Nanny in your room." The older woman blew her nose into a hanky. "Not showing any symptoms, thank the Lord."

Jennie clutched her chest. Meanwhile, Hugh braced himself against the wall, about to collapse at any moment.

"Help me move him to the study."

Crushed under the weight of the former athlete, the two women struggled down the hall. They eased Hugh onto the leather couch. Jennie grabbed an extra pillow off one of the Queen Anne's and tucked it under his neck.

"If you don't mind, ma'am," Cook rasped, "I'll take the first shift. Closest I have to a son, he is."

Jennie grabbed her hand. "I know he's fond of you, too. We both are. I…" She touched his burning forehead, the gravity of Hugh's condition all too real. "I've been at the hospital all day. I don't think it's safe for me to be anywhere near Molly."

"What can I do?"

"I'll need linens. Water. Any ice we have left."

"Of course."

"Can you listen for Nanny? Keep me updated."

The servant nodded, her eyes red from crying.

"Thank you, Cook."

Once Hugh was settled, Jennie peeked in on her aunt. The woman remained inconsolable. Curled up next to Samuel on the table, Gertrude attempted to hum him a lullaby while petting the top of his head.

"Remember this one, darling?" she asked as if expecting an answer. "It used to be your favorite."

Jennie marched to the dining room, measuring a double amount of brandy into one of the tumblers. If only she'd kept a bit of laudanum. Too late now.

"Here," she said, feeling very much like Lady Macbeth as she lifted it to Gertrude's mouth. Her aunt tried to push her away, but Jennie remained firm. "I know it doesn't taste good but it'll help."

For now. There would be the funeral to get through, and Jennie prayed they'd only be burying one Callaway. Once Gertrude had quieted, she crept back to her patient.

Hugh was in bad shape. Fever raging, his body convulsed under the blankets. He drifted in and out, in and out, in and out. Jennie did the best she could, keeping cool rags in all the necessary places, sponging water into his cracked lips. Still, there were times he was utterly delirious, his fragile mind ripping itself apart.

"Shannon," he murmured in agony.

"Yes," Jennie lied. She had to. Because maybe, just maybe, somewhere some Red Cross nurse was lying to her Danny, too. She touched his cheek to let him know she was there, and her cousin flinched with relief.

"Can't see you. It *hurts…*" A whimper. "It hurts to open my eyes."

Except Hugh's eyes were open. Glazed and bloodshot, yes. But wide open.

"Shhh," she cooed, stroking his saturated hair back. What else could she say?

Thankfully, Cook tapped on the door, relieving her momentarily.

They switched back and forth like that for three days, sanitizing the house in between— every surface scrubbed and scrubbed, the rags boiled and re-boiled yet again. Jennie wasn't sure how much longer she could last. Her hands were raw, their cuticles cracked and red from the bleach. She couldn't remember the last time she bathed, her hair limp and oily.

Gertrude, meanwhile, refused to leave Samuel's side. They'd have to bury him soon, Jennie knew, but the morgues were still full. At this point, though, she wasn't above digging the ditch herself. Theirs not being the only family on the block stricken with the illness, the stench of the dead was drawing flies and vermin of all kinds to the once prestigious neighborhood.

Hugh's fever finally broke sometime on the fourth day.

"Jennie?" he asked weakly as she applied a fresh compress. "Where am I?"

She was pouring him a cup of tea when a big black car pulled up across the street. It was odd, seeing a vehicle on the road after the city had been a practical ghost town.

Jennie suddenly felt cold. Handing her cousin the cup, she crossed her arms against herself. A man got out, tucking a white envelope under his arm before vanishing from view. Seconds later, the doorbell rang.

CHAPTER 76

"I'll get it," Shannon flew down the stairs to answer the lobby phone, but it stopped ringing before she could reach it.

Her heart sank. There'd been no word from Hugh in days, and her nerves were raw. The reports in the papers, optimistic initially, took a dark turn as the insidious illness spread faster than anyone imagined.

"Josephine! Sal, stop!"

A copy of the *Star and Wave* tucked under her arm, Shannon marched the Rossini kids right back up to their apartment. Knowing Marian couldn't read (in English, anyway), she paraphrased the paper's front page for her.

"You need to keep them home from school."

"But it is Monday, yes?" her friend questioned.

"It is," Shannon explained. "But there's no school today. They're closed."

"Closed?"

"Yes. For two weeks, at least."

"Two weeks?" her friend repeated, and Shannon could see the look of terror in Marian's eyes as she tried to imagine what to do with all five children cooped up in the tiny apartment for that length of time.

"I'm headed to Kennedy's now for some odds and ends. Can I get you anything while I'm out?"

Soon, the Hotel Cape May was turned into a hospital, the facility quickly reaching capacity by the close of the first week. It was the same story in every county across the state as merchants and military personnel brought the flu home from their recent trips into Philadelphia. Meanwhile, food flew off the shelves faster than the stores could get it in, all shipments on hold until the shutdown was lifted. If things were this bad on the island, she couldn't imagine what the cities looked like.

Keeping idle was difficult. Shannon wasn't sure she could do it for one week, let alone two. Her nervous energy required her to move, to do. She'd go crazy if she didn't. Even those auxiliary luncheons sounded appealing in comparison.

It was so peculiar. She grew up in isolation. A fortress she'd created for her own sanity. Except for Danny, Shannon spent her whole life pushing others away. Under quarantine, genuinely secluded from the rest of the world, all she wanted was Hugh. To hear his voice say her name. She tried to remember what it sounded like, playing it over and over in her head for fear she'd forget. Given a chance, she'd tell him all the things she held back, even if that meant telling him about Pa. She didn't want any more secrets between them. She just wanted him. And that's what made the waiting near impossible to bear.

But now the phone was ringing again. Ringing and ringing— her neighbors were terrified to exit the safety of their cocoons.

Shannon couldn't take it anymore. She made a mad dash for the stairs. In her haste, she forgot the handkerchief she usually used to cover her face. Too late now, if she turned back, she would miss the call.

Reaching the landing, she almost tripped, grabbing the banister to steady herself before whirling around the corner to the last flight.

"Hello?" she panted into the receiver.

"Now connecting from Philadelphia," the operator's nasal tone confirmed.

This was it.

It was him.

It had to be him.

Dear God, please. Let it be him.

"Shannon?"

Hugh sounded so far away, making the hundred miles between them feel like a thousand. Her eyes filled with tears, but she wouldn't let him hear her crying. Not now. Not only was the operator listening, but Shannon wasn't sure how much time they'd have on the call, and she didn't want to waste a second of it.

"Hugh?" she blinked furiously, hoping he didn't pick up on her staccato.

"I'm here," he said quietly. "Are you well?"

"Yes. Are you? I've been so worried."

As it turned out, she'd been right to be concerned.

Samuel. Sweet, sweet Samuel. One of the kindest people she'd ever known. Of course, the boy hadn't exactly been strong before but to be dead? At eleven? She couldn't even begin to wrap her head around the injustice of it, feeling a rage she hadn't felt since she lost her mother.

And Mr. Martin, dying in prison on bogus charges to begin with. Shannon balled her fist around the telephone cord. Evidently, one of the guards unknowingly brought the virus to work with him and infected the entire cell block. They were so close to proving his innocence. She shook her head, angry tears bubbling over the apples of her cheeks. Jennie must be beside herself.

She asked as much, and Hugh confirmed they were all taking it really hard. By the time he told her of Rutherford, Shannon was almost sorry he even called. Was there no end to this madness? For all that he said, though, Hugh never answered her initial question. So, drawing a deep breath, she asked again.

"How are you? Are you alright?"

There was silence on the line.

"I am," he said finally. "It was a close call, but I made it through."

She gulped. A close call? He made it through? Shannon wrapped a clammy palm around the telephone cord. He wouldn't be calling if he were still at Death's Door.

"When are you coming home?"

Not back. *Home.* Where he belonged. With her. And Snowball. In that tiny one-bedroom apartment where she occasionally burnt his toast and Hugh, darling Hugh, never wanting to risk her feelings, not only ate it anyway but made sure to tell her it was delicious.

Home. Where he would've been safe all along if it weren't for Will barging in on their dinner. No. It really wasn't Will's fault. He was only trying to help, after all.

A fire crackled deep in the pit of her stomach. Shannon felt that flame before. It should've frightened her, but it didn't. Instead, she welcomed it, the darkness beckoning; meanwhile, her whole body shook with anger. There was only one person to blame.

Joseph Fucking York.

The parade, the papers said. What had they called it? A "breeding ground for the flu"? The same Liberty Loan parade Gertrude wouldn't have been absolutely obsessed with if Mr. Martin hadn't been arrested.

None of them would've even been in the city if Walter were a free man as far as Shannon was concerned. The war effort on the island was in full swing, something she could attest to herself no thanks to Gertrude. Who was to say the family wouldn't have stayed on at the cape after the summer this year? Harnessed their volunteering locally. The sea air had proved beneficial to Samuel, didn't it? The family would have Hugh within arm's reach, and she could've helped Jennie with the baby. It sounded beautiful when she played the scenes through her mind. Scenes that would never be.

Samuel, Walter, Rutherford. She flashed through their names, all lost forever. And Hugh. *Her* Hugh with his close call.

"Shannon," he was saying now. "Shannon, are you still there?"

She scolded herself for not paying attention. There was a weakness to his tone. Her heart hurt. Physically ached inside her chest. *He's struggling.* It was just like him to try to cover it up.

"I'm here."

"I'll be home soon," he wheezed. "Soon as they lift the travel restrictions." The last part, barely audible, Hugh cleared his throat. "I love you. Stay safe."

"Love you, too," she croaked, squeezing her eyes shut. "And I will."

But Shannon had no intention of staying indoors even a minute longer. The call no sooner ended, she rushed back upstairs to grab the keys to the Model T. She turned the crank furiously, the car only used sporadically as of late to save on fuel.

"C'mon, c'mon," she banged on the steering wheel, demanding it to start. Finally, she heard the engine catch and popped the clutch, the ancient machine lurching forward, black puffs of smoke wisping out the tailpipe.

Her first stop was the farm. She had to warn Will. Who knew how York would react to the news of Mr. Martin's death? Shannon shuddered, remembering the night he showed up at Juniper Grove. This was a man who was used to getting his way, no matter what. He'd already killed once. Appeal or no appeal, what was stopping him from doing so again?

I will, you son of a bitch. The car crept around the turn from Higbee Beach to the west side of the cape. She parked along the gravel road, walking the rest of the way so as to not disturb Mr. and Mrs. Barkley.

Shannon climbed the ladder and stepped into the nook Will set up for himself in the loft. It was cozy, a small oil lamp and flannel blanket taking up the back corner.

"You have to leave town," she urged. "Now. Tonight."

"Where am I s'posed to go?"

"I don't know. But you can't stay here."

He had kin on the mainland. Some cousins out in Woodbine. That settled it.

She took him as far as the Shunpike, watching with a heavy heart as Will's lanky silhouette faded from view.

The guard stopped her at the toll heading into the Wildwoods.

"Bridge is closed," he said in an official tone. Or, about as official as one could sound through a mask.

"Heard they need volunteers at Mace Hospital."

He furrowed his brows.

"I just want to help."

A few bats of her eyelashes, and he waved her through. It was only a white lie. Shannon had almost forgotten how easy they were to tell. Like slipping into an old, comfortable sweater.

Frank beamed as she strode into his office. "Just couldn't stay away, huh doll?"

"And miss all this?" she grinned, gesturing the docks outside with one hand and playfully holding her nose with the other. Usually bustling, the fishery, too, was silent amidst the flu outbreak.

He pointed at her usual seat opposite his desk. "You shouldn't be out."

"Neither should you."

"That's what I like about you, Shannon. You never hold anything back."

She smiled politely. "Funny you should mention that…."

This was Frank, after all. She knew she could be honest. He'd never judged her before; why would he now? And before she could stop herself, Shannon spilled everything, starting with the blackmail. How York not only tried to steal her brother's sweetheart, he'd also stabbed Hugh in the back with a smile. He framed Walter. Manhandled the poor maid. Threatened one of her oldest friends.

"Something needs to be done, Frank. He needs to be called to account."

He leaned back in his chair, hands folded over the shiny buttons on his vest, and let out a deep chuckle.

"What?" she asked, somewhat annoyed.

"You. Wanting to put a hit on this York fella, that's what."

"I'm not joking," Shannon quipped, the voice not of her own.

The darkness took hold. She couldn't escape it; wasn't sure she even wanted to. Frank cocked his head, regarding her with caution as it began to dawn on him that she was serious.

"That man," she continued, "hurt every person I care about in some way or another. Every. Person."

"So he should die for it?"

"Why not? Walter did. So did that precious little boy. And Hugh…" The reality of almost losing him again was still too raw.

"You really love him, don't you?"

"I told you that when I quit."

"Thought you wanted to play house."

"Well, you were wrong."

"Apparently so." He offered a stiff nod and looked out the window. "You're fiercely loyal to the people you care about, Shannon. It's one of the things I admire about you."

"So you'll do it?"

"*I'm* not doin' anything, doll."

"But you know someone who will?"

"Let's just say these things have a way of …working themselves out." Frank locked eyes with her over the desk. "With more and more cars on the road, there's crashes all the time. A pity, really."

"Tragic," Shannon agreed with a wicked grin.

"There is the matter of payment, of course."

"Right." Now it was she who broke the stare, looking down at the top of the desk. She'd spent all her savings and wouldn't dare ask Hugh for the money. *So much for no more lying to him.* "Perhaps I could come back to work? Put my earnings toward whatever's owed."

"You could. Or," he reached across the desk, softly grazing the top of her glove.

"I'm engaged, Frank." Still, Shannon didn't pull her hand away.

"I know."

"When?"

It was for all the right reasons, she told herself. She had to. A small part of her even wanted to, and Shannon never hated herself more.

Frank bit his lower lip, and she felt her blood run cold. Now. He didn't need to say it out loud; the greedy look in his eyes told her everything she needed to know. Pa had looked at her like that once, her back stiffening at the recollection. With staggered breath, she began undoing the buttons on her collar.

Her hands shook, making it difficult. She was only on the third one when he started laughing again.

"Stop," he commanded.

Was he really mocking her? Cheeks burning, Shannon held her head as high as she could. Maybe she was taking too long. She wouldn't know; she'd never done this before. A thrill shivered somewhere deep inside her. Perhaps he wanted to help.

"Something wrong?" she asked as nonchalantly as possible.

"No. Quite the contrary." Frank smirked. "Congratulations, doll. You passed."

"I *passed*?"

"Fiercely loyal, like I said."

"You bastard! You were testing me?"

"You didn't say no."

He had a point. Still, she had her pride. She wanted to slap him.

"What do you want, Frank?"

"I want to be on the other side of that loyalty." He sighed. "I don't wanna be the guy you run to with your problems, Shannon. Surely, on some level you must know that. Do you ever wonder why I didn't kill you that night on the docks?"

Frank pouted across the desk, his gray-blue eyes searching her.

"Are you going to take care of York or not?" she asked through gritted teeth.

"Consider it done. But Shannon, someday I'm going to ask you for a favor in return. And when I do, you're going to say yes."

CHAPTER 77

"N o."

The plea was desperate. A cry for mercy. Danny tried to force himself not to listen, but he couldn't help it. The field hospital was crammed, its beds pushed close together to allow for the never-ending influx of wounded. Men all around him in agony. Missing arms, legs, sometimes both. Nurses rushed to and fro around the church basement they were using due to the latest evacuation.

"Please, Doc, please. Don't send me back."

"Son, your burn's healed. Nicely too. You're very lucky. Not many men can say the same."

"But you can't—"

"I have my orders. Now you have yours." With that, the doctor continued down the endless line of beds.

There was nothing physically wrong with the man next to him. Nothing that the eye could see. Shell shock, they called it. Or cowardice, depending on who you were talking to. Danny suspected that the physician's opinion was on the latter side by his demeanor.

Danny knew better. He had his own demons.

⋯⊷═◯═⊶⋯

The Army found him two days after the shelling on a recovery mission. It was only when he moved spontaneously that they realized he was still alive, however barely; his unconscious state just as severe, if not more so, than any of the physical injuries plaguing him.

His memories blurred together, a vicious assault on his crumbling psyche. Close range, hand-to-hand combat. Visions of his German opponents struggling and begging for their mothers would give way to those of Jennie smiling sweetly. Stomach swollen, she glowed.

Daddy. A child's voice echoed from beyond, and Danny saw a young version of himself torn fretfully between his sister and their father. Little Shannon was terrified. She cowered by their bed, holding tightly to one of his toy soldiers as Pa undid his belt. The figurine came to life, and, all at once, he was back in a trench, listening for the whistle and ready to go over the top.

The scenes continued on a loop, daring him to surrender. Oh, how desperately he wanted to. It was so tempting. He was so tired of fighting. He'd done it all his life; he had nothing left to give. Defeated, Danny resolved this was the last ladder he'd ever climb, and a strange peace befell him. At that, the wall grew higher and higher, enshrouded in mist.

Up, up, up he went; faces of the lost swirling furiously around him in the darkness. They were all there: Huns, Jones, and Smitty, the little pup chasing her tail. And there was Pa. A demon maestro, his skeleton hand outstretched in the forefront as if a wand, leading the cries of the damned. The chorus rose to a deafening pitch as they beckoned him to join them.

Yet one voice, soft and nurturing, stuck out. Danny stopped climbing to listen closer.

"Come back to me," Jennie begged.

Home. A piece of his heart would always be there. Buried in the sand by the lake with Captain Kidd's treasure.

Danny's eyes snapped open. Panting, his pulse pounded. At first, he didn't realize where he was. The pungent odor of camphor was his first clue, a scent he remembered well from his stint at Mace. As he tried to sit up, a sharp pain tore through the left side of his torso, his chest and arm trembling. He groaned, catching the attention of a nurse a few beds down.

"Sergeant, you're up." The petite blonde offered a warm smile. She finished checking the vitals of her current patient then made her way over. "Everything's intact," she advised matter-of-factly.

"Why's it…." Danny grimaced, "…hurt so much?"

She put a hand over his, squeezing it reassuringly. "I'll get you something for the pain."

The girl returned a few minutes later with morphine. Before administering the syringe, she reached in her pocket and pulled out the watch Jennie gave him, gently placing it in his palm.

"It was taped to your chest when they brought you in," she explained. "Cleaned it up best I could."

Stunned, Danny looked down at it, rubbing his thumb over the engraving. *I'll love you until the end of time.* Would she really, though? He wasn't the same man anymore. Hadn't been in a long time.

"Thank you," he whispered.

"All in a day's work," the nurse shrugged before plunging the needle into his right bicep.

That was a month ago. Danny kept the watch tied to his dog tags ever since. He wasn't going to lose this one; couldn't chance someone stealing it while he was asleep. The way he'd knotted it, there was no way anyone could snag it without waking him. Sometimes, if he were feeling blue or bored or just plain exhausted, he'd graze the inscription, an instant calm washing over him as he remembered Jennie's sweet smile that day on the veranda. He was touching it now, he realized, finally forcing himself to look over at the private beside him.

Freddie. Seemed like a nice enough kid. From Alabama, he'd said when they were playing cards together a few nights back. Had a girl back home waiting for him in Mobile. The talk of the town, she was.

"Outta all the fellas, she picked me. Me," he bragged in a slow drawl as he tossed a Lucky into the pot.

Danny raised the bet with a cigarette of his own along with a small piece of chocolate. "She sounds swell."

"She is."

Now Freddie was rocking back and forth on the bed, a glazed look in his eyes. He must've felt Danny's stare because his lips began to quiver.

"I wanna go home," he whined.

Danny wasn't sure what to say. His damn collarbone refused to heal, or it might be him going back to the front.

"Me too, Fred." The funny thing was, as soon as he said it, Danny felt a relief of sorts which both surprised and scared the hell out of him. "Me too."

CHAPTER 78

The war ended in November, celebrations popping up all over the country, but Hugh was in no mood for ticker tape or champagne. None of them were. The grief was all-encompassing, slowly gnawing away their every fiber.

He committed Mother to a sanitarium following Samuel's funeral after she refused to let them lower the coffin.

"He's afraid of the dark, Hugh," she begged. "Don't let them. You can't—please! He'll be all alone down there."

Hugh caught his father's eye across the open ditch. *Control her.* Message received. Noticing the way Minnie smirked beneath the black netting of her veil, he clenched and unclenched his fist. Now wasn't the time nor the place. Instead, he gently looped an arm around Mother's shoulders in hopes of leading her away with at least a shred of dignity.

"Come now, let's just take a little walk."

Still weak himself, he'd take her as far as he could and pray it was enough. But Mother balled her fists, easily breaking apart from him in his diminished capacity. She frantically sprinted back to the gravesite.

"No!" she wailed, hurling herself atop the casket.

Jennie wasn't faring much better, though her emotions were on the other end of the spectrum. With her father in the ground and her husband's whereabouts unknown, she was little more than a ghost herself. She clammed up, going through the motions of her everyday activities in a haze and hardly acknowledging Molly. Meanwhile, the Spanish Flu disappeared as quickly and mysteriously as it started.

Shannon, through it all, was an angel. She'd met him at the train station, leaping into his arms as soon as he stepped on the platform.

"I've missed you so much," she cooed, nestling herself against his pea coat.

Hugh craved her touch, the best medicine in the world. Pulling her close against his chest, he lowered his head, so it rested atop her blonde curls. They had to postpone the wedding due to mourning, but she took it in stride like she did everything else.

"Just for a little while," he promised. "Then we'll never be apart again."

"Never?"

"Never."

The months rolled by, one after the other. Hugh had so much to do, and there never seemed to be enough time. In addition to his naval duties, he had to keep up with the regular reports of his Mother's physicians. Then there were the calls and meetings with Biddle to manage her estate and what was left of Walter's for Jennie.

Worse, there was no word on Danny. He'd made inquiries where he could but didn't expect any accurate results. The final numbers were trickling in from France, and they weren't good. His regiment was part of the final offensive against the Germans, which lasted forty-seven days. The Americans suffered heavy losses—120,000 casualties, 26,000 of whom were killed in action.

That's just the bodies they could identify. Hugh shoved the report in a desk drawer. There was no way he could go to the girls with that information.

It offered none of the closure they deserved.

"I'm sorry, friend. I'll take good care of them, I promise."

Ready or not, at twenty-two, Hugh was the man of the house. The glue holding them all together, the pressure was so much at times he thought he'd break. He could feel the cards in his hands. Smell the stale smoke and cheap perfume that lingered in the air. Hear the chips being stacked. This was his life now. The proverbial odds against him, but Hugh played to win.

Fortunately, a larger apartment opened up at the boarding house just after the New Year. He wouldn't call it exactly kismet, but he also couldn't deny how secretly pleased he was either, the logistics making things a bit easier.

The two-bedroom was just down the hall from Shannon's current studio. His fiancée in one room, his cousins in the other. With Snowball, of course. He'd never separate his beloved from her faithful friend. The scrapper was even growing on him, sleeping on his lap in a tight ball when he read the newspaper. Cook, meanwhile, took Shannon's old room.

Molly took to the change of environment like a duck to water, which was good because Jennie was becoming more and more withdrawn. As professionally as she handled the flu epidemic, Nurse just couldn't hold a candle to Shannon when it came to the baby. No one could ever convince him otherwise, so he let the servant go.

Hugh loved coming to visit, the little one toddling across the room, her chubby arms outstretched to greet him, semi-toothless grin slightly asymmetrical like her aunt's. He'd scoop her up, holding her high above his head and twirl her around; Molly's giggle was the sweetest song ever sung.

Shannon was so good with her. A natural. He cherished the nights they'd take her up to the boardwalk, Molly sitting atop his shoulders with a taffy from Roth's, the rainbow sphere nearly as big as her head.

"You're not the one who has to put her to sleep," Shannon teased as they approached the confectioner but always acquiesced in the end. Who could say no to those dimples?

Soon they'd have a family of their own. Start trying on the honeymoon, if he could wait that long; restraining himself proving more and more painful with each passing day.

Hugh lost his own virginity years before college, a quintessential Knickerbocker birthday present from his father when he turned sixteen. They were at the Union Club, Father grinning beneath his mustache as the whore led him upstairs to one of the private rooms.

"Go easy on him," he instructed as if Hugh were one of his yearlings.

If he could do it all again, he'd have waited. Shared that first experience with Shannon. He'd dream of it. The two of them, back at the old beach bungalow in that tiny little room. So close. Nothing between them but love.

Love. It was beautiful. Miraculous. But it wouldn't put a roof over their heads.

Hugh still had to figure out how to support all of them. He wouldn't come into his settlement for another three years. There was practically nothing left from the Martin holdings, and he was careful with Mother's money being that, technically, it was still hers. Hugh was only a custodian.

Some of his men had already re-enlisted, but he wasn't sure if he would join them. On the one hand, the Navy offered the structure and stability he needed after flunking out of school. On the other was the number of mouths he needed to feed on a military salary. He'd have the new cottage after the wedding, but there was still the matter of utilities, staff, clothing; Molly seemed to grow leaps and bounds overnight, and she was just one child.

Sure, Pat Rossini made it work, but not without sacrifices. As far as Hugh was concerned, he'd already sacrificed enough. He didn't want to make do. He wanted to give his family the kind of life he'd had as a child. Little Molly deserved that. And Shannon? She deserved everything.

Hugh strode up the dock one warm June morning, same as he did every day, and pushed open the door to his office. To his surprise, it wasn't empty.

Father was sitting in his chair. Minnie stood beside him, her back turned as she looked out the window into the harbor. He rose, offering Hugh a handshake as the door swung shut.

"Morning, son."

"Father." Hugh accepted his hand but wasn't sure what to do next. Feeling stupid, he said, "This is a surprise."

"Indeed."

"Hughie," Minnie gushed, planting a revolting kiss on his cheek. "Our war hero," she continued, gazing around the office. "We're so proud of you, darling. So, so proud."

"I haven't really done anything aside from what's been asked of me."

"Nonsense!" she winked.

His father nodded in agreement, ushering Hugh to the tufted leather chair he'd previously occupied. "Sit," he commanded.

"He was just keeping it warm for you, dear," Minnie explained.

Hugh remained standing, clasping his hands in front of him to convey the false confidence he wished were absolute. Minnie Blackwell had never been kind to him. Never. Fearing he'd run to Mother about the affair, she did everything she could to keep him under Father's thumb. It was she who plied him with copious amounts of champagne at Delmonico's for that birthday dinner all those years ago. Minnie, who smiled knowingly as they left for the Union Club. But Hugh wasn't sixteen years old anymore. All the 'dears' and 'darlings' in the world could never change the part she played in destroying his innocence.

"What brings you?" he asked in the tone usually reserved for his men.

"We wanted to tell you in-person, darling, being he was a friend."

"I was speaking to my father."

She feigned indignation.

Father looked from one to the other. "It's alright, my pet." He cupped Hugh's shoulder. "Joseph York."

Hugh stifled a cough. A friend? These two didn't know him at all. His *father* didn't know him at all. Never had. He lived in his own little world. One that was far away from reality, where money reigned supreme and values were nonexistent if you bore the correct name.

"He's dead," Father relayed matter-of-factly.

"Dead?" Hugh mouthed.

"Car accident. T-boned by a fruit truck on his way up Madison. Driver went right through the signal. Claimed his brakes failed."

Minnie procured a handkerchief from her purse, deliberately shaking it before dabbing the corner of her eye. "He was so young."

"Services are this weekend. St. Thomas's, of course."

Hugh should've felt bad. It was a gruesome way to die. Joseph *was* relatively young. He was also an unimaginable bastard.

"That's..." He exhaled long and slow before meeting Father's eye. "I'm sorry to hear. His *mother* must be beside herself."

The older man clicked his tongue. "Some women... *Most,*" he corrected himself and glanced at his wife, "are able to bear such things with grace."

Hugh narrowed his own eyes at the woman. "Since when is it graceful to laugh at a child's funeral, Father?" It came out with a force Hugh hadn't expected from himself. Years of fury, all bottled up.

"We've traveled all the way down here to see you. Is that any way to show gratitude?" Minnie frowned. "I suggest you watch your tone."

"And I suggest you take some air out on the docks."

Father clenched his jaw then nodded. "Go on, Minnie. It's probably best I speak with my son alone."

She slithered toward the door and slammed it closed.

Again gesturing they sit, Father took his place in the chair opposite Hugh's desk.

Defeated, Hugh plopped down, raking a hand through his hair. "Why are you really here?"

"It's been a long two years, Hugh. I know you don't think much of

Minnie but she wasn't lying. We are proud of you, son. I'm proud of you."

Hugh felt the Earth move under him, gripping the top of the desk to steady himself.

I'm proud of you.

He'd waited twenty-two years to hear those words. Twenty-two insufferably long years.

"Father," he gulped.

"I should've told you sooner, I know. I'm sorry, Hugh."

"Why now?"

"York." He frowned. "Same age as you, gone in an instant. Gets a man thinking. And Samuel, of course," he added solemnly.

"Samuel…" Just saying his name hurt.

"The thing is, Hugh, you're the last of our line. I'm not getting any younger. The will's been updated. Minnie will get a settlement—when the time comes, mind you, though hopefully not in the foreseeable future—along with the house on Fifth Avenue. As for the rest, son, it's yours."

Hugh had long stopped checking the price of Callaway stock. He thought he'd made peace with the estrangement years ago. Still, the money was tempting, and his mind wandered about how he would use it, starting with the girls.

"Are you sure? Harvard. Father, you were so angry…"

"Not important. Never was. You're my son, Hugh. My sole heir. My legacy. *That's* what matters. Minnie helped me see that."

Minnie. Of course. That didn't take long.

"Doesn't she want her own children?" Hugh ventured.

"She's," He stroked his chin. "Well…let's just say she's at a certain point in her life where that's not exactly ideal."

Hugh opened his mouth to agree, but apparently, Father wasn't finished.

"Cornelia, on the other hand…."

"What about her?"

"Have you heard of eugenics? Minnie finds the movement so fascinating.

Her bloodline goes back to the *Mayflower*."

"How nice for her."

The sarcasm seemingly lost on him, his father offered a doleful smile. "Indeed."

Hugh felt like he missed some kind of inside joke. Father was acting so strange. Mouth dry, he stood, pouring himself a glass of water from the basin and eager to move the conversation along so he could get on with his day.

"Would you like anything while I'm up?"

"No."

Father was leaning on the desk when he turned around, his hands folded neatly in front of him. The smile was gone, a stern look in its place. Hugh took his seat with caution; all he could do to not fall into the snake pit.

"We have quite a storied pedigree ourselves. The Browne line on your mother's side. Newer money on mine, not that it's relevant anymore. Two generations from now no one will even care." Father cocked his head. "You've had your fun, Hugh. Not that I blame you. The Culligan girl—"

"—Shannon."

"Shannon."

"What about her?"

"She's beautiful, son. You can even keep her if you like. You know I don't care about such things." He waved a nonchalant hand. "But you can't marry her."

"Mother didn't object."

"Not the best counter argument considering she's in a mental institution right now."

Hugh could feel his cheeks flush with rage. "I love her."

A low chuckle. "And you can keep her. Did you not hear me the first time?"

"As my mistress? Father, do you even hear yourself?"

And then it hit him. The inheritance was nothing more than a bribe. His pride tumbled, Father's knife twisting in his heart. The Queen's gambit paid off, stripping him of the dignity and respect he'd felt mere minutes before. All these years, and he was still just another pawn in Minnie's game. Teeth clenched, he glared at the man across from him.

"Get out."

"I didn't mean to offend you, son. But you have to be practical. It's a good match. One I strongly suggest you consider."

"Did you not hear me the first time?"

The older man stood, meandering back to the door. "You can keep the divorce settlement from your mother. No strings. The ink's long been dry on that paperwork and I can't be bothered. As for the rest, I trust you understand the conditions."

Hugh bit his fist so hard he drew blood. His chest heaved, cold sweat dripping from his temples in the hot summer air. He gave it a few minutes, maybe more, he wasn't counting, to make sure Father was gone before hurling his water glass across the room.

CHAPTER 79

"*Whew*—what a racket!" Shannon jogged across the apartment, Molly lagging behind her.

"Whack-it!" she parroted.

"Yes, exactly."

She opened the door where Sal and Vinnie Rossini were elbowing each other across the threshold. Miniature versions of Pat, so close in age one might even mistake them for twins. Shannon knew the feeling all too well, which was exactly why she couldn't be angry with them despite the noise.

"Boys," she said, trying her best to sound stern and failing miserably, "was all that banging really necessary?"

"It's his fault," Vinnie poked his older brother, who, in turn, stuck his tongue out.

"*Na*-ah."

"Ya-*huh*."

Shannon cleared her throat, turning her eyes down the corridor where Marian peeked out her head.

"Salvatore! Vincenzo!"

"*Full names,*" Shannon thought, "*never a good sign.*"

"You woke up your brother." Their mother waved her hands furiously. "How many times do I have to tell you to be quiet in the hallway?"

Sal was quick to apologize. "Sorry Ma. There's some swell outside. Real highbrow. Said she'd give a quarter to the first person to bring this to Mrs. Culligan."

He handed Shannon a note addressed to Jennie. "She said she'll wait for her response."

"Thank you, Sal." She took two pennies of her own and handed them each one. The boys left, and Shannon scooped up the baby. "Let's give this to Mama."

They found Jennie on her usual spot on the bed. Knees hugged against herself, she stared at the lace curtains wafting in the summer breeze. Snowball was curled up next to her at the hip, and Jennie absentmindedly stroked his long, super-soft fur.

"This just came for you," Shannon said, handing her the card.

Jennie opened the envelope. She didn't even bother to hide her look of disgust. "Cornelia Blackwell."

Hugh's stepsister?

"Like her that much, do you?"

The joke did little to lighten the mood.

"We ran in the same set," Jennie frowned. "That was a long time ago." Agitated, she let out an exasperated sigh.

Snowball scurried off the bed with Molly hot on his tail. Jennie started to rise to follow them, but Shannon sat down beside her.

"She's fine. Cook's in the kitchen."

Jennie twisted the paper in her hands. "Cornelia wants to go to lunch. I can't imagine what she could possibly want."

Shannon silently agreed. Lips stalwart, she recalled that awful girl's insinuations at the Officer's Ball. It was one of few conversations she actually remembered; what drove her to drink so much in the first place. *He's marrying you.* Still, something didn't sit right. Miss Blackwell hadn't even telephoned or written following the funerals last autumn.

"Jennie," Shannon said as gently as possible, "an outing might do you good."

The other woman shrugged sheepishly and looked away. Shannon didn't mean to embarrass her. She hoped Jennie understood. The loss of Mr. Martin rocked her sister-in-law to the core. Even now, she wasn't fully herself. Shannon looked after Molly where she could so the other woman could rest and recover.

They went out occasionally, though nothing like the regiment Gertrude had either girl tied to the previous summer. Molly and Enzo being relatively close in age, the women of the boarding house strolled the babies along the promenade on warm evenings. The sun stayed in the sky longer, a mild ocean breeze caressing their cheeks while Marian's boys chased each other up and down the sand.

It was nice. Being able to enjoy one's self again. To hear Sal Rossini's laughter and smile at the simple joy he'd brought Samuel, almost as if the boy's spirit was dancing in the wind alongside them.

Better still, being able to go out in public without those dreadful masks. Shannon winced at the recollection, hoping those days were long gone.

Now summer was here again. The first after the war, shiploads of doughboys all on their way home. More and more returned each day, a fact neither she nor Jennie dared mention aloud. They needed to move on. To let Danny go.

If not for Hugh, Shannon would be just as droll as the woman who sat on the calico quilt. She chanced a look through the curtains where an enormous silver car was parked outside. His stepsister. Like it or not, that's who Miss Blackwell was. They'd have to meet eventually, right? It was just a lunch, but it might just be the small step Jennie needed to take before she took another. It would only get easier.

"I'll come with you, if you want."

"Would you?" Jennie asked gratefully.

"Of course."

CHAPTER 80

Jennie dressed with ruthless determination, pulling her best frock from the closet. Dusty rose always flattered her skin tone; the dress was perfect for the warmer temps that settled on the cape. Her weight was returning slowly but surely, no thanks to the delectable dinners Cook served up nightly. There were some additions to the menu, too; the macaroni Marian taught her how to make quickly became a weekly staple they all enjoyed. Still, Jennie hoped she didn't appear too thin; her serpentine hostess never one to hold back. Hopefully, the drop waist would do the trick.

She twirled in front of the vanity. No corsets! *The only good thing to come of the war.* No one missed them.

The length of the dress showed her calves, a fact that still made some women feel scandalous, but if she remembered Cornelia correctly, her own hemline might have been even shorter. She piled her hair high on her head, pinning on a wide-brimmed hat adorned in large pink and purple velvet flowers.

Jennie felt a pang of guilt to be out of her mourning clothes. Had they waited long enough? This was Daddy, after all. And Samuel. And...*No.*

Danny could still be out there somewhere. Maybe on a homebound ship right at this instant. There would be no more black in this household. God willing, not for a long time.

"Is lip rouge too much?" She asked Shannon, who appeared in the doorway looking just as smashing in the pale blue tea dress and matching cloche of her own.

Her sister-in-law smirked. "Never."

Five minutes later, they were hurrying down the stairs.

"I should warn you," Jennie began when they reached the lobby. "Cornelia can be prickly."

"If you mean like those dreadful committee girls, you needn't worry. Nothing I can't handle."

The chauffeur already had the door open for them.

"*Dah-ling*," Cornelia gushed. She planted an air kiss on Jennie's cheek and squeezed her gloved hands. "I've so much to tell you."

Jennie offered a demure smile. "My sister-in-law, Shannon Culligan," she said as the other woman scooted in.

Cornelia winked, flashing a toothy smile. "Charmed, I'm sure."

"Thank you for having me," Shannon said politely.

Cornelia completely ignored her. "James!" she screeched to the driver, "the Iron Pier, please."

The lunch was phenomenal, not that any of them expected less. With rationing over, chefs across the nation rejoiced in the return of sugar, flour, and meat. Waldorf salad, lamb chops with mint jelly, bread baskets overflowing with warm, fresh rolls. And butter. Creamy and delicious and so terribly, terribly missed.

What did surprise Jennie, though, was the champagne flowing like a fountain. The war was over, but the Navy base was still very much operational, and she didn't think the moratorium had been lifted. Then again, she supposed, savoring a sip from her own flute, she wasn't going to complain about it.

Cornelia hadn't changed much since the last time Jennie saw her. Looking at her, it was like the war never even happened, dressed as immaculately as ever in a celery green lace number. Like Jennie's, the waistline was lower, favoring a boyish silhouette but daring enough to show her calves.

Her jet black hair was swept up under a cloche, an ornately embroidered silk band the same color as the dress around its brim. Cornelia's lips were just as red as the other ladies, though they were flapping through most of the courses.

On and on, she droned, as Jennie knew she would. She'd meant what she told Shannon, they weren't friends. Still, she reminded herself the outing wasn't really about catching up with Cornelia. It was about her. About moving on with her life. Dragging herself if she had to. Shannon was right in suggesting they go; these little stints became easier each time she tried. And Jennie had to keep trying. If not for herself, then for Molly.

"How is your aunt, dear?" Cornelia asked in a false soprano.

As if you really care.

"Wonderful," Jennie replied with an equally fabricated smile of her own. "I got a letter from her earlier in the week. They think she's well enough to be released."

"So soon?"

"Eight months in an asylum is a long time."

"A *week* in an asylum is a long time," Shannon chimed in.

Cornelia cocked her head. "Speaking from experience, Nellie Bly?"

Seeing Shannon's cheeks flush, Jennie stopped her just as she opened her mouth for a rebuttal by clearing her throat. Never one to name drop, in this instance, she couldn't resist. This was Cornelia Blackwell. The girl quoted *Town Topics* the way others quoted scripture.

"As I was saying, she plans to summer in Rhode Island. At Marble House."

Cornelia took the bait, her brown eyes twinkling. "With Mrs. Belmont?"

Jennie mentally added a tally to Team Culligan. "Well, who else, *dah-*

ling?" she purred.

"And you really think she's up for social engagements?"

"Oh, certainly. Her letters are replete with the suffrage movement. I think it's the one thing keeping her going right now. You know Gertrude. She has to keep busy."

"Well, I'm glad to hear it," Cornelia said, almost sounding authentic for once.

"Will you be in town long?" Jennie asked. *Please say no.*

Cornelia waited for the busboy to finish clearing their plates and let out a shrill. "I didn't want to lead with this, and spend the whole luncheon talking about myself, I could *never*. But…."

She grinned.

The pianist in the corner of the room seemed to play a little louder, the refrain of Puccini's *Un Bel Di* echoing across the black and white marble floors.

"*But*," Cornelia rubbed her palms together. "Mother and Edmund are at the yacht club now working out all the details."

"What details, exactly?" Recalling her uncle's notorious spitefulness, Jennie was more than a little confused.

Cornelia didn't miss a beat. "Why, for the wedding, of course. I *do* hope you'll serve as Matron of Honor. I'd love your thoughts on the color scheme. Right now, I'm leaning towards lavender for your dresses. Hugh likes lavender, doesn't he?" She tilted her head. "I think he told me that once. I'm sure of it."

Jennie plastered on the sincerest smile she could possibly muster and kicked Shannon under the table. *Let me do the talking.* She waited until she received her response, a hard jolt to the shin, then proceeded.

"Cornelia, I'm flattered. Perhaps you didn't know," she patted Shannon's hand atop the table, "but, my cousin is spoken for."

"That. *Please*." The other woman snorted. "Just another one of Mann's trash stories. Almost as bad as the ones they wrote about your father, rest his soul." She rolled her eyes. "I didn't believe a word of it."

Jennie hadn't seen or heard from this woman, or any of her former peers, since her own wedding. Trash stories. Why stay away if one didn't believe them? Unless, like Cornelia, your favorite sport happened to be double talk.

Gertrude would know precisely how to respond. Jennie, on the other hand, was woefully out of practice. Meanwhile, she caught Shannon's eye out of her peripheral. She was wild, Jennie knew; the color on her cheeks almost the same as Marian's famous Sunday sauce.

"Cornelia—" She tried again, but their companion wouldn't have it.

"Just think, Jennie. We'll be family," Cornelia's triumphant smile akin to the pictures of barracuda she used to find Samuel pouring over in the library. "I've always felt so close to you. And, in a few years— *if* we even wait that long—maybe I'll have a little boy for your daughter. Samuel. Or do you think that's too soon?" She drew her index finger to her ruby lips. "No, no, Samuel's perfect indeed. Anyway, won't little Samuel just be a match made in heaven for your... Your?"

"Molly," Jennie reminded her, eager to get this little speech over and done with. Skipping dessert was looking better and better.

"Right, Molly." Cornelia started to nod then cringed. "*Molly?*"

"That was my mother's name," Shannon sneered.

"It was?" replied the viper. "How very...Irish."

"And?"

"Eugenics, Miss Culligan." Cornelia sat back like a queen. "Mother's just *wild* about the new science." She jutted her chin at Jennie. "Your uncle, too. It's all about keeping the lines clean, you see. I shan't get into the figures—better to leave all that to the men, so long as I get carte blanche when it comes to shopping, that is—but," she cackled at her own joke and lowered her voice, the sides of her mouth curling, "Hugh is his sole heir."

Jennie ran the numbers in her head. Uncle Edmund's fortune was greater than Father's had been on his best day.

"So," Shannon asked before Jennie could interject, "when you say 'clean', what you really mean is 'not Irish'?"

"No," Cornelia replied flatly. "I mean 'not poor'. However, I suppose they're one in the same."

Jennie struggled to stay calm, arching a brow in reproach.

The other woman huffed with annoyance. "It's high time somebody said it, Jennie. Why, to think of you—a Browne no less, reduced to living in that dreadful apartment. Little street urchins running all over." She shook her head in disgust. "You belong in New York. We'll get you a nice place, dear, don't worry. My Samuel, your...*Molly*. Raise them to inherit their birthright. Pass it on to their own children and so on and so forth. Though, she does have a middle name, doesn't she? Perhaps we could use that?"

"Her name is Molly," Jennie snarled as the waiter approached with the dessert cart. "Her name will *always* be Molly."

"Ladies," the server interrupted, "can I interest you in any delicacies?"

Having lost her appetite, Jennie declined.

"I really shouldn't," Cornelia purred. "Watching my figure, you know."

"That's funny," Shannon remarked as she rose from her seat. Eyeballing the nearest pie, she grabbed it by the rim and strode around the table, stopping just short of her rival. "Didn't you say earlier you were fond of lemon meringue?"

Cornelia couldn't answer for once, whipped crème and custard smeared all across her face.

Shannon dabbed an index finger into the mess, sliding the sugary sweetness across her lower lip in a deliberate display. "Mm. Tastes good."

CHAPTER 81

One look at Jennie, and Hugh knew he was in for it. Arms crossed against herself, she blocked the doorway. "This isn't a good time."

"C'mon, Jen. I'm tired. Had a helluva day." Frowning, he tried to brush past her, but she moved with him, putting her hand on the door jamb.

"You're not the only one."

"What's that supposed to mean?"

"Cornelia stopped by."

Hugh groaned.

"So you did know she was in town."

"Not exactly."

Before Hugh could say anything else, Molly pitter-pattered between her mother's legs. "Hi," the baby smiled, accentuating her dimpled chin.

"Hey Molly," he grinned back. "How's my girl?"

"Pie?"

Well versed by now in her toddler-speak, he replied, "Why yes, I do like pie."

"Good."

"It *is* good. Especially with some ice cold milk." Hugh reached down and picked her up, Molly's chubby legs curling halfway around his torso. Knowing he'd get nowhere with her mother, he turned to the little one, "Y'know, your aunt makes a delightful beach plum tart. One of my favorites. Is she around?"

The toddler pouted. "Her sad."

Hugh turned down his own lips. "She is? Do you think this calls for a tickle?" His fingers danced across Molly's potbelly, and she squealed. "Let's get her shall we?"

Defeated, Jennie could only glare as they waltzed into the parlor. The door to Shannon's bedroom was closed as the pair approached. Hugh tried the handle, but it was locked.

"Shannon?"

Nothing.

Jennie plopped down on the couch, drumming her nails along its arm. "She was quite upset."

He furrowed his brow. "Cornelia can be...."

"Vicious? I know." Her jaw tightened. "I should've never agreed to lunch."

Hugh winced. "That bad?"

"Yes," Shannon quivered behind him. Silhouetted against the doorframe, she looked so tiny.

Jennie looked from one to the other and took Molly out of his arms. "Why don't we go see if Enzo wants to play outside before bedtime?"

The baby clapped her hands together in delight, and the two of them disappeared down the hall.

Hugh stepped closer to the bedroom, stopping just arm's length from Shannon. Head cocked, he extended his hand, long fingers grazing the side of her dewy cheek. "What did she say to you?"

Shannon sniffled. "It's not what she said, Hugh. It's that she was right."

"About what?"

"I'll never be good enough for you," Shannon started, backing herself into the room. She blinked furiously and lowered her head.

"To hell with Cornelia."

"There will always be someone like her. We're from two different worlds, you and me. We can't keep ignoring that."

Hugh shook his head. "Your brother and Jennie were happy."

"For what? An hour before he got called up? There's no comparison."

"The money never bothered you before." He took a step toward her, but she recoiled.

"It always bothered me, Hugh. You just chose to ignore it. Have you forgotten the Officer's Ball?"

"You certainly did." He bit his fist as soon as it slipped out.

Her blue eyes flared.

"I'm sorry. I—I didn't mean…"

Shannon stormed across the room, yanking dress after dress out of her closet and hurling them in a heap on the floor.

"I've tried, Hugh. I really have," she choked. "I can't do this anymore."

"You can't do what anymore?"

"Pretend to be someone I'm not. Someone I'll *never be*. You weren't at those charity luncheons. You didn't see the looks they gave me."

"That was months ago. Why didn't you just tell me?"

"I couldn't disappoint you. Not to mention what your mother would've said." She grabbed another frock and tossed it into the growing pile.

"Shannon, please. Stop," he motioned for her to sit on the bed. "I know you're upset but let's talk about this."

Another metal hanger clanked against the wood. "What is there to talk about, Hugh?"

"You could never disappoint me. Never," his voice cracked.

She cackled. "You're wrong. There are things about me you don't know. Things I've done." She gulped and shook her head sideways. "I'm not who you think I am."

"Who you are? Shannon, you're—"

Kind. Affectionate. Generous. Hardworking. Beautiful.

"—worthless. Completely worthless." Her face raw with contortion, Shannon buried it in her hands and sank to her knees in the mountain of clothes.

A heaviness arose in his chest. Is that how she thought of herself? No. It couldn't be. This was the girl who doted on dear Samuel. The one who took in strays, be they animals or people, like himself. The girl who went without to ensure the comfort of others, who was great in a crisis. Level-headed and steady, Shannon did what needed to be done for Jennie before being asked, rising to the challenge when the trial and after-effects uprooted all their lives. Hell, he couldn't have made it through the last six months without her. If only she could see what he saw.

Looking at her now, though, folded into herself, trembling, what Hugh saw was a girl who was broken. *"I don't need fixing…"* He thought of the Officer's Ball, his earlier remark stinging even more. Shannon had always been fragile; a bone china teacup hastily pasted back together. She knew it, he realized now, kept it hidden from the world under sarcasm or distance.

It snuck out in flashes, that brittle vulnerability. He'd seen it in her interactions with Danny the day of Samuel's rescue and the meltdowns when her brother was drafted and ultimately left for Camp Dix. Hugh always reasoned they were far and few between, a natural response to a tragic set of circumstances. Women were emotional, he'd told himself. Mother and Jennie, no different. In retrospect, there was nothing natural about Shannon's over-eagerness to please Mother. What he'd thought of as bonding, sweet, was really just another weapon in the arsenal she used to fortify her perceived shortcomings.

Hugh knelt down beside her and put his hands on her shoulders.

"You're not worthless. You hear me? You're *not.*"

"I am," she sobbed. "I always have been and I always will be."

"Don't say that."

"It's true. My own father didn't love me, Hugh. It was wrong of me to expect anyone else to." Shannon looked at the floor and wrung her hands. "Let me go. *Please*. Leave me be."

"I won't. Not now. Not ever." He caressed her cheek with his knuckles. "Shannon, I love you. All of you." Hugh stroked her golden hair, choosing his next words with caution. "As for your father—"

She sucked in air.

"Listen to me, okay?" he whispered. "Give me that much before you throw us away."

"Fine."

"I never told you this. I always thought… always felt horrible about it, but…." A deep frown slashed across his face. "I wasn't sorry when he passed away." He clasped her hands. "I saw what he did to you, Shannon. Knew it wasn't the first time. Don't ask me how. I just felt it. Like lightning."

Her eyes brimmed with a fresh round of tears. "You don't know," she whimpered, "what it was like growing up in that house. I deserved it."

"You *didn't*," Hugh cupped her cheeks. "No one deserves to be abused, Shannon. You didn't deserve it. You didn't deserve any of it."

Shannon tucked a stray hair behind her ear. "You're wrong." Her voice shook. "I tried to stay out of his way. Danny, too." She shook her head sideways. "Look where that got him, huh? From one hell to another."

Hugh didn't know how to respond. Thinking it best to say nothing, he tilted his head in solemn acknowledgment.

"I always thought, if I were good, things would change. That some miracle would befall us. I never talked back. Kept the place spic-and-span." She shrugged. "Nothing I did was ever enough."

He pulled her close, holding her tight against his chest. They settled into a quivering silence, and he stroked her hair.

"I try not to dwell on it, some of the things Pa said or did. Most of the time…I don't even think about it. But listening to Cornelia today?" Shannon sighed. "I was right back in that house again. I can't explain it,

Hugh. I know it must sound so strange."

Hugh couldn't help but think of his interactions with Minnie that morning. "It doesn't," he said in a gruff tone.

She gulped down another steadying breath.

"I'm here, Shannon," he rubbed her back. "There's nothing you could say that would make me stop loving you. I didn't realize you were under so much pressure. I'm sorry I didn't see it." He released a stout exhale. "I don't expect you to be anyone other than yourself."

"What if I don't know who I am?"

Hugh kissed the top of her head. "Well, then I'll be here to remind you. Today, tomorrow, and the day after that. Always, Shannon. Until someday you see yourself the way I do. The way I always have. The way I always will."

"I'm no picnic sometimes."

"Neither am I."

"You have your moments."

He snickered. "Do I detect a grin?"

"Maybe."

Hearing her voice return to its regular timbre gave him hope.

"Your past is your past, Shannon. We all have one. I can't change yours, so help me God I would if I could, but I can promise you a future full of love and happiness."

Snowball hopped from his place on the bed. He rubbed against their legs, kneading into the linens. Hugh glanced down at him, scratching behind the cat's ears.

"He's growing on me," he admitted.

"He likes you, too. Knows you're a good guy."

"Yeah?"

"Yeah."

Hugh gently pulled away from her. Shifting his weight from both knees to only one, he took her left hand in his, thumbing over the ring Mother picked out.

Shannon bit her lower lip. "What are you—"

"—Something I should've done a long time ago but took for granted."

The muscles in her throat constricted.

"Marry me."

The cat let out a soft mew, and she giggled. "Pretty sure that was directed at me."

"Shannon," he breathed. "Please say yes."

She cast her dark lashes down and rose, tugging him into an upright position. Chewing that lip again, she strolled back to the bed and sat down on the edge.

Hugh could hear his pulse in his temples as he lowered himself beside her. Eyes wide, like he'd never done this before. But really, he never had. Not with someone he loved and certainly never sober.

Shannon kissed his forehead, cheeks, and lips; her touch soft as rose petals as she traced a finger along his jaw. She peeled herself back, her staggered breath warm on his neck.

"Yes."

He kissed her again. Harder this time, one hand supporting her back as he swung them onto the mattress. He'd wanted her for so long. Waited for this moment with every fiber of his being. Hugh wouldn't trade her for all the money in the world. This warmth, this intimacy. You couldn't put a price on it.

Hugh spooned her closely afterward, just like he'd dreamt about, softly combing his fingers through her hair and admiring the tiny freckles on her nose while she snuggled beside him.

The post-war markets were already looking up. And if they took another dip? Well, there were always numbers and cards and ponies. They'd be fine. More than fine. And once his settlement came through, they'd never have to worry about anything.

"I'll spend the rest of my life making you feel like a queen," he silently promised.

CHAPTER 82

Danny leaned against a lamp post in front of the boardinghouse, intensely scrutinizing a crack in the sidewalk, the cap on his head so low it almost touched the bridge of his nose. An olive-green Army coat hung on his bodice, and he'd turned up the collar to counteract the breeze blowing off the water. A small satchel the same color as the coat sat to the left of his feet. Feet which were currently glued to the pavement.

Cool salty air caressed his stubbled cheeks, and he inhaled the sweet scent. He never thought he'd set foot on the cape again. Yet here he was, after all this time. If only he could bring himself to knock on the damn door.

The possibility that Jennie moved on hung in the air like the smoke from his last cigarette. Danny rubbed the watch in his pocket and reminded himself of their vows so long ago. She loved him then, and he hoped against hope she still loved him now.

And if she didn't? Well, then he had no one to blame but himself. He hadn't written her in ages. He'd understand if she couldn't forgive him for that, he couldn't even forgive himself.

His thoughts were momentarily interrupted by chatter up the block.

Two boys tossed a baseball back and forth across the sidewalk. A woman, presumably their mother, scurried after them, another little boy on her hip. A welcome sight, seeing children behaving their age. The villages outside of Paris were frighteningly quiet. Little men of the house, the boys there helped their mothers in the fields. They'd long forgotten how to play, how to smile, even.

It was dusk, and the sky above them swirled in hues of heather and deep violet. The moon hadn't risen yet, but, judging by the clouds on the horizon, he didn't think they'd be seeing it anytime soon.

Suddenly, another figure strode up behind them. Danny held his breath.

It was Jennie. She smiled and laughed with the brunette beside her. He couldn't hear what they were saying, but it didn't matter. The smile he'd dreamed about. The woman he loved. Not fifty feet away.

One of the boys pointed. "Who's that, Mama?"

The group paused. Jennie clapped a hand over her mouth, grabbing the other woman's shoulder with the other. The two women embraced, and her companion quipped something in another language. The boys took off in the opposite direction, their mother soon trotting not far behind.

Jennie didn't move. She just stood there, frozen.

Danny gulped. All the times he'd envisioned this moment, and he didn't know what to do. He'd seen reunions before, of course. At the docks and the train depot. Sweethearts clamoring through the crowds. Sweeping kisses worthy of the pictures. But those fellas had probably kept in touch with their wives while they were gone. Once, at least.

He offered a broken smile.

"Danny?" she said in a voice he didn't quite recognize. "You're *alive*."

He slowly walked toward her, stopping just a few inches away, already feeling the heat between them.

Danny cocked his head to the side, tenderly grazing his thumb along her cheekbone. "Lemme look atcha."

Jennie's hair was swept haphazardly up under her hat, a few flyaways escaping and framing her face. She gulped, smiling and holding his gaze as if she were afraid he'd disappear.

"You're really here."

He nodded solemnly in response, then furrowed his brow, looking around them.

"Where's the baby?" he asked.

Jennie cast her eyes down, where a small child clung to her left leg, happily sucking away on a peppermint stick. Danny followed her gaze, shocked to realize he'd been expecting an infant. That, for him, time and space had stopped since they'd last seen each other.

He grinned, swelling with pride, as his daughter looked up at him for the very first time. She had big blue eyes and rolls of baby fat, so much so it almost appeared she didn't have a neck. The toddler smiled back, a dimple in her chin, rows of tiny teeth stained red from the candy.

Danny reached in his bag and pulled out a small Teddy Bear. He moved slowly so as not to scare her and lowered himself to the girl's level. Jennie stepped backward, allowing them space.

"Hi there, Molly," he said softly, offering the stuffed animal.

But the child looked shyly away, burying her face in Jennie's skirt. She quickly glanced at Danny again, her eyes huge, before pulling the fabric over them a second time. *What did I expect?* Swallowing hard, he stood back up and shuffled from one foot to the other.

Jennie came to his rescue, looking hopefully from one to the other. She took the bear, eyes welling up as she ran her hand along its fuzzy head. "Looks just like mine."

"You remember?"

"Remember?" A rickety laugh escaped. "It was the night of our first kiss. How could I ever forget?"

Danny let out a ragged sigh.

Jennie picked Molly up, holding her tightly on the hip. She ran the bear along her daughter's cheek. "So soft, isn't he?" she practically sang, bringing forth a muffled giggle.

Another nuzzle, and the baby grabbed it from her. Molly squeezed the bear with all her might, the corners of her little mouth curling into an asymmetrical smirk.

"What are you going to name him?" Jennie ventured, putting her down again.

"Bear," the child responded.

"That's a nice name," Danny added thoughtfully. "Got somethin' for you, too." Reaching into his satchel again, he retrieved a small box of fudge from Roth's. "I'm sorry it's not more…."

She blushed. "No, they're my favorite. How very sweet of you."

Just then, the clouds above them gave way as the summer storm made landfall. Molly squealed with delight, the warm rain falling in large drops. Holding her arms perpendicular—candy in one hand, Bear in the other— she threw her head back and twirled, giving her parents a private moment together. A broken smile quavered across Jennie's lips, and Danny pulled her against his chest. She buried her face in his jacket, poorly suppressing a sob as she leaned into his protruding collarbone.

"It's okay, Jen," he whispered. "I'm home… I'm home now."

She looked up, smiling through her tears. He nodded, the weight of his words an anchor threatening to pull them both under as thunder rolled in the distance offshore. Jennie cleared her throat, attempting to collect herself. Entwining the fingers of her left hand in Danny's, she reached out to gather Molly with the other.

"C'mon. Let's get you out of this rain and I'll fix you some supper."

And so, the three of them made their way down the sidewalk, the first few steps in their new lives together.

CHAPTER 83

"Shannon…" Hugh's husky voice was a symphony in her ear. "Shannon, wake up."

Cradled in sheets, she rolled over and grinned. "Did I dream it?"

He shook his head and smiled back, planting a kiss on her forehead. "No."

Shannon giggled, nestling her head against the pillow. Hugh, meanwhile, was busy buttoning his shirt. The muffled voices eking out from the sitting room answered her question as to why. She doubted Jennie would judge her too harshly. This was, after all, the same girl who'd met Danny for those late-night trysts before the war.

And there it was, that same dull stabbing every time she thought of him. It would always be there, she supposed; a phantom limb. Danny crossed a bridge she couldn't follow. *He broke his promise.* Not intentionally, she knew—that was Pa's doing. But broken just the same. Her brother's absence at birthdays and Christmases was felt keenly before, now he'd be missing her wedding, too. The birth of her children. The rest of her life.

She threw a wistful side-eye at Hugh, now combing his black hair back.

He caught her, smiling back with those dimples she adored so much. She hoped she hadn't told him too much. At the same time, it felt surprisingly good to finally talk about her upbringing. Cornelia may have reduced her to that pigtailed little girl, but Shannon gave her that power. In opening up to Hugh, loving him, allowing herself to be loved in return, she took it back—a schooner freed from her mooring. Sails wide. Nothing but an open ocean before her.

Maybe someday she'd tell him more, but never their secret. No, never that. Danny carried it with him to his grave. So too, would she. The blood on their hands would always be thicker than water.

"Get dressed," Hugh mouthed, handing her the blue frock she'd worn earlier. "You know how impatient Molly can be. Only a matter of time before she comes looking for you."

One.

Shannon slipped into the dress.

Two.

Hugh zipped her back and slid into his loafers.

Three.

The baby pounded on the locked door. "Surprise!"

"No, no," they heard Jennie admonish. "Not yet, *Schatz.*"

Hugh smirked. "Clockwork."

Shannon playfully swatted him. "After you?"

"One more kiss."

"Thought you'd never ask."

Holding Hugh's hand, Shannon exited the room first, where an exuberant Molly was dancing in circles with a stuffed animal.

"Surprise," the toddler chirped again.

"What a cute bear," she smiled at her niece. "Is that for me?"

Molly grinned, crinkling her button nose as she shook her head no.

"Brought you something even better," Jennie gushed. She stepped out of her room. Lights out, a shadowy figure stood behind her.

Shannon's throat closed. The rest of her body went completely limp. *No, it can't be.*

Her thoughts swirled so quickly she couldn't keep up with them.

She was leaning on someone. Hugh. He was beside her, his strong arm around her shoulder. Holding her. Never letting her fall.

"Hey sis." Danny's voice rippled across the hall.

Shannon reached out to him, her face erupting with delight. "You came back." She exalted, forcing her legs to move. "You came back to me."

Danny traced an index finger over his chest and wrapped his arms around her.

ACKNOWLEDGEMENTS

Much like raising a family, writing a novel takes a village. I'm blessed and humbled to have so many wonderful people in support of this work.

To Karen Berdoulay, my dear friend since childhood, thank you. It seems like yesterday we were on the beach together in Ocean City, catching up about our children and day-to-day lives, when I (albeit shyly) first told you I'd written a short story. Your support and encouragement since that time means the absolute world to me.

To Jo Salow, who has championed this project from its inception, thank you for believing in me.

To my beta readers (a group which also includes Karen and Jo): Sarah Sebuchi, Ellen Zuckerman, Lilian Ledoux, Erin Hensh, Michael Quinn, Adrian Bestndworld, Erin MacMinn, Rosalyn Briar, Patty Quinn, and Dan Saunders. Thank you for the time you took reading my early manuscript. The feedback you provided was invaluable. I could not have done this without you.

To my editorial team: Lauren Shute, Shannon Henesy, and the staff at LTS Editorial, thank you for the suggestion to develop the Culligans' story into a series, as well as the hard work and dedication you put into helping me expand and improve the characterization, theme, and overall plot.

To my design team: Sarah Davis and the lovely group at Elite Authors, thank you for your patience in answering my (many) questions when it came to cover design and formatting.

To my in-laws, Steve and Christine Quinn, thank you for sharing my passion and vision for this series. Your love and support helped take TTW from a dream to a reality, a legacy I'm proud to leave for our family.

To my children, Cameron and Mackenna, thank you for inspiring me daily. I am a better person because of both of you. Always follow your heart, and never stop dreaming.

Finally, to my devoted husband, CJ. Thank you for taking my craft seriously. For listening to me brainstorm and plot. For seeing the best in me. For reading (and re-reading) the early drafts of this work, to reading (and re-reading again) the final versions. I'll always look back and smile at our late night proof sessions, hearing you quote certain sections in a character's voice. None of this would have been possible without you by my side. Here's to our next adventure!

AUTHOR'S NOTES

There are several characters in **Thicker Than Water** who lived during the time period in which the novel is set. These include (in order of appearance): Dr. Margaret Mace, Frank Hilton, Augustus "Gus" Hilton, and Joy Bright Hancock.

You may also recall my references to John Wanamaker. In addition to his responsibilities as Postmaster General, he was also a successful American merchant and credited with the founding of Sea Grove (which is now Cape May Point, New Jersey).

Also mentioned in passing is Alva Vanderbilt Belmont, whose life served, in part, as the inspiration behind Gertrude's character development (particularly as it pertained to her relationship with Jennie).

Additional information about these historical figures and how they factor into the narrative can be found on my website: www.lauraquinnwrites.com. May I further recommend the following works:

Remarkable Women of the New Jersey Shore, Clam Shuckers, Social Reformers and Summer Sojourners by Karen Schnitzspahn

Prohibition in Cape May County Wetter than the Atlantic by Raymond Rebmann

Millennium Philadelphia, The Last 100 Years by the Philadelphia Inquirer staff

The First Resort (Fun, Sun, Fire & War in Cape May, America's Original Seaside Town) by Ben Miller

Consuelo and Alva Vanderbilt: The Story of a Daughter and a Mother in the Gilded Age by Amanda Mackenzie Stuart

The Husband Hunters: American Heiresses Who Married into the British Aristocracy by Anne De Courcy

The Glitter and the Gold: The American Duchess In Her Own Words by Consuelo Vanderbilt Balsan

Some of the settings that appear in the novel are or were real places. In Philadelphia, these include: the Bellevue-Stratford Hotel, John Wanamaker's Department Store, and Reading Terminal Market, which all have storied histories. The Bellevue was acquired by Hyatt, and Wanamaker's by Macy's, but both buildings are still operational (as of 2022), as is the market.

With regard to the New Jersey locales, Consolidated Fisheries was once a thriving business on Otten's Harbor in Wildwood. It also, however, operated as the early headquarters of Frank Hilton's rum ring.

Camp Dix is now Joint Base McGuire-Dix-Lakehurst in Wrightstown, NJ. Cape May Section Base Number 9 and the Wissahickon Barracks are the grounds of what is currently the United States Coast Guard Training Center in Cape May. At the time of this printing, the Corinthian Yacht Club remains in operation.

Lake Lily (sometimes spelled "Lilly" on period specific postcards of the era) is now part of Cape May Point State Park.

The Cape May Country Club was only a nine-hole golf course. For the sake of the narrative, I extended it to encompass a full eighteen.

The home that previously served as Jackson's Club House now operates as the Mainstay Inn Bed & Breakfast. A servant (the inspiration behind Bess) did keep watch on the second floor and alerted patrons by rocking back and forth in her chair.

The architecture and interiors that inspired the fictional Juniper Grove are loosely based on those of the Weightman Cottage. Built in 1850 by William Weightman, Sr. (the Philadelphia chemist responsible for quinine), the "cottage" was split in two and moved in 1881. Beautifully restored, the buildings are now the Angel of the Sea Bed & Breakfast.

The Iron Pier and Hotel Cape May are no longer in existence, as is the entirety of the Culligan's hometown, South Cape May.

With regard to historical events in narrative, I tried to stay as close to source material as possible based on my research. A NJ resident myself, making sure these details were accurate was a matter of utmost importance to me from the beginning.

Fellow history buffs may appreciate how I arrived at Danny's physical description. He is based on the "For Your Boy" YMCA poster by Arthur William Brown circa 1918. I originally saw the poster while visiting the U.S. Army War College in Carlisle, PA, and the image made quite an impression. His Army regiment, the 315th, was really nicknamed "Philadelphia's Own."

In July 1916, there were several shark attacks along the northern coast of New Jersey. Resources suggest they were likely carried out by different animals (versus a single shark), one of which was presumably a bull shark given that it swam up the Matawan Creek. Located over a mile inland, the creek empties into Keyport Harbor along the Raritan Bay. Though sources conflict as to whether or not the attacks served as the inspiration behind Steven Spielberg's *Jaws*, I will leave it to the reader to draw their own conclusions regarding any parallels.

The explosions at the Eddystone Munitions Plant, Black Tom Island, and Wissahickon Barracks, sadly, did occur as described. While sabotage was suspected (and confirmed) in the first two bombings, it was ultimately ruled out with regard to the fire in Cape May.

The German submarine, *U-151*, attacked and mined the southern NJ Coast in the spring of 1918. The attack was known as Black Sunday, and resulted in the sinking of seven vessels.

Finally, Philadelphia's Liberty Loan Parade, on September 28, 1918, resulted in a catastrophic outbreak of the Spanish Flu. Writing about a pandemic while living through one was particularly difficult. My research and outline for TTW was completed prior to the COVID-19 lockdowns. There were times in the last two years where I strongly considered changing these chapters (or eliminating them completely from a reader-sensitivity standpoint). My only hope is that I did justice to those lives impacted in both outbreaks.

Those interested in learning more about these (and other) regionally specific events during World War One, might consider the following nonfiction:

The Great Influenza: The Story of the Deadliest Pandemic in History by John M. Barry

US Coast Guard Training Center at Cape May by Joan Berkey and Joseph E. Salvatore, MD

A History of Submarine Warfare along the Jersey Coast by Joseph G. Bilby and Harry Ziegler

Remembering South Cape May by Joseph Burcher

Philadelphia the World War I Years by Peter John Williams

ABOUT THE AUTHOR

Laura Quinn currently resides in southern New Jersey with her husband, two children, and spoiled tabby cat. When not writing or consuming copious amounts of coffee, she enjoys hiking, the beach, and spending time with her family.

Thicker Than Water is her debut novel, with two additional books planned to round out the Culligans' saga. For exclusive updates on the sequels, stay connected with Laura by subscribing to her blog at www.lauraquinnwrites.com. You can also follow her on social media:

Instagram: @lauraquinnwriter

Facebook: @lauraquinnwrites

Pinterest: @lauraquinnwrites

Goodreads: @lauraquinn_author